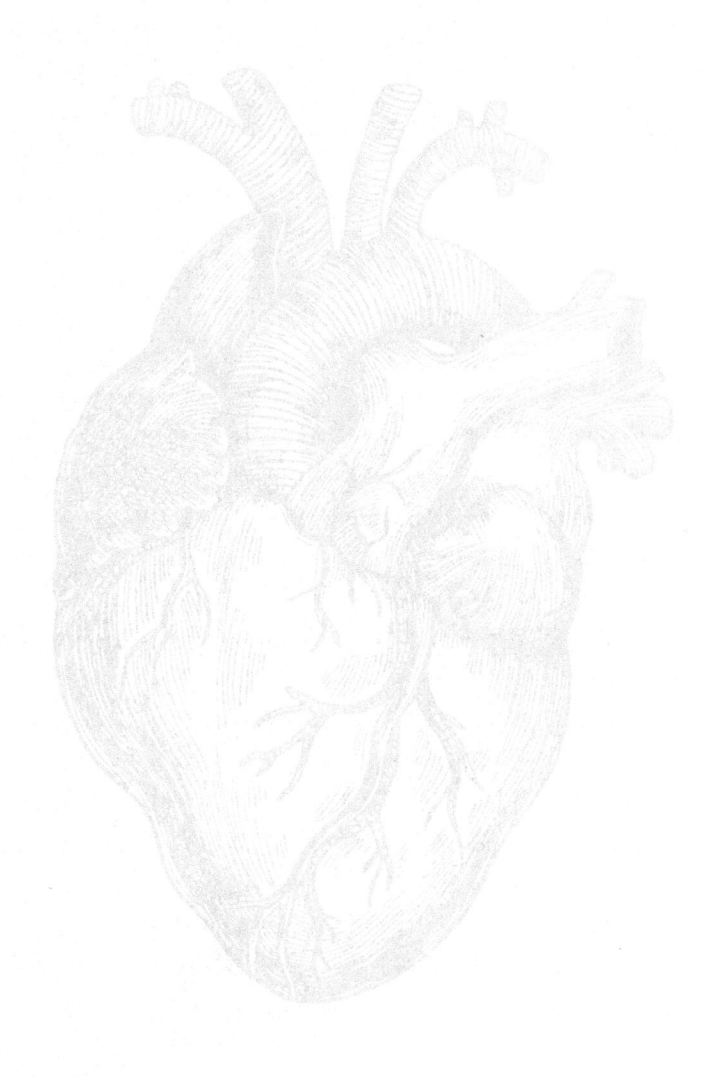

TAKE MY HAND   1

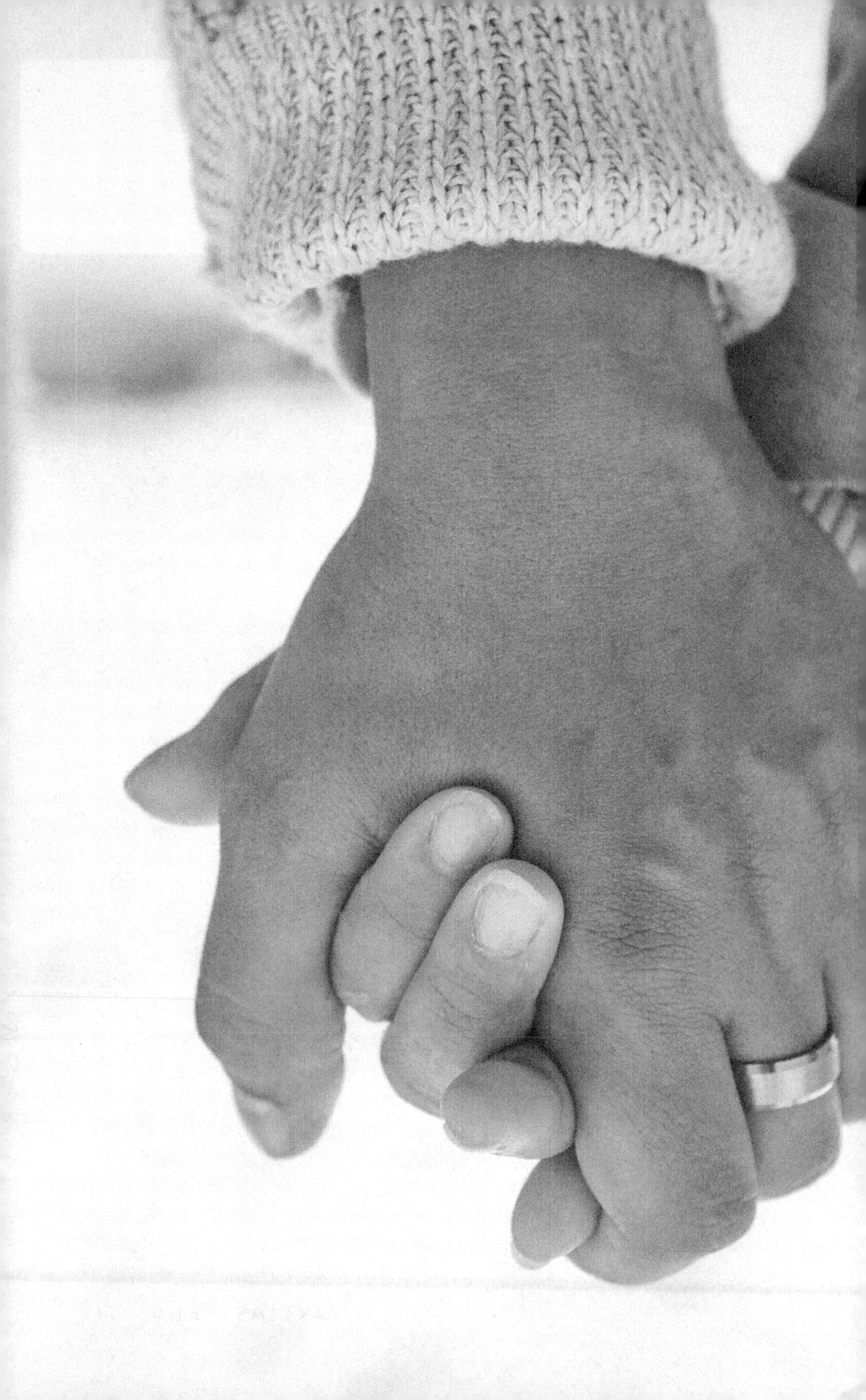

TAKE MY HAND

NIKKI ASHTON

Copyright © Nikki Ashton 2024 All Rights Reserved ©
Take My Hand

Published by Nikki Ashton
Bubble Books Ltd

This book is licensed for your personal enjoyment only. This book may not be re-sold or given away to other people. If you would like to share this book with another person, please purchase an additional copy for each recipient. If you're reading this book and did not purchase it, or it wasn't purchased for your use only, then please return to your favourite book retailer and purchase your own copy. Thank you for respecting the hard work of this author.
All Rights Reserved ©
This is a work of fiction. Names, characters, places, brands, media and incidents are either the product of the author's imagination or are used fictitiously. The author acknowledges the trademark status and trademark owners of various products referred to in this work of fiction, which have been used without permission. The publication/use of these trademarks is not authorised, associated with, or sponsored by the trademark owners.

Cover design & Formatting – Lou Stock of LJDesigns

TAKE MY HAND   5

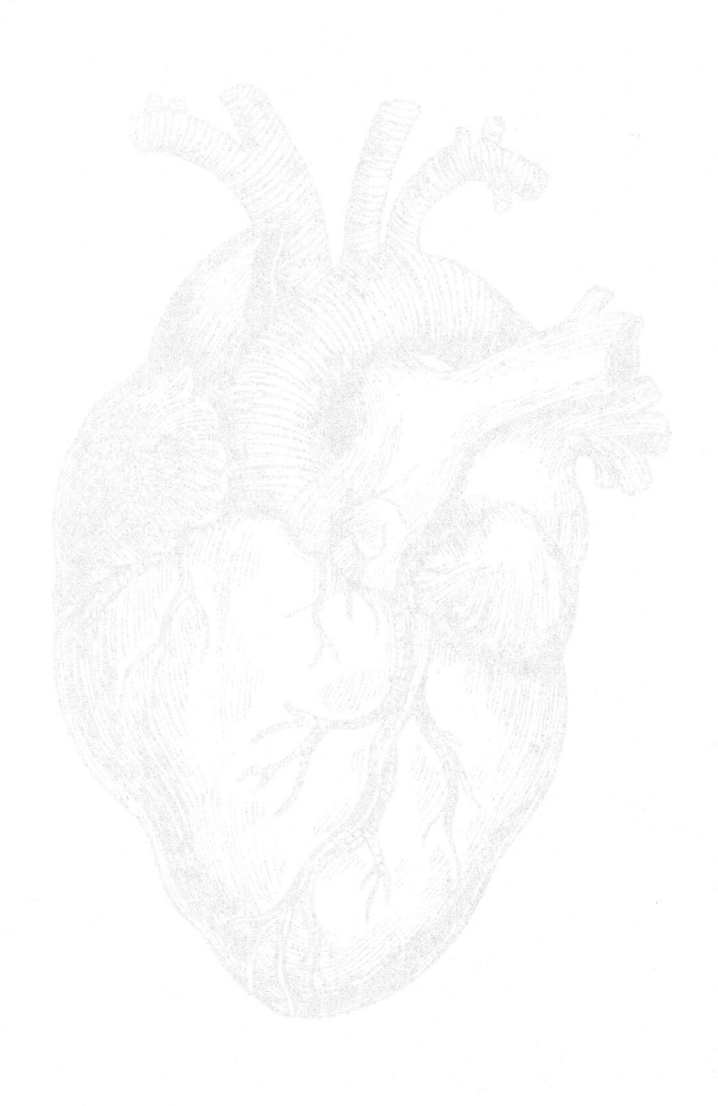

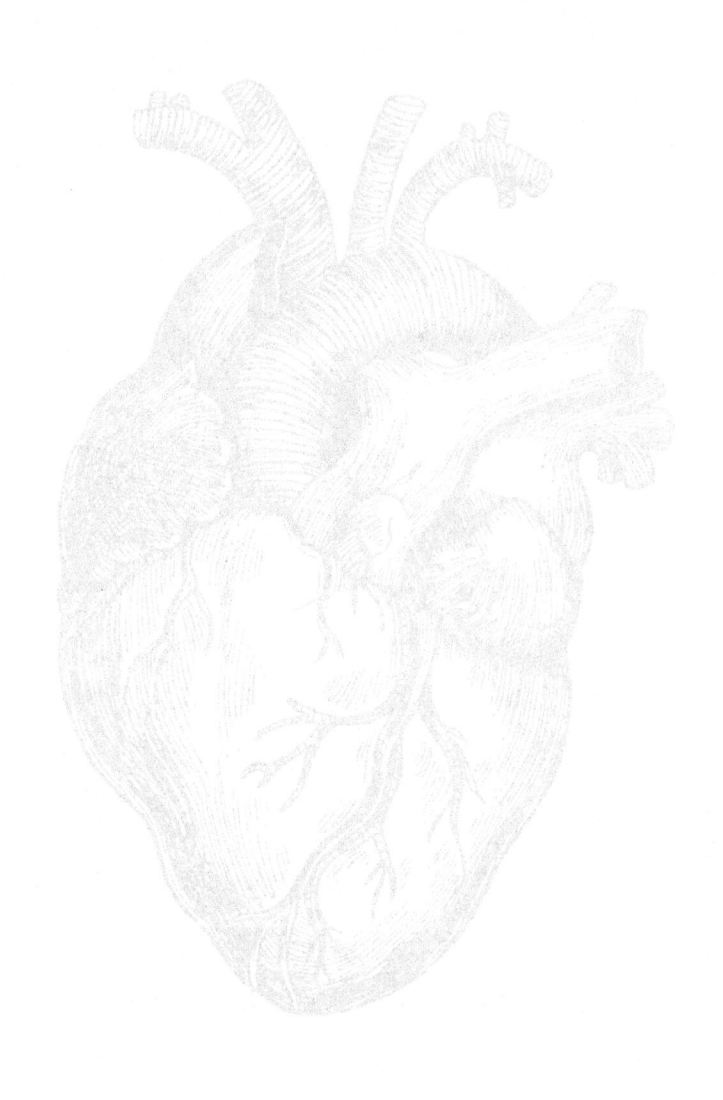

To Dad.

I miss your laugh.
I miss your voice.
I miss hearing you say I love you.
I miss you rolling your eyes.
I miss your smell.
I miss holding your hand.
I miss you.

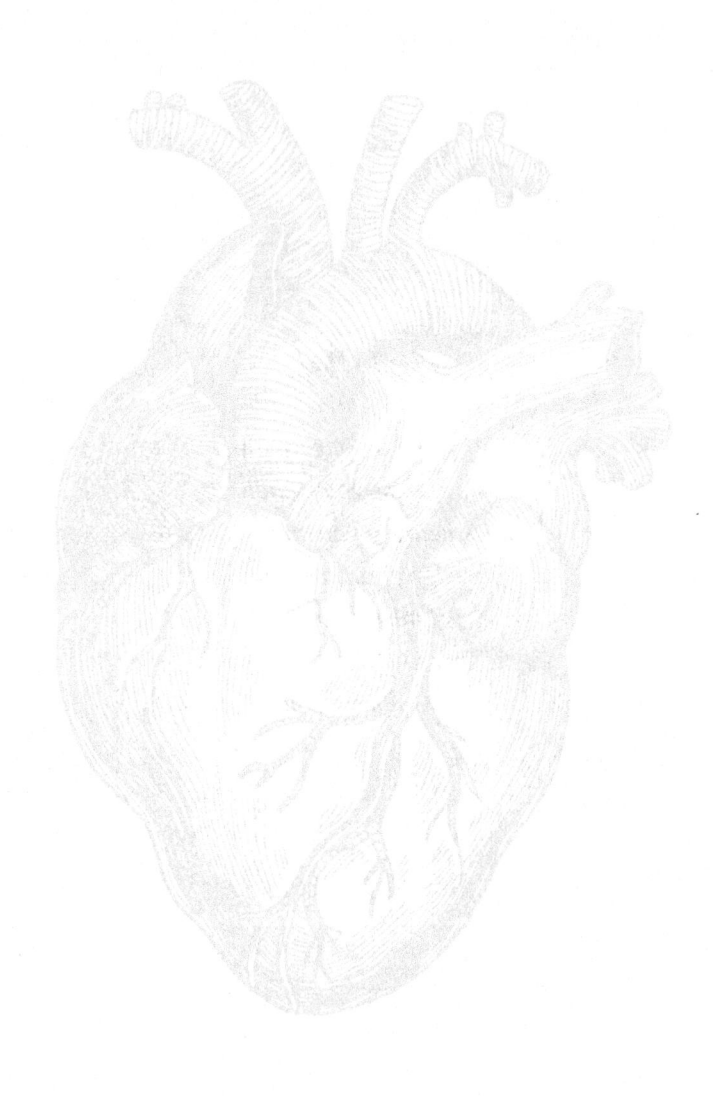

PROLOGUE
Will

As the wind whipped around the people who walked slowly away from the graveside, I couldn't help but think about the warm bed and body that I'd left to come to the funeral of someone I hadn't seen in ages. It wasn't like Andy and I had been in touch over the last year, not since she'd ended things between us. I wasn't heartbroken by it, in fact she did me a favour. I'd been wanting to end things for a while. Two weeks of dating someone was usually my limit, but Andy and I had been together for almost two months. My feet were itching, and then she told me that it was over.

"Will?" A tall woman with hair greying at her parting cleared her throat. "You're Will Newman?"

I nodded, and instantly I saw she had Andy's eyes—startling blue with tiny flecks of grey. She had a kind smile, just like Andy's.

"I'm Andrea's aunt, Miriam." She held her hand out to me. "I'm the one who sent you the message and the... I suppose you'd call it an invite." She shrugged.

I blinked. "Ah, okay. Thank you for letting me know." I took her hand and shook it. "I'm sorry for your loss." And I was. Andy was a nice girl, and it had been a shock to hear she'd been killed in a car accident.

"Thank you, thank you." Miriam looked down at the ground and sniffed.

"Well, it was nice to meet you, although not in these circumstances." I made to leave, but she grabbed my arm.

"Will, I think we need to talk."

I frowned at her. "We do?"

She looked around and then nodded. When I followed her gaze, I saw a guy in a black wool coat, buttoned up, with a grey-and-black-check scarf around his neck. The guy mouthed 'okay' and then left.

"That's my neighbour," Miriam explained. "Eric. He gave me a lift here. There didn't seem much point in having a limo for two of us."

I nodded, as if it mattered to me how the aunt of my ex-girlfriend got to her funeral. I wasn't even sure why I was there. I mean, I'd had the message or invite, whatever you wanted to call it, but I didn't need to go. I wasn't sure what had made me, especially when Nicole was lying naked in my bed.

"Are you coming back to the pub for the wake?" Miriam asked.

"I wasn't planning on it," I replied, looking back to the where her neighbour had been standing. "I have work later. I actually work *in* a pub."

"Ah, okay. Well, if you change your mind, I'm sure we'll still be going late into the night. You know what these funerals are like when the family has Irish roots."

I didn't, but I nodded anyway. "Sure. So, I'd better get going."

"Oh, we still need to talk." She chewed on her lip. "Do you have a few minutes?"

I looked down at my watch, because I was the old-fashioned sort of guy who still wore one. I had a couple of hours before I had to open up. It would take me half an hour to get home, fifteen minutes to get to the pub. That would leave me just enough time to fuck Nicole one last time—we'd been seeing each other for two weeks, so her time was pretty much up.

"I have a couple of minutes," I replied.

Miriam nodded and pointed. "There's a bench there. Perhaps we could sit?"

"Yes sure."

I followed her to the bench, and then we both sat. Miriam didn't say anything, and I was beginning to wonder whether she was a little crazy from her grief. I knew she and Andy were close because Andy had mentioned her a few times. It had been something about how Miriam had taken Andy in when she was seventeen, after her mum killed herself.

"So, when was the last time you saw my niece?" she finally asked.

I shook my head. "I don't know, maybe a year ago. We didn't really have any contact after she ended things."

Miriam rolled her eyes. "Yes, that was my Andy. Once you were out of her life you were out of her life."

I smiled, not sure what to say. I hadn't cared that Andy cut me totally out of her life, but maybe Miriam would like to think everyone loved her niece as much as she did.

I pulled my coat closer around me as the wind picked up. "What was it that you wanted to talk to me about?" I wanted her to get on with it because Nicole was silently calling me like some sort of siren of the sea.

Miriam grimaced. "I'm not sure how to tell you this, so I guess I'll just come straight out with it."

My brows knitted together. "Okay."

"The thing is, Will… well, however I tell you this, it's going to sound… God, I could kill Andy." She gasped and closed her eyes. "Oh, bloody hell."

"It's okay." I tried to hide my smile. That sort of inappropriate shit made me laugh. "Just say what it is that you have to say."

"Okay well the thing is, Will, I'm just going to come out and say it. You have a daughter."

At that moment, I knew how it felt for the arse to drop out of your world.

My chest felt tight, as if it was too small for my heart. Sweat formed on my top lip, and I thought that I might puke. I was twenty years old—I couldn't have a kid. I was just a kid myself.

"W-what?" I leaned forward and pinned my gaze to her lips so I could see the words as they came out of her mouth. "Say it again."

"You have a child."

Yep, I heard and saw it right. Miriam opened her bag, pulled out an envelope, and passed it to me.

"These are some pictures of her. Sorry, she's a girl, or did I already say that. I said you had a daughter, didn't I?"

I nodded and looked down at the white envelope in my shaking hand.

"Her name is Maddy and she's adorable. She's just five months old." Miriam took the envelope from me and opened it. She pulled out a picture and held it up in front of me.

I looked at it but barely took it in. A dark haired, chubby kid was all I saw. I didn't notice whether she looked like me or her mother. I wasn't aware of whether she was cute or not, or what she was wearing. The image swam in front of my eyes.

"What do you… shit." I rubbed a hand down my face. "I mean, I don't want to speak ill of Andy but is the kid… fuck."

"Yours?" she asked. "Yes, I'm pretty sure she is. Of course, we can arrange a DNA test, but Andy didn't lie, and she told me right from the beginning that Maddy was your daughter. She found out she was pregnant right after she ended things with you. I mean, she might have known before. She was always trying to do everything on her own. You know, losing her mum, I think she just felt that—"

"I don't know what to say," I said interrupting her. "I mean, I have a job in a pub. I don't know if I can take care of a kid."

Miriam took a deep breath and then took my shaking hands in hers. They were cold and soft, and something about them reminded me of my mum, even though I hadn't held her hand in over ten years.

"Will," she said softly. "I know that this all seems scary to you, but I'm sorry, son, you're going to have to step up."

I shook my head. "No, I can't. That's not possible. Can't she stay with you?" I pulled my hands free from hers and gripped my hair. "I'm twenty, Miriam. I live in a shitty flat above a betting office, and I work nights in a pub. I don't get home until three every morning."

Miriam shrugged. "I don't know what to say, Will, but I'm sorry—you're going to have to deal with it."

"How the hell can I deal with it? What do you suggest that I do?" I leaned forward to take a deep breath, gasping in air because I felt like I might collapse from a heart attack.

"I'm sorry, Will. I know that this is a huge shock."

"You reckon?"

"The thing is, you really need to figure this out soon."

I looked up at her, and she was chewing her lip again. Her blue eyes were brimming with tears, and I knew that what she was about to say wasn't going to be good for me.

"Why?" I asked, swallowing back the scream of fear balled in my throat.

"I'm dying, Will and if you don't take Maddy, then she'll end up in care, and I don't think you want that."

I felt like I'd been punched in the gut—at Miriam's news, but also the mention of my child going into care. I'd been brought up in the system from the age of nine, and it had not been good. It had been fucking hideous. Foster parents who only wanted me for the money they could earn. Being passed over for adoption because I wasn't a cute little baby and had been labelled trouble. All I'd wanted was to be fucking loved. Playing up had been my way of getting attention. It didn't take some prick with a degree to realize that.

"She's a baby. She might get a good family," I replied, hating the vile taste of the words in my mouth.

Miriam took a deep breath. "And she may not. Are you willing to take that chance?"

I stood up and took two paces away from the bench. "You can't just put this on me, Miriam. I had no damn clue. She doesn't know me."

"I know, and I'm sorry, Will, but I have no other choice. I can't let her go into care. Yours isn't the only awful story I've heard. You know Andy went into care for a little while." She shook her head. "Of course, you know.

That's where you originally met, wasn't it."

It was true. Andy and I had been in the same kid's home when we were thirteen. Her mum had gone missing, and I'd been sent back by another foster family because I was too much for them. Andy was only there a month or so, and then Miriam came for her. I stayed another two years until Mrs Powell fostered me until I was eighteen. Then, a year later, Andy and I bumped into each other at the pub I was working at, and we got together that same night.

I thought about Mrs Powell and wondered whether she could maybe take the baby. She was almost seventy, and I'd been the last kid she fostered. I still had dinner with her once a week and saw how much her joints hurt and how bent her fingers were getting, so I knew deep down that it wouldn't be fair to ask her. I also knew that to help me, she'd say yes without even thinking about it.

"I am sorry, Will." Miriam's voice was soft and full of emotion, and I realised it must have been hard for her, too.

I stopped pacing and looked at her. "How long do you have?" I asked.

"Not long. Six months at most. It's bowel cancer that I foolishly didn't get checked out. This big coat hides the fact that I'm skin and bone underneath, and then there's the miracle of makeup."

As I looked at her, I could now see how sunken those bright blue eyes were and how pale her skin was beneath the blusher on her cheeks.

"If it helps, I've left everything to Maddy—my house, my car, my money. There's enough for you to be able to take care of her, as well as some going into trust for when she goes to university."

I vaguely recalled Andy telling me that her Aunt Miriam was well off. Her late husband had been some sort of financial wizard who'd made a fortune in investments. When he died of a heart attack at just fifty-four, Miriam had become a wealthy widow.

"Will, I always regret that I couldn't help Andy's mum get off the drink and drugs. I'll always regret that Andy had to spend a single day of her life feeling scared or alone because my sister refused my help or to even talk to me. When I took Andy home from that children's home, I vowed that she'd never suffer ever again, and that now includes Maddy. If I could change anything I would, but when I got my diagnosis just after Andy's death, I knew that you were the only person who I could trust that baby with."

"Even I don't know if you can trust me, Miriam," I cried. "I know nothing about babies."

"You can come and live with me, and I'll show you the ropes. It'll give you some time to adjust before I'm gone. Some time with some support."

I looked up to the sky and wondered what the fuck I'd done to deserve this shit to be landed on me. Then again what had Maddy done to deserve it too?

"When I get ill, you won't need to take care of me. I've organized for a nurse, and if necessary, a place in a hospice."

I looked at her and could see the weight of everything was firmly on her sloping shoulders. If nothing else, I supposed I could do it until she was gone—to give her some peace. Then, maybe, if it was tough, I could think about putting Maddy into care. She was a baby; she'd get a nice family who'd want to love her. Yeah, that's what I'd do—play the game until Miriam was gone, and then get my life back. I could make sure I didn't fall in love with her. I never fell in love. Two weeks was my max, after all.

"Okay," I sighed. "You'd better give me your address, and I'll be around tomorrow."

Miriam sighed, and a serene smile broke out over her face. I knew at least I'd given her some peace for the time that she had left.

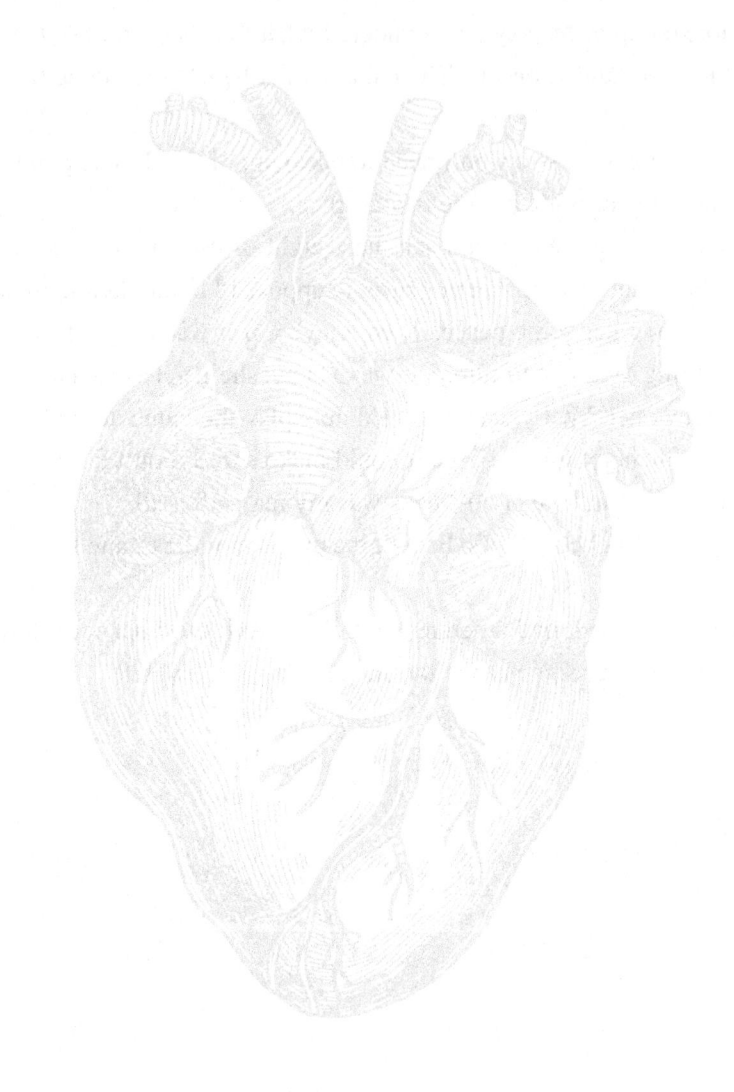

INTRODUCTIONS

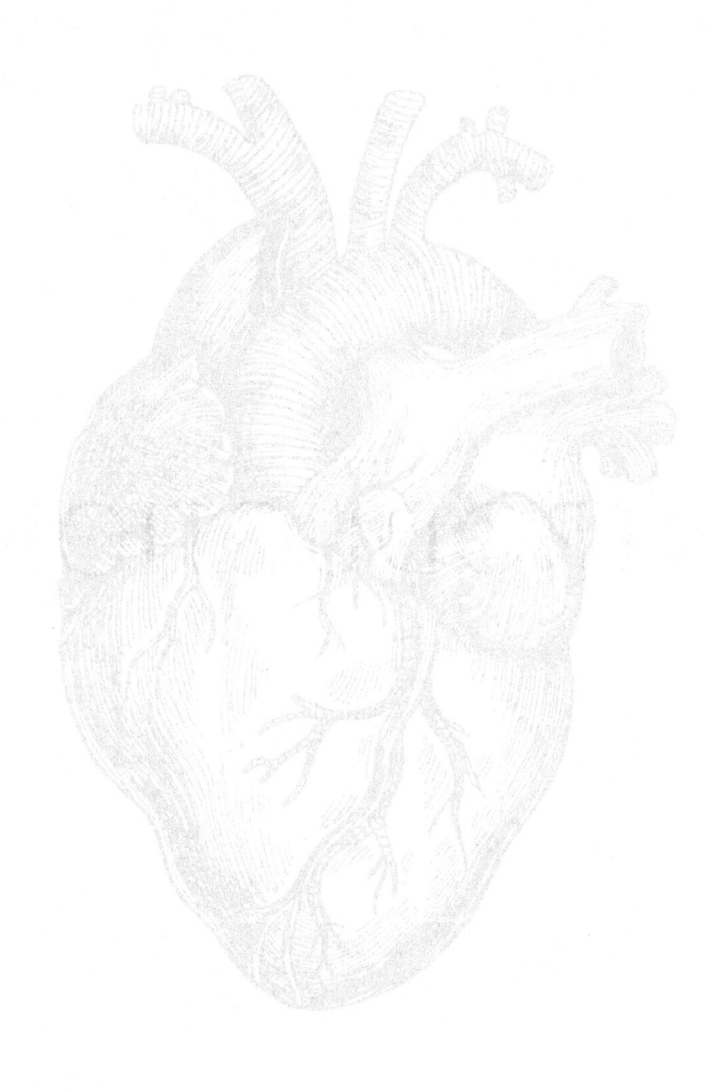

CHAPTER 1

Will

17 Years Later

"Shit," I hissed as I snatched my watch up from my bedside table. I threw back the duvet and dropped my feet to the floor. "Maddy, sweetheart, you'd better get up. We're late."

Grabbing yesterday's jeans from the floor, I pulled them on and then snagged a t-shirt, quickly smelling it to make sure it would survive at least the school run. Thank fuck I only had one more year of battling with the mums who all wanted a fucking piece of my arse.

I didn't have to take Maddy to school, but it seemed ridiculous not to when my bar was only around the corner from it. The problem was, at only thirty-seven and still being in great shape—even if I did say so myself—they surrounded my car like flies on shit. It was a wonder I wasn't a stone heavier with all the cakes and pies they gave to me. As for the sexual propositions, I felt violated daily. One woman even bruised my arse after Maddy left her bag in my car, and I had to run after her with it. She had an iron grip, and I didn't think she was going to let go.

"Dad," Maddy's yell made my ears ring. "Get your arse out of bed, or we're going to be late."

I shook my head and ran down the stairs to where her voice was coming from. When I skidded into the kitchen, I wasn't surprised to see she was already tucking into her breakfast, with mine waiting for me at the place opposite hers at the kitchen table.

"Morning, sweetheart." I grinned as I sat down and picked up the spoon for my cereal. "I should have known you'd be up and ready."

My seventeen-year-old daughter rolled her eyes and then grinned. Damn, she was beautiful. She looked a lot like her mum, but a lot like my mum too because Maddy had her smile. *My* smile and my lips.

"Did you do pay roll?" she asked.

"Yep. Sure did." I took a spoonful of cereal and watched as she delicately nibbled her toast.

She may have been brought up by a neanderthal, but I'd taught her manners. In fact, I taught her a lot; manners, how to punch a guy who made her feel uncomfortable, how to put a mean girl down with one short sentence, and most importantly how to make the best damn Long Island Iced Tea known to man.

I was so damn proud of her. I was proud of myself for sticking with it, even when times were hard. To be honest, sticking with it hadn't been hard, mainly because I loved her more than life. From the moment I saw Maddy in her cot at Miriam's house, I fell, hook, line, and sinker. There was no way she was going to be a two week thing. We got to keep Miriam for almost nine months before she died, and I had to say, they were probably some of the best months of my life. I felt loved and wanted, and it turned out I was pretty good at the whole dad thing. It had been hard work, especially when Miriam got really ill, but I'd managed to keep it together. I even helped take care of Miriam when the nurse wasn't around. Those nine months made me a man.

Maddy also had amazing organisational skills and made sure that I kept on top of business with my bar. I'd bought it when she started her last year of primary school. Mainly because she had joined drama club, and that, along with sleepovers and a nice group of friends that she had, I found myself with a lot of free time. Also, Miriam had changed her will and had left me a bunch of money to be received when Maddy was five. I had no fucking clue until Miriam's solicitor called me on Maddy's birthday. Apparently, she knew me better than I thought because the stipulation had been that Maddy was still with me. I'd never mentioned my plan to put Maddy into care once Miriam had gone. I'd never thought about it again once I saw her, not until the day Gordon, her solicitor, told me that there was a cool quarter of a million quid waiting to be transferred into my bank account.

These days, drama club had been replaced with fashion, music and, I hated to say it, boys. They seemed to be mentioned in every hushed conversation that I heard between Maddy and her friends. I was only grateful that her school didn't have a sports team of any note. Imagine if the star striker of the school football team started hanging around her. I'd either be grey or bald. The thought of my baby going after or being seduced by some dickhead who rated himself, filled me with dread. It was just every other hormonal teenage lad I had to keep an eye on instead.

"You know that I'm going over to Emma's on Friday night, right?"

"Yes, I do because I won't be here." I grabbed my coffee mug and took a long swig. It was hot and strong, just how I liked it. "I also know that you want to know if I can get you booze to take, but you've been building up to ask me."

Her eyes went wide and then she blinked slowly.

"How did you know that?" she asked.

"I'm your dad, it's my job to know this stuff."

She narrowed her eyes on me and then pointed. "You were listening in, weren't you? When Emma, Ana and Liv were here."

I shrugged and then took another spoonful of cereal. I wasn't going to tell her that Emma had let slip to her mum, and her mum had told me, thinking that maybe us sharing secrets might lead to us sharing a bed too. It also didn't hurt for my kid to think that I had special hearing skills.

"*Dad.* I can't believe that you've been listening in." She gasped. "Were you listening last night?"

I wasn't, but there was enough giggling for me to know that boys were being discussed. Oh, to be seventeen again and getting that first rush of attraction to the opposite sex. Okay, so I wasn't naïve enough to think she hadn't already kissed a boy. She was seventeen, which was like a twenty-year-old of my generation. They grew up so fucking fast these days. I'd drilled into her the importance of keeping herself for the one. Insisted on it, in fact. That was ironic coming from me, of course, but she was my baby and there would be plenty of time for that when she was like... thirty.

"I might have been," I replied. "But I guess you'll never know, because I won't tell."

"Dad," she whined. "I need my privacy."

"Yes, you certainly do, but I also need to be sure that you're safe. Which is why I will always listen in on your conversations. Even when you're sixty and I'm eighty."

"You might be dead when I'm sixty," she replied, a little too casually for my liking.

"Never. I will survive as long as I can just to annoy the shit out of you."

Maddy grinned, and her naturally plump lips parted to show the tip of her tongue between her teeth. Her chocolate brown eyes sparkled.

"So, the booze? Will you get some for me from the bar?"

I shook my head. "Nope."

"Dad!"

"No Maddy. You want booze, then you get some yourself, like any other teenager. It's a rite of passage. Get alcohol behind your parents' back, drink too much of it, puke and then clean it up without them finding out. Or so you think." I winked at her and then swigged back the last of my coffee. "Okay, let's go or you're going to be late and will get a detention."

"Please, I never get detention. I'm like a star pupil at that school."

She wasn't wrong. Maddy had clearly inherited brains from elsewhere in her family tree because she was a straight-A student. Her teachers told me regularly that she could easily go to a top university if she wanted to. My little angel wanted to make a difference, though. She wanted to become a children's counsellor, or a social worker and was adamant that she was going to do an online degree. I'd tried to dissuade her, telling her that she needed to go to a 'real' uni to get all the experiences. She could still be close to home if that was what she wanted, but Maddy was adamant. Only time would tell if she'd change her mind. I just hoped she wasn't saying it because she didn't like the idea of leaving me alone, because I would be perfectly fine and would in no way be lonely. My sex life had been sketchy, to say the least, in the last seventeen years. Occasional hook-ups when Maddy was on sleepovers or away on school trips had seen me through, but I was more than ready for something a little more than occasional.

"Okay, star pupil. Let's go."

We both quickly put our dishes in the sink and then grabbed jackets and bags, and I led us to my Range Rover that was almost as old as Maddy.

"You know, if you let me buy a car, you wouldn't have to drive me to school every day."

"We've talked about this, Maddy," I sighed as I started the engine. "Aunt Miriam's money is for uni, not a crap car. It's my job to buy that for you."

"Exactly," she snapped, looking out of the window as I touched the edge of the speed limit. "You'd buy me something awful. Something safe and ugly and bright yellow. I want something decent."

I shook my head. "When you go to university and need a car, I'll get you one. Until then I'll drive you or you can walk. Besides which, you've only had a handful of lessons."

We lived in a small town about forty-five minutes from Manchester, and the places that Maddy went to were all within walking distance. If she needed to be somewhere after dark, I took her. There was absolutely no need for her to reduce her lifespan by having a car at the age where she feared nothing. Since her seventeenth birthday, she'd been desperate to drive and had booked lessons straight away. I, on the other hand, didn't understand the rush. Besides which, the lessons had stalled with her finding other things to spend her money on, so she obviously wasn't that desperate.

"I won't need a car if I do Open University." She turned in her seat and poked me in the arm. "So that's another two years I'll be the sad douche without wheels."

"Shit, life is tough, sweetheart." I took a left and within a few seconds was pulling up in front of the school. "Okay, munchkin. Have a great day."

Maddy growled at me and then leaned over the console for a kiss. "You're a dick, Dad, you know that, right?"

"I do indeed." I offered my cheek, and the little shit licked it. "Ugh, you're disgusting."

"Bye, Daddy." She grinned and then she was gone.

"Christ, I love that kid," I muttered to myself and put my car into drive and headed toward my bar, The Jumping Frog—the thing that aside from my daughter, was my biggest pride and joy. I just had no idea what crap was going to meet me when I got there.

CHAPTER 2
Maddy

"**B**loody hell, Maddy," Liv breathed out with her hand on her heart. "Was that your hot dad who dropped you off?"

I groaned. "Liv, my dad drops me off every day. You know that."

"I know but he's just so dreamy."

Emma burst out laughing. "Who the hell says dreamy?"

"Liv, obviously," Ana replied as she swept black polish along her short nails. "I don't know why you just don't say, 'wow, Maddy your dad gives me a raging lady boner. I really want him to smash my back doors in.' You know, something like that."

"Ana," I cried, smacking my hand against her arm. "Really. That's my dad."

"He shouldn't be so hot then should he," she replied, frowning at me. "You do know half our year wants in his pants, and that includes the boys."

She was right of course. My dad was hot. Even I could admit that. He was six five with short dark hair and stubble, and had, according to my friends, 'a-may-zing arms'. Best of all though my dad had an incredible smile. It lit up the whole place and was infectious. It made me feel warm and safe. Like if Dad was smiling then everything was okay. My dad always smiled. I'd rarely seen him sad or upset, or worried. I'm sure that he did feel all those things, but he never ever showed me. Everything that he did was for me.

I knew the circumstances of him and my mum and how come Dad came to take care of me. He'd never hidden it from me. He'd told me about Aunt Miriam and her sister, my grandma; he told me everything. I'd even been introduced to one or two girlfriends over the years. I say girlfriends but they were more like hook-ups. Although he was always at pains to try and keep that fact from me. They'd been introduced as, "this is my friend 'insert name', she's just popped in for breakfast." I wasn't stupid though.

"Hey, suckadickable boy nine o'clock."

My heart lurched at Emma's words. I knew that it would be Zak Hoyland. I knew because even without seeing him, my skin was goose-bumped and a shiver was running down my spine. That was the affect that he had on me. He had ever since he'd joined our class last year, when he'd moved from London. As well as being as hot as hell he also had an amazing accent. Ana assured me that he was a real cockney from the East End of London. She knew because she watched *Eastenders*.

Intel, i.e., Liv, whose mum worked in the school office, said that he was from Paddington, and his dad had transferred to work as a transplant surgeon at a new private hospital just outside of Manchester. According to Liv, or rather her mum, Dr Hoyland was heading up the surgery unit of the new hospital. He'd brought the whole family, Zak, his wife, who was a dentist, and Zak's little sister, up North.

"Now that is someone who could smash my back doors in," Ana sighed.

"Yes," Liv sighed. "That boy's face card is never declined, and I don't say that lightly."

"Please. Do we have to?" I asked, feeling a swarm of butterflies in my stomach. "He's not a piece of meat."

They all burst out laughing, and when I glanced at each of them, they looked like they might pee their knickers. I had no idea what their problem was.

"What?" I asked, dropping my bag to the floor. "Why are you all so hysterical?"

"You," Emma said. "Acting like you don't want him to rub his dick all over your vagina."

I felt the heat creep up my neck. "No, actually I don't."

"Bullshit," Ana growled out, screwing the cap back on her nail polish. "I can practically smell your reaction to him from here."

"Ugh, you are gross," I replied, giving her a look that I hoped made her quiver. Ana was a hard nut to crack though. Her mum and dad taught mixed martial arts and she knew how to take care of herself. Nothing scared Ana.

"It's just the truth." She slipped her polish into her bag and then turned toward the main entrance of school. "Let's go bitches. Collard will have our arses if we're late for Maths."

With a sigh we all turned to follow her. It was then that I got full sight of Zak in all his glory. Today he was dressed all in black with his dark hair ruffled at the front. I'd like to think it was because he'd run his hands through it in frustration at not being able to rush up to me and ravage me in front of the whole school. It was more likely he'd fixed it like that on purpose because he knew it made him look good.

"Just put one foot in front of the other, Mads," Emma whispered in my ear. "Don't give him eye contact and you won't turn to a mushy jelly."

"Funny," I hissed. "I have no clue where you got it from that I think he's hot."

"Oh, come on, Mads," she replied with a grin. "Every girl in this school thinks he's hot. You just happen to deny it too much and too often. And, get this, I heard a couple of first year girls talking about who was hotter, Zak or your dad."

I burst out laughing. "No, you did not."

She arched her eyebrows and shrugged, daring me to argue. I linked my arms with hers and followed Ana and Liv down the path. As we got closer to Zak my heart rate increased and I just hoped that Liam Jeffreys who was standing with Zak didn't speak to me because my voice would definitely give the game away as to how Zak made me feel.

Liam and I had gone all through school together and were like family. His dad and my dad were friends and me and Dad had spent a lot of time with him and his family.

"Maddy."

Shit. Now I had to talk to him. Fuck it.

"H-hey Liam. You okay?" I flashed him a smile, trying hard not to catch Zak in my line of vision.

"Mum asked if you wanted to come for tea on Friday night, seeing as our dads are hitting the town."

It was the stag night of one of their friends, so they were going to Leeds for the night which was why I was going to Emma's.

"That's really kind of her but I'm staying over at Emma's." I pulled on Emma's arm, bringing her into the conversation.

"You could come over though," she said.

What the actual... why the hell did she ask that? We never had boys over on sleepovers. Never, ever, and we'd been having them since we were eleven!

"It's just a stupid girl's night," I added.

"Er, my mum is out. We're getting booze, don't forget. What's stupid about that?"

I gave her a stare to warn her to take the invitation back, but she didn't.

"So, come. I mean, it's not a party or anything like that, but we're getting pizza, maybe watch a movie."

I wanted to kill her. She knew that since he'd moved here, Zak and Liam were joined at the hip. If Liam came to her house on Friday night, then so would Zak.

"What do you think?" Liam asked, and although I wasn't looking directly, I knew he was talking to the suckadickable boy.

"Yeah, alright. Sounds good."

His deep, accented voice sent a heat through my body—a heat that lodged itself deep in the pit of my stomach. I risked a peek at him, and he was just as handsome as he'd been yesterday, and the day before, and the day before that. From the way he stood, tall and straight, how he rolled up the sleeves of his shirt to show off his forearms, the tiny beauty spot on his neck just below his left ear, how he carried his backpack off one shoulder, to the thick silver rings on his thumb and ring finger and the chain around his neck—all of it made him spectacular. He even smelled good. Nothing like the rest of the seventeen-year old balls of hormones in our class who reeked of cheap aftershave and candyfloss vape. No, Zak Hoyland didn't do stupid things like vape. He smoked real cigarettes. Well, I'd only seen him smoke once at Liam's party when his parents had gone away for the weekend to visit his grandma.

"Should be decent," he said, looking directly at me. "Booze, pizza and films sounds cool. Thanks for asking."

I loved how he pronounced asking, it was more like arsking, and it was sexy.

"Top, Zak," Liam said with a laugh. "It's top, not decent."

"Whatever." Zak grinned back and hit Liam on the arm. "Come on then, you wanker, let's get to class."

Wow, there it was again, clarse, not class. I could listen to him for hours.

As they walked off, Emma sighed. "Oh, dear, oh dear," she said, falling into stride with me. "What are we to do about you?"

"Me? What about me?"

"How on earth do we resolve this unrequited love?"

"Don't be so ridiculous," I replied. "There's no unrequited love."

"No," Ana said, over her shoulder. "Just an innate desire for him to smash your back doors in."

As my friends all burst out laughing again, I couldn't be bothered to argue with them. They were pathetic and didn't want to hear the truth. That was what I was telling myself anyway.

CHAPTER 3
Will

When the bar came into view, my breath caught as it usually did. Still unable to believe that it was mine. I knew I'd had a leg up from Miriam, but I'd still put my heart and soul into it. It hadn't been the best of places when I'd bought it. It had been a pet shop at one time until the owner had done a bunk, leaving behind a load of birds and guinea pigs. Being abandoned for years, it was run down, full of rotten wood and an infestation of rats, courtesy of the bird food still stored in there. That almost made me throw the towel in—I fucking hated rats. It was the tails and those beady little eyes. The place was mine, though, and when it came on sale in the little town that I lived with Mrs Powell I knew that I had to have it.

I knew that the cash from Miriam would only go so far with the money pit that I'd decided to buy. That meant for a long time I carried on with my pub job in the day and a little night security work at a factory that made steel valves. Thankfully, my old friend and neighbour, Sam, and his wife Louise were more than happy to have Maddy stay with them a few nights a week. It wasn't ideal, but for a couple of years it was necessary.

Now, though, the bar was finished, and aside from Maddy, it was my biggest pride and joy. Finished to a quality standard, it was a cool place to hang out for a whole range of Norford inhabitants. It wasn't like a typical pub, so we tended to get the younger crowd at night and the older ones during the day to drink coffee or the odd bottle of wine. We also seemed to be on a good route for minibuses of hen and stag parties going into Manchester, so unlike a lot of pubs and bars, we were doing okay.

Flicking through the post that I'd picked up on my way in, I lifted the bar flap and made my way to the back office. I could hear the clinking of bottles coming from the cellar and knew that Marcus, my head bar tender, had already arrived. Going to the door at the top of the stairs, I shouted down to him.

"Marcus, you want a brew?"

His blond head appeared, and he looked up at me, wiping the sweat from his brow. Cellar work was hard, and I didn't envy him in the stifling heat of the cellar. I made a mental note to look into a portable aircon machine for down there.

"Yep," he replied. "Make it a strong one."

I grinned. "Heavy night?"

"Could say that." He winked and then disappeared.

Marcus was me twenty years ago, before I knew I had a daughter. I'd lost count of the number of women I'd seen leave his flat, which was above the bar. Women of all ages and sizes had been in the guy's bed, and he showed no shame for it. And why should he, if they were willing? Each one I'd seen looked happy, leaving with a smile on her face.

I threw the post down on my desk and then doubled back to the kitchen to get us some tea. We didn't do meals as such, mainly because it was a pain in the arse trying to find and then keep a decent chef in such a small place. Those who were any good didn't stay long because they got poached by one of the big bars in Manchester or Liverpool. We therefore served chips, bacon and sausage butties, and the odd burger that the bar staff could easily throw together.

When I saw the dirty dishes on the side, I sighed heavily. Dylan was our dish washer and glass collector and wasn't supposed to go home until the kitchen was clean of plates and glasses. This was the third time in two weeks, and I was getting a little pissed off. He was a thin, wiry guy who I had a feeling had a drug habit. If he didn't, he had the longest lasting cold in history. He never stopped sniffing.

"Fuck," Marcus said from behind me. "Did he leave dirty plates again?"

I half-turned to him and sighed. "Yeah, I think I'm going to have to give him a warning."

"Let the fucker go," Marcus replied, reaching for two mugs from the shelf. "He was late twice last week as well."

I set about making us a cup of tea each, thinking that I needed to find a new dish washer like I needed to a hole in the head. Norford was small, once upon a time being just a small village of about three thousand people. It had grown over the last fifty years but was still small. With two major cities only one or two hours away, and the nearest large town only eight miles up the road, the place was not awash with people who wanted to work for minimum wage and free booze six nights a week.

"I'll have a word with him," I said as I watched the kettle boil. "Unless you know someone who'd like the job."

Marcus laughed. "Sorry, boss. Although I think my grandad is looking for something to get him out of the house. Grandma is hormonal as fuck apparently."

I groaned inwardly because Marcus' grandparents were only twenty five years older than me. When I thought about how fast the last twenty five years had gone by, I knew it wouldn't be long before I could be in their shoes. Not that any guy would be getting his hands on my little girl until she was at least forty or fifty.

Marcus nudged me. "You've got that look on your face. The one you get when I tell you how pretty Maddy is getting."

I narrowed my gaze on him. "I will cut your dick off, believe me."

"As if I'd even attempt to go there," he scoffed. "Like you said, you'd cut my dick off."

"She wouldn't look twice at you anyway." I turned back to the kettle, which was ready, and poured water into both mugs. "Sugar, seeing as you had a big night?"

"Yep, I need the rush. I didn't get to sleep until five this morning. Then I had to meet the delivery at seven."

"Poor baby," I said with no hint of sympathy.

"I heard you used to be just as bad." I handed him the mug and watched as he took a sip, wincing at the heat and the sweetness, since as I'd overdone it on the sugar. "Shit, we really need to buy better tea bags."

"No, we don't." I took a drink and had to agree it wasn't great. "We get better tea bags, and the staff will drink more of it and then I'll have to buy more and that will cost me money."

"Shit, it's a good job you're a great boss because that's just mean."

I shrugged. "Times are hard, mate, and I have to save cash where I can." The next sip was better as my taste buds started to adjust to it. "Anyway, who's been talking about me?"

"Lucas Tandy."

"Little fucker needs to concentrate on his own life instead of gossiping about mine." Lucas Tandy and I had gone to school together when I lived with Mrs Powell, and he liked to make out that we were good friends. We were not, and he had no clue what I got up to after I left Norford. I came back once a week to have dinner with Mrs P, God rest her soul, not to party with Lucas.

"I hear his wife caught him with Debbie Godfrey again."

"Yeah I heard. She really needs to kick his arse into touch."

"She's pretty cute actually," Marcus said with a faraway look in his eye. "I don't think I've ever had a woman fifteen years older than me."

I shook my head, despairing of him but knowing I'd been just the same. Although I never hooked up with an older women. "Steer clear of Alice

Tandy, Marcus. That's a whole load of trouble that you do not want to get involved in."

He winked and pulled out a stool. "Maybe. I'll see if she needs a confidence boost."

"I mean it, Marcus. If Lucas decides to get nasty with you do not come to me asking for help."

He held his hand up, palm facing me. "Okay, okay, I get it. No porking Alice Tandy."

"Fucking hell, Marcus," I groaned. "No wonder you manage to get a load of women with that charm and silver tongue."

"Hey," he said. "There's nothing silver about my tongue, it's pure platinum." He wiggled his tongue around. "You ask Ella from last night."

Rolling my eyes, I decided I would be much better off in my office dealing with bills. Moving into its semi-darkness, I opened the blinds and then rolled out the chair to sit down. The first envelope I opened was a bill, as was the second and the third. Finally, when I'd mentally cleaned out my bank account, I opened an invitation for the wedding of Amber a girl who had worked for me a couple of years before.

"Everyone is getting fucking married," I muttered to myself, throwing the invitation to one side. It was for me and Maddy, which made me laugh. That was how good my love life was—people seemed to think that the only date I could get was my daughter.

I really needed to do something about it, for my own sake as much as anything. The long-term relationship I had with my right hand was beyond boring. Norford was a small town, and I had a seventeen-year-old in the next room to me. Options were limited. Maybe the stag party at the weekend was coming just at the right time.

CHAPTER 4
Maddy

I found maths to be boring at the best of times, getting easily distracted because it just didn't hold my attention. I was good at it, but Mr Collard had one of those dull, boring voices that, if you hadn't had a good eight hours sleep and a couple of pints of coffee, would put you to sleep. His drone on algebra usually resulted in one of our class taking a nap.

Today's lesson was no different, except from one major thing. Zak Hoyland was sitting at the desk in front of me, leaning forward and giving me a glimpse of the waistband of his underwear. Now, where most guys in school wore Calvin's Zak did not. His waistband said *Oddballs*. Seeing them, I found myself grinning. It just showed how rad he was, that he could get away with it.

"Hey."

I turned to the whispered voice on my left to see Ana's raised brow.

"What?" I glanced up to the front of class to see Mr Collard was writing on the board.

"Stop looking at his arse." She pointed at Zak and shook her head.

"I'm not."

"You so are." She leaned across the small divide and pulled me closer by tugging on my jumper. "You're looking at that fine arse and wondering what it would look like if it was pumping between your legs."

The gasp I let out wasn't supposed to be so loud, but I could practically feel the wind created by the whip of heads. I quicky looked forward, seeing that half our class were looking my way. That included Zak and Mr Collard.

"Do we have a problem, Miss Newman?" He couldn't even chastise without sounding boring. "Hmm?"

"Nope. No problem here."

"You think we can concentrate, then?" He didn't even wait for an answer before turning back to the board.

I blinked slowly and deliberately at everyone else and waved my hand, indicating for them to turn back around. They all did except for Zak who smirked sexily.

"You okay, Maddy?" he asked, tapping his pen against his bottom lip. "Anything bothering you?"

Swallowing hard, I searched desperately for an answer, but his blue eyes were too magnetic and mesmerizing. Trapping me in a vortex of silence.

"I'll take that as a yes," he added when it was clear I wasn't going to reply.

"I'm fine," I added quickly, desperately hoping he wouldn't turn around and move his attention back to his textbook.

He studied me, and it felt like he was looking beyond the clothes, the skin, and the bones, right into my soul. My blood warmed as his stare intensified. He was beautiful and dark, with perfect teeth, a straight nose, a little dimple in his right cheek, and a tiny scar on his chin. It was so small it was almost unnoticeable, but I'd seen it.

"What about you?" I asked. "Are you okay?"

His eyes twinkled with a whole host of things, and I imagined all of them were bad, but in a good way.

"I'm a little stuck on the problem which Mr Collard has set. Do you think you could help me? I hear you're a bit of a brainbox."

I frowned. I'd heard he was so clever that had his pick of universities. "Didn't I hear that you wanted to be an accountant or something?"

His shoulders shook with silent laughter. "No way. I want to be a vet. Who wants to be a boring accountant?"

I nodded to the front of the class. "Mr Collard, apparently."

"Not surprised. He's a boring bastard."

Wow that accent was just the sexiest thing ever. Having lived in Norford since infant school, no one I knew sounded any different. We all had the same flat Cheshire accent with a hint of Manc, which made Zak's all the more interesting. He was the exciting new boy. He made my stomach a little bit squishy despite how much I denied it to my friends.

"You should go and sit with him," Ana said as she looked down at her black painted nails. "Help him with his…" she looked Zak up and down, "problem."

I narrowed my gaze at her and silently told her that I hated her. Ana shrugged and grinned.

"Well," she sighed. "What the hell are you waiting for?"

"*Ana.*"

"What is going on back there?" Mr Collard asked.

Zak turned around to face him. "I'm stuck on a problem sir, and Maddy was just offering to help."

"I can help you," Liam offered from his desk in front of Zak.

"It's fine, mate." Zak pointed a thumb towards me over his shoulder. "Maddy offered." He leaned forwards. "No disrespect but I think she's a bit cleverer than you."

Liam laughed, balled a piece of paper and threw it at his new friend. "Dick."

Their banter was good-natured, and it made me smile. I liked Liam and, in many ways, he was like a brother to me—or the very least, a cousin—and he'd often hung around with me and my friends when we were young. Now, though, it seemed that he and Zak had become really good mates.

"That's true," Liam answered. "She's got all the brains. Sit with her, but keep your hands to yourself."

"Liam," I hissed.

He grinned and turned back to his desk, leaving me to the deal with the discomfort he'd created.

"You going to help me, then?" Zak asked.

"Yes, she is," Ana replied.

"Whatever you've decided to do, Miss Newman," Mr Collard droned, "do it quickly."

Rolling my eyes, I stood and moved my chair next to Zak, ignoring the giggles from Liv and Emma two rows down.

"Okay," I sighed as I sat down. "Tell me which one you're stuck on."

Zak's long fingers pushed the paper of twenty problems toward me and he tapped at the one third from the bottom.

"How come you did all those others but this—probably the easiest one of them all—you can't?" I asked.

"It's just really hard," he groaned, with a hint of the bad I'd seen in his eyes.

"Okay, if you multiply this number by—"

"This film night you girls are having," he interrupted me. "Is it a pyjama party? Where you all wear skimpy pj's and nighties?"

I turned to him. "Do you really need my help?" He didn't. All the other answers written in his neat, blocked handwriting told me that much. "And yes, maybe."

He grinned and shrugged one shoulder. "Good to know."

"So, the maths problem."

"What should I wear?" he asked not interested in the maths problem. "My *Oddballs* undies?"

I felt the colour rise in my cheeks as I looked down at the test paper. I cleared my throat. "Can we just get on with this?"

"Sure." I heard him chuckle beside me. "But make sure you get back to me on the outfit situation, won't you? I'd hate to look like a prat." He swivelled the ring around on his thumb, and for some stupid reason, it made my stomach twist with excitement.

As for the sleepover, I wasn't sure that he was being serious. But as he leaned closer, I stopped thinking about it because his pure presence overpowered me. I had no idea how to be around this boy. My dad had taught me to be strong and independent and take no shit from anyone, yet I had a feeling that Zak Hoyland might just test everything that I'd ever learned.

CHAPTER 5
Will

It had been a long day, and I was knackered. As Maddy had messaged to say she was going over to her friend Ana's, to study and stay for tea, there didn't seem much point in going home, so I'd stayed to help work the bar. It was great we'd had a busy night, but I was glad when it was time for me to go and pick up her up.

Pulling up in front of Ana's house, I could see that Maddy was already waiting outside the front door. I parked and leaned across to open the car door for her.

"Why are you waiting outside? It's almost eleven-thirty, Maddy. What have I told you about hanging around the streets alone late at night?" I shook my head, feeling a tightness in my chest that was a mixture of irritation and anxiety.

"Dad, this is Norford," she protested, throwing her bag down by her feet. "Who the hell do you think is going to be hanging around waiting to kidnap me?"

Driving away, my jaw tightened. "Don't fucking joke about it, Maddy. Even the smallest town has its share of sickos. And don't roll your damn eyes at me." I didn't need to look at her to know that was what she was doing.

"I wasn't."

"And don't lie to me, that's not what we do, Madeline."

"Wow, you Madeline'd me." She sighed. "*So unfair*"

I glanced at her to see her feet were up on the seat. "And get your feet off my leather."

After a couple of minutes of silence, she leaned over and kissed my cheek. "Sorry, Daddy."

"Don't try and get around me, Maddy. I set rules for a reason, not just because I'm the parent and you're the kid."

"I know, and I am sorry. For standing outside and putting my feet on your seats."

"I don't give two shits about the seats. I do, however, love you, so when I tell you things like stay inside your friend's house until I get there, it's because I want you to be safe." Pulling up at the traffic lights, I turned to her. "Do you understand that?" She nodded and pulled her feet back up, which made me smile. "Don't be a little shit and get your feet down."

"Did you eat tea?"

There she was, looking out for me as usual while changing the subject. "A couple of bacon butties earlier."

"Dad, really?"

"We were busy."

"All that fat and carbs is not good for you. Why didn't you order out from Bennetts?"

Bennetts was a sandwich and salad place and made *the* best Chinese Chicken salad.

TAKE MY HAND 41

"Like I said, we were busy. There was a birthday party in."

Maddy snorted. "Female, I'll bet."

I chose not to answer because she wasn't wrong. There'd been about twenty of them, and Marcus and I had garnered a lot of attention. I figured we had around ten drinks each owing to us from them, not to mention an overflowing tip jar.

When we pulled up to the house, I leaned into the back seat for the day's takings while Maddy got out. I looked through the windscreen to see her open the letterbox attached to the wall by the front door. She took out the contents and she handed it all to me.

"Bills and a letter from Lancaster University," she said nonchalantly.

"What?" I flicked through to find an envelope addressed to her with the Lancaster Uni logo on it. "Did you apply? When did you apply? You didn't tell me. Why didn't you tell me?"

"It's no big deal," she sighed, taking my keys from me, shoving them in the lock, and pushing open the door. "I don't even know if I want to go. I just thought that I should apply. You know… just in case."

As I followed her into the house, I grinned. It was what I wanted for her. I didn't want her to go to do an online course when she was bright enough for better things.

"You didn't wait for clearance?" I handed her back the envelope. "You applied first round? You told me you didn't want to go. You know, the fact that you did must mean it's your preference." I grinned, and she sighed.

"I know, but I have until June to decide. *If* I get my grades." I'd have preferred if she'd said she was committed, but at least she was considering it. I shoved the envelope back at *her*.

"Open it."

"Dad I—"

"Maddy, open the damn letter. Please."

Chewing on her bottom lip, she took the letter back and stared at it for a few seconds. I nudged her shoulder with my finger, and big brown eyes—an image of mine—looked up at me.

"I'm scared, Dad."

"Why, sweetheart?" I asked, cupping her cheeks. "All I wanted was for you to apply. I won't love you any less if you don't get in. Besides, you weren't even sure that was where you wanted to go anyway."

She shook her head. "That's not it. I'm scared in case I *do* get in."

"Well, if you do, I'll be the proudest dad alive, you'll go, have an amazing time, and take the world by storm."

"But you'll be all alone here." Her cupid's bow lips pouted, and she suddenly looked like the four-year-old cutie who got upset when her snowman melted before she'd had a chance to build him a wife.

"Maddy, I'll be fine. It's not even two hours away, so you can come home whenever you want to," I grinned, "or whenever I need you to."

There was that eye roll again. "Like you'll care when you're living the life of a single man and every woman in town wants to take care of you."

"Not going to happen." I shook my head. "Just like you're not going to meet some guy who wants you to be his girlfriend."

Maddy groaned, but even in the pale light of the lamp I'd left on in the hallway, I could see the blush on her cheeks. I saw how she kicked her toe against the floor and then scratched the back of her neck. Shit, there was already a boy. Of course, there was. She was beautiful, sweet natured, and funny, so why wouldn't there be a boy?

"I want you to do what makes you happy, Maddy," I whispered, stooping down to look her directly in the eyes. "But I think this would be good for you to go. Isn't Ana going to Sheffield and Emma to Nottingham?"

"Well, yeah, but—"

"Which means you're not going to get to see them much anyway," I explained.

"Yes, but Liv will still be here, she's going to Manchester and living at home. Liam is doing that Business Apprenticeship at Bentley Motors, so he'll be home, too."

I pressed a kiss to her forehead. "Just open the letter, and then we can talk about it tomorrow." I knew that there was no point in pushing her. If there was anything predictable about my daughter, it was that she could be as stubborn as a mule, especially if she knew that I wanted her to do something that she didn't want to do. "If you don't want to go, then don't."

"I know what you're doing, Dad," she replied giving me a wry smile.

"But it won't work."

"I have no clue what you mean. Now, open the letter and I'll make us some hot chocolate." I rubbed her arms and moved away. "You want cream and marshmallows?"

With the envelope on the table between us, Maddy and I drank our hot chocolate. It was almost midnight, and with what was possibly some great news sitting there, my tiredness had disappeared. My nerves were jangling and my leg bouncing up and down as Maddy took her sweet time.

"Fuck it," I grunted and reached for it.

"Dad, no," she snapped, slamming her hand down on top of mine. "I'll do it." She pushed her mug away and pulled the letter to her. "Whatever it says I don't want you pressurising me, okay?"

"Okay. No pressure."

"Promise?"

I didn't want to promise but knew if I didn't, we'd be there until the next morning with the damn thing unopened.

"Promise. Now, take my hand." It was our thing. It was what I always told her to do when she was scared, ever since she was a little girl. When she took her first steps, her first day at school and the time an older boy, Jordan Campbell, tripped her up just before the bean bag race on sport's day. She missed the start of the race, so I told her to take my hand and I walked up to Mrs Beaker, the head, and told her to restart the race. As for Jordan Campbell, I waited a long ten years to get him back when I refused to serve him in the bar because he didn't have any ID, even though I knew he'd turned eighteen the week before.

Maddy gave a single nod and wrapped her tiny fingers around mine, squeezing them. After a few seconds, she breathed in, then slowly let it go, ripping open the envelope. As she took out the letter, wary eyes looked at me before unfolding it and holding it to her chest.

"I don't want to look."

"Maddy, sweetheart, come on you are much braver than that."

She swallowed and slowly lowered the paper, glancing down at it. Squinting, her lips moved as she read.

"Maddy, why don't you wear your glasses?" A hand was held up to silence me as she continued reading. "Well?"

I leaned across the table and tried to look over the top, but Maddy just lifted it higher so that her face was hidden. When I heard a sharp inhale, I had no idea whether it was good or bad news. She gave nothing away as she carried on reading.

I scrubbed a hand down my face and groaned, "Oh come on, just tell me will you."

The letter fluttered to the tabletop, and when Maddy's face was revealed I was still unsure how to react.

"Well?" I finally asked, linking my hands at the back of my neck. "Did you get in?"

Maddy nodded. "I got in, Dad. Three B's required." She licked her lips as her brown eyes went as big as saucers. "I got in."

Pride swelled in my chest as I watched the girl who I loved more than life itself. She was my whole world, and I'd vowed seventeen years before to help her to find her wings and soar. University could be the beginning of a whole new world for her—her ticket out of tiny little Norford, where she could make a better life for herself. She would never need to rely on the kindness of a dying woman to make something of herself, or work for hours every day to make sure she kept a roof over her family's head.

"I'm so proud of you, sweetheart," I whispered. "And your mum would be too."

I'd never hidden the details about Andy from Maddy. She knew about the childhood that Andy and I had and how we'd met, and why we had separated. She was also fully aware that Miriam had been very persuasive in getting me to meet her and to accept the responsibility of fatherhood.

"Would she?" Maddy whispered, tears brimming against her lashes.

"Yes, she would. Whether you decide to go or not, I will always," I tapped my finger on the table, "always be proud of you. You could clean the streets or become a brain surgeon and I'd be equally proud."

"Dad." Her voice cracked as she grabbed my hand. "I don't want anything to change. I want to be seventeen forever. Live with you forever."

I chuckled. "You're not thinking straight. I think you'll realise when you're about eighty and wiping my arse that isn't a good plan."

Laughing, she swiped at her eyes. "Nice vision, Dad."

"I'm right, though."

Smiling, she picked up the letter with her free hand and gave it to me. "You might want to frame this, then, because it might be the last great thing that I do… besides wiping your arse."

My daughter was beautiful, clever, funny, and she was going to rule the world, whatever she did with her life.

CHAPTER 6
Maddy

"Did you get the booze from your dad?" Emma asked as she opened the door to me, excitement shining in her eyes. "You said he'd give them to you from the bar."

I shook my head. "No, you know that I didn't. I told you that he said he wouldn't. That I had to get them some other way, like every other teenager."

Emma groaned quietly, and the look of excitement was replaced with one of irritation as she looked over my shoulder to my dad's rear lights disappearing down her street.

"He won't get us any even if I begged him." I shrugged. "We'll have to go to the shop."

"Oh, like Mr Monroe will let us buy booze. He knows us, Maddy. He knows that we're seventeen. Like he's going to say, 'Oh hey girls get whatever booze you like. It's on the house.'"

"Now, you're being ridiculous." I put my hand against her chest and pushed her back into the hallway. "We can work something out."

"Like what?" she demanded, putting her hands to her hips. "My mum locked all her booze away. Not that she has that much; she's so boring."

"Not so boring," I offered with a raised brow. "She's letting you have boys to a sleepover."

Emma looked away and scratched the back of her neck while shuffling from one foot to another.

"Emma! Shit, your mum doesn't even know that Zak and Liam are coming over, does she?"

"She'd have said no."

"Yet you still invited them?"

"I did it for you."

"Hah, really? Is that so? The fact that you've got the hots for Liam isn't why you suggested it, then?"

Emma's mouth dropped open, and she blinked slowly. "I do not."

"You liar." I laughed and punched her playfully in the shoulder. "It's about time that you admitted that you're so hot for him I could fry bacon on your stomach."

"As a vegetarian, I find that offensive." She gave a little shudder. "It doesn't matter anyway why I invited them. The point is, they'll be here in thirty minutes, and, like real lame dicks, we have no booze."

"What about Ana and Liv?" I asked. "Aren't they bringing any?"

"No, you and I were booze, and they are pizza and popcorn." She dropped her face to her hands and made a noise like she were in pain. "I may as well have asked my mum to make sandwiches, cake and ice cream."

"Christ," I muttered. "Drama queen much." I dropped my overnight bag to the floor and contemplated our options. "Do you have cash?"

Emma nodded. "About fifteen quid. Why?"

"I have twenty-five, so when Liam and Zak get here, we give Zak the cash and get him to go to the shop. Mr Monroe doesn't know him, and he looks old enough."

"Mr Monroe will still ask him for ID; you know he will," she snapped.

"Well, we obviously can't get it ourselves, so what do you want me to do?" I threw my hands in the air, beyond frustrated with one of my best friends.

"Your dad owns a bar, Madeline."

I gasped and stared at her open mouthed for a few seconds. "You Madeline'd me."

Emma looked suitably apologetic. "I'm sorry, okay, I didn't mean it. I really didn't. I'm so, so sorry."

"Oh, for God's sake, Emma, stop acting like you just killed my pet puppy. Now," I said. "how do you feel about that plan? About asking Zak to go and try and buy us some booze."

She thought about it for a second and then nodded. "Okay. We'll ask Zak."

"No," Zak said a little later as he stood in the doorway, arms folded over his chest. "It isn't happening, love."

"W-what?" I asked, totally distracted by the way his hair, sticking up in all directions after he'd pulled off his blue beanie, looked. It was a mess, but he looked amazing. He smelled amazing.

"I said," he leaned forward, arms still folded and his noses inches from mine, "I won't go and get your booze, *love*."

"But why not?" Emma asked, her voice a high-pitched screech of despair. "We don't have any if you don't go and get some." She shoved her hand into the front pocket of her jeans and pulled out some notes, holding them in the air. "I have cash. Maddy has cash, so why not?"

"We can't have a party without booze," Ana said, pushing past Zak into the living room to throw herself down on Emma's mum's pink leather sofa. "I mean, Liv and I kept to our side of the bargain. We brought the food."

"And we brought this." Liam grinned and gave a little bow as he presented himself to us. "And this." He then pointed at Zak, who smiled

TAKE MY HAND 49

and showed his straight white teeth. I guess that was the benefit of having a dentist as your mum.

"We did bring something else." Zak unfolded his arms and held out his hand to Liam, who hooked a black rucksack over it. Zak brought it to the front of him and with his eyes on me the whole time, unzipped it and reached inside before producing a couple of bottles of vodka from it. It was like he'd lifted a rabbit out of a hat as we all gasped. "Keep your money, love."

"Yes," Emma screamed. "I think I fucking love you."

The bottles were snatched from Zak's hands, and Emma darted off into the kitchen, with Liv following close behind. Ana sighed, as if bored, and got up from the sofa. When she reached Liam, she placed a hand on his back and pushed him.

"Come on, Wilfred, let's go help with the food and drink."

Liam shook his head and said over his shoulder, "I told you my middle name in secret, Ana," he growled, narrowing his eyes. "Don't ever call me that again. And I haven't forgiven you for telling everyone."

"Whatever."

Once they'd all disappeared, Zak laughed. "She's quite bossy, isn't she?"

"Ana?"

He nodded. "You've all got your place in the gang though."

"We do?" I frowned not sure what he was talking about.

"Ana is the bossy one, Emma is the organiser and Liv is the dramatic one." His denim blue eyes perused me. "I'm trying to make my mind up about you, though, love."

The way he said 'love' made my heart thud double-time and my stomach flip.

"You are?" I asked, almost in a whisper.

"Oh yeah, I am." He grinned and then turned to follow everyone else into the kitchen.

I was rooted to the spot wondering what the new hot boy at school meant, and once he made his mind up, would he like it?

We were playing Never Have I Ever, and it was a toss-up between who was most drunk, Liv, Ana or Liam. It appeared my friends were a lot wilder than I realised. I had no idea that Liam had even had sex, never mind in a field. I'd barely seen him with a girl. I knew that Ana and Liv weren't virgins, but Liam shocked me. As for Zak, he sat there staring around at the rest of us with a huge shit eating grin, like he was a kid memorising every moment, taking pictures with his mind to flick through later. He listened to everything we said, watched everything we did, and joined in with every note of our laughter.

I'd learned that he'd skinny dipped in the sea, skipped school—or 'bunked off' as he called it—kissed an older girl, kissed a boy for a dare, and stolen from a shop. The most interesting part, though, was that he sipped his vodka with a stony expression during questions about sex. He was gorgeous, funny, clever, and got me all hot and bothered when he looked at me, so I should have known he wouldn't be a virgin. I was just surprised that I didn't like the idea.

"I'm bored of this game," Emma slurred. "Let's watch a film."

She was also drunk, not because she'd done a load of things, but because she had continued to down vodka like it was going out of fashion.

"Which film?" Liam asked, smiling lazily as he lolled drunkenly.

"No chick lit shit," Ana said, pointing a wavering finger. "I want to watch a horror movie."

"No," Emma protested. "I get scared."

Liam leaned into her. "I'll take care of you. Keep you safe."

Emma blushed and fluttered her eyelashes.

"Horror movie it is then," Ana said with a smirk.

"I need to pee," Liv said and got to unsteady feet.

We all watched as she swayed out of the room.

"She won't come back down," I said as we heard a hiccup from the hallway. "She'll be asleep within five minutes."

"True story." Emma stood up and held herself steady with her palms on the table. "Okay, let's go into the living room and get this film started. And I've decided it's romance we're watching. My house, so my choice."

Decision made, I went over to the sink, deciding that I wasn't a big fan of vodka and wanted a glass of water instead. I assumed Zak had gone into the living room, so almost jumped out of my skin when he came up beside me as I ran the tap for cold water.

"Can you get me one of those, too, please?" he asked, emptying his vodka into the sink and then holding out his glass.

"You not a vodka lover?" I asked, filling his glass first.

"It's okay. I prefer a lager." He looked at my frown. "What? It's refreshing."

"It's awful, that's what it is."

"What about you? What do you prefer?"

"Cider or beer." I filled my glass with cold water and flipped off the tap. "Or water."

"Wow, your dad must be so proud. He owns a bar, but his daughter prefers the soft stuff."

I tilted my head and shrugged. "I do drink, just not vodka. It makes me sick, to be honest. As for Dad, he makes it a rule not to drink before eight at night if he's working, but even then, he limits it to one or two drinks a night."

"Sounds sensible." He leaned back against the cabinet, his long, strong fingers gripping his glass as he took a sip. "My dad says that most of the liver transplants that he does are because of booze."

"He's not just a doctor, then? He's a surgeon?"

"Yeah, he is. A transplant surgeon."

"And your mum's a dentist?"

"Wow, you have been researching me, haven't you?'

I huffed. "My dad told me because Liam's dad told him. My dad and Liam's dad are best friends, which makes me and Liam kind of like cousins I guess."

"Cousins," he repeated, nodding slowly. "Good to know."

I wasn't sure what that meant, but the heat in my blood made me think it might be something important. Something that maybe one day would lead me to taking a shot of vodka in a game of Never Have I Ever.

"You smoke?" he asked, reaching into the back pocket of his jeans and pulling out a packet of cigarettes.

I shook my head. "Never felt the desire."

Another smirk. "You know, Maddy, we should all have desires in life."

"You think?"

"I do. Now," he said, nodding toward the back door, "keep me company outside."

He placed his hand on the door handle and paused, looking back at me. "Do you need a coat? It's cold out there," he said.

"I'm good."

Outside, I felt a slight drizzle against my skin. Nothing too hard, but enough to make my naturally wavy hair frizzy, and I almost ran back inside at the sheer horror of the thought. Zak, though, was already sat on the garden bench, so I approached him as he lit up his cigarette. His cheeks hollowed as he drew on it, holding the smoke in. After a few seconds, he blew it out and patted the seat beside him.

"Come and talk to me," he said. "Tell me what your plans are."

"My plans?" I asked, surprised.

"Yeah. After A-Levels. What are you planning on doing?"

"Uni," I replied. "It's just which one."

"What are the choices?"

Did I have a choice? Was there any better than Lancaster for me that wasn't hours away? The only other one I'd considered was even further away—Edinburgh, not that I had any chance of getting in there.

"Lancaster or Open University."

"Bit different," he said with a laugh.

"I know. My dad is desperate for me to go to Lancaster, but I don't know." I pulled the sleeves of my jumper down over my hands. "It's all a little scary."

"What's scary about it?" Zak took another draw on his cigarette. It was long and hard and then he immediately threw it down and stamped on it. Pushing it into the ground.

"I like my life," I admitted. "And I don't know whether I'm ready to give it up." I shivered against the cold and almost yelped when an arm came around me. Zak pulled me into his side and rubbed my arm. "Erm, thanks."

"No problem. Now carry on telling me why you've got such a difficult decision to make." He stretched his legs out in front of him, crossing them at the ankles. "What is it you want to do for a career?"

"Social work or counselling," I replied without pause. I didn't have to think about it; it was what I'd wanted to do for years, ever since Dad told me his story—how he and my mum had met in a children's home. When he told me he'd have probably gone down the wrong path if it hadn't been for Grandma Powell, I knew that I wanted to help people like him somehow. When Grandma Powell died when I was eleven, there were almost a hundred of the kids she'd fostered at her funeral. It just proved to me that working with kids who needed help was what I wanted to do. "Both are dedicated professions." Zak gave me shoulder a squeeze. "I don't know you very well, but I'll bet you a tenner you'd be good at both."

I shrugged. "Well, I hope so."

"Yeah, I reckon so. I also know that Lancaster is one of the best degrees for Social Work, alongside Edinburgh."

"How on earth do you know that?" I asked, wondering if he could read my mind.

"I wanted to know all the courses available in case I change my mind about being a vet." He brought his legs up and nudged my knee with his. "Okay, why Open Uni then? Why's that in the mix rather than going away?"

"Because I can stay home, and it won't cost a fortune and because… I can stay home because I'm scared of leaving my dad." I turned to look at Zak, expecting him to be looking at me like I was an idiot. He wasn't, though. He was studying me and had a soft, understanding smile.

"Your dad will be fine without you, Maddy. As for the cost of uni there are such things as grants."

I cleared my throat. "I don't need a grant. My great-aunt left me enough money." I looked up at him and grimaced. "Even more stupid, hey? I just don't want to blow it all on my education."

"Worse things you could blow it on." Zak grinned. "As for the rest, well, life is good now, and you don't want it to change, and I get that."

"You do?"

"Hmm, I do. I didn't want my life to change and come here. I had a great life in London. Great friends, girlfriend, went to a great school—but then…" He shrugged and I felt a little pain in my stomach that he had a girlfriend. "Now I'm here, there are most definitely advantages."

He was grinning at me and had one eyebrow raised and I felt that squishy feeling in my stomach again.

"Why Norford, it's so small?"

Zak rolled his eyes. "Because my mum likes the idea of living in a place called Norford. Plus, she and Dad like peace and quiet when they're not working."

"Did you live in the centre of London?" I asked.

"Paddington, but my parents worked in the city. Like I said, this place has definite advantages. I mean, the girls here are prettier, for a start."

My face heated up and I cleared my throat. "We, erm, we should get back inside," I said tentatively. "I should probably check on Liv. Make sure she's sleeping on her side."

Zak nodded and removed his arm from around me, and instantly I regretted my suggestion to move from the bench. We both stood up, and as we got to the back door, he turned around to face me.

"Oh, and just in case you wanted to know, love, I don't have a girlfriend any longer. We ended things before I left London."

My heart began to beat in double time, and as I watched Zak disappear through the door, I couldn't help but wonder which uni he was going to.

CHAPTER 7
Will

"No," I said to my mate Sam Jeffrey's. "I'm not doing it."

"Why not, it's just a fucking t-shirt?"

I worked my jaw as I stared at him, wondering whether I should just punch him on his stupid nose and be done with it.

"There is no way I'm wearing something which says, 'Wet Willy Will' on the front of it." I snatched the t-shirt that was in his hand and held it up. "How come you get 'Cocky Sam'?"

"Because my name is Sam, why do you think?"

"'Sam is a Cock Head' would be better." I threw the t-shirt back at him. "What about our guest of honour anyway? What's Gary got?"

Sam grinned. "Genital Wart Gary."

"For fuck's sake, Sam. That's just mean. No woman is going to go near him with that plastered across his chest."

"And they shouldn't. It's his stag night."

"Yeah, but you don't need to throw him under the fucking bus because of it. Genital warts, my arse," I muttered, getting Sam a bottle of beer. I popped the top and then slammed it on the bar in front of him.

"Changing the subject," he said pausing the bottle halfway to his mouth. "Did you get Maddy booze for tonight?"

"How do you know?" I asked.

"Liam and his new mate Zak are going over there."

"Two things: who is Zak, and why are boys going over?"

"He's the kid from London. I told you about him. His dad is a surgeon, and they moved here toward the end of last year."

I nodded. "Oh yeah, I recall you mentioning it. So, to the second point, why is Diane letting boys in the house when she's not there?

"I'm guessing that she doesn't know. I only know because I heard Liam on the phone to Zak."

"And you didn't think to stop him?" I shook my head and took a long swig of my beer.

"Because they're fucking kids, Will. It's their last year before uni—let them live a little."

"Fuck, Sam I've been a seventeen-year-old boy. I know what is going on in their heads." I felt my heart rate speed up at the thought of what could be happening at that very moment in a house full of teenagers and no adults. "Did Liam take alcohol?"

He shrugged as he took a drink of beer.

"Why am I even asking that? Of course, he did."

"Will, just calm down. Maddy is a sensible kid, and it's Liam we're talking about. They're practically brother and sister."

"I don't know this kid Zak, though," I protested. "And in thirty minutes we're getting on a fucking bus to go an hour and a half away. What if she needs me?"

Sam rolled his eyes. "She'll be fine. I'll get Louise to check in with them."

"Maybe Louise could go and pick her up."

"No, Will," he snapped. "Let her have fun. Besides, Louise is taking Darcy to the cinema and then pizza."

I rubbed my chest and groaned. "I'm being an overprotective dick, aren't I?"

"Yes, you are. Christ knows what you'll be like when she goes off to uni."

"Oh shit, don't remind me." I was the one who wanted her to go. I was clearly a masochist.

Laughing, Sam put his beer down on the bar and handed me my t-shirt. "Stop fussing and get this damn shirt on before everyone else get here." I opened my mouth to object, but he held his hand up to silence me. "No. You're wearing it and if you do, then I'll consider asking Lou to go round and check on them."

I snatched the white cotton from him, deciding that wearing a shit slogan t-shirt was worth it if it meant I got to find out my daughter was safe.

***

We were in a bar which sold craft beers and great food, but it was dark and had a slight tackiness to the floor. The music played quietly in the background, making it ideal for twelve blokes on a stag party. We were at the bar, chatting the usual crap after having eaten a meal, and, just as I'd predicted, everyone was flagging.

"I've got a stomach ache," Gary complained rubbing a hand under his Genital Warts t-shirt. "I think that I need a lie down."

"Me too," Gary's future brother-in-law, Casey, groaned.

"I told you not to eat that extra slice of chocolate cake," Luke said, as he patted his flat stomach. "Right, where next?"

Luke dragged Gary into the mele of some of the other blokes in our group, with Casey following closely behind. As I watched them, I pulled out my phone to check the time. It was almost ten-thirty, which, by my calculation, meant we had another three and half hours before we could get back on the bus home. It was good to be out and enjoying myself, but I was still worried about Maddy. I had to trust her though, she'd be gone to university soon enough, and then I could be almost two hours from her if she went to Lancaster. Further, if I managed to persuade her that Edinburgh was better—or so my research over the last couple of days had suggested. Seeing as she'd shown interest in Lancaster, I thought it might be a good time to see what else was out there. Trying not to think too much about my daughter and what she might be doing, I turned to the bar to order another drink.

"Stag party?"

The voice coming from my right was soft, sultry and definitely interested me. I turned with a smile and was glad I'd stayed at the bar. She was stunning. Chestnut-coloured long hair that fell down her back and golden-brown skin garnered my attention. She smelled good too.

"Yes, it is," I replied and thumbed behind me. "The one with the genital warts."

Her head whipped around in the direction of Gary, and she smiled. Her teeth were straight and white but had a little gap between the top two. I recalled Mrs Powell telling me once that it was lucky to have a gap like that. When her gaze landed back on mine, I felt like I was the lucky one.

"You're really beautiful you know that?" I couldn't help myself; it just came blurting out.

"Thank you."

I liked that she didn't deny it coyly or preen like some influencer looking for followers. She just smiled as she gave me thanks.

"I'm Will, by the way." I held out my hand and watched as she looked down at it.

"You don't have genital warts too, do you?"

She was grinning but still didn't move her hands from the bar, where they were resting.

"Nope. I'm," I said, opening my jacket, "I'm Wet Willy Will."

"Wow, a wet willy. Nice." She looked at it with a raised eyebrow and laughed before taking my hand and shaking it. "Maya."

"Pleased to meet you, Maya."

"Whose idea were the t-shirts?" she asked.

"Cocky Sam's." I pointed directly at Sam, who was urging Gary to down beer from a jug. "I think he gave me a shit one on purpose because I am and have always been, so much better than him in every way, right from when we met as teenagers."

"You sure have confidence in yourself."

I shrugged and smiled, enjoying the feeling that talking and flirting with a beautiful woman gave to you. There were no bills, no employee issues, no worries about stock—just a level of freedom that made you glad that you were young. Glad that you were healthy. It was that feeling of anticipation of what might be about to come.

"I find the best person to back you is yourself in this life."

"Very true." She turned to face me, resting her elbow on the bar. "So how come you're standing alone and not with the rest of the guys, knocking back beer and singing Oasis songs."

I looked over to the guys to see they had indeed moved onto singing.

"I guess I'm not a singer." I copied her stance, placing my glass on the bar between us. "What about you? Who are you here with?"

She glanced over her shoulder. "I'm with two friends. It's kind of a divorce party."

"Ah, okay." I nodded slowly. "Yours or one of your friend's."

"Morgan's, my friend. I've never had the pleasure of being married." It was at that moment that the barman came up, throwing a towel over his shoulder.

"Sorry to keep you folks, what can I get you?"

"Another of these, please, and..." I held my hand out to Maya, but she shook her head.

"It's fine. I'm getting another bottle of wine."

"That's okay." I turned to the bartender and handed over my card. "Get the lady her bottle of wine too."

"Honestly," she said, "I can't—"

"Yes, you can. But could I buy just *you* a drink, too?"

She paused, looked at me and then back to the bartender. "I'll have a rum and Coke, please, but let me just take the wine back. Is that okay?"

"Sure, as long as you promise to come back."

"I will." She gave me a smile that made her eyes sparkle and took the bottle from the barman. "I'll be two minutes."

I watched her walk over to her friends and put the wine on the table. She crouched down at the side of the table and the three of them put their heads together. First one friend looked my way, and then the other one. They then huddled their heads together again until her friend closest to me dropped her head back and roared laughing. Maya rose slowly with her eyes on me, and I smiled at her. When she gave me a little wave, I stood up straighter and smoothed down my shirt.

"Hey, Will," Sam's booming voice got me swinging around in his direction. "We're heading out to the bar next door."

I glanced back at Maya who was flicking her hair over one shoulder. "I'm going to stay here."

Sam blinked. "What?"

"I'm staying here," I repeated. I looked over my shoulder, and when I looked back at him Sam's eyes were also in that direction.

"Oh right," he said his face breaking out into a grin. "Don't forget, minibus leaves at two."

I shook my head. "I'll find you before then. I just want to finish my drink."

"Whatever. Just message me and I'll let you know where we are." He slapped my back and gave me a wink. "Be careful."

I couldn't say that I always was, because I had a seventeen-year-old daughter to prove otherwise. "I'm just finishing my drink," I stressed, but Sam laughed and started to round up the rest of our party.

I kept my eyes on the door, watching them leave when I felt a hand on my shoulder. I turned to see that it was Maya.

"Okay?" I asked.

She nodded and lifted her rum and coke. "Thanks for this."

"My pleasure." I looked around the bar and spotted a booth. "You want to sit down?"

"Yeah, sure."

As I led Maya to the booth, I knew that I wouldn't be joining the party again until it was time to go home.

CHAPTER 8
Will

"I don't normally do stuff like this," Maya said, her slim fingers circling the rim of her glass. "Ditch my friends for a man I've known for a whole five minutes."

I had to be honest, I liked that she had. Five minutes wasn't long enough, and if she hadn't agreed to have a drink with me, I might have camped myself at her table. Admittedly, she was beautiful, but I was desperate to get to know *her*.

"I can go and find my mates if you want to go back to your friends," I offered, hoping she wouldn't agree.

She frowned and shook her head. "No. In any case, if I did, my friends would go crazy. In Loretta's words, 'go and get a piece of that fine arse, girl.'"

I burst out laughing and looked over to her friends, who were sneaking glances at us. "What about your friend who's getting divorced? Did she warn you off me?"

"That's rude," Maya said with a smile. "Assuming she's a man hater just because she's getting divorced."

I looked at her through one eye and groaned. "Yeah, sorry, you're right it was."

"It's fine, she actually jokes about it herself." She turned to look at her friends who gave her a little wave. "Oh no, they're going to be grilling me for hours."

"How long have you been friends?"

"Morgan and I went to nursery school together and we met Loretta in our first year at high school. We just clicked and have been best friends ever since. We were Morgan's bridesmaids."

"How long was she married?" I asked, unable to move my gaze off her face. Even in the light of the lamp on the table, I could see that her eyes were a gorgeous shade of green with tiny flecks of brown.

"Five years." Maya shrugged. "He's a nice guy, but they should never have married. They are so different."

"In what way?" I loved her teeth too. That little gap was cute.

"Morgan is a party girl, and Ben likes to stay home. They met at uni, and I think they thought that it was the natural order of things, but as they grew up, they grew apart."

"Are you all from around here?" Despite it being Winter her skin was a gorgeous bronze colour that glowed, and it was taking every bit of my self-control not to touch her. Just to see if it was as soft as it looked

"Yep, born and bred," She replied. "Although Loretta is only visiting this weekend. She lives in Newcastle with her fiancé, Matt. What about you? Where are you from?" When she leaned closer, I got a hint of her perfume again and made a mental note to ask what it was.

"I live in a tiny little place called Norford, not far from Manchester. As for growing up, well, it was a few different places. Until a lady called Mrs Powell fostered me and she was from Norford." Maya's neck was long and slim, the sort that looked good adorned with jewellery, or that you could spend hours kissing.

"No family then?" She caught her bottom lip in her teeth, and two concerned creases appeared between her brows.

"Yeah, I have family." I smiled feeling my heart expand. "I have a seventeen-year-old daughter. Madeline, although she prefers Maddy."

"Seventeen? Wow."

"Yeah, me and her mum were young and careless, but I wouldn't be without her. She is my world that's for sure. Her mum died when she was only a few months old."

"Oh no," Maya said, laying her long, elegant fingers on top of my hand. "I'm so sorry."

"Thank you, but we weren't together at the time. In fact, I didn't even know that I had a daughter." I looked at the sympathy in Maya's eyes and let out a chuckle. "Bloody hell, I've known you about a minute and I'm already giving you my life story."

"I must have one of those faces," she replied. "The kind that makes someone want to spill their guts."

Maybe she did, but for me it wasn't her face. It was just her. I felt like I wanted to talk to her about everything and keep talking and talking until we were hoarse. I had no idea why, but I felt like I knew her but not enough. It wasn't that comfortable feeling you had with old school friends, but it was exciting, like I was discovering a whole new world. It was new and strange, but good. I'd liked lots of women over the years but had never seen myself having anything other than a sexual relationship with them. But this girl, this woman—she already had me wondering, 'What if?' Ten minutes in, and I was hooked.

"What about you?" I asked. "What about your family?"

"Where to start." She rolled her eyes. "Brief history is, they're big and brash. My grandpa was Scottish and came to Leeds sixty years ago when he was twenty-two. He met my grandma two days later and a month after that they got married. Ten months later, they had my dad. He was followed by three more sons and two daughters. My mum and dad have been married for thirty-five years and I have an older brother Jack, and a younger brother, Charlie. Jack has three kids, and Charlie probably has about ten but officially none."

"He's a party boy?"

"Yes, he bloody well is. Well, he was, he's now met *the* one and is engaged. Mum even booked him into a sexual health clinic a couple of years back because she was so worried his dick might drop off. He didn't speak to her for a month because of that."

"She was just looking out for him."

"I know." Maya banged her hand down on the table. "That's exactly what I said. I told him, 'Charlie Mackenzie you are one big slut and Mum only wants to be sure you don't have genital warts or some such."

"Like Gary," I added.

Maya grinned and her green eyes lit up. "Just like Gary." She narrowed her gaze on me. "He doesn't really have genital warts, does he?"

"No," I said around a laugh, "he doesn't have any sexual disease of any kind. At least none that I'm aware of, not that I inspect his genitals regularly."

"When does he get married?"

"Three weeks on Friday. To Amy, she seems lovely, although I don't know her well. Gary is more Sam's friend than mine."

"Really? That's exactly a week before my brother." She wriggled down in her seat like she was getting comfortable. "Anyway, so tell me about your daughter. What's she like?"

"Amazing." I didn't need to think about it. "Sweet, funny, smart, opinionated."

"Aren't all teenagers?"

"I guess so. She also knows how to wrap me around her little finger, so sometimes," I winced, "she gets too much of her own way."

"That's what dads are for. Mine still spoils me."

I sat back in my seat and watched her carefully. I bet with everything in me that she deserved to be spoiled. She looked like the sort of woman who should be treated like a queen. The sort that you cherished every single day.

"Do your brothers spoil you too?" Linking my hands in front of me, I relaxed back into my seat, getting comfy just like Maya was.

"Oh my goodness," she cried. "You have no idea."

She was right, I didn't, but was anxious to find out. "Hold it there, and I'll grab us some more drinks."

She sat up straight and smiled. "Great."

As I walked to the bar, I hated that it was time wasted. Time away from the woman who appeared to already have me tied in knots.

CHAPTER 9
Maddy

Everyone was asleep. Liv was snoring, Ana was sucking her thumb like a toddler, and Emma was muttering about unicorns and Harry Styles. Whereas I couldn't shut my eyes because there was far too much going around in my head.

My conversations with Zak. How Zak laughed. How he held his head to one side as he listened to me. How when he left Emma's house, he walked backward down the driveway, talking to me until he disappeared around the corner.

Did any of it mean anything? Did he like me? When he gave me a hug before he left, was it a little longer than the one that he gave to the others?

I turned on my side, away from Liv on the blow-up mattress we were sharing, and flicked on my phone to scroll through the pictures I'd taken earlier. I quickly flicked through the ones of everyone else, until I got to the three or four that I'd taken of Zak on his own. The first one he was smiling with his perfectly straight, perfectly white teeth showing, and his blue eyes bright. Liam had been talking to him, but Zak's eyes had been on me as I snapped away. The next one was Zak smoking a cigarette in the garden. He was sitting on the bench again and I'd caught his side profile. His strong, square jaw and the little dimple right at the corner of his mouth. The smoke was swirling up in front of him, and if I'd had any talent as a photographer, it could easily have been the cover picture on one of the books that Louise, Liam's mum liked to read.

I stared at it and wondered what he was thinking about in that moment. Maybe it was me. We'd been getting along, chatting, laughing. Perhaps he was thinking about asking me on a date. I thought about how he only ever took a couple of drags on his cigarette and then put it out. What was the point of smoking? Glancing back at the picture it struck me how cool he looked with a cigarette in his mouth. Maybe that was why. Yet he didn't strike me as a boy who cared whether he looked cool or not. What if it was all an act and he was sweet and funny and, what…

"Shit," I groaned and rolled onto my back, holding my phone to my stomach. A small chink of light escaped lighting up my chest for a few seconds before it faded out.

I was being stupid. He could have any girl in school that he wanted, so why would he be interested in me? I wasn't anything special. My eyes were a little too big, and my top lip was bigger than my bottom one. I couldn't dance for shit—I got that from my dad, he was awful. I was hopeless at sport too. Zak Hoyland would, and probably should, end up with a girl like Becky Marshall. She was Head Girl and captain on the school netball team. She was much more Zak's level.

"What are you doing?" Liv's voice was muffled by the pillow she was face down in. "What time is it?"

I lifted my phone and brought it back to life. "Three."

"Morning or afternoon?"

"Morning. You've been asleep since nine-thirty. You really are a lightweight."

"Everything feels wrong." She moaned like she might be about to puke.

I turned my head to face her. "Do you need a bucket or something, because you know Emma's mum will kill you if you vomit on her carpet."

"Nope." She lifted her hand to swipe at her mouth. "I need water."

I reached across my body and picked up the bottle of water I'd taken to bed with me. "Here, have this."

She shuffled around until she was in a sitting position and took the bottle from me. "Thanks, you're a life saver. Vodka is a bitch."

I lay on my stomach, still watching as she gulped back almost all the bottle in one go. Her blonde hair was a messy halo around her face, and she had mascara smudged under her eyes, yet she still looked pretty.

"Liv."

"Hmm," she said around the rim of the water bottle.

"You know when you dated Joshua, how did you know that you liked each other?"

Her little button nose wrinkled. "You told me," she said, holding the bottle against her forehead. "You came up to me in PE and said, 'did you know that Joshua Brooks wants in your knickers?' I said no, and you said that I should go speak to him, so I did." She grinned and pushed her messy hair from her face. "And you were right. He did want in my knickers."

"I remember," I said. "I caught you with your knickers down, if I recall."

"Do you think you two could stop talking about knickers," Ana complained from Emma's bed. "Some of us are trying to sleep."

"Sorry," I whispered. "Go back to sleep."

"I can't now. Not until you tell me why you want to know how Liv knew she liked Joshua."

Shit. Liv was a little self-centred and I could have easily got her off the subject by talking about, well, Liv. Ana was different though. She wouldn't stop hounding me until I gave her something.

"I was just wondering that's all," I replied, rolling onto my back.

Ana snorted. "Wow, you're some sort of English wizard and you can't come up with anything better than, 'I was just wondering'? Shit, Maddy, up your game girl."

"What's going on?"

"Oh crap, now we've woken the monster from the deep." Ana sighed. "Go back to sleep, Em."

"I can't not if you're all talking about something. You know that I hate being the last to know." She reached over and flicked on the bedside lamp. "Spill."

"I was just asking Liv how she and Josh knew they liked each other." I dropped my forearm to my forehead and sighed. "It was nothing important, you can all just go back to sleep now."

I heard the bed clothes rustle and then feet land on the floor. I turned my head to see Emma sitting on the edge of the bed. Ana lay next to her on her side with her head propped up on her hand. Both were staring at me expectantly.

Liv shifted so that she was also watching me. "Okay, the gang's all here. Go for it."

"Go for what?" I asked.

"Go for the full deets on why you were asking about me and Joshua."

"I'm just curious that's all." All three of my friends burst out laughing. "You know I hate you all, right?"

"Whatever," Ana said with a yawn. "Tell us so we can get back to sleep."

"I'm not stopping you."

"But you are, Maddy." She yawned again, stretching out the arm that wasn't supporting her head. "You know we'll lie awake wondering."

"She's right," Liv added. "So, just tell us why you're asking."

These were my friends. My best friends who would have my back through thick and thin, so why was it so hard to tell them?

"Does this question have anything to do with a certain cockney boy with a nice arse?"

"No," I answered too quickly, seeing as they fell about laughing again. *"Why are you laughing?"*

"Sush," Emma whisper hissed. "You'll wake my mum."

"Sorry, but you were the ones laughing."

"Because you're lying to yourself, and us," Ana sighed, dropping to her back. "Now, let's start again. Are you asking because of Zak?"

There was no point in lying. "Yes. Okay. It's to do with Zak. I don't know whether he likes me or not."

"He likes you." Liv snorted a laugh and then moaned. "Shit, that hurt my head."

"She's right, he likes you," Emma added. "He spoke to you more than anyone and he gave you're a really long hug when he left."

I sat up. "You saw that? I didn't imagine that, right?"

"Oh yeah, we saw it. I thought he was going to drag you from my house and make you go home with him."

I pulled up my knees, hugging them to my chest, wondering whether I'd have gone willingly. It didn't take long for me to decide, I would have.

"I just want to talk to him all the time," I admitted. "Look at him all the time."

"Totally understandable," Liv replied. "Like Emma said, he's extremely good to look at. Like a juicy burger."

"I wish you wouldn't liken him to food," I groaned. "For one thing, it makes me hungry."

"Yeah, for his big cockney dick," Ana said, laughing.

"She wants him and his big cockney sausage for breakfast," Liv added, in a dubious cockney accent, which made us all laugh.

"His huge pork sausage with beans on the side."

"Ugh gross. Who has sex covered in beans?" Ana asked.

"I didn't mean that she… oh fuck off," Emma said, turning to poke Ana in the leg. "You know what I meant." She lifted her shoulders and pouted. "Why do you always do that. All of you pretend that I've spoiled the joke. You do it every time."

We didn't; she either went too far or just didn't get the joke.

"The point is," I said to avert some sulking on Emma's part, "how do I know if he likes me? And if he does like me, what do I do about it?"

"That's easy," Ana replied. "You flirt with someone else, and he'll get jealous and ask you on a date."

"No way," I objected. "I'm not doing that. Besides I'm no good at flirting."

"Liv could teach you," Emma announced, scrambling over Ana to get back into bed. "She does it with your dad all the time."

"That's just gross." I shuddered and threw Liv a narrow-eyed glare.

"Maddy," she sighed. "We've discussed this. You know I think he's hot, but I would never do anything about it. I could never have sex with a man *that* old. Fantasise about him, yes, but actual sex…" she shuddered and shook her head, her lips all pinched.

"Wow," I murmured. "It's great knowing you think about my dad while you touch yourself."

"What, don't tell me you don't have a visual when you're flicking your little bean?" She actually sounded annoyed.

I closed my eyes and slapped my hands over my face. "Let's just go to sleep," was my muffled response. "I really don't want to talk any longer."

"Yeah," Liv agreed. "I think I need to sleep before I vomit."

"My mum will kill you if you do."

"Your mum will kill all of you if you don't shut up," Emma's mum yelled from her room across the landing.

We all giggled and settled back down, and within minutes they were all back to sleep, whereas I continued to think about the blue-eyed boy with the perfect smile and cute dimple.

ZAK'S WHATSAPP MESSAGES

ZAK

How's your day been mate? Missed me?

OSCAR

Like bad farts, mate!! No, it's weird without you here. How's the new place?

ZAK

Yeah, like I said, it's good. Liam is top.

OSCAR

TOP!!! Stop you sound like a proper Manc.

ZAK

That's nothing. When you kiss someone, around here they call it NECKING ON! Necking on, have you ever?

OSCAR

Weird! Makes you sound like a vampire! Anyway, what about that girl you like? Any progress? Had the balls to talk to her yet? Necked on with her yet?

ZAK

I've always had the balls. I was playing it cool. And yeah some progress. No necking on... yet. She's cute.

OSCAR

CUTE??? What about her tits lol???!!

ZAK

I wouldn't be such a dick as to tell you... but they're nice from what I can tell. She's gorgeous actually. Funny. A bit shy, yet confident. Nothing like the girls at school.

OSCAR

Nothing like Connie then!! She's got a new bf btw. Danny Spencer.

ZAK

Not that I care as we finished before I even left, but WTF is she doing with him?? I know she's a bitch, but he's a prick and he's a druggie.

OSCAR

Precisely. Anyway, back to the new gf. Have you made a move?

ZAK

Kind of and she's not my gf.

OSCAR

Tell me you've at least made it clear you like her!!!

ZAK

Yeah. Well at least I think I have. I just hope I haven't got it wrong cos she's proper mint!

CHAPTER 10
Will

"Favourite film?"
"The Longest Ride."
"Wolf of Wall St."
"Favourite book?"
"I don't read a lot. I'd have to think about it. What about you?" I asked.
"Easy, Daisy Jones & The Six."
"Okay, I heard of that. Maddy read it and loved it. Maybe mine would be Misery."
"As in the film?"

"Yeah. When I was about fifteen, I read this old copy that Mrs Powell had on her bookcase. It was almost falling apart, but I loved it. Couldn't put it down."

"Longest relationship?" Maya asked making me wince inwardly.

"Two months. It was with Maddy's mum." I held my breath, but she was still smiling. "You?"

"Eighteen months and he cheated on me pretty much the whole time. Right next question." She took a few seconds to think and then asked, "Biggest regret?"

"Easy," I sighed, feeling the familiar pull in my chest. "Thinking that I couldn't be a father to Maddy."

Her eyes softened as she watched me carefully. "But you did a good job."

It was more a statement than a question, so I smiled and nodded. "Yours?"

"That's even easier than my favourite book. Letting Peter Carson take my virginity on my fifteenth birthday. It was awful. It took less than three minutes, he yelled out 'mother fucker' as he came and then told the whole school that I'd begged him for it."

"Sounds like a real charmer." I raised a brow, wondering how anyone could treat her as anything but a princess. "I hope you got your revenge somehow."

Maya giggled. "When we were eighteen, I let him think he had another chance, so enticed him to the college theatre hall for sex. I got him on stage and stripped him down to nothing, and then Morgan turned on the stage lights while Loretta marched in with most of the sixth form singing '*Oops!... I Did it Again*'. It was brilliant."

We both started to laugh loudly, and the guy behind the counter of the cafe we were in tutted and turned up the sound on the TV. We had been in there for a couple of hours after the bar across the road had got a little too noisy to hear each other. Now, after endless cups of coffee, two pieces of chocolate cake, and a few rounds of twenty questions, it was almost time for us to say goodbye. Maya had already called an Uber, and I needed to head for the minibus home.

Bizarre as the feeling was, I wasn't sure that I was ready, and staring down at the mug of coffee in front of me, I felt my stomach roll with anxiety.

"I need to go to the bathroom," Maya said.

As she pushed up from her chair, I wanted to grab her hand and pull her back down, or at the very least, beg her to let me go with her and wait outside the ladies.

"I'll be two minutes."

I nodded. "I'll be waiting."

And I would. I'd sit around for hours waiting for her if she asked me to.

"You know I'm closing up soon," the guy behind the counter yelled, his eyes still on the TV in the corner.

"Yep, we're going soon." The idea that we had a few minutes less made me look toward the door to the toilets and will it to open.

After another couple of minutes of me acting like a stupid preteen with a crush, the door swung open. A vision of pure sexiness appeared. She sashayed back to our table, grinning like she didn't have a care in the world, and I began to wonder if I'd imagined our connection.

"Okay?" I asked, looking up at her as she pulled out her chair.

She nodded and smiled brightly. "They have the most amazing hand lotion," she said, planting her perfect arse back on the seat. "I took a picture of it to see if I can find it online." She thrust her hand across the table and waved it in front of me. "Smell."

I gave a quiet chuckle as I caught hold of her fingers and brought them up to my nose. "Nice." It smelled flowery and clean. Although, it wasn't the aroma that I'd remember of my time with Maya. That would be her perfume. It was feminine yet heady and sensual, everything that I would recall every time I thought about her. "What's your perfume?"

"My perfume?"

"Yeah, your perfume." I didn't let go of her hand, but kept her fingers entwined in mine. "I like it much more than I like your new favourite hand lotion."

"It's my going out with the girls when I want to feel badass perfume."

"It must be a pretty big bottle to get all that on the label."

Maya giggled. "Chanel No. 5. That's what it's called."

I nodded. "I've heard of it. My friend Sam bought some for his wife a couple of years back."

"It's expensive so either he's a great husband, or he did something really bad," she replied, arching her eyebrows.

I laughed and lifted her hand. "He gave her wedding dress away to some kids for a jumble sale." I ran my thumb over the knuckle of her ring finger. "It was a two-thousand pound dress eighteen years ago, and she wanted their daughter to wear it for her wedding someday." I shrugged. "So, it was the perfume or a horrendously expensive designer bag."

Maya crossed her legs and leaned her body closer to me over the yellowing Formica table. I got another whiff of her perfume, and I felt myself get hard. I'd been on the edge of it all night, just watching her and listening to her sultry voice, but knowing that our time would soon be up, playful flirting and easy chat no longer seemed enough. I had a need for something more. Something important. Something bigger. A raw, basic need that I knew could become all-consuming and overpowering. Yet all we'd done was talk. My fingers on hers was the most contact that we'd had, yet I knew sex with Maya would be earth-shattering.

"I need to get going soon," I sighed placing her hand between both of mine. "When does your Uber get here?"

She looked down at her phone lying face up on the table and clicked on the screen bringing it to life. She groaned.

"He's two minutes away."

"Two minutes?" The sudden feeling of breathlessness alarmed me. "You sure?"

She nodded and gave me a small shrug. We'd had nowhere near long enough. Three hours couldn't possibly see me through the rest of my life. I knew I'd be craving her by the time I got on the bus, never mind the next day or the next. I knew after just three hours that Maya was the sort of woman that even a lifetime wasn't long enough.

"Can I see you again?" I blurted out, panicking that our two minutes was almost up.

She blinked. "You live over an hour away, almost two."

"We could meet halfway," I offered, conscious that I sounded desperate.

She didn't answer straight away, and my hopes rose. Then she immediately dashed them. "I know it's not far, Will, but I'm busy with work, you're busy with your bar and your daughter."

"Don't you think that after spending three hours together we owe it to all the effort that we put in so far to try?" Yep, I was pathetic.

"I'm not so sure we should if it's been such hard work for you." She grinned and pulled her hand from mine. "I really have to go."

I followed her gaze over my shoulder and saw a car parked outside. When the driver waved, I turned back to see Maya had one hand up while she grabbed her jacket from the back of the chair with the other.

"I guess that's it then." I stood and pulled a twenty from my wallet and threw it onto the table.

"Yeah, I guess so." She came around the table a reached up to kiss my cheek. "I had a great time. It was good getting to know you."

"Me too," I replied, inhaling her scent again. "Come on, I'll walk you out."

As we got to the exit the guy behind the counter barely looked away from the film he was watching, just managing a mumbled thanks as I opened the door. The temperature outside had dropped dramatically, and I dug my hands deep into my pockets as Maya shivered.

I should have hugged her to help stave off the cold, but touching her, even for a minute, scared me. I couldn't become addicted to her because who knew if I'd be able to touch her again or taste the sweetness that she had to offer. So, instead, I reached in front of her and opened the back door of the Prius.

"It really has been great," she said. "Although I can't believe I quit girls' night for a guy I met standing at a bar."

"And we didn't even have sex."

We both started laughing, and I felt a deep regret that we hadn't. Regret that was laced with pride that I hadn't been that bloke for once.

"It was a great night," she said, a cold, smooth palm cupping my cheek. "A really great night."

"I just wish it could last longer." I shrugged. "I guess that's life."

She looked up the street and then swung her gaze back to me. "You could come home with me." She sounded tentative, scared almost.

"Is that what you really want?"

"I know three hours isn't enough," she replied, wrapping her arms around her body. "And I know the idea of not seeing you again is making me feel a little weird." She rolled her eyes and sighed. "Shit, that sounds like I'm some sort of creepy person doesn't it. I mean… I have no idea what I mean."

My hand went to the back of her neck, and I pulled her to me. As her scent got stronger my heart gunned faster and the hand at my side tremored with anticipation. Leaning closer, my lips barely grazed hers as I whispered, "I understand totally. I don't want to think about this being it."

"But it's ridiculous. We don't know each other."

"I know that you like sexy perfume and have a soft spot for Nicholas Sparks' films. I know that you're beautiful, and that the idea of leaving now and not seeing you again makes me want to get in that car and go home with you."

"But?" Her lips turned into a small smile.

"But, I have Maddy to think of. She's on a sleepover, but it'd still feel wrong not being home if she needed me." I let out a long breath, wishing things could be different. "It's our thing we always have breakfast at a local cafe on Sunday morning, and I don't want to miss any until I absolutely have to."

Maya nodded, her nose brushing against mine, and the brief contact set my pulse into overdrive. Never had I felt such a need before, and *never* had I wanted to call my little girl and put off Sunday breakfast.

"I think I need to kiss you."

"I think I need you to kiss me," Maya said in a breathy whisper.

Her lips were soft and pillowy, and when they parted, I thought I might fall to my knees in gratitude. Our tongues touched, and she tasted of chocolate cream. She tasted sweet *and* hot, and full of sin—if only we had the time. My hands moved into her hair so that I could hold her in place. Now that I was tasting her, I wasn't letting her go easily. When she let out a little moan, I pushed her back against the car and she gripped at the front of my shirt, dragging me closer. Parting her legs, I pushed my thigh in between them and felt her thrust her hips. The hot, sexy, woman was getting herself off and I fucking loved it. It took me all my time not to flip open her jeans and do the job for her.

When I was hard to the point of bursting my trousers open, I heard a clearing of a throat and a voice from inside the car yelled, "Ah, c'mon on guys, I just got my car washed and waxed."

Maya and I both laughed, and even though it killed me to, I pulled my mouth away. Her lipstick was smudged, so I reached up with my thumb and rubbed at the side of her mouth. I grimaced.

"I think you may need to take a look yourself. I fear I might have made it worse."

Maya shook her head and swiped a hand across her mouth, following the line of her lips with her finger, rubbing as she did.

"Sorry."

"No, don't be." She ran a finger down my cheek. "It's proof that I've been thoroughly kissed."

"I'm sorry, miss, but we really need to get going," the uber driver complained.

"Go," I said, taking her hand and giving it a squeeze. "Before I jump in there with you and disappoint my daughter and make myself feel a whole load of guilt for the rest of my life."

"Okay, damn it," she said with a shake of her head. "Let me take your number." She tapped at her phone and then looked at me expectantly.

"Lady, please just get in or I'm going to have to go without you."

I leaned one hand on the car and looked inside toward the front. "Hey, big man, she'll be one minute, okay. So, stop yelling at us."

I didn't wait to hear his response but straightened up and reeled off my number to Maya. As she entered the numbers, the car started up, and my need to kick out his rear lights was great.

"What's yours?" I asked as Maya got into the car.

"I'll message you."

I had to be content with that because the driver started to pull away. "Don't forget."

"I won't."

I just managed to stand back to avoid being hit with the door as Maya pulled it shut and then waved at me through the window. As the car drove away from the pavement, she twisted in her seat and continued watching and waving from the window until she was just red lights way off in the distance.

Feeling deflated, I looked at my phone. I tried to tell myself it was to check the time but really it was to see if I'd had a message from Maya. There wasn't one, but I had ten minutes to get to the bus, so feeling annoyed, I set off at a jog with half of me hoping that I missed it.

MAYA'S DIARY ENTRY

I did something stupid tonight! I met a guy and dumped Morgan and Loretta for him. I'd only been talking to him for five minutes when I told them I would see them later—only I never did. I stayed with him all night. Well, not all night. He put me in an Uber about an hour ago and sent me home alone. I asked him to come with me, but he couldn't, and I'm quite glad because it's too soon. He's so gorgeous, though. Beautiful brown eyes and a beautiful smile.

I've got to admit he was hot and made me want to jump him! His name is Will, he's 37, and he's got a 17-year-old daughter. Her mum isn't around as she died when his daughter was only a few months old, but he says they weren't together at the time.

I can't stop wishing he'd come home with me, but I know that would be stupid. I'm pretty sure he's not a mass murderer or anything like that, but who knows. Bloody hell, he's sexy. I can just imagine what his body is like under his clothes. He was on a stag night and wearing a T-shirt that said 'Wet Willy' on the front, which was hilarious. Once his group of friends left him with me, he took it off. He wasn't happy about wearing it, but I thought it was funny. I was instantly drawn to him—his slow, easy smile, the dimple in his cheek. Everything about him was gorgeous. Handsome, but not in a classic way. Rugged. He was wearing suit trousers with shoes, but I got the idea that he would look incredible in jeans and boots, too. He had a cool, casual way about him, but there was a hint of nervousness in his confidence when he talked to me. If he hadn't had that, I'm sure I'd have done anything to get his attention. He was that hot.

I told him I'd message him, and I want to do it now, but I know Morgan and Loretta would kill me. It's hard not to, though. My stomach is full of butterflies. I need to act my age and force myself to wait, not act like an impatient teenager. I hate playing games, though—I've had enough guys do that to me. Still, an hour after saying goodbye might be a bit too soon!

I should get to bed. Loretta has persuaded me to do a car boot in the morning. All I want to do is watch tonight's telly I've recorded and eat junk, but she won't take no for an answer.

I hope he does like me and is happy when I finally call him!

CHAPTER 11
Maddy

I threw my backpack down on to the kitchen table and guessed from the stillness in the house that Dad was still sleeping. I'd left Em's house before anyone else had woken, because I couldn't see the point of lying there with the various noises my friends were making, especially not when I had a breakfast date with my dad.

I opened the blinds at the window, letting in the pale light of the January morning, and sighed. Hopefully, in a month's time, the weather would be getting warmer with Dad getting busy at the bar as people started to venture out more. Not that he wasn't ever busy. During the winter, he was rammed most days. Dad always said that there were some people he only ever saw during those months when they were using his bar to keep warm and saving on their heating bills.

The garden outside was looking drab, not that we ever did much with it. We had a cherry tree, Grandma Powell's favourite, but I had no clue how we managed to keep it alive every year. Our skills at gardening totalled us being able to cut grass. I usually cut the front and Dad the back, mainly because if he cut the front, all the women in the neighbourhood came out to ogle him, especially when it was hot, and he took his shirt off.

"Hey sweetheart, good night?" Dad's tired voice drew my attention from the garden, and I swung around to face him.

He rubbed both his eyes with the heels of his hands and yawned, looking all dishevelled and sleepy.

"Good, thanks, and you?"

A smile brightened up his face. "Yeah, pretty good actually." He walked over and pulled me into a hug, and I melted into him, wrapping my arms around his waist. He smelled of bed and traces of his favourite aftershave. Like home. "You didn't tell me that boys were going to be there."

I looked up at him, resting my chin on his chest. "How did you know?"

"That doesn't matter, but what does is that you didn't tell me." I attempted to pull away from him, but Dad kept a tight hold. "Stay right there, young lady, and explain to me about the doctor's kid."

Stiffening, my throat went dry. "W-what?"

"Sam told me that the new kid was joining you last night. What's he like?"

What was he like? Wow, how to answer that without sounding like a love-sick idiot. "He's nice." I shrugged. "He wants to be a vet."

"Great career choice, kid, but was he respectful to you?"

"Dad!"

"You're my baby, so I'm entitled to ask." He put a finger under my chin, keeping my attention on him. "Was he respectful to you and your friends?"

"Yes, he was. He's nice. Liam wouldn't hang out with him if he wasn't."

Dad nodded. "Very true." He dropped a kiss to my nose. "I wish you'd told me boys were going to be there but I'm glad you had a good time."

I blinked at him. He normally questioned me like a murder suspect where boys were concerned.

"Did you kiss a pretty lady last night, Daddy?" I grinned, tipping my head to study him.

"No."

I burst out laughing and slapped his chest. "You liar, Dad. You did, didn't you."

"Alright, alright." His lips were tipped up at the edges, and there was a definite glint in his tired eyes. He started laughing. "Her name was Maya, and she *was* pretty and lives in Leeds."

"Like you said, a couple of hours' travel is nothing. You did get her number?"

He winced. "She took mine and said she'd message me, but I haven't had anything yet." He reached down to the pockets of the sleep pants he wore and pulled out his phone. When I escaped from his arms, he tapped at his phone, looked at the screen and shook his head.

"Nope."

"Maybe she wants you to know what it's like to be left hanging." I raised an eyebrow at him. "Hmm?"

"I've never left a woman hanging," he protested, and I almost choked.

"Lizzie, Maria, Bonnie." I counted the names off on my fingers. "And they're just the ones I know about."

"Lizzie wanted to marry me after one date, Maria wanted to marry me after two and Bonnie kept making a weird noise with her throat."

"And Maya? Do you think she'll want to marry you?"

"I guess I'll never know," he said before kissing the top of my head. "Now, I'm going to get showered so we can go for breakfast."

Watching him leave the kitchen, I hoped she called him because he deserved to be happy. If he got that with a lady called Maya maybe I wouldn't be so worried about leaving him alone.

"Hey, Monique." Dad flashed our waitress a smile and got a huge smile back, along with a flirty wink. "The usual, please, love."

"You, too, Maddy?"

I nodded. "Just the orange juice for me today, please."

"Be right back."

She gave Dad a lingering smile, but he was too busy looking down at his phone.

"Still no message?" I asked, leaning across the table and trying to look at his screen.

"No." He looked up at me and threw his phone down onto the bench seat next to him. "I wasn't expecting one." He shrugged. "It was just one of those one-night things."

I grinned. "Oh, Dad, you are such a liar. You're devastated, aren't you?"

"Don't be so stupid. And I am not a liar."

"And I beg to differ." The bell of the café door jingled behind me as I watched him take a surreptitious look at his phone. "Bloody hell, Dad, just call her."

"I can't. I don't have her number. *She* said *she'd* message *me*."

Smiling up at Monique as she placed two glasses of juice on the table, I prodded Dad's arm. "That is a huge school boy error, William."

He also gave Monique a smile, then once she disappeared back to the kitchen, he turned his attention to me. "I know, you don't have to remind me, Madeline." Bringing his glass to his mouth, he paused and raised his eyebrows. "I think you might have a visitor."

Frowning, I swivelled around in my seat. When I saw Zak walking towards me, I felt the blood drain from my face. My hair was just piled on top of my head, I was wearing my White Fox hoodie and sweatpants, which were one wear away from the washing machine, and my make up consisted of eyeliner and mascara.

"Z-Zak," I stammered. "What are you doing here?"

He grinned. "Would you believe, breakfast." He turned to one side. "Amelia didn't fancy my burnt toast."

It was then that I noticed a pretty, young, dark-haired girl standing next to him. She gave me a shy smile as she slipped her hand into Zak's.

"This is my little sister."

"Hi, Amelia." Dad cleared his throat, and I swung my gaze between him and Zak. "This is my dad, Will."

Zak took a step forward and held out his hand. "Pleased to meet you, Mr Newman."

My eyes widened as I watched Dad push out of his seat and accept Zak's handshake. "Will is fine. I take it you're the new boy, Zak."

"Yes. Yes, I'm the new boy." He looked a little unsure as my Dad sat back down. "My parents are both working this morning, so breakfast is my responsibility, and like I said, Amelia doesn't like burnt toast."

I looked over at his sister, who was gazing up at him, and I could totally understand why she was looking at him so adoringly. He clearly hadn't suffered from lack of sleep after a night drinking vodka. His eyes were bright, his hair was sexily dishevelled, and he smelled gorgeous. My heart slammed against my chest as he turned his smile on me.

"What do you recommend?" he asked.

I swallowed and then licked my lips as I tried to regain some composure. Nothing came out, though, when I tried to speak.

"The full English," Dad said, rescuing me. "With toast." He winked at Amelia. "And it's not burned."

She giggled and buried her face in her brother's arm. Another woman charmed by my dad, it seemed.

"In fact," he continued. "I would ask Monique to make you one of her special milk shakes to go with it."

Amelia gave a little gasp and looked up at Zak. "Can I?" she asked, her voice soft and sweet.

He rubbed a hand over her head and nodded. "I think we can manage that."

If I thought I'd liked him the night before, it was nothing to how I was feeling watching him interact with his little sister. Not only was my heartbeat erratic, but my stomach felt like it had a million butterflies. Then, when he glanced at me, I thought my lungs might have seized up because I couldn't breathe.

Zak's tongue flicked along his bottom lip. "We should leave you to your breakfast."

Unable to speak, I nodded and felt a small sense of relief when he turned to Amelia to lead her away. It was short-lived, though, because Dad decided to send me into complete turmoil.

"Why don't you join us. We've only just ordered."

My head spun around to see him frowning yet smiling at the same time. He seemed torn as he looked between me and Zak. He wanted to be polite, but he was my Dad, and he knew that I liked the boy he'd just invited to our table.

Monique appeared with Dad's coffee. "Everything okay here?" she asked.

"Yeah, yeah," Dad replied. He nodded in the direction of Zak. "We've got two joining us."

"Oh, okay. Take a seat, guys, and I'll get you a menu." She smiled at Amelia and ran a hand down her hair. "I think you look like a milkshake sort of girl. Am I right?"

Amelia nodded and then looked up at her brother who was looking at Monique. "I'll have a tea, please and a full English. Could Amelia have toast and peanut butter, please?"

"Absolutely," Monique replied.

Zak hovered at the end of the table, looking at the seat next to me, but when Dad coughed, he pushed Amelia towards me.

"You sit next to Maddy," he said softly, his eyes firmly on me. "I promise she's nice."

As I moved along the bench seat to let her in, I caught Dad staring at me, and when I smiled at him, his shoulders sagged as if regret appeared to weigh him down.

CHAPTER 12
Will

Irrationally, I wanted to punch the little shit's lights out. Irrational because I quite liked him. He was attentive to his sister, respectful to me, and polite to Monique when she checked in on us. My biggest problem was the way he looked at my daughter. It wasn't creepy or salacious, but there was something in his eyes. Something I'd seen before. I'd been a teenage boy. It was the look that told me he liked her, a lot. A look that told me he was having thoughts of what could happen between them. He was also making a big effort not to touch her in any way. I could see under the table that his legs were tucked under the seat, and when they both reached for the ketchup at the same time, he drew his hand back like the bottle was on fire.

If he'd just been some kid who wanted to... shit, I couldn't even contemplate it... I would have probably felt better about it. I could have warned him off with threats to his balls. Zak wasn't like that, though; he was serious about his studies and his future, which meant he would probably become serious about Maddy. That also meant the probability of a broken heart somewhere along the way.

As for Maddy, it was clear she felt the same way. She was looking anywhere but at him and anything I said she either rolled her eyes at or laughed a little too loud. Fidgeting and restless, her fingertips tapping incessantly like she was drumming a trance beat on the table. She could fall big time for this boy, and I didn't want her being derailed.

Then again, he might be good for her. He was talking about going to Edinburgh University. If they got serious maybe she'd follow him there. I scrubbed a hand over my face and groaned inwardly. Who the hell thought being the parent of a teenager was easy? Maddy was a good kid, and yet bringing her up was still filled with jeopardy.

"So," I said, pushing my empty plate away, "how are your parents settling in?"

"Great," Zak replied. "At least they seem to be. They try not to talk about work when they get home."

"Daddy works a lot," Amelia added.

We'd established that she was nine years old, loved Harry Potter and doing colouring books and had gradually lost some of her shyness as the minutes had passed. Her voice was quiet and clear but every time she spoke she aimed it at Zak. Not like she was checking it was okay, but just that she was still a little shy.

"He does," Zak replied, grinning at her. "But if he didn't we wouldn't have all the nice things we have, would we?"

He leaned forward and took a piece of toast that she'd left on her plate, taking a bite out of it. I glanced over at Maddy, and she was watching him, while pretending not to. She definitely had a crush on him, even if I didn't know my daughter, the blush on her cheeks would give it away.

"I have a trampoline," Amelia announced.

"Wow," Maddy replied. "I always wanted a trampoline."

Did she? I didn't know that. I would have got her one if I'd known.

"Want to have a go on mine?" Amelia asked.

Zak laughed. "I think maybe Maddy has grown out of wanting a trampoline."

Amelia's head whipped around so she could look at my daughter. "You don't want to go on it? Why not? Everyone loves trampolines."

Maddy was obviously torn between upsetting Amelia and annoying Zak. Blind to the fact that he liked her, she must have thought he would hate her becoming friendly with his little sister. I was torn between telling her that she should have more self-confidence because she was beautiful and keeping her away from the teenage boy with raging hormones. I went with throwing the two teenagers together, hoping I didn't regret it.

"I think she'd love to go on your trampoline," I offered, picking up my mug of coffee. "You're never too old for trampolines."

Zak looked at me, his eyes wary, and then over to Maddy. "You can if you like. I just thought…"

"Yes," Amelia cried, bouncing on her seat. "When can you come to our house?"

Maddy stared at me, unsure of what I was doing or why I'd said what I said. Maybe it was the possibility of never hearing from or seeing Maya that had made me soft. Losing out on something that I knew could be great, I wanted to be sure Maddy didn't go through the same thing.

"Well," I announced. "I need to go to the bar for a couple of hours, so if Maddy wanted to go back with you, I could pick her up later." I placed a hand on Zak's arm. "Unless you're busy."

His eyes went wide as he shook his head. "No. No. We were just going to watch a film until Mum and Dad got back."

I looked back at Maddy, who was bright red and chewing on her lip. "Do you have plans?" I asked her.

"No." She finally locked eyes with Zak. "If you're sure you don't mind. I mean if you'd rather do something else. Or maybe I could stay with Amelia for you, until your mum and dad get back."

I wanted to shake her and tell her to have more belief in herself. To back herself because this boy next to me didn't want to do anything else. He wanted to spend time with her. I just hoped that Zak had the balls to take control.

"No, I have nowhere else I want to be. It would be good if you could come back to the house with us." He cleared his throat. "Maybe play on the trampoline, and then we can all watch a film together?"

I couldn't help but smile, and I liked him a little bit more. I just hoped he didn't let me, or more importantly, Maddy, down. Maybe I wasn't ready to let her go, but knowing it was time meant that I had to trust him.

CHAPTER 13
Maddy

I had no idea what my dad thought he was doing, but when I got home I would kill him. Mortified wasn't the word. He'd practically forced Zak to invite me over to his house. The poor boy had no choice.

"Listen," I said, as Zak pulled his keys from his jacket pocket. "I can leave you to it. My dad shouldn't have suggested I come home with you both."

Amelia was skipping up the gravelled driveway ahead of us, seemingly excited that I was going to be visiting the Hoyland house.

Zak turned and walked backwards. "I'm glad he did. So, stop stressing about it."

"You're sure you don't mind?"

"One hundred percent," he called over his shoulder as he turned back around. "I'll give you half an hour on the tramp with Amelia, and then you're mine."

My heart thumped wildly, and my stomach swooped while Zak walked nonchalantly away, totally unaware that he just sent me into a state of anxiety.

"Come on," he yelled, pushing the door open and letting Amelia run inside. "Time is passing, Madeline."

He had Madeline'd me, and for once I didn't mind. In fact, I liked the sound of it in his accent. Quickening my steps, I reached the front door, where Zak was waiting for me. He had his finger hooked on the chain around his neck, and his eyes were twinkling, and I wondered what he was thinking about.

"Romance or horror?" he asked, looking over his shoulder at Amelia who was skipping down the hallway.

I shrugged. "Didn't we have this conversation last night?"

He tilted his head on one side. "Yeah, and if I recall, romance won. Maybe horror then."

"What about Amelia? She can't watch a horror film."

"She won't watch it. She'll sit through the first two minutes and then go to her bedroom to read Harry Potter, like she always does."

The idea that we might be alone later made my nerves spike, and a huge boulder in my throat stopped me from swallowing. The thought was exciting, but what if he was just being nice? What if there was nothing in it and I got myself worked up for nothing?

"Honestly, Zak, I can go once I've spent some time with Amelia."

He frowned and shoved his hands into his jeans pockets. "Do you want to leave?"

"Well, no, but I thought…"

Zak stepped closer, one cheek pushed into a half smile. His whole body was relaxed, and he had an air of confidence that I'd never seen in a boy before. In fact, I'd never met anyone like him before. Admittedly, I'd lived in a small town all my life but even so, he was nothing like the stupid, childish boys I usually spent time with at school. Maybe it was what all southern boys were like; I had no idea, but I liked it.

"Maddy," he said, his voice soft and coaxing. "Stay and watch a film with me. I want to watch a film with you. *I* want *you* to stay." He ran a hand down my arm, stopping just short of my hand, and then walked away. "Now, get out there before Amelia starts worrying you've done a runner." He pointed to a door off the large entrance hall, to the right of an oak staircase. "You can get to the garden through the kitchen."

"Okay."

"I'll be in the lounge when you're ready." He pointed to another room and then ran up the stairs, leaving me alone, wondering how the hell I'd gone from Sunday breakfast with Dad to playing on a trampoline with the new hot boy's little sister.

***

Zak was right, Amelia disappeared up to her room within minutes of the film starting. I don't think the intro music had even finished before she said she was bored and going to read. Once she went, the atmosphere in the room changed. It became highly charged—well, I felt like I was on high alert at least. Zak still appeared relaxed at his end of the sofa, whereas I was pushing myself as close to the arm as possible. It was a huge, comfy, dark green velvet one, and it felt like I was miles away from him.

When we heard Harry Styles blasting from above us, Zak paused the film and turned his body to look at me.

"What are you doing all the way over there?" he asked.

The butterflies in my tummy took flight, and my heartbeat sped up. "S-sorry?"

"Why are you sitting right at the other end of the sofa from me? Don't you want to be close in case you get scared?"

"How scary is this film?" I frowned because I was a wuss. Horror films weren't my thing, but we had made the poor guy watch a romance film the night before... so...

"Enough that you'll want to hide your face. Oh, and you might feel the need for me to cuddle you." He said, arching an eyebrow and rolling his lips inwards.

My heart sank at the thought, but then the idea of snuggling up to Zak was a bonus.

"Is it gory?" I shuffled down until I was sitting next to him.

"There's one part with the grandfather and a nappy, but that's all I'm saying." He took my hand and pulled on it. "Besides which, I like your perfume, and I want to be able to smell it."

God. I felt sick. Excitement. Nerves. Trepidation.

Before I could think about it any further, Zak pulled me into his side, wrapped an arm around my shoulder, and turned on the film. I went as a stiff as a board. Even my eyes stopped moving. Then, when his thumb began to rub up and down, gently tickling my arm, I thought I might squeal.

"There's a Coke there for you," he whispered into my ear. "On the coffee table."

In front of me was a can of coke and a glass with ice cubes in the bottom. "T- thanks."

"Wasn't sure if you'd want a glass or not."

His accent. His deep, raspy voice. His thumb sending messages around my body.

He then shifted a little, propped his feet up on a footstool, and poked me gently in the side. "Relax. I'm not going to murder you."

Then the film properly started, and we fell into silence. After a few minutes my body settled against Zak's and I watched the film, but after only half an hour, I'd decided I didn't like it. It wasn't scary as such, but creepy. The cushion I'd grabbed was in front of my face more than not and Zak kept chuckling beside me.

"It's funnier than it is scary," Zak said with a laugh. "I can't even take it seriously."

"Why are we watching it then?" I jumped as the grandmother went scooting past the screen on all fours like some sort of animal. "Shit, this is weird."

Zak let out a belly laugh. "You really are a wimp." His hand came to my waist and tickled me. I squealed, squirming to get away from him.

"Zak, don't."

"Ticklish are you?" His eyes were shining with mischief.

"No."

He grinned. "Liar."

Scrambling back, I managed to evade his long fingers, which were grabbing for me. I fell onto my back, kicking my socked feet out to try and push him away, but he managed to bat them from him, grabbing hold of my ankles. With a huge smile, he pulled me back down the sofa to him. We were both laughing, play fighting with one another, a mass of feet and hands, and I loved it.

Zak's hand's then went for my wrists, and his rings were cold against my skin, making me gasp. He paused, his eyes dark and enquiring as he looked down on me. Neither of us spoke, the only sound coming from the TV in the background, as we stared at each other.

When his thumb began rub gently over my waist, I think I stopped breathing. I know I stopped breathing. His head dipped lower until our mouths were inches apart, and I didn't dare hope that he was going to kiss me. And he didn't; he just looked at me, his eyes moving over my features but lingering on my lips. When his tongue darted out, I braced myself, but nothing happened because the moment he moved, the lounge door swung open and Amelia marched in.

"Zak, the Wi-Fi has gone down." She stalked inside looking down at her phone. "I was playing my music."

Without any urgency, Zak pulled himself away from me and got off the sofa. I watched, still on my back as he walked over to his sister and gently pulled the phone from her hand. When Amelia's head came up, she looked over at the TV and I took the opportunity to sit up, acting like I hadn't been about to kiss her brother.

"He's making you watch *The Visit*," she cried and swung her gaze to me. "It's hideous, isn't it?"

"Did he let you watch it?"

"Hey," Zak protested, his eyes concentrated on Amelia's phone screen as he tapped at it. "It's nothing to do with me. I was watching it, fell asleep, and she sneaked into my bedroom." He looked up and grinned at me. "Mum and Dad thought she was being murdered she screamed that loud, and I almost shit the bed." He handed the phone back to Amelia. "You'd disconnected from it somehow. I've told you, download stuff instead of using the Wi-Fi."

She rolled her eyes at him and then turned on her heels. "Oh, and by the way, Mum and Dad are back."

Instantly, my nerves spiked again, but Zak simply sat down, back at the opposite end of the sofa. He kicked his feet up on the footstool again, looking like nothing in the world ever bothered him.

"I should go," I said, shuffling to the edge of the cushion. "If your parents are back."

Zak turned to me and frowned. "Why? They're very friendly, you know."

How could one person seem so unbothered by anything? He hadn't cared that Amelia caught us about to kiss, or that his mum and dad were home, and some random girl was sitting on their sofa.

"Won't they be mad? That I'm here. They've just got home from work, Zak."

"Mum was reorganising her surgery and Dad was doing follow ups on a couple of surgeries. It's hardly been a taxing morning for them." He laughed, and it was deep and rumbling. Another reason for him to set the butterflies off again.

"Zak, I—"

"This is where you're hiding."

I looked up to see a small, pretty woman standing in the doorway. Her dark hair was tied back with tendrils escaping the side. She was wearing jeans and a plain white t-shirt with a streak of dirt on the front, and her feet were bare.

Instantly, I looked down at my trainers that I'd kicked off, lying haphazardly next to the coffee table, and I reached for them.

"Mum, this is Maddy from school. She's a friend of Liam's and now mine, too."

I blinked rapidly, wondering how I was going to slip out now that she'd been alerted to my presence.

"Oh hi, Maddy." I turned to look at her. Her smile was just like Zak's, and she had a dimple in her cheek, just like him. Her accent was the same, just maybe a little more refined than Zak's. "It's lovely to meet you." Her eyes crinkled at the sides, and I genuinely believed she was happy to meet me.

"You, too," I replied. I wanted to apologise for imposing on their Sunday, but my mouth was too dry to say anything else.

She looked back into the hallway and then back to Zak and me. "We brought back pizza. Would you like to stay for some, Maddy? You'd be very welcome."

The lump in my throat grew bigger and my mouth went drier as I squeaked, "I don't want to impose, Mrs Hoyland."

"Don't be daft," Zak said. "Mum wouldn't have asked if she thought you were." He gave his mum a thumbs up. "She'll stay. Did you get Mexican beef?"

She laughed quietly and then shook her head. "Of course, we did, darlin'. Ten minutes and it'll be out in the kitchen. And Maddy, please call me Lisa."

Once she'd gone, Zak grabbed my arm, pulling me close again. "Good, we're just coming up to the nappy scene. It's just what you need before you tuck into a Mexican beef pizza." He burst out laughing, full, deep and long, and I couldn't help but join in. Until the scene came on the screen, and then I decided that maybe staying for pizza wasn't a good thing. Then I glanced at Zak and realised that even grimacing he was still more handsome than any other boy I'd met before, so perhaps I would manage it after all.

CHAPTER 14
Will

Waiting for a message from a woman *and* wondering what your teenage daughter was getting up to did not contribute to a relaxed Sunday afternoon. My nerves were shot to pieces. I'd spent most of the day checking my phone, turning it on and off to ensure it was working, even sending myself an email and a WhatsApp message from my PC.

When I wasn't doing that, I was considering all sorts of scenarios between Maddy and Zak and none of them were good, especially as she'd messaged me earlier to say she didn't need a lift. I had to keep reminding myself that

Maddy was sensible, and Zak seemed like a respectful kid. As much as I adored my daughter and would give my life for her, I didn't want her to have to go through what I had. It hadn't been a struggle because of Miriam, and I'd make sure it wouldn't be a struggle for Maddy. That didn't mean I wanted her to have to make choices that hadn't even been a consideration before. I loved my life, and I fucking adored my daughter, but would I have chosen to run a bar if she hadn't come along?

That probably made me sound ungrateful, and I most definitely wasn't. I had so much to thank Miriam for. I had my own bar because of her. I was a respected member of our community because of her. I just felt at times, if I hadn't needed to do that for Maddy, I might have explored other things. I might have actually kicked my arse into gear and travelled or even studied to find my perfect career. I might have spent time to consider what would benefit me the most.

Suddenly, guilt swilled like poison in my stomach. I was a stupid idiot because who was I kidding? Without her, I would probably still be serving behind someone else's bar. I knew, as she had, that I would never have changed my life if it hadn't been for the responsibility of Maddy. My daughter was a lot brighter than me, though. More driven, more courageous, and more ambitious. Even if she did find herself with a kid, she'd be fine. That didn't mean that I wanted some cocky new kid doing things to her that shouldn't be allowed until she was at least thirty. Better still, once I was dead and gone and didn't have to know about it.

Glancing at the clock on the cooker, I was surprised to see it was almost five. Funny how quickly an afternoon of worrying and pacing went by. I looked at my phone again. There was still a signal and still no message.

The noise of the front door opening took my attention away from the phone. I didn't want to crowd her or come on too strong, so just called out to her.

"In the kitchen, sweetheart."

"Hey, Dad."

Instantly, my body sagged with relief. She sounded happy and relaxed, not like she was hiding anything from me. When she walked in, with a huge smile, I knew that I was right, especially when she came over and wrapped her arms around my waist.

"Did you enjoy your peace and quiet?" she asked.

"Not bad. I finished off some paperwork," I lied. "How was your afternoon." I stiffened in anticipation.

"Good. Played on the trampoline, watched a film, and then had pizza with his mum and dad." Maddy pushed out of my arms and slapped at my chest. "You thought I'd had sex with him, didn't you?"

"No."

"Liar." She frowned and shook her head. "Give me some credit, *Dad*."

"I'm not sure how comfortable I am having this conversation, *Maddy*."

"Seriously?" she asked, stepping back a couple of paces and crossing her arms over her chest. There was a determined jut to her chin, just like when she was a little girl who didn't want to wear a coat when it was cold outside. "We've always talked about this stuff, ever since you took me to buy sanitary towels when I was thirteen."

"Sanitary products are different from sex."

"You gave me the talk, Dad. You even showed me how to put a condom on a banana when you said school hadn't done it properly. So, how come now you don't feel comfortable talking about it?"

I shrugged. "Because now it seems real."

"Well, it hasn't happened." Her eyes were narrow. "It's not even like I've had a date with him. We're not even talking, Dad."

"What the hell does that mean? I thought you'd been there all afternoon. Did you spend the day in silence or something?"

She rolled her eyes. "Oh, for goodness sake, Dad. It's what we do. We talk, then we date, and then we become boyfriend and girlfriend. What's so difficult to understand about that?"

"In my day, you asked a girl out, and if you liked each other, you then you became girlfriend and boyfriend. If you didn't, then one of you came up with an excuse not to see each other again."

"Ugh," Maddy groaned. "So Neanderthal."

"The point is, Maddy, if you spent an afternoon with a girl in a house, where there were no parents, you did a lot more than watch a film."

"Well, we didn't. And did you miss the part where I said we had pizza with his mum and dad?"

"Yeah, I did." I blinked slowly. "So, breakfast with me and then lunch with his mum and dad. When's the wedding?"

"Ugh, you're so annoying." She turned around and headed for the door. "I'm going upstairs to do some homework, give me a shout when tea is ready."

Then she was gone.

"Bloody kids," I muttered, going over to the fridge to decide what to cook.

Deciding on a chicken with all the trimmings, I gathered everything together. I was halfway through peeling potatoes when my phone buzzed in my pocket. Considering that I'd been on high alert all day, I took my time taking it out and looking at it. Disappointment had shadowed me for almost twenty-four hours, so expected it to be Marcus or Sam. When I saw it was an unsaved number, hope soared. It might be Maya, and if it was someone asking me about an accident I'd never had, I'd go ballistic. Answering, I almost dropped the damn thing with the nerves of anticipation.

"Hello." My heart was hammering so hard, I wondered if I might be having some sort of attack—panic or fatal, I wasn't sure.

"Hey, it's Maya."

Finally. My nerves turned to excitement.

What the hell had happened to me?

"Hey, Maya." I tried to sound calm, but doubted I'd succeeded.

"Hi, how are you? Sorry it's taken so long to get back to you."

I'd forgotten how sexy her voice was. Like every word was a dirty secret, told only to me.

"No problem at all," I lied. "It's great to hear from you, though. Glad the Uber driver got you home safe. He did, didn't he?"

Her laugh tinkled down the line. "Yeah, he did. He was a bit grumpy and I'm pretty sure he gave me a bad rating, but never mind."

"And what about your friends? Were they okay with not seeing much of you last night?"

"They were fine. Wanted all the gory details, though."

"Gory?" I pulled out a chair at the table and settled down. The smile I had was hurting my cheeks. Just hearing her voice had my stomach swooping like I was riding a rollercoaster. It was pathetic, but I was already mad about her. Barely knew her, yet I already liked her a lot and knew I wanted to see her again—more than once.

"You know what I mean." She laughed again, and it hit me in the right spot. Unlike a teenage boy, it was in my chest rather than my dick. That surprised me, because sex had always been my natural instinct when I was attracted to someone. My dick was a bit like a divining rod, but instead of twitching when water was around, mine stood to attention at the sight of a great pair of tits or a perky arse. Butterflies were not my usual reaction.

"I agree. There was nothing gory about it," I assured her. "I had a great time, and I hope you did, too."

"I think you know that I did. I wouldn't have called you otherwise."

"To be honest, I was beginning to think you weren't going to bother." I grimaced wondering if I sounded whiny and needy. "I mean it wasn't like I was waiting or anything."

I closed my eyes and groaned silently. I sounded pathetic, like I'd been crying into my hankie for the last twenty or so hours. Admittedly, I'd had my phone stuck to my hand, but I didn't want to sound desperate.

"I hope you were," Maya replied with a laugh. "I did something wrong if you weren't."

Laughing felt good. Laughing with *her* felt better. It was stupid, but it felt like I'd never laughed before.

"I can promise you, you did absolutely nothing wrong." I ran my hand through my hair, wondering what the hell had come over me. Why was my heart beating out of my chest? Why was I struggling to breathe? Why the hell was my mouth so dry?

"That's good to know." Maya exhaled, and I wondered whether it was from relief. I hoped it was and not frustration or boredom from talking to me. "Anyway, I was erm…"

"If you need to go then it's fine. Thanks for checking in." I didn't want her to go. What I really wanted to do was yell at her to just talk to me for a little longer. *Then* she could go back to her own life and forget about me.

"No. No. I have nothing to do except watch last night's telly that I recorded and eat a bar of Dairy Milk chocolate." She cleared her throat. "No, I was wondering whether you'd like to meet up."

I sat up straight, gripping my phone so tight I thought I might shatter the screen. It was not what I'd been expecting. The brush-off yes, but definitely not the suggestion we meet up.

"When?" I shook my head at how quickly I'd responded.

Maya didn't pause, though. "I happen to be off work for the next week."

"A software developer, right?"

"You remembered?"

"I remembered. In fact," I said, lowering my voice, "I remember a lot of things about you." As I thought about her soft skin, her smell, her gorgeous eyes, my natural instinct kicked in. I shifted my chair closer to the table, petrified that Maddy might walk in and see what was happening in my kecks. "You're unforgettable, Maya."

There was another soft sigh on the other end of the line, and then silence. Like we were both knew it could be the start of something but didn't want to spoil it with words. Didn't want to ruin the perfection of it.

After a few moments, I was the first to speak. "When and where?"

"Like I said, I'm free all week," Maya replied, her voice strong and confident because she knew I would go wherever and whenever to see her again.

"Tomorrow. I can come to you. I can be in Leeds for eleven."

"That's good for me. I'll message you the address of a coffee shop close to me." Voice strong and confident. Assured and certain.

"See you then."

When the line went dead, I wondered whether I should have played it differently. If I should have suggested later in the week, not come across so desperate. Then I realised that I was desperate, so why bother lying?

CHAPTER 15
Maddy

After getting home on Sunday evening, I'd replayed what had happened at Zak's house that day. Not so much having pizza with his family, even though they were lovely, but all the other stuff was on repeat in my head.

His thumb gently rubbing my arm. Him pulling me closer. Tickling me. I kept going over and over it, all with a huge smile that I couldn't get rid of. It was Monday, we were back at school, and I was still thinking about it, and still beaming. Then I realised that I was about to see Zak for the first time since the day before, and my grin melted away.

"Oh, bloody hell."

"What's wrong?" Ana asked as we walked across the concourse towards the canteen, to the weekly sixth form meeting.

"Erm, nothing." I hadn't told her, or any of my friends, that I'd spent the day with Zak. It wasn't that I didn't want to; I just didn't have time. That was what I was telling myself, anyway. The real truth was that I was too embarrassed—embarrassed that I might have imagined it all and that when I saw Zak, he would act like it was nothing. I would hate that because, to me, it was something.

"Your face says different." We both stopped walking, and I stared at Ana as her lips, painted a deep purple, broke into a grin. "Wouldn't have anything to do with a certain boy, would it?"

How the hell had she worked that out. I stiffened and gave a quick shake of the head. "No idea what you're talking about."

"You liar," she gasped and nudged me. "You've been weird since Emma's sleepover."

"How would you know?" I protested. "I haven't seen you."

"I've spent all morning watching you." She raised an eyebrow. "In Psychology you went all funny-looking while we were talking about the memory. Like you had a special memory of your own."

"I was not." I rolled my eyes and carried on walking.

"And in Social Care, you were gazing outside when we were talking about nutrition. Were you thinking about Cockney boy's arm around you on Saturday night?"

She laughed, and I was glad I was two paces ahead of her and she couldn't see my face. Ana would see straight away that I looked guilty. She was wrong, though; it was everything from the day before, not the sleepover, that had me daydreaming.

"Just hurry up, Ana, we're going to be late."

"We've got ages," she said, running up beside me. "Hey, did you see Emma and Liam chatting this morning before they went into History? Looking very cosy. In fact, I almost suggested they get a room—they were so close, their lips were almost touching."

We were nearly at the canteen, and my stomach was doing somersaults.

Zak would be in there. He would be sitting there, looking gorgeous, with the rest of the sixth form girls hanging around him. All gazing at him and flirting. Milly Rogers would definitely be flicking her hair and fluttering her false eyelashes. No doubt she'd be wearing a low-cut top, too. Showing off that stupid bright pink bra she liked to wear.

"I didn't see them," I replied.

I had, and I'd felt a hint of jealousy that they felt comfortable enough to openly flirt with each other. I wouldn't dare do that with Zak. I had no idea whether he had been flirting with me because he liked me, or just because he could.

"Well," Ana continued, searching in her bag, "they needed to get a room. It was hot, but she needs to spill the tea. She's never told us she likes him."

"Right," I said, distracted by the fact that we had arrived at the canteen.

"Are you listening to me?"

Ignoring her, I pushed the door open and took a huge breath. Right inside was Zak, leaning against the wall, looking down at his phone. Everything about him was beautiful—his fingers tapping at the screen, his thick lashes fluttering, pouty lips that his tongue licked seductively, and his long legs crossed at the ankle. When he coughed, he put a fist to his mouth to cover it, which made me smile. So many of the boys in our year just spluttered their germs over everyone. He was full of rizz, and so different, so gorgeous, that I doubted there was any chance he liked me.

"Bloody hell, Maddy." Ana banged into me from behind, almost sending me flying. As I stumbled forward, Zak looked up and grinned.

"Falling for me, Maddy."

"Christ, Zak," Ana groaned. "That's the shittest line I've ever heard." She shook her head and walked towards the table where the rest of our friends were sitting. Liv was smiling at something on her phone, while Emma chatted to Liam, who was leaning over the back of her chair.

Pushing lazily off the wall, Zak grinned at me. "Hi."

"Hi," I replied, clearing my throat, putting a hand against the butterflies swarming my stomach. "You okay?"

"Yeah. Not bad. You?"

"Good, thanks." I looked over his shoulder to see Ana joining the others.

She said something and Liam threw his head back and roared laughing.

"Something has amused him," Zak commented, glancing over his shoulder before bringing his gaze back to me. "You look nice today, by the way."

I blinked and ran a hand over the front of my leather jacket, grateful that I'd worn my newest jeans with a crop top. Not like I hadn't planned it, because of course I had.

"Thanks. So do you." I groaned inwardly, wondering whether I'd said the right thing. Was I being too obvious? Would he think I was an idiot for saying it? Blooming heck, fancying boys was hard!

A beautiful smile lit up Zak's face, and he took a step closer to me. "How long do these meetings go on for, anyway?"

His hand reached out, and he lifted my bag higher on my shoulder, from where it had slipped down my arm.

Trying to ignore the way my stomach was doing somersaults, I shrugged. "Depends on whether anyone has been caught vaping in the toilets or with weed in their pocket."

Zak raised an eyebrow. "Does that happen a lot, then?"

"Not really. Well, the weed not so much but the vaping probably once every two weeks."

"And if they have been caught?" Zak asked, shoving his hands into his jacket pockets.

"Then we have to watch a video about the effect vaping has on your lungs and we'll be here for almost an hour. If not, then forty minutes tops, and we get to go home early."

With his blue eyes firmly on my face, Zak nodded. "Looks like it might be an hour then because Mr Anderson caught me smoking coming into school this morning."

His smile was carefree, and his relaxed stance said he wasn't worried one bit about it. If I'd been caught smoking I'd have been shitting myself in case they told my dad.

"What did he do?" I asked. "Has he called your mum or dad?"

Zak shook his head. "Nah. It was on the street outside the gates, I'm not that stupid to smoke on school property. I still reckon he'll give us a lecture about it, though."

"Do your parents know you smoke?"

"Dad does, but he agreed not to tell Mum if I gave up." He grimaced because he clearly hadn't.

"Does he think you have?"

"Yeah. And I will. Maybe when I've finished the pack I've got left."

I rolled my eyes and grinned. "Then there'll be another excuse."

"Nope. No. There won't. I've got six more left, and then that's it." When the muttering behind him went quieter, Zak turned around. "Looks like it's starting. We should get over there."

Mr Anderson, our head of year, was standing in front of the food counter where the shutters were down. He had his hands on his hips and was looking around expectantly, waiting for individual conversations to finish.

"Yes, sooner it's over, the sooner we can go home," I said with a sigh.

As I passed him, Zak leaned in and whispered close to my ear, "By the way, what are you doing tonight?"

Instantly, my breathing sped up and became shallower as his question penetrated my brain, and I thought I might pass out.

"S-sorry?" I asked, wanting him to say it again so that I could be sure.

Catching hold of my bicep, he gently pulled me to a stop. "What are you doing tonight?"

My head whipped around so I could look at him, and I was faced with sincere blue eyes staring at me while his tongue swept along his plump bottom lip. He didn't look nervous or unsure, and I would have bet money on the fact that he wasn't feeling sick.

"Nothing. Well, except for some course work for social care."

"Do you need to do that tonight?"

Did I? I usually did my work the day it was handed out, but it didn't mean I *had* to do it then. I shook my head.

"Fancy going out for a Maccies?"

I did, but I knew Dad was making a curry. "My dad has organised dinner." As soon as I said it, I regretted it. I could have gone and not had a burger. I could have said yes and stuffed myself to the point of feeling sick if it meant spending time with him. I could have asked Dad for a small portion of curry. My shoulders dipped with regret.

He gave me a sexy smirk. "That's okay, we can just go and get a drink."

"We can?" I swallowed, conscious that his eyes seemed to be staring at my lips. "Yeah, that sounds good."

"I'll pick you up at seven." Dumbstruck, I nodded, and Zak smiled, giving me a quick wink before walking away.

As Zak sat down next to Liam, resting his arm on the back of the empty chair next to him, it struck me that he had no idea where I lived. Rushing over, I plonked myself down next to him and leaned closer to whisper, seeing as Mr Anderson was clapping his hands for silence.

"You need my address," I stated.

"No, I don't," he whispered back. "I got your address from Liam."

It was said with such confidence, in that super sexy accent of his, and my nerves kicked in again, realising I needed help from my friends. I was confident in so many ways, but not where Zak Hoyland was concerned, and I wasn't going to risk missing out on something good.

ZAK'S WHATSAPP MESSAGES

OSCAR

Did you watch the match earlier? What a bag of wank. We couldn't score in a titty bar atm.

ZAK

No I didn't watch it. I saw the result though. Another draw isn't great.

OSCAR

Hang on! Why didn't you watch it? Please don't tell me you're not supporting City or United? If it's United you're dead to me!

ZAK

Lol. No. I had Maddy round. We watched a film.

OSCAR

Back the fuck up. Maddy the girl you're not sure likes you?

ZAK

Yeah and it seems she does! We might have had a moment!!!

OSCAR

A moment! WTF is a moment? Have you turned into a teenage girl?

ZAK

Fuck off. I read it somewhere 😂😂😂

OSCAR:

Did you show her your tiny dick? That will only take a moment!

ZAK:

NO! And you know it's not tiny. I was about to kiss her, but my sister walked in. Then my parents came home.

OSCAR

She's met your family!!! It must be serious! What do they think of her?

ZAK

...

OSCAR

Where are you? Why are you ignoring me???

ZAK

Was just asking if I could borrow Mum's car. Yeah they liked her. Mum says she sweet and very pretty.

OSCAR

Run now mate while you can. If Lisa likes her you're in trouble.

ZAK

Well Amelia loves her so...

OSCAR

Aww shit. I've been the victim of Amelia's love. Being trapped in that Wendy House when we were 12 and made to drink pretend tea has scarred me for life!!!

ZAK

You do know she still thinks she's going to marry you one day and have your babies.

OSCAR

I've just puked in my mouth you fucker! I'm going. I can't talk to you anymore.

ZAK

So you don't want to know about how I'm going to ask Maddy on a date then!

CHAPTER 16
Will

I was a confident man, especially where women were concerned. Self-assurance was something I'd been born with, and I always used it to good effect. Waiting for Maya, though, I felt like I might be sick with nerves. I had no idea what the hell was wrong with me. I'd met the woman once, spoken to her for a few hours and yet was acting like a lovesick teenager.

The coffee place we were meeting in was rammed, and I'd been lucky to grab a table that became available just as I was served with my drink. It was also opposite the door, so I would have a good view of Maya walking in.

Five minutes later, when she did, I wasn't prepared for the sight of her. She looked amazing when I'd met her, but my mouth dropped open as she headed inside. She was wearing tight jeans tucked into brown knee high boots, a tan-coloured polo-neck jumper and a short brown leather jacket. Her bag was slung across her body, and her hair was pulled into a high ponytail, and she looked beautiful. I was already thinking things that I probably shouldn't. Mainly about her wrapping her legs around me while I fucked her. When she grinned and waved, I felt my heart speed up.

"So sorry that I'm late. I got stuck talking to my neighbour."

"No problem." I stood up and pulled out a chair for her. "What do you want to drink, I'll get it for you."

She glanced at the menu of drinks and then turned back to me. "Cappuccino please. *With* chocolate."

Her eyes twinkled, and I couldn't help grinning. "I'll be right back."

Five minutes later, I was putting a large mug down in front of her. Maya immediately picked it up with both hands and took a sip. She closed her eyes and sighed.

"Ooh, perfect."

Yeah, she really was. "It's nice in here. Do you come in here often?" I asked.

Maya giggled. "That sounds like a cheesy chat-up line."

"Oh, I'm full of them."

She studied me and then her beautiful face melted into a smile. "I bet you are." She shrugged her jacket and bag off and turned to hang them on the back of the chair. Her jumper wasn't skin tight, but moulded to her body, showing off the perfect curve of her tits. I wondered what her nipples were like, if they were pink or brown, big, or small. When she suddenly burst out laughing, I was snapped out of my daydream.

"What's so funny?" I asked.

"Just something Morgan said." She took another sip of her coffee.

"Morgan is the one getting divorced, is that right?"

Maya tilted her head on one side and grinned. "You remembered."

"I remember a lot about you and Saturday night." And I did. Especially her perfume. I'd even looked it up on line but stopped short at buying it because that would just be weird. She was wearing it again, and I knew that it would be forever my favourite smell from then on.

"Same here." Beautiful green eyes shone over the rim of her mug. "How was your daughter's sleepover?"

I scrubbed a hand over my head, rubbing it, as if I could erase the thoughts and worries. "Boys were involved."

Maya raised her eyebrows. "Boys?"

"Yeah, well, one boy in particular." I grimaced. "He's a nice kid, though, which makes it worse."

"Really? Oh dear." She picked up her spoon and scooped some of the froth from the top. When she slipped it into her mouth, her tongue flicked out and seductively licked it before darting back behind plump, pink lips. "Handsome, is he?"

I shrugged. "It appears my daughter thinks so. His dad is a surgeon and his mum and dentist."

"Good stock." She winked at me. "So, what's your problem?"

"She's my little girl. That's the problem."

Maya's laugh sounded out, mingling with the chat in the coffee shop. "Unfortunately, Will, Maddy has to grow up at some time. She can't stay seventeen forever."

I was amazed that she remembered everything about my daughter. I could only hope that I'd been as memorable to her.

"I know you're right," I groaned. "It just feels shit."

She laughed again and reached out her hand and patted mine. "It'll all be okay, love, don't you worry."

The smile I gave her was genuine because she'd made me feel a little bit better about things. Mainly because she was right. I couldn't stop Maddy growing up. I couldn't make her do anything, which was why her choice of university had to be exactly that, hers. All I could do was be there for her and hold her hand when she needed it.

"So," I said, pushing my mug away. "Are you free all day?"

"I might be." She curled her lips inwards, as if she was trying to hide a smile.

"Maybe we could grab some lunch. You could show me around Leeds."

"I could, could I?"

Nerves swirled in my stomach, wondering whether I'd misjudged the situation. "Unless you'd rather just stick to coffee?"

Maya wrinkled her nose and shook her head. "No. I think that I like the sound of that."

I sighed with relief and sagged back in my chair. "Perfect. Now, what do you fancy to eat?"

***

As we'd walked around the city centre, I couldn't remember when I'd felt so relaxed. My mind had barely wandered back to the bar, all the bills that I needed to pay, Maddy and her future. I'd been fully invested in Maya, listening to her, talking with her, just watching her smile. Even the weather had done us a favour. A pale Winter sun had come out and almost fooled us into thinking Spring was already on its way. It was bright outside, and warm at our table next to the window of the small Italian restaurant we were eating lunch in.

"I love the colder weather," Maya said, looking through the window. "But you can't beat the sun, can you?"

"You can't, not that I've felt any on my back for a couple of years."

Her gaze whipped back to mine. "You haven't had a holiday?"

"Not for…" I closed one eye and tried to figure out when it had been. "Seven years."

Maya's eyes widened. "Seven years? That's a long time."

I sighed because I couldn't have agreed more. Once Covid hit I couldn't justify a holiday, seeing as I wasn't sure I'd be able to keep the bar. Instead, I'd concentrated on offering a takeout service, and an outside bar at the weekend if the weather allowed. We also served hot drinks and bacon baps outside during the day, and while it hadn't made me a millionaire, it had all kept us ticking over.

"The dreaded Covid," I told her. "Maddy has been. Her friend's parents offered to take her to Spain with them."

"That's kind of them." Maya's face softened. "Has it been hard being a single parent?"

I shrugged. "Some days are worse than others. Some years have been worse than others." I laughed, shaking my head. "She makes it worth it, though, or so she tells me."

Maya grinned. "When she's not kissing boys."

My heart dropped. "I never said she'd kissed the boy."

"Oh, come on, if she's as pretty as I'm guessing she is, then he'll have kissed her." She put a forkful of pasta into her mouth and raised an eyebrow.

I rolled my eyes. "Now you've made me feel worse."

"Ah, don't worry, she'll be fine." She nodded at my plate. "How's the steak?"

"Good. And the Carbonara?"

She nodded and licked her lips, distracting me. Her lipstick had disappeared ages before, and she hadn't reapplied it. She didn't need it anyway; she had plump, pink lips that I was desperate to kiss.

"Actually," Maya said, pushing her bowl away, "you haven't shown me a picture of Maddy. I'd like to see one."

"You would?" Most women I'd been with changed the subject whenever it moved to my daughter. There'd been a couple who had been desperate to meet her, but I'd soon figured out that was just a way to get me to like them. If they loved my daughter, then I'd love them. It didn't work out like that, though. Yet with Maya, I did want her to get to know Maddy and not be freaked out that I had a seventeen-year-old daughter.

"So?" she prompted. "Can I see one?"

Putting my knife and fork down on my empty plate, I reached for my phone and flicked to the album of Maddy photos. I picked one taken a few weeks before when she was sulking and not talking to me. I wouldn't let her go to a house party of someone she didn't know. She'd given me the 'I'll be the only one not there' speech, but I'd soon found out that was a lie. One quick call to Ana's mum had confirmed she wasn't allowed either.

I turned my phone screen to Maya. "This is my Maddy."

She looked at the screen and then her fingers gently prised it from mine. "She's beautiful." Smiling, she tapped at the screen and zoomed in on the picture. "She looks like you around the mouth. It's the pouty lip thing." Maya looked up at me and grinned.

That made my chest swell because mostly she was Andy, her mum. I also liked that Maya had obviously been studying my lips.

She looked up at me. "Do you have any others?"

I chuckled. "Hundreds, just swipe."

Maya spent the next couple of minutes looking at pictures of Maddy, oohing and aahing at the baby and toddler ones, and commenting on her beauty as she got to the teenage ones. Eventually, she passed the phone back to me.

"That boy has definitely kissed her, and if he hasn't, then he's a nice boy who'll treat her well."

"Is that what you think, he's a good one if he hasn't tried to kiss her yet?"

She nodded and relaxed back into her seat. "I do."

"What does that say about me then? I kissed you." I leaned forward, my forearms on the table. "Are you saying I'm not a nice boy?"

She studied me and then also leaned forward, adopting the same position, our faces inches from each other. I was so close that I could see the tiny whisky coloured flecks in her green eyes and how her long eyelashes curled up. How smooth and perfect her skin was.

"No, I don't think you are." She licked her lips, her voice a deep, sultry tone.

Watching her watching me, it made me want things. Things that I didn't think either of us were ready for, because I didn't want it to be some sort of brief fling between us. She was worth more than a few bunk ups, plus if I rushed things with her then she might get the wrong impression of what I wanted.

"However," Maya continued, rousing me from my thoughts, "I never said I liked nice boys."

I grinned and reached for her hand, linking our fingers together. "I can be nice, very nice, in fact, for the right person. Besides, nice is such an inadequate word for what I could be."

Dragging in a shaky breath, she nodded. "That's good to know because, to be honest, I'm so sick and tired of the not-nice men."

A shadow passed over her face, and it was clear there was a painful memory behind her words. When she exhaled slowly, like she was letting go of something, I knew for certain that we were most definitely not going to be a brief fling. I liked this woman a lot, and for the first time in ever, I wanted her to like me, too.

"So," I said, reaching up to tuck a loose strand of hair behind her ear, "how about after this we do something else?"

She narrowed her eyes on me. "Like what?"

As much as I wanted to ask her if we could go back to her house, I wouldn't. "I don't know bowling, cinema, shopping, a walk?"

Her nose wrinkled and she shuddered. "Ugh, not shopping. I hate it."

"That's a relief." I blew out a breath and smiled. "I hate it, too."

"Yet, you'd have gone for me?"

"Told you, I'm nice." I winked at her and was rewarded with a beautiful, bright smile. "So, if not shopping, what?"

Her shoulders shrugged up to her ears as she asked tentatively, "Could we go bowling? I haven't been since I was a teenager."

"Good for me. Although," I said with a groan, "I'm not sure I like the idea of wearing those shit shoes."

"I promise not to take any pictures of you wearing them." She giggled and the sound went straight to parts of my body that I shouldn't have been thinking about.

"Okay, bowling it is." I looked around and caught the attention of the waiter, indicating for the bill. "And lunch is on me."

"No, I'll—"

"Maya, it's just me being nice, so no arguments."

She patted the table. "Okay, but I'm paying for bowling."

"We'll see." No way was she paying for anything, because I was determined to treat her well—treat her well and show her how nice a man I could be, because, for some reason, I felt like she hadn't had one before.

CHAPTER 17
Maddy

I was annoyed with my dad. He had sent me a message to say he wouldn't be home for dinner, but there was curry in the slow cooker, and I had to make sure I ate some.

It wasn't that I was mad that he wasn't home, but that he hadn't messaged me until I was walking through the door. I could have said yes to Zak's invitation to McDonald's. I could have been enjoying a bloody burger with him instead of my dad's curry, *alone*. It wasn't like I could call him and say my plans had changed. That would have looked desperate.

At least dad not being home meant that I could get ready without him questioning me every five minutes. Or him hanging around the front door when Zak arrived, or even worse, asking Zak a thousand and one questions about the evening and warning him to take care of me.

Annoyance, though, was soon replaced by nerves as I realised the time. It was almost five to seven and Zak would be arriving soon. Unless, of course, he stood me up. My stomach dropped at the thought. What if he did? Maybe he'd changed his mind? What if it was just a joke and he didn't like me at all? What if Liam had dared him?

"Shut up, Maddy," I muttered to myself. "You're being stupid."

When, just seconds later, there was a loud banging on the door, I knew I hadn't been stood up. At least I hoped it was Zak. With one last look in the mirror, I ran down the stairs, took a quick breath at the bottom and then pulled open the door.

Zak was standing very straight, with his hands behind his back, grinning. "You look good." He looked me up and down. "Gorgeous, in fact."

My heart beat erratically as I stared at him. I wasn't used to boys being so confident and saying what they thought. Most of the boys I'd talked to, or had dates with, liked to mess around with a girls' head. Talking in some sort of stupid boy code and expecting the girl to understand. And never had one told me that I looked gorgeous as soon as I'd opened the door. One boy, Toby Jacobs, who had since left our school, told me once I looked quite nice, but only after I told him that I liked his jacket.

"Thanks. I like your jacket."

Shit, I was an idiot. Who told a boy they liked his jacket? Me apparently, *to two different boys.*

He gave his sexy grin again. "Cheers." When he held his hand out to me, I gasped, and he smiled. "I won't bite."

I could feel the heat rising in my cheeks as I tentatively took his offer and let him curl his fingers around mine.

"I borrowed my mum's car, so sorry if it's a bit..." Zak shrugged his shoulders.

I looked past him to see a Mini parked at the curb. "I like it."

"Yeah," he said, rolling his eyes. "It's great, but not the best when you're six foot two."

Swallowing, I looked up the full length of him, finding everything about him hot. He was gorgeous to look at, but I liked him as a person too. So far, he seemed like he was nice and wouldn't do the usual dickhead boy things. What did I know, though; he might be the biggest player in the world.

"Anyway, let's go," he said, tugging on my hand. "I'm starving."

"You haven't eaten yet?"

Pulling me down the path to the car, he groaned. "No. Mum made this awful lentil thing because she thinks we eat too much meat. Even Dad wouldn't eat it, and he eats everything."

I thought about his parents and how slim his dad was. He didn't look like he ate everything. He was nothing like my dad; he was older and had been wearing suit trousers and a white shirt—something you'd never see Dad in. Mr Hoyland's hair—Mister, not Doctor, because he was a surgeon—was greying at the temples, and he had a short beard also speckled with grey. He was also very tall, which was obviously where Zak got his height from, because his mum was tiny, not much taller than Amelia.

When we reached the car, Zak opened the door for me. He didn't do it with flourish or make it cheesy; he just did it like it was a normal thing for him to do. Not at all like the other boys my age, who let a door swing back in your face without caring.

"Thanks." I flashed him a smile and got into the car, and when he leaned inside, I felt my breath rush from my lungs.

"I'll just fasten you in." His breath whispered against my ear, making me shiver. "Make sure you're safe."

"Is your driving that bad?"

His face was inches from mine, and I could smell the mint of his toothpaste on his breath as it mingled with his aftershave. When he smiled and showed his perfectly white, perfectly straight teeth, I had to hold back a moan. He was beautiful.

"Nope, I'm a great driver. In fact, my dad says I'm a little bit slow at times."

"My dad will be pleased," I breathed out.

"Where is he, by the way?" he asked, clicking my seatbelt into place. "I expected him to be out here warning me about being safe and getting you home on time."

"He's out. He went to meet a supplier." And he had no idea that I was out with Zak. Otherwise, I was sure he'd have made sure to get home as soon as he could.

"That explains it." I got another flash of teeth, and then he disappeared before closing the door.

I watched him run around the front of the car and then open the driver's door, folding himself into the seat. It was all done with confidence, and I wondered if I could handle him. His long fingers wrapped around the steering wheel, and he bounced in his seat.

"Right, let's go." He grinned at me again, and as soon as we were on our way, I opened my WhatsApp and messaged Ana.

MADDY
Zak just picked me up to go to McDonalds!!!!

ANA
WHAT!!! Like a date?!!

MADDY
I don't know. I think so. He asked me at school. I'm scared!!

ANA
Why! Has he done something to scare you?

MADDY
NO! He's just so…beautiful.

ANA
Do you look good?

MADDY
What do you think?

ANA

Of course you do! What was I thinking!! Just enjoy it and make sure you message me later. I want all the gossip on how he kisses and whether he uses the right amount of tongue.

Smiling, I put my phone back in my pocket and glanced over at Zak, who was concentrating on the road. If he did kiss me, I'd probably pass out before I had time to figure out what his tongue action was like.

"Put the radio on if you like," Zak said, nodding at the dashboard. "Or you can go through my playlists. My phone's hooked up."

With his eyes still on the road, he reached into the console, and, taking hold of his phone, handed it to me.

"Passcode is one, two, three, four."

I burst out laughing. "That's not very safety-conscious."

Zak shrugged and chuckled. "I wouldn't remember anything else."

"Are you sure you don't mind me knowing it?" I asked, looking down at the screen, trying to decide whether to open it or not.

"No. Why would I? I don't have any secrets. Everything else is Hoyland123."

"Wow, okay then." I licked my lips and tapped at the screen. Once I opened the music app, I scrolled. "How many playlists have you got?"

"I like music, and I like to make playlists. In fact, I have one for almost every occasion." He indicated to turn the corner, and I loved how easily he made driving look, how manly his hands were, how his rings clinked against the metal strip on the steering wheel. "Check out my 'Food Shopping for Mum' one; it's brilliant."

Laughing, I did as he suggested and found it. Reading through the songs, I had to agree with him. It was full of banging tunes.

"I'm putting this one on," I told him. "I can imagine you pushing your trolley listening to it."

"See, told you it was good."

I looked over at him, and he had the biggest smile. As the music kicked in, he started to move around in his seat, looking happy and not one bit embarrassed that he was doing a head move that looked like some sort of excited chicken.

"It is," I replied. "Really good."

Zak looked at me briefly, and his eyes were twinkling. "See, I told you a night out with me would be a good one."

I frowned. "Did you?"

"Maybe not," he said, laughing. "But it will be. Promise."

Relaxing back in the seat, I couldn't help the huge smile that hurt my cheeks. I wasn't sure what Zak taking me out meant, but I was determined to enjoy it, even if my stomach was in knots.

CHAPTER 18
Will

"You didn't tell me you were a bowling champion," Maya complained, her lips pouting. "That's not fair."

I chuckled, shaking my head. "I haven't played for years. Probably since Maddy had a bowling party for her eighth birthday."

Putting a hand to her hip, Maya narrowed her eyes on me with a hint of a smile. "I don't believe you."

"I swear." Grinning, I wrapped an arm around her waist and pulled her closer, whispering in her ear, "You're just not very good."

Laughing loudly, she slapped my chest. "You cheeky beggar."

Her eyes were full of amusement as she leaned back to look at me, and I had to kiss her. Cradling her face in my hands, my thumbs gently stroking her chin, I laid my lips on hers and gave her the softest of kisses. Maya melted into me, snaking her arms around my neck as her tongue flicked out, prompting me to deepen the kiss. When she gave a little moan, it encouraged me to pull her closer. I was hard behind the zip of my jeans, and when Maya pushed her hips forward, I knew that she felt it. I knew that if we were somewhere else, we would probably be naked within seconds. We weren't somewhere else, though, and I didn't want to ruin things, so I gently pulled away.

"We should get back to the bowling," I whispered.

She licked her lips and nodded. "I suppose so. Although, I'm a little disappointed that we do."

"Yeah, and me." I sighed heavily. "But you still have a few games to try and win back some pride."

"Will, I'm four-nil down. How the hell do you think I'll do that?"

"I might let you win the next few games."

"No way," she said, gasping. "I don't want any favours."

"Okay, if you say so." I gave her waist a squeeze. "Let's see what you can do."

"Right. Let's do that."

I let her go and watched as she wiggled her gorgeous arse to the lane and picked up her bowling ball. When she sashayed into position, there was definitely an extra sway to her hips. As she got ready to send the ball down the lane she pushed her backside out further than necessary and practically did a slut drop. I didn't care whether she won every one of the next games, especially if she styled it out in the same way.

She glanced over her shoulder and winked. "Here we go." The bowling ball flew out of her hands and trickled down the centre of the alley for a couple of feet and then slowly dribbled into the gully at the side. "Shit." Maya stood up and whirled around to face me. "Stop smirking."

"I'm not." I rubbed a hand over my mouth to try and hide the smirk that she'd spotted.

"Yes, you are." She put her hands to her hips and sighed. "Come on then. Show me how it's done."

Sauntering over to the rack of bowling balls, I picked one up and walked to the spot. Maya moved out of the way, waving her hand in front of her.

"Off you go, Mr Bowling Champion."

I let the ball go and watched as it ran down the aisle knocking eight skittles over. "I didn't get a strike out," I said almost apologetically.

Maya burst out laughing and walked up to me, wrapping her arms around my shoulders. "Maybe you're not that good then." Getting onto her tiptoes she gave me a quick kiss. "I don't think I'm going to beat you after all, so do you fancy going somewhere else?"

I did, but it was probably time I went home. I'd left Maddy her dinner and had messaged her that I wouldn't be home until later, but I couldn't leave her alone all night.

"I really should be getting back. It'll take me a couple of hours, and there's Maddy."

"That's fine." She stroked my cheek and smiled. "I had fun today. Thank you."

"It's been my absolute bloody pleasure." I had to kiss her but was afraid that if I did, I wouldn't stop. "Can we do it again, soon?"

She grinned. "I'd love that."

"As soon as I get home, I'll call you and sort when. Is that okay?"

"Perfect."

Heavy with disappointment, I let her go. "Do you want a lift home? I'm parked on Templar Street."

"I'm parked just around the corner from the café, so don't worry."

It was only six-thirty, but it was dark outside, and I didn't like the idea of her going back to her car alone.

"Then I'll walk you back to your car."

She slapped at my chest. "You don't need to. It's through a crowded shopping area."

"Nope. I want to. I insist."

She thought about it for a moment and then nodded, taking my hand in hers. "I'd like that. It would be very kind of you."

I gave her hand a squeeze and pulled her a little closer. "I told you, I'm a very nice man."

Her eyes grazed over my face as she sighed, "You know, I actually you think you are."

"I am," I said, staring into her beautiful green eyes. "And I'm looking forward to showing you exactly how nice I can be."

As she smiled at me, my chest warmed, and I knew she was *the* one woman I'd want for much longer than two weeks.

***

"Well, this is me," Maya said, pointing at a newish, white Kia SUV-type car.

The fact that it was a big, sturdy car gave me a strange sense of relief. I liked the idea that she would be safe while driving.

Beeping the lock, she opened the passenger door and threw her bag onto the seat before turning back to me. "I've had a great day," she stated, leaning back against the car.

I moved closer, not ready to have a distance between us just yet, but knowing I had to go. Then, when she smiled at me, I knew I had to kiss her before I did, so placing my hands on the roof of the car I confined her with my arms.

"I don't really want this day to end, but…"

"You have to go home for Maddy," Maya said. While her smile was only faint, her words weren't said with blame but stated. I was sure she understood, at least I hoped that she did because Maddy was the most important thing in my life. The most important person in my life.

"Can we meet up again?" she asked.

I was shocked, expecting that I would have to beg her to see me again. "Definitely. Yes," I said on a breath of relief. "When?"

Maya shrugged. "Like I said, I'm off all week." She dropped her gaze to the floor, with a hint of a smile. "I could come over to you." Green eyes flashed back up at me. "Or not, whatever you prefer."

Pressing my body against hers, I pushed my leg between her thighs, noticing how her hips thrust forward like she needed the relief. I know I did.

I was desperate for her, but there was time for what I needed.

"I'd love you to come over to me." I took a deep breath. "Maybe meet Maddy?"

I had no idea why I'd suggested it. We'd had one bloody date. It should have been so wrong, to want her to meet my daughter so soon, but it felt so right. Everything inside of me was desperate for them to get to know each other, because the warmth in my chest told me it would be amazing.

Maya's cheeks pinked as she laid her hand over the top of my thudding heart. "I'd like that, but only if you think it's right. If Maddy will be okay with it."

"I think she would." She was always telling me to take women seriously and that it was time I settled down. "I think she'll like you. I mean, only if you want to. If you don't, then I erm…" I scratched my head. "It's probably too soon, I probably shouldn't have said anything."

Maya shook her head and smiled. "Will, it's fine. I'd like to meet her, but only if she's ready." Exhaling slowly, she licked her lips. "I know it's stupid after just one date, but I think this could go somewhere. I think," she rolled her eyes, "God, this sounds so cheesy, but I *know* this is something good. Too good not to give it a chance."

My exhalation was full of relief that she felt the same way. "I agree, so let me speak to her, but I'm sure she'll be happy to meet you."

"Honestly?"

"Honestly." Nodding, I leaned in closer and kissed her softly.

When our mouths met, everything around us melted away, and all I could feel was Maya's soft lips against mine. All I could hear was my heart thudding against my breastbone. All I wanted was more time with her.

"I'll speak to her as soon as I get home."

"Okay," she whispered. "I should let you go."

She was right, but the idea of moving my body away from hers was hard. For the first time ever, I was torn about putting my daughter first. It wasn't an option, though; it was ingrained in me to be there for her.

"Yeah, I suppose you do." With a defeated groan, I pushed away from Maya with our fingers still linked, unable to totally let go. "I'll call you."

"You better." She grinned and took a deep breath.

"Speak later." I took a step back. Only one.

"We have a family Zoom call later, so if I don't answer leave me a message and I'll call you back." She chewed on her bottom lip.

Nodding, I took another step back and our arms stretched out. "Is there a good time to call?"

"After eight. We do it after *Coronation Street* has finished. Mum is mad on it. Actually, so is my brother Jack, but he won't admit it."

Earlier, Maya had told me her parents had gone to live in Scotland, going back to her dad's roots after he retired, and they kept in touch with weekly video calls with her and her brothers.

"I'll call about half nine. That okay?"

A huge smile broke out, showing me the cute gap between her teeth. "Perfect."

I couldn't leave without tasting her lips one more time, so took a quick kiss and loved the little moan she gave.

It took me five more minutes before I watched her close her car door and start up her car. Then I legged it back to my own car and went home, hopefully to get my daughter to agree to meet the new woman in my life.

MAYA'S DIARY ENTRY

Oh shit. I am in so much trouble. I really, really like Will. He's just... argh, there aren't enough words to explain what's going on in my head, in my chest and in my stomach. I have never liked anyone this much so soon. I know I'm a romantic, and I'm probably making a tit of myself, but I could see myself falling in love with him. He was so lovely, insisted on paying for everything, held my hand, kissed me against my car. He's an amazing kisser. Morgan will kill me for using the word amazing. She'd tell me it's lazy vocabulary!! Anyway, he was an incredible kisser. I was so turned on, I think I almost came, lol. I asked him to come home with me, but he couldn't because of his daughter. I like that he seems like a good dad. It's clear she's the most important thing in his life, and that shows what kind of man he is. At least, I hope it does. He said he was going to call me, and I'm panicking. What if he doesn't call? Should I call him? I hope he isn't stringing me along. I don't think he seems the sort of guy that would. Oh shit, I think I might be sick now!!

CHAPTER 19
Maddy

As we sat at the table, I couldn't stop looking at Zak. Who would have thought that eating a burger was sexy? Maybe it was the way he licked burger sauce from his fingers that made me all hot and bothered. Or how he sucked hard on the straw of his coke. Whatever it was, I couldn't take my eyes off him.

"This is so rude," Zak said, wiping his hands on his serviette. "You not eating while I stuff my face."

"It's fine." I shook my head, unable to take my eyes off his fingers. There was ketchup on one of them, and I was almost tempted to grab his hand and lick it off myself. "I'm enjoying my milkshake."

"I know, but it's not much of a date watching me eat."

My stomach knotted. "A date?" I asked tentatively.

He grinned and then his tongue snaked out and licked off the ketchup, leaving me disappointed.

"Yeah, what did you think it was?"

I shrugged. "I don't know." Zak raised an eyebrow. "Okay, so maybe I'm a bit dense."

"You're not dense. Maybe just a bit slow."

When my mouth dropped open, he started laughing and grabbed my hand, pulling it closer to him. He threaded our fingers and rubbed his thumb up and down mine, every single stroke sending my temperature higher and my nerves spikier.

"I really like you, Maddy." His bright blue eyes twinkled as he leaned across the table. "Do you want to be on a date with me?"

My throat felt dry, and my lips stuck to my teeth as I smiled. "Yes."

He laughed, throwing his head back, showing his Adam's apple, and there was something about it that made me feel all tingly.

"You don't sound very sure."

"No, honestly, I am. Do you? Do you want to be on a date with me?"

He sighed and shook his head, frustrated. "Of course I do. I asked you didn't I?" He leaned further across the table and whispered, "I've been wanting to ask you for ages."

"You have?" I wiped my spare hand on my jeans, trying to ignore the nervous roll of my stomach.

"Haven't you realised? Didn't you notice how I kept staring over at you?"

I shook my head, aware that my mouth was gaping. "No. I mean, I did wonder at Emma's house but wasn't sure."

"And when I nearly kissed you at my house? Didn't that prove it to you?" He gave me a sexy smirk. "Was it that bad?"

"*No*." I cringed at my eagerness, wondering whether he thought I was lame.

His smile seemed to say that he didn't, and when he took my other hand,

I was sure that he didn't. When he reached over to kiss me quickly on the lips, I knew that he didn't.

"You taste of chocolate." Slowly pulling back from me, his gaze was firmly on my lips. "It's nice."

"T-thanks."

"So," he said, letting go of one of my hands, "where do you fancy going next?"

"I don't know." I shrugged.

"Not that there's much for seventeen-year-olds to do around here."

"I bet you wish you'd never moved here, don't you?"

Zak frowned. "No, because I wouldn't have met you if I hadn't, would I?" He grinned. "I like it here. I like how easy it is and the fact that no one is rushing around, stressed out."

"I think my dad might argue that one with you."

"Really?" He looked down at our joined hands and smiled at them before looking back up at me. "I'm surprised. He seems so laid back."

"Don't let him fool you. He gets very stressy when it's time to do his year-end accounts."

"He seems like a nice guy, though."

I waved him off. "He's okay."

When Zak smiled at me, my heart started to beat so fast I felt like I'd run a marathon. I was full of nervous energy and could feel it edging into my fingers. Fingers that he was holding onto, so I gently pulled them from his. He frowned and then looked down at my hand as I slid it towards me.

"Don't you like PDA's?" he asked.

Pushing both shaking hands under my thighs, I shrugged. "I don't mind them."

"I was enjoying it. Holding your hand. I liked it." He pouted and then grinned, holding out his hand, palm up. "Come on then, give it to me."

"What?"

"Your hand," he said with his eyebrows raised. "I'd like to hold it. If that's okay with you." He leaned closer and whispered, "Is that okay with you?"

Biting on my top lip, I nodded and gave him back my hand. He linked our fingers again and then lifted them, resting his elbow on the table. Everything inside of me felt… strange, fizzy almost.

"You have really soft skin," he said, stroking my palm, tickling it and making me squirm. He grinned mischievously. "Oh, I forgot that you're ticklish. I'll stop."

The instant that he stopped doing it, I wished I wasn't, because I'd liked it. Relief came, though, when he started to rub my thumb instead.

"Better?"

"Yeah," I whispered. "That doesn't tickle at all."

"Good." He moved his head closer to mine and gave me the slightest of kisses, yet my heart almost exploded with the surge of adrenalin that it created. "So, any idea where you want to go after here?"

"My house?" I suggested, without thinking.

Zak blinked slowly. "Your dad isn't home. Are you sure?"

I had no idea whether I was or not, I just knew I wasn't ready to say goodnight to him. I wanted to spend more time with him, talking to him, looking at him.

"Yes, it'll be fine. It's not like we're going to raid his drink cabinet or anything. Not that he has a drink cabinet."

His shoulders shook as he laughed. "What does it say about my parents that they do?"

"That they're more grown up than my dad."

"How old is he, by the way?"

"Thirty-seven. What about your mum and dad?"

He thought about it for a couple of seconds. "I have to work it out from my age because I always forget." After another brief pause he said, "Dad is fifty-five, and Mum is forty-nine. They met at some sort of medical exhibition and were married six months later and had me a year after that."

"A bit older than my parents then." I didn't really care that they were only young. Dad had proved that age and experience didn't mean you made a better parent, but I knew some people still judged him for being a young parent.

"I just think they were both tied up with their careers, but Mum always says that if she had her time again she'd have had children younger. Says she'd have like to have had more than two."

"And what does your dad say about that?" I asked, grinning.

Zak gave a quiet laugh. "He says she couldn't have because she hadn't met him, the love of her life. Although, I do think he'd have liked a couple more, too. I think they tried between me and Amelia, but it didn't happen." He frowned. "I have a feeling Mum might have had a couple of miscarriages, but she never mentions it. What about you? Do you miss having brothers or sisters?"

"I've never thought about it to be honest. It was always just me and Dad, and he did everything he could to make sure that I didn't feel any different to my friends. I think that was why he encouraged me and Liam to be friends. It felt like Liam and his mum and dad were family. My dad and Liam's dad have known each other for years. They were neighbours when my dad moved here. So it's always been like I had an auntie, an uncle, and a cousin."

Zak sighed and shook his head. "I take my big family for granted. I have eleven cousins."

"Wow." My eyes went big. "Eleven?"

"Yeah. My mum has two brothers, and my dad has a sister and two brothers."

"That's a lot."

He nodded. "It is. Yet you know, we barely see each other because we're always too busy. And now we've moved here, I bet we'll see even less of them."

"Another reason to miss the big city." I smirked.

Zak raised an eyebrow as he looked at me. "But like I said before, I wouldn't have met you if we hadn't."

"Very true."

"Hey, I know, let's take your dad some nuggets back with us."

"What?" I couldn't help but laugh at such a strange suggestion. "My dad?"

"Yeah. He does eat meat doesn't he?" Zak's eyes were full of excitement like he'd had the best idea in the world.

"He does, but I'm not sure how much meat is in their nuggets."

"Agreed, it's questionable, but even so, what do you think?" He asked, peering over my shoulder towards the counter. "Ten or twenty?"

I shook my head. "Ten would be fine, Zak, but you don't have to." I started to giggle at the idea of him presenting my dad with ten chicken nuggets.

Letting go of my hand, he stood up. "Shall I get him fries as well."

"No," I replied, my giggle turning into a full-on laugh. "The nuggets are fine."

He bounced on the balls of his feet, like an excited toddler. "Sauces! What sauces shall I get? Tomato or barbeque?"

"Barbeque."

"Right. I won't be long."

He leaned down, gave me a quick kiss, and went off to the counter. As I watched him looking hot and gorgeous as he ordered the food, I realised that I liked that he had rizz, but I also liked that he was a little bit nerdy, too.

***

Zak parked next to the kerb just as my dad drove onto the drive. I was surprised because it was almost nine, and I'd expected him to be back well before us. His meetings never usually went on so late.

"Oh good," Zak said unbuckling his belt. "He'll be able to eat them hot."

I loved how it made him so excited. I just hoped my dad didn't act up because I'd brought Zak home.

Opening the car door, he turned to me just before he got out. "He won't mind me being here, will he?"

"No. Not at all." I wasn't sure, but if he did, he wouldn't say anything in front of Zak.

As I rounded the front of the car, Dad was unfolding himself from his. As Zak reached out for my hand, my dad looked from him to me.

"Hello. Where've you two been?"

"Maccies," Zak said, holding up his bag of nuggets. "We got you some chicken. Maddy said no fries, but…" he looked at me and grinned, "I didn't listen."

Dad smirked and crossed his arms over his chest. "That's very kind of you."

Zak pushed the bag closer to him, and Dad slowly unfolded his arms and took it from him.

"Didn't know you were going out," Dad said, moving towards the front door with his key in his hand.

"You weren't here to tell," I replied, raising an eyebrow. "How was the supplier?"

Dad paused for a second and then continued up the path. "Yeah, good. I'll talk to you about it later."

That was odd because he never spoke to me about suppliers. Maybe he'd decided to make a big business decision and wanted to run it past me.

We followed Dad into the house, through to the kitchen, my heart thudding with unease at how the unexpected meeting between him and Zak would go. Dad had seemed to like him at the café, when we'd had breakfast, and he was pretty easy going, so I shouldn't have worried. I was his little girl, though, and Zak was a boy who clearly had an interest in me.

Dad reached for the kettle, switched it on, and then turned back around. "Brew?"

I glanced to my side where Zak was standing. He didn't exactly look relaxed, but he certainly didn't look scared or nervous.

"Please, Mr Newman."

"I told you, Will is fine." Dad flashed him a smile and then looked at me. "Maddy?"

"Tea, please." At least he hadn't full named me, so I wasn't in trouble for going out without telling him. If I was, it would only be a safety thing with him. He just liked to know where I was.

"Anyone want a nugget?" Dad opened the bag and peered inside before putting his hand inside and bringing out a couple of fries.

"No, thanks." Zak moved a little closer to me and I almost leapt as his little finger linked with mine. "I just had a burger."

I glanced at him, aware that my face was burning, but when I looked at my dad he had turned back to the making the mugs of tea.

"Are you going to sit down?" he asked over his shoulder. "I don't fancy eating this while you're both standing over me."

Letting out a breath, I moved towards the table, aware that Zak hadn't let go of my finger. When I looked at him he was grinning, like he knew I was loving it and hating it in equal parts. Pulling my hand away and rolling my eyes, I sat down at the table, my stomach instantly flipping when Zak took the chair next to me. His thigh nudged mine just before his fingers tickled my side.

"Oi," I hissed, trying to sound annoyed, but unable to hide a smile.

Zak raised an eyebrow and then turned to look at dad's back. "I can make the tea for you Mr Newm—, sorry, Will. You can eat your nuggets then."

"Dad's very particular about his tea," I told him.

"I am." He reached into the brown bag and pulled out a piece of chicken, popping it whole into his mouth, chewing it as he continued making the drinks.

Zak linked our fingers again and my heart started jumping around in my chest. Everything he did made it go fast, made me feel excited inside. Made me want to smile until my cheeks ached.

Eventually, Dad turned around and placed two mugs in front of us. Then he got his own and brought it to the table along with his nuggets.

"I really appreciate this," he said, peeling the lid off a barbeque sauce pot. "I didn't realise that I was hungry." He looked up. "So, what else have you two been up to tonight?"

"Not what you're thinking," I muttered, earning one of Dad's looks that said I'd better not be lying to him.

"Just McDonald's," Zak replied. "But Maddy only had a milkshake."

"You had the curry?"

"Yes, I had the curry. You left it for me so why wouldn't I?" I narrowed my eyes on him. "It was very nice, by the way."

"I know. I make a good curry." He winked at me and then ate another piece of chicken as we watched him in silence. It wasn't uncomfortable as such, but I didn't like it. Who knew what Zak was thinking, but worse still, who knew what my dad was thinking? And if he was thinking the worst, what questions would he start asking?

Dad took another bite and then took a long sip of his tea.

"Lovely," he finally said. "Thanks for that." He slapped his hand on the table. "So, Zak, how are you and the family settling in? The people of Norford can be a little inclusive at times."

"It's great. We're really liking it here." He looked at me and grinned, making it obvious why he particularly liked it in Norford. At least, I hoped that *I* was the reason.

"And your mum and dad like it?" Dad cleared his throat, peering into his mug.

"Dad says the hospital is great, especially the staff. As for mum, well," Zak chuckled, "she's happy as long as teeth are involved."

"Same as Dad and beer," I muttered, earning a nudge in the shin under the table.

"I serve it, it doesn't mean I love it."

Giving him a wry smile, I sat back in my chair. Then I realised doing that gave Dad a view of mine and Zak's linked fingers, so quickly pulled my chair closer to the table.

"Anyway," Dad said, picking up the bag. "I'll leave you to it." He looked directly at Zak. "Don't stay too late. You've both got school tomorrow."

He winked, but there was no disguising the warning as he got up and put his mug into the sink and the bag in the pedal bin. Walking slowly to the door, with his usual confident swagger, he called over his shoulder.

"Don't forget I need to speak to you later, Maddy, so don't go to bed until I have."

I glanced at Zak and then back to my dad who was disappearing into the hallway. "Okay."

Once I heard the living room door click shut, I swivelled in my seat to face Zak. "What do you think that's about?"

Zak shrugged. "I have no idea." He laughed and wrapped my hand in both of his. "How would I know? It's not like I'm his best friend and he confides in me." He leaned closer to me. "If I was, he'd let me stay late."

I rolled my eyes. "Take no notice. He's a pussycat deep down. Stay as late as you like."

"I don't know, Maddy. I don't want to make him mad right from the beginning."

"He's not mad. Honestly." I shook my head and grinned. "Don't be scared of Big Bad Will."

Zak's eyes turned serious. "I'm not, but I do respect him."

Wow, I did an excited internal dance. I knew that if he'd said that to Ana she'd have laughed in his face and told him he'd given her the ick. Not me, though, I liked that he cared what my dad thought.

"Okay," I said, swallowing back the moan of appreciation. "But that doesn't mean that you have to go yet."

He frowned. "I wasn't planning on." He nodded towards the oven, specifically the clock glowing orange. "It's only half nine. I think I have at least an hour left before he starts coming in and checking on us."

"Really?" I smirked. "What shall we do during that hour?"

Zak watched me carefully, his head tilted on one side, eventually exhaling long and deep. "This." Then he leaned in closer, his lips landing on mine. "Is that okay?"

I drew in a breath and nodded. "Yeah. I'd like that."

"Good," he whispered. "Because I've been wanting to do it for weeks."

His admission surprised me and made my cheeks heat up.

"Weeks?"

"Yeah, bloody weeks, love."

The way he said, love, made me want to jump him and wish that I had the confidence of Ana or Liv. They'd have kissed him as soon as they opened the door to him.

I straightened my back. "I suppose you'd better kiss me some more then."

Instantly, Zak's hands cupped my face, his fingers laced into my hair and his lips, soft and gentle, touched mine. It was the most perfect, most romantic of kisses. It was the best of all the first kisses that I'd ever had. It was everything that I hoped kissing Zak Hoyland would be like. As he leaned in closer, and his tongue pushed against the seam of my lips, I hoped that it would go on forever. His soft moan sent a message to the pit of my stomach, and I pressed my thighs together.

Wanting to show him that I was just as into it, I moved onto his lap, wrapping my arms around his waist, and holding on to his hard back muscles. There was smooth dip down the length of his spine, and I let my fingers moved slowly towards his jeans. When they reached the cotton waistband of his boxer briefs, I dipped a coupled of fingers inside, rubbing the tips of them along to one of the dimples at the bottom of his back.

"Maddy," he whispered, shifting me so that I was straddling his thighs.

No more words were said as we continued kissing, my fingertips digging in as it deepened, as we both gave more soft moans of pleasure.

After what seemed an eternity, I heard the living room door open, and my dad clear his throat, giving us a few seconds warning.

I quickly moved back to my own chair and leaned nonchalantly on the table with one elbow, my head resting in my hand. Zak grinned and readjusted his jeans, moving his chair closer to the table.

"Yeah, so Amelia jumped in the deep end and nearly drowned," he said, in a slightly too bright voice.

Quickly latching on, I joined in the conversation. "Did you go in after her and save her?"

"Yeah, of course I… oh hey, Mr Newman, erm, Will."

"Hey, Zak." Dad looked at me and frowned. "You okay?"

"Yeah, why?"

He shrugged. "Look a bit flushed." He moved over to the thermostat on the wall and turned the dial. "No bloody wonder, it's turned up to twenty-three. I've told you, Maddy, it only needs to be twenty at the most." He whipped around to look at me. "And I'm not made of money."

I rolled my eyes and turned back to Zak. "Anyway, you were saying."

He hesitated and looked at my dad.

"It's fine," Dad said. "I'm just coming in for a glass of water." He ran the tap and filled a glass. "You can come and sit in the living room if you want to."

"We're fine thanks," I muttered.

Dad grinned and shrugged. "Okay. Whatever. See you later."

Once he'd gone, Zak breathed out a sigh of relief. "I lied. I am a bit scared of him."

We both started to laugh until Zak leaned in for another soft kiss, and everything but him fell away from my mind.

CHAPTER 20
Will

Just before quarter past ten, Zak popped his head around the living room door and said goodnight. A minute later, the front door opened. Twenty minutes later, after lots of giggles interspersed with too-long silences, I heard it close. One minute later, Maddy entered the living room with a big, soppy grin on her face.

"Boyfriend finally gone has he?" I asked, shifting the cushion behind my head.

"If you mean Zak, yes. And he's not my boyfriend."

Turning the sound down on the TV, I sighed heavily. "Oh, yeah, I forgot you talk for a while first. Although," I said, turning my head to look at her, "there wasn't much talking going on at the front door, Madeline."

"Am I in trouble for something?" she asked, flopping down into the armchair. "He didn't stay too late. We stayed in the kitchen. We didn't do drugs or drink alcohol."

"I know." God, she was a little shit at times. The looked on her face would scare most grown men. Narrowed eyes and pinched lips that said, 'fuck with me if you dare'. I mean, I was glad in many ways that she'd never be walked over by a man, but it wasn't so cute when it was aimed at me. "And less of the attitude."

"I'm not giving you any attitude."

"The face says it all." Pushing myself up, I dropped my feet to the floor. "Now, shall we try again. Has Zak gone home, finally?"

She paused, only for a second, but long enough to show a little defiance. "Yes, he's gone home. You said you wanted to talk to me before I went to bed."

Pointing the remote, I turned the TV off and turned to her. "I do." I had no idea why I felt nervous. It wasn't like she didn't already know about Maya. It wasn't like she didn't want me to get a girlfriend and settle down. She was always banging on about my love life and how I should stop having inconsequential relationships.

"Remember I told you about the girl I met on the night out in Leeds?"

She frowned, her nose scrunching up like it did when she was little and was told no and didn't understand why.

"What's happened? Has she got you into some sort of trouble? Is she pregnant?"

"How quick do you think it takes?" I shook my head in disbelief. "No wonder you dropped biology, you're crap at it."

"I do know about procreation, Dad. I'm just wondering why you're looking so serious, that's all." She hugged a cushion to her stomach, putting her legs over the arm of the chair. I opened my mouth to tell her stop abusing the furniture but decided against it. I'd learned over the years when to fight my battles with my daughter.

"I just wanted to ask if you'd like to meet her." I knew I sounded rushed and breathy, but I'd never wanted to introduce Maddy to someone before. I had, but it didn't mean I always wanted to. "I met up with her today."

"Not a supplier?"

I shook my head. "I met Maya. In Leeds."

"So, Maya finally messaged you." She raised an eyebrow and smirked. "Nice work, Dad."

"Will you, then? Meet her."

"Wow, you do like her." Scratching her chin, she glared at me. "Why are you so nervous? Is she an ex teacher of mine?"

"No!"

"She's not under twenty-five, is she?" Maddy's face went white, and if I didn't want to get the conversation over with, I would have let her think I'd found a woman closer to her age than mine.

"She's thirty-two."

"And she's not married?"

"No," I replied. "Never been married."

"Children?"

"No."

"Well, she's getting on a bit, Dad if you do decide you want babies together."

"Maddy," I groaned. "We've had one date."

"And yet you want her to meet me." She shrugged. "Sounds pretty serious already if you ask me."

I was slowly losing my patience. "Madeline, are you happy to meet her or not?"

She considered it for a minute. "Yes, I'd like to. If she's special to you, then I'd love to meet her."

"Seriously?"

She dropped her feet to the floor and stood up. "I am very serious. I'd love to meet her." Throwing the cushion back onto the armchair, Maddy moved over to the sofa and sat down next to me, putting her hand on top of mine. "Dad, I'm glad you've met someone that you like enough that you want me to meet her. I've been telling you for ages."

"I know, sweetheart, but it's always just been us. Me and you. I wanted to be sure that were okay with it." I ran a hand down my face, not sure why I was finding it so hard. I liked Maya and I wanted to see where it could go. I wanted her and Maddy to get along. To really like each other. It was just bloody difficult realising that things might be about to change in a life that I'd become so comfortable with. I wasn't normally someone who stood still. I believed in moving forward and relishing change, but introducing a woman into the life that Maddy and I had forged together, well, it seemed like a huge leap.

"I'm more than okay with it. Honestly, Dad." She leaned in close, hugging my arm. "At least if I go to uni, I'll know that you're being looked after. That someone is feeding you."

"I can feed myself, you know." I leaned back, taking Maddy with me, settling against the cushion. "You're not a little girl anymore, and I'm struggling a little bit with that. There's a boy you're *talking* to…" She slapped me playfully on the chest. "And then you might go off to university."

"And I might not."

"Maddy, sweetheart, we've talked about this. Going away will be better for you than studying online. You'll have a better experience than if you stay here with me."

"We'll see," she said with a sigh.

"It's just bloody scary."

Grinning, she held out her hand. "Take my hand, Daddy."

I smiled, hearing the words that I'd said to her since she was a little girl, and placed my large, calloused one in her small, smooth one. I loved that now she was older she knew that sometimes I needed to hear it too.

"I know it's scary, William, but we all have to grow up."

I narrowed my eyes on her. "You're a little turd."

Giggling, she reached up and kissed my cheek. "So, when do I get to meet her?"

"I don't know, but soon. I hope." I thought back to my afternoon with Maya. I wanted more of it. More afternoons spent laughing and flirting with each other.

"You'd better call her then, hadn't you."

"Are you sure?"

Sighing, she rolled her eyes. "Yes, Dad. I'm sure."

The relief rolled through every muscle in my body, like I'd been given a sedative. The realisation at how tense I'd been feeling, waiting for Maddy's reaction, made me blink.

"You okay?"

Stirring myself, I turned back to my daughter. Her expressive eyes showed concern as they grazed over my face, searching for whatever it was that she thought was bothering me.

"She's not pressurising you into meeting me, is she?"

"No, honestly, Mads, I'm fine." I leaned forward and kissed her forehead. "It's just a big thing, you know. Introducing a woman that I actually like to you."

"As opposed to..."

"A woman who begs to meet you because she thinks I'll like her more."

"Maya isn't like that?"

I shook my head. "Nope. She's nothing like any other woman I've ever dated."

Maddy burst out laughing. "Dad, you don't date. You have one night stands that last a couple of weeks."

She wasn't wrong. It didn't mean that I wanted to admit it, though. "Whatever, Madeline. Now, get to bed." I smiled, just so she knew I wasn't being serious, but also didn't want to talk about it any longer.

Yawning, she stood up and gave me one last hug. "Night, Dad. And ring her." She raised both her eyebrows—eyebrows that I had paid a stupid amount of money for her birthday.

"I will. I'll call her now."

That earned me a kiss on my cheek, and as she disappeared, I grabbed my phone and called Maya.

MAYA'S DIARY ENTRY

Panic over, he called me at about half ten. He was waiting for Maddy's boyfriend to leave so he could speak to her.

I'm going over there and he's going to call me tomorrow to finalise the details!

There's something about him that makes me feel like this could be going somewhere. Like maybe he could be the one who treats me properly. The one who I could have a future with. Is that stupid? One meeting and a phone call?? I'm an idiot. I can't rush this. I can't make it more than it is. I've been excited about a relationship before, and it turned to crap, so I need to stop getting ahead of myself on this one.

CHAPTER 21
Maddy

The last thing that I expected to see, as I walked towards the school gate, was Zak. He stood out amongst the hordes of kids milling around. Our sixth form didn't insist on us wearing school uniform like a lot did, but even if he had been dressed in grey trousers and jumper with a white shirt and burgundy tie, I'd have spotted him anywhere.

Leaning casually against the metal mesh fence, he had an unlit cigarette dangling from his mouth, a sexy grin keeping it in place.

"Hiya gorgeous." He took the unlit smoke from his mouth and shoved into the top pocket of his thick padded jacket. My stomach and heart battled with each other as to which could flip the most, and my cheeks felt like they were burning.

"Hi. What are you doing here?"

He looked around as he pushed off the fence, stretching his long limbs in a stride towards me.

"Erm that would be waiting for you. What else?"

I shrugged. "I don't know. I just didn't expect it."

"We both have maths first thing, so…" He held out his hand for me.

I hadn't even told Ana, or any of the others about Zak kissing me at the kitchen table. Ana knew that we'd gone out, but that was it. By the time Dad had spoken to me about Maya, all I'd been ready for was to get in my bed and fall asleep. Admittedly, dreaming about Zak.

"Are you sure you're ready for everyone to…" I looked around. "I don't know. I mean…"

"Maddy," he whispered, leaning in close, "I like you. I don't mind who knows. Do you?"

I would have been happy to scream it to everyone. Hijack the sixth form weekly meeting and add it as an agenda item.

"No, I don't mind." I gave him a shy smile. "I was just thinking, you know, we've not been talking for long and—"

He laughed. "I don't believe in all that talking shit. I like you. I like kissing you. I like spending time with you. So as far as I'm concerned we're together. Are you okay with that?"

Swallowing, I nodded.

"Good." He gave me a wink, which in no way whatsoever gave me the ick, and then grabbed my hand. "If we hurry, we can have a quick snog before everyone else gets there."

I snorted out a laugh, embarrassment making me hide my face behind my hand. Zak didn't seem to mind, because he pulled me closer and then wrapped his arm around my neck while still holding my hand, and walked us in through the school gates.

More than a few people stopped to stare at us, but Zak kept marching forward while telling me about a school talent show that Amelia had entered.

With each step my confidence grew and by the time we reached the door to the sixth form block, I had the biggest smile and felt pride like I'd never felt before.

I wasn't bad looking. A lot of people had told me I pretty, my dad always said I was beautiful, even Zak had called me gorgeous, but I wasn't sure that counted as it was in a greeting. The point was, being with him, with his arm around me, made me feel like I'd suddenly become the coolest, prettiest girl in school. He was stunning to look at, was sweet and had rizz, and rightly or wrongly him picking me made me feel like I mattered. It wasn't a great advert for me being an independent, strong woman, but I was a seventeen-year-old girl who was liked by the hottest boy in school, so at that point I didn't really care. I wanted to enjoy the moment.

As we pushed through the doors, Zak kept his arm around me, manoeuvring us sideways so he didn't have to let go.

"Do you think your dad would let you go to a party at the weekend?" he asked, as we walked down the corridor towards our maths class. "One of the lads from the football team is having one. His mum and dad are going away for a few days."

"Who's the lad?"

Zak's brow furrowed as he thought about it. "Jack someone."

"Dawson? Jack Dawson?"

He nodded. "That's him. So, you fancy it? You think you'll be allowed to go?"

"I'll just tell him I'm going. He won't mind." He might warn me about drinking too much, or not doing anything stupid with Zak, though, "He would only say no if I don't know whose party it was."

"I know, but I don't want to piss him off. I told you; he scares me."

Rolling my eyes, I poked him gently in his side. "He does not. There's nothing scary about him."

"Hah," he scoffed. "That's easy for you to say. You're not the one seeing his daughter."

That sent a little thrill through my body, jolting my heart to take an extra beat. When I looked up at Zak and saw two lines furrowed between his eyebrows, I couldn't help but laugh. Even concerned he still looked gorgeous.

"Honestly, Zak, he's a big softy. Don't worry."

"Well, I don't want to risk it, so make sure he's okay about it." He kissed my cheek, sending me into another hot mess. "Maybe *I* should ask him?"

"No, don't do that," I snapped, pulling us to a stop outside our classroom. "Don't you dare."

He burst out laughing. "Okay, okay. Chill." He held up his hand, clearly amused. "I won't."

"No, you bloody well won't." I shuddered. "No one needs to ask him."

"He'll know anyway, Liam is going, and his dad is bound to tell yours."

He wasn't wrong. They told each other pretty much everything, especially where Liam and I were concerned.

"We don't have to go," Zak offered tentatively. "We could do something else."

"No, I want to go. It'll be fun, and honestly, my dad will be fine." Looking at him and his earnest face, I had a massive urge to kiss him, but not the nerve.

Zak narrowed his eyes on me and smirked knowingly. Leaning closer his mouth slanted over mine and *he* kissed *me*. It wasn't deep or rushed but sweet and slow, his tongue lazily sweeping against mine. As I was about to push against him and possibly ride his thigh, Zak pulled away, smiling.

"Bloody hell, that's a development."

At the sound of Liam's voice, we both turned to see him, Emma and Ana standing watching us, each of them grinning.

"Alright," Zak said, clutching my hand he brought it in front of him, a clear signal to anyone watching that we were together. It gave me a thrill.

"When did that happen?" Emma asked, blinking like she was sending Morse code with each flutter of her eyelashes.

"He's liked her for ages," Liam informed her knowingly.

"They went on a date last night," Ana added.

Emma whipped her head in her direction. "How did you know that? How did I *not* know that?" She glared at me. "Does Liv know?"

I shook my head. "I only told Ana last night. It was a last minute thing."

"The date or telling Ana?" she asked, sounding a little hurt.

"Both." I shrugged. "I didn't mean to keep it from you, but I just…"

Emma threw her hands in the air. "I get she's your very best friend, Maddy, but you could have told us."

Pouting, she hitched her bag further up her shoulder and turned towards the classroom. Liam gave us a tight smile, and then watched her throw the door open.

"She'll be fine," he said. "I'll talk to her." He jogged after her, leaving Ana staring at us with a raised eyebrow.

"Date went well then?"

Zak chuckled. "Yeah, definitely."

"If I was you, I'd message Liv," Ana suggested. "She's gone to the dentist and is back at lunchtime."

I nodded and looked towards the classroom that Emma had disappeared into. She was right, Ana was my very best friend, but I could have easily let Emma and Liv know later in the evening. I would have been upset, too, if she hadn't told me.

"She'll be fine. You know she's a drama queen," Ana added. "Now come on before we get into trouble for being late."

I looked up at Zak, unease making my chest tight. "I should have told her, and Liv."

"Like Ana said, she'll be fine." He gave me a quick kiss. "Now, come on let's get in there."

Nodding, I let him tow me in, sad that I'd upset my friend, and that it had marred my excitement of what was starting with Zak.

***

"I am sorry," I told Liv and Emma as we sat eating our lunch. "He asked me, and I just messaged Ana after he picked me up."

Liv shook her head. "Don't worry about it." She winced and touched her cheek, the side where she'd had a filling in her tooth. "Emma, stop being ridiculous. Now, this party on Saturday. Are we all going?"

"Jack Dawson's?" Ana asked, poking a fork at her salad and practically snarling at it.

"Yes. The football team are going, obviously, and Harry Mayhew," Liv informed us, the subject of Zak and me clearly no longer of any importance.

"So, we need a plan."

"For what?" I asked.

She huffed and placed her hands on the table. "To get Harry to notice me."

"Just wear your lowest-cut top," Emma muttered.

"Or that leather skirt that barely covers your bum." Ana popped a tomato in her mouth and winced. "I don't know why they insist on serving these shitty, sour tomatoes."

Liv flicked her long blonde, poker-straight hair over her shoulder and lengthened her spine. "Can we be serious?"

My attention moved to the double doors leading into the dining room as Zak, Liam and a couple of other boys strolled in.

"Maddy!"

Liv's voice snapped my gaze back to her. "What?"

"A plan. We need a plan for me to get Harry's attention."

"We've told you," Ana stated, peeling a banana. "The clothes will do it."

"Yeah," Emma added. "The skirt and the top together will seal the deal."

As Liv continued talking about her latest crush, I sensed that I was being watched. The hairs on my arms stood up and a shiver ran through my body. I turned my head and saw Zak looking at me from across the room. Toby, one of the boys he'd come in with, was talking to him, but his attention was definitely on me. There was a beautiful smile on his face as soon as our eyes met.

"Oh, for shit's sake," Ana groaned. "Just go and speak to him."

"No." It was hard, but I tore my gaze away from Zak. "He's having his lunch."

"Yeah and he looks like he wants to eat you." Emma snorted at her own joke, and I felt myself shiver with excitement.

The anticipation of doing more than kissing Zak took my breath away. Already, I could imagine going further with him than any other boy I'd been out with before. I mean, I'd done things, more than kissing, but I'd never gone all the way. I'd never felt enough for someone to have sex with them. It wasn't like I was waiting for 'the one' or for marriage, but I just hadn't ever felt like I wanted to before. Yet Zak was different. I wanted more with him, even if he wasn't the boy I'd end up with.

Turning my gaze back to him, I was disappointed to see his attention was back on whatever the boys were talking about. I watched him for a few seconds and then sighed, still unable to believe that he seemed to like me as much as I liked him. About to turn back to the girls, I instantly stopped because Zak's head swivelled in my direction. When he winked and gave me a broad smile, I knew for definite he was going to be my first.

CHAPTER 22

Will

My mouth felt dry, and the silence seemed to have stretched for hours. It was actually only seconds—ten to be precise. I knew because I was counting.

"I told you, honestly," Maya said, sounding breathy.

"And you're sure that Maddy is okay with it?"

The relief that she was okay with Maya coming over was immense because this relationship was different.

"She's totally on board. Honestly."

"What do you think? Shall we all go out for dinner?"

The vice-like grip around my chest loosened, and nervous air rushed out. "That would be fantastic. I'll book somewhere." My mind was already racing ahead to where we could go. "There's a great pub in the next village along."

"Sounds good." Maya paused for a second. "I'm wondering whether to come on the train."

"Yeah, you could." I didn't like the idea of her going home on a train late at night—or driving, for that matter, so I second guessed myself. "Why don't you stay over in our spare room. That way you don't have to travel home on the train or in the car late at night."

Maya chuckled. "In your spare room?"

"Of course. I wouldn't assume anything." Besides which, I wasn't sure that I fancied fucking her until she screamed, with my daughter across the landing. Didn't mean I hadn't thought about it, a lot. "That will happen when we have more time and a little more privacy."

"Okay," she said breathily. "I'm happy with that."

Instantly, my dick twitched, and I had to readjust myself. Thank the fuck Marco and our other bartender, Dilly, were busying themselves with the lunchtime rush. It was old-age pension day, and, as usual, we had a horde of people aged sixty plus wanting tea, coffee and bacon sandwiches. We always took a delivery of cakes and pastries on a Tuesday as well, and so, without selling much alcohol, it was one of our busiest days. I was lucky to have escaped for a few minutes to call Maya.

"Well, maybe we can discuss that tomorrow," I suggested. "How does getting here for five sound?"

"Brilliant. If I'm staying over, I'll drive to you. You sure that's okay? Maddy won't mind me staying the night?" She sounded unsure again, and so I couldn't wait for them to meet. That way, she'd soon realise that everything was going to be fine.

"She will be great about it. I promise."

"Okay," she said, exhaling. "Can you message me your address?"

"I'll do it as soon as we finish on the call."

"Great."

Grinning, I puffed out my chest. "I can't wait to see you." And I couldn't.

Twenty-four hours was too long.

"See you tomorrow, Will."

Her honey-toned voice sent a message to my chest and my dick, and it was difficult to end the call. Eventually, though, we did, and I left my office, messaging her my address, to go and do some work. Marcus was wiping down the bar as Dilly chatted to a couple at their table.

"Hey, sorry about that. It took a bit longer than I thought."

He shook his head. "No problem. We've got it covered. Robbie, helped out with serving food."

"He turned up on time?"

Marcus had finally had enough of Dylan when he'd been over two hours late on Sunday, and then he'd gone missing for an hour. He eventually found him dealing weed to a bunch of teenagers on our car park, hence Robbie.

"In fact," Marcus said, turning to throw his wet rag into the small bar sink, "he's quite good at cooking. He made some great sandwiches."

I frowned. "A bacon butty is a bacon butty, mate."

"Yeah but add a bit of rocket and mayo and it becomes something else." He grinned, wiggling his eyebrows.

"You're not making something sexual out of a bacon butty, are you?"

"Fuck off. What sort of freak do you think I am."

"I choose not to answer that one." I moved along the bar and snagged a glass to pour myself a Coke. My mouth was dry still from the nerves at calling Maya. Once poured, I took a long gulp.

"Hang over?" Marcus asked.

"Nope. Just thirsty." I looked over his shoulder to see Dilly coming back to the bar. "Hey, Dill, weren't you off half an hour ago?"

"Yes, but we had a rush on while you were on the phone."

"Sorry about that." I scratched the back of my neck, feeling bad that I'd spent almost an hour on the phone to Maya. "Get yourself off now and come in later tomorrow."

"It's fine. I'll save it until I need it." She gave me a bright smile, running a hand through her short, cropped hair. "I do need to go now, though—Dan can't pick the kids up from after-school club, so I need to."

"Yeah, get going. See you tomorrow."

She left us with a wave and Marcus staring after her.

"It's not going to happen, mate."

I wouldn't say he had a crush on Dilly, it was more like she was a challenge. I was right, though, it wasn't going to happen. She was divorced from Dan and was seeing a guy she'd met on the internet. Plus, she was ten years older than Marcus, and while he liked an older woman, she was not interested in a younger man.

"I can dream." He shrugged nonchalantly and leaned against the bar. "Anyway, what about you? How was the stag night? You never said."

That would be because I didn't want to say anything. I was worried that if I did, it might put a curse on the thing with Maya.

"It was a good night. Gary enjoyed it. Apart from the bloody t-shirts we all had to wear."

"Did you get lucky?" Marcus leaned one elbow on the bar and waited expectantly. He knew that on nights like that, I usually did. "Meet a nice young lady?"

I almost told him no, but I was sure it was too obvious. It was idiotic to think telling someone would spoil things. I wasn't normally superstitious.

"Yeah, I did actually. Her name is Maya."

Marcus raised an eyebrow. "Sexy name."

I chuckled and shook my head. "Not sure I understand what you mean, but she is pretty sexy."

"Picture?"

I reared back with the sudden realisation that I didn't, but I should have. It might have made the last couple of nights tossing and turning easier to deal with.

"I'll take that look of pain as a no," Marcus said, grinning. "Just a mental image then?"

What a mental image it was. Her golden skin, long, luxurious dark hair and her forest green eyes had kept me awake every night since I'd met her. Even banging one out each night hadn't help.

"Yeah." I scrubbed a hand down my face. "She smells great, too."

"Wow, you do have it bad. You seeing her again?"

"Have already," I informed him. "Yesterday."

Blinking slowly, he moved so his back was leaning against the bar. "And here was me thinking you were trying to get us a better deal on lager."

Shrugging I reached for my glass of coke and took another sip. "I wasn't sure how it was going to go, so…" I shrugged.

"But?"

I couldn't help but smile as I thought about our day together. "It was good."

"And have you told Maddy about her?" Marcus might have been seemed like he didn't care about much, but he did care about my daughter. Since he'd started working for me, he'd taken on the role as unofficial big brother to her, even if he did try and goad me about how beautiful she was.

"She knows and has said she'd like to meet her."

"What?" He pushed his body off the bar, his arms braced as he gripped the wood behind him. "Already?"

Nodding, I felt my chest tighten, wondering if I'd done the wrong thing. "You think I've been too hasty?"

"I don't know, mate. Do you? Because what you think is what matters, not my opinion." He returned to leaning against the bar. "I've just never known you be like this over a woman before. Shit, you barely see anyone more than twice, never mind introduce them to Mads. This one must be special."

It didn't take me long to think about it. "Yeah, she is. I like her a lot." I grimaced at the fact I was laying myself bare to Marcus. Sam was usually my go-to person with sharing, but I wanted anyone who would listen to know about Maya. "It's a weird fucking feeling, but I like it. I like her."

Marcus shrugged. "If it feels right, then go with it. Let's just hope that Maddy likes her."

My stomach tilted at the thought, but I pushed it to one side. Maddy and I tended to be on the same wavelength, and I hoped that this was one of those occasions. If I liked Maya, then I had to be confident that Maddy would, too.

"I suppose we'll find out, won't we," I replied, sighing heavily.

Marcus gave me a wry smile. "I suppose you will, mate. And if Maddy doesn't approve you can always introduce her to me."

It was illogical, but I wanted to punch my friend in the face for even thinking it. And I knew that if Maddy didn't like Maya, I would be devastated.

MEET THE FAMILY

CHAPTER 23
Maddy

My dad looked like he might be about to puke. I'd never seen him so nervous. He was the one who was always confident, always telling me everything would be okay—not at all like the anxious man staring out of the window.

"Dad, it's going to be fine. I'm sure I'll like her."

His head whipped in my direction. "Don't know what you're talking about."

Watching him frown, I walked over to him and held out my hand. "Take my hand, Daddy," I said the words he always gave to me when I was upset or worried.

Without thinking, he did just that but when I giggled, he shook me away. "I'm fine, you idiot."

"You're the idiot," I scoffed. "Getting so worked up to point of nearly passing out."

"I am not." He returned his gaze to the window, and instantly his back stiffened. When his hands linked at the back of his neck, I knew Maya had arrived.

Placing my hand on his back, I patted it gently. "Breathe, Dad."

He blew out a breath. "What if you don't like her?"

"What if she doesn't like me?"

He turned to me and frowned. "Then she's not the person for me. Anyway, she will. What's not to like, you're like me?"

"Exactly!" I jumped back to dodge his hand that I knew was going to tickle me. "Want me to let her in?"

"No, I'll go." He pulled his shoulders back and left.

Waiting for them to come back into the room my own nerves hit. Dad was clearly smitten by Maya, and I didn't want to let him down. I was genuinely worried that she wouldn't like me because if she didn't, I knew it would upset Dad. As much as he liked her, I knew that I was the most important person in his life. The pressure to be perfect for him was making me feel a little sick, too, but I hoped that I'd masked it from him.

Having no more time to worry about it, the door to the lounge opened and Dad led Maya into the room. My instant impression was how beautiful she was and how jealous I was of her hair. Long, thick, wavy and shiny hair was what I aspired to have. As for her clothes who knew that a brown flowered smock dress would look so good with thick tights and brown Dr Marten boots? She had the sleeves pushed up to show off an armful of bronze bangles, and I made a mental note to try and find some for myself.

"This is Maddy," Dad said throatily, dragging my attention away from Maya.

"Hi." I gave a little wave.

"Hi, Maddy. Great to meet you." Maya tucked her hair behind her ear and took a half step forward. She hesitated for a split second but then opened up her arms and pulled me into a hug. She smelled lovely, too, and I knew I had my new female crush, style-wise at least. I just hoped that her personality was as gorgeous as she looked.

"Lovely to meet you, too." I looked over her shoulder at my dad, not before noting how great her extra-large hoop earrings were. He was almost bouncing on his toes, desperate to know whether Maya and I were going to hit it off.

We pulled apart, and Maya took a step back, glancing at Dad over her shoulder. "She looks like you."

"Gorgeous then," he stated with a chuckle.

I rolled my eyes, but when his shoulders dropped I was glad to see that he'd relaxed a little bit.

"I really don't know what you see in him," I muttered.

Maya laughed and shrugged. "I think maybe I was drunk."

Dad grinned, and I knew that I already liked her. Unless she was the best actress in the world, or I was the most stupid person on the planet, she seemed lovely, and I was glad for my dad.

"So," he said, sounding tentative again. "Do you want me to show you your room?"

I wanted to laugh, loudly, because I doubted whether she'd stay in her own room. Especially, not if the way they were looking at each other was anything to go by.

"If we have time." She looked between us. "What time is the table booked for?"

"We have time," Dad told her. "We have an hour at least before we need to leave."

"Then, yeah," Maya replied with a bright smile, "you can show me my room."

As they disappeared up the stairs, excitement spiked. I loved that Dad was finally going to get some happy. And, yes, maybe Maya staying over might have seemed quick, seeing as they'd only just met, but I wasn't worried. It felt right.

Just as I wondered whether I should follow them, my phone rang, and I was shocked when I saw it was Zak.

"Hiya."

"Alright, gorgeous."

Instantly, my face split into a grin, and I felt butterflies. "Everything okay?"

"Yeah, I just wanted to check you were good."

"Me?" I asked.

"I knew you were nervous about meeting your dad's new girlfriend. I wanted to check-up on you. Make sure you're not freaking out."

My hand rested over my thudding heart, and my cheeks ached from smiling. "I'm fine. She seems nice."

"She's already there?"

"About five minutes ago."

"And?" he asked with a chuckle. "Does she really meet your approval, or are *you* just being nice?"

"No, she meets my approval. She's lovely in fact. Or at least she seems to be in the short time I've spoken to her." I looked over to the door to check that I was still alone. "She's gorgeous, Zak. I can see why Dad likes her."

"What was she like with you?" Zak asked, as a door closed in the background. "Sorry, just shutting Amelia out."

"Aww don't be mean to her."

"I'm not, she keeps asking me about Taylor Swift, and I have no idea what to say."

I gasped. "You don't know anything about Swifty. I'm appalled."

Zak groaned. "Ah shit, not you as well."

"I think maybe Amelia and I need to educate you."

"No, you're alright thanks. I'll stick with Stormzy."

"Ugh, how do I live with that?"

"What?" he asked, his laugh resonating deep down the line.

"That my boyf—" I instantly stopped myself just in time. "That you're a rap boy."

"I'm sure you'll cope."

I breathed a silent sigh of relief that he hadn't picked up on my slip up. "But to answer your question, yes, she was lovely with me. Gave me a hug, said she was pleased to meet me and said I looked like my dad."

"That sounds good. Sounds like she seems nice. Although, you looking like your dad makes me feel like I might vomit."

"I hope you think I'm prettier than him."

Zak's laugh trailed off. "Much prettier. Gorgeous, in fact."

The butterflies started up again and I wasn't sure what to say. I went for, "I'd better go before they come back from the bedroom."

"From *where*?" he asked, shocked.

"He's just showing her the spare room," I told him, rolling my eyes. "You and your dirty mind."

Zak laughed and I had a sudden desire to see him. "Want to come over later?"

"Won't it be late?" he asked, and I could detect a hint of excitement at the idea.

"Well, I'll call you when we're back and you can decide then." I bit down on my lip, waiting anxiously.

"Yeah, that sounds good. Maybe persuade them to skip dessert."

More relief flooded through me at his idea. Surely it meant that he wanted to see me later. He wouldn't say that if he didn't want to, would he?

"I'll call you later, then." I tried to make it more like a statement than a question, conscious of sounding like I was desperate.

"Definitely," Zak replied. "Speak to you later."

"Okay, will do."

"Oh, and Maddy," he added.

"Yes."

"It's okay to say I'm your boyfriend, because I am."

As my heart thudded loudly in my ears, I barely heard Zak say goodbye. All that I could think of was the fact that I was his girlfriend.

***

It was official: my dad was halfway to being in love. In fact, he might already have reached the point of no return. It was the way he gazed at Maya, a bit like she was made of twinkling diamonds, and he couldn't quite believe it. To be fair, she wasn't much less obvious in her feelings for him either. I could honestly say that not everything Dad said was hilarious, but Maya appeared to think it was. Her laugh had tinkled like a little bell all evening.

They were quite sweet, really. At first they'd tried desperately to not appear too besotted with each other, avoiding eye contact, talking mainly to me, but I wasn't fooled. Within ten minutes Dad had moved his chair closer to Maya's and they were holding hands on top of the table, stealing glances at each other and being generally cute. It didn't even induce sick in my mouth—they were so adorable.

"So, you want to be a social worker," Maya said, her little finger linked with Dad's while her spare hand held onto the stem of her wine glass.

"Yes, I do." I glanced at Dad who already had a raised eyebrow. "I'm planning on doing my degree from home. Open University."

"My friend did her teaching degree with the OU," Maya replied. "She said it was great, loads of boozy parties at Summer School."

"Shit," Dad groaned. "And there was me thinking at least if you didn't go away, you would never end up in A&E with alcohol poisoning."

"See, Dad, there are benefits to staying at home. I only end up getting my stomach pumped once a year."

"I still think Edinburgh or Lancaster are the best options," Dad said with a sigh. "I hear their emergency departments are top notch."

"You don't want her to stay at home?" Maya asked.

I rolled my eyes. "We've been having this battle for months," I told her. "He wants me to have the full uni experience, but I want to stay at home."

"She thinks I can't cope without her." Dad cocked an eyebrow making Maya giggle. She'd giggled a lot during the last hour or so.

"And do you think you can?" she asked him.

"Of course I can," he scoffed. "She's the one who can't even make decent scrambled eggs."

"Dad, who would get you out of bed on time for work if I wasn't here?"

He narrowed his eyes on me and then grinned. "Maybe you have a point."

I turned to look at Maya, and my breath hitched. She was gazing at both me and dad and her eyes were glistening. She'd told me that her mum and dad lived in Scotland and that she missed them, so maybe that was what had made her emotional.

"What about you, Maya?" I asked. "Where did you go to uni?"

"Sheffield. Not the best for my course, but," she laughed and shook her head, "believe it or not, I didn't want to leave home either."

"See." I pointed at Dad. "Not everyone wants to go away to Uni."

"Exactly." Maya laughed and nudged Dad in the ribs. "Not everyone wants to leave their dad."

"Don't encourage her." The smile that he gave to her was as gentle as I'd ever seen him give. It was just like the ones he gave to me when I was worried, or scared, when he wanted to reassure me. He'd give me that smile and then say, 'Take my hand.'

I didn't want to spoil their moment, but suddenly I felt like I shouldn't be there. It wasn't exactly a private moment between them, but it was obvious they were both falling quickly for each other, and they should have been able to do that without me ogling them.

"I'm just going to the loo," I told them.

Dad's eyes tore away from Maya's and met mine. "Do you want a desert, sweetie pie?"

I almost told him my favourite, brownie's with ice cream, but then remembered that maybe Zak might come over.

"I'm fine, thanks."

"Maya?"

She shifted in her seat and licked her lips before shaking her head. Dad blew out his cheeks, and I realised that the *private moment* was fast approaching. Me disappearing for a few minutes would be good for them.

"Just get the bill, Dad," I told him. "If we fancy anything we've got some ice cream in the freezer."

Dad swallowed and then cleared his throat. "Good idea."

As I left them alone, I would have put money on Dad creeping across the landing later, and it made me smile. I was happy for him, and even if he and Maya only lasted a short time, he'd experienced something with someone who was more than just a hook up. He deserved that because it was time he thought about himself for once and maybe me going away to uni would be good for him, too.

ZAK'S WHATSAPP MESSAGES

ZAK
It's official I have a girlfriend!

OSCAR
That was quick. You haven't even been talking to her for long.

ZAK
You know I hate that talking shit. She's out with her dad and the woman he's seeing tonight but think I'm going to go over later.

OSCAR
Message me the deets!

ZAK
Fuck off!

OSCAR
Shit you really do like her. I'll call you tomorrow just off out with Sarah.

ZAK
SARAH JACOBS!! When did that happen?

OSCAR
It's not! We're in charge of prom after party so we're checking out venues.

ZAK
I thought Luke's parents said you could have it there??

OSCAR

Changed their minds because he got caught smoking a spliff! He's a dick anyway.

ZAK

Told you that in year six! Speak tomorrow mate. Say hello to Sarah for me. Oh and tell her to tell Deacon I'll message him about him staying here when he comes to check out the Uni.

OSCAR

Will do.

CHAPTER 24
Will

Maddy had gone up to her room, leaving Maya and I alone in my living room. The fire was on, flickering artificial flames, the lights were down, and we were both nursing a beer. We'd been talking so much we'd barely taken a drink since we'd sat down almost an hour before. I didn't think I'd ever felt as at peace as I did then.

There'd been times of great happiness in my life, mostly since I'd become a dad. Maddy was a constant joy. Times at the bar had been fun—some nights we'd laughed until our sides ached. I think Marcus had actually snorted beer down his nose on one occasion. Peace, though, that I'd never felt. There'd always been a worry in the back of mind while I was laughing or watching my daughter with pride. There'd always been bills to pay, orders to place or worries if Maddy was happy or being bullied.

Sitting next to Maya, knowing Maddy was safe upstairs, happy and enjoying her life, everything felt… fuck, I didn't know how to describe it other than serene. Like I was lying in the warmest pool, feeling boneless, floating around with not a single worry in my head.

"But my brother Jack's mother-in-law, Carol, is a horrible woman," Maya said, continuing the story she'd been telling me.

I laughed, loving hearing about her family. Maybe it was because I didn't have one of my own, or maybe I just loved hearing her voice.

"Why is she horrible?"

She screwed up her face. "Apart from the fact that she was my history teacher in secondary school and hated me, she's too strict with Jack's kids and Daisy's only six, George, is four and Claudia is two. They should be allowed to have fun before real life starts." A giggle erupted. "Although Daisy did wrap her favourite necklace in toilet paper and flush it down the loo."

"Sounds like she deserved it. Spoilsport."

Humour flashed through her forest-green eyes. "I might have wrapped it in tissue for her."

She giggled again, and all the sweetness and joy of it wrapped around me, making me want to stay there with her for as long as humanly possible.

"Anyway," she continued, "this boyfriend of Maddy's, what's he like?" She pulled the thick wool throw over her shoulder and looked at me expectantly.

"You cold?" I asked, leaning towards the fire. "I can turn it up."

"No." She hugged her shoulders up towards her ears. "I'm lovely and toasty."

"Just say if you are."

She shook her head. "I will, but tell me about Maddy's boyfriend. What's he like? Do you like him?"

I shrugged. "He seems like a nice kid. Has ambitions to be a vet, comes from a nice family, and is polite."

"And he treats Maddy okay?"

I felt myself tense and my skin start to itch. "As far as I know. They're pretty new. Just talking, or so I'm told." I thought back to them sitting close to each other in my kitchen. Then how they'd pulled apart when I walked in. "I think there might be more than talking going on, though." I shuddered, and Maya laughed.

"She's seventeen, Will. There's a good chance she's kissed more than one boy."

"No, she hasn't." I knew that probably wasn't true, but in my head it was.

"Okay, what about your bar? Tell me about that." She put her bottle down on the coffee table and scooted a little closer to me. "I know it's in the centre of the town and that it was run-down but what's it like inside?" She waved her hands around and shook her shoulders. "What's its vibe?"

I groaned. "Don't ever ask that question again or do that action." I circled my finger around. "That was weird."

Maya grinned. "Was it unattractive? Have you gone off me?"

"Too bloody right."

Laughing, our eyes latched on each other's, and when a tiny tear appeared at the corner of Maya's, I reached up to wipe it away with my thumb.

"You're beautiful," I whispered, stretching my fingers to lace into her hair at her temple. "I don't think I've ever seen eyes as gorgeous as yours before."

"I'm sure that's not true." She curled her lips inwards and looked down at my hand resting on her thigh over the blanket.

She looked a little shy, but she *was* the most beautiful woman I'd ever seen. I wasn't lying.

"How about your friend, Morgan?" I asked, grinning at her shyness. "How's she feeling after her divorce?"

"Loving life." She rolled her eyes. "Too much. Every time I speak to her, she's either hung over or getting ready to go out to a party."

"Enjoying herself then?"

"Seems so. Who knew divorce could be so much fun." She moved a little closer. "And you've really never fancied it? Getting married?"

"Nah. Besides, I had Maddy. She took up all my time and to be honest, I never met anyone who I wanted to settle down with." Until now…maybe.

"You didn't want to find a mum for her?" Maya asked, resting her chin on her hand, listening intently to me. "It must have been hard, though, just you taking care of her and running the bar."

"Yeah, at times, but my friends Sam and Louise have been brilliant. More like an aunt and uncle to her. They had her overnight, after school, they even took her on holiday a couple of times when I couldn't get away from the bar."

"Were they the ones who took her to Spain?"

I smiled that she remembered I'd told her about that. "No, when she was younger. Her and Liam are like cousins, so they had a great time." I grinned, recalling how she'd come back from a week in Cornwall full of tales of catching crabs in rock pools, swimming in the sea. and eating huge pasties covered in sand.

"They sound like good friends to have."

"They are."

I knew I was lucky, not many twenty-year-olds who found themselves with a baby had the opportunities that I'd had. Not everyone had a Miriam or a Sam and Louise. The blessings I'd been given were nothing short of miraculous. Maddy and I could quite easily have been living in poverty, struggling from day to day, wondering how I was going to pay the bills, or even put food on the table. My life had been charmed somewhere along the line, and the gratitude I felt was endless.

Just the flip of a coin. If I hadn't trusted Miriam, if I hadn't been desperate to move on from the bar I was working in, I might have still been working in other people's bars. I could still be bringing home a shit wage each week, relying on my smile to get some decent tips so that I could afford more than Pot Noodles to eat. Maddy might be living with a nice family, but she could have equally been shipped from one foster family to another and be a troubled teenager. No, I was definitely blessed.

"I don't think I always realise how lucky I am to have my family," Maya sighed. "How easy my life has been. No family drama, my parents are still together, I actually get on with my siblings, and when I wanted a Barbie bike when I was seven, I got one. No questions asked."

"I had a Barbie once," I informed her, recalling the worst Christmas I'd ever had.

"You did?"

I nodded. "The foster family I was with didn't really want me there at Christmas. They hadn't bought me anything and I was lucky they even let me sit down to lunch with them. I think the wife felt a little guilty, so gave me one of the dolls they'd bought for their own daughter."

Maya gasped. "No way. That's awful, Will. Did that happen a lot? You going to foster families that didn't really want you?"

"One or two. To be fair to them, I was an emergency placement, seeing as I'd pissed my last foster dad off big style when I threw a brick through his car windscreen. He said he didn't care that it was two days away from Christmas—I wasn't welcome any longer."

Maya's eyes filled with emotion, and I took her hand in mine.

"I was my own worst enemy, Maya. Don't feel bad for me. I threw the brick just because he asked me to tidy my room."

"I just feel awful that you were brought up in the system." She frowned. "How are you so together?"

I laughed, not sure that was true. "If I am, which is debatable, it's down to Mrs Powell."

"The lady who fostered you as a teenager?"

"Yeah. She was brilliant. She was an incredible grandma to Maddy, too." I sighed heavily. "We both still miss her a lot."

"Tell me about her."

"Not much to tell, really."

"There must be," she argued, poking me in my side. "I've told you about my family, so you tell me about yours."

I thought about Mrs P and her shiny blue eyes that twinkled when she smiled and went steely when she was telling me to stop being a dick. For a long time, I'd just seen her as another adult who told me what to do, but I'd been so wrong. Within six months she'd managed to change me from a moody, insolent brat into a... moody, well-mannered brat who did whatever

I could to gain Mrs P's approval. I did all that because she listened to me, she gave me a hug when I needed it, a bollocking when it was deserved, and she encouraged me at every opportunity.

"She was the mum I hadn't had since I was a little kid," I told Maya. "Never once was I made to feel unwanted by her. She knew that I wasn't particularly academic, so helped me to think of jobs that I would be good at, like bar work. Well, actually she suggested retail or even care work, but I wasn't sure that looking after other people was my thing."

"How did you get into bar work then?"

"Started washing glasses in a pub, and then when I was eighteen they offered me a shift behind the bar, and I loved it. Loved that my feet were always wet and that my clothes stunk of beer."

"And the women flirting with you?" she smirked.

I shrugged. "It helped. I never looked back really. Took one bar job after another, and with each one, took on more responsibility. Until finally I got my own place. I wouldn't have done any of that without Mrs Powell."

"You never called her, Mum?"

"It had never crossed my mind to, mainly because even though I'd mostly grown up in the system, my mum had tried her best and she'd loved me." I shrugged. "I had a mum."

Maya licked her lips, and while I knew it wasn't meant to be a turn-on, it was, and I had to concentrate hard not to kiss her.

"What happened to your mum, if you don't mind me asking?"

"Heart attack." As always the word came out full of indifference. It had been over twenty-five years since she'd died and with each passing year, she'd faded more and more into the past. Memories of her had become fainter. "She was only thirty-two but had a congenital heart condition." Maya's eyebrows rose. "Maddy and I are both fine, we've been tested."

She exhaled and nodded. "That's good."

"Mrs Powell got me tested, and then I got Maddy tested when she was about four. And before you ask, I never knew who my dad was. He disappeared before I was born. All I have of him is a letter to her saying he wasn't interested in being a dad. Mum did her best, worked a couple of jobs and provided for me as much as she could. I was clean and fed and happy. I was a little shit, but I was happy. It was just us seeing as her mum kicked her out at sixteen and then moved away without telling her where she was going. She was a good mum to me, though, from what I remember."

"And then she died."

Her words were said with sadness, and I hated it. I'd stopped feeling sad. Yes, I loved my mum, but I barely knew her, and she'd become a kind of a myth a long time ago.

"She did and then I eventually found Mrs P." I grinned, still wondering how I'd been so lucky.

"No wonder you're so dedicated to Maddy."

"I just want her to have as normal a life as possible, even if it is with only one parent."

Maya's eyes softened. "I think you've managed it."

My chest tightened as I thought about my daughter. The love I had for her was too big to contemplate. It was hard to describe how it made me feel. Fulfilled, proud, lucky, scared were only the edges of the emotions she evoked in me.

"She's my biggest achievement."

Maya's head rested on the back of the sofa, her eyes latched on mine, and instantly the atmosphere changed. What had been soft and easy became intense and electrified. The rhythm of my breathing changed; it sped up but was shallower with each inhalation. Never had I ever wanted a woman as much as I wanted Maya. Never had I ever felt so desperate to kiss someone yet been so scared to do it at the same time.

We'd kissed before, but it felt like the next one between us would be life-defining. It would determine how our lives might change. If it wasn't perfect, she might decide to disappear, and already I knew that if she did, it would be an opportunity lost for something incredible.

Unable to hold back any longer, I leaned forward and cupped Maya's face. My thumb rubbed along her bottom lip, pouty and pink and desperate to be kissed.

"You're so beautiful," I whispered. "The most beautiful woman I've ever met."

"I don't know about that."

"Yeah, you are." I studied her, my eyes taking in every inch of her clear complexion, losing myself in the depths of the green jewels staring back at me. "I don't want to sound cheesy, but I really need kiss you."

"You don't need to ask."

In one swift, smooth move, I planted my lips on Maya's and did what I'd been desperate to do all night.

It started off slow and gentle as my tongue pushed against the seam of her pillowy soft lips. When Maya opened up to allow me in I increased the pressure, and her arms came around my neck and pulled me closer. With her fingertips brushing the nape of my neck, I wrapped my arm around her waist, pushing my hand into the small of her back. She tasted like the sweetest honey, and it took my breath away. My heart and lungs battled with each other as I struggled to stay calm. Not to rush the ending of the best kiss that I'd ever had.

Like magnets, we pushed closer to each other. The kiss became more forceful. Maya's hand gripped my shirt, bunching it between her fingertips, while her other one cradled the back of my head, keeping me in place as our tongues danced together.

"Will," she whispered, as she threw the blanket to one side and moved to straddle me.

As she rode my rock hard dick, my brain turned to mush, and every single thought left my head. My hand went to cup her breast, my thumb rubbing over her dress against her tight nipple, so tight that I could feel it through the fabric. My heart was beating hard and fast, almost out of my chest, like any minute it would burst through my shirt.

"I think I'm going crazy, how much I want you," I told her, lacing my fingers in her hair. "I've thought about you every minute of every day since we met.

"Same," she gasped out as I thrust my hips upwards. "But we need to stop."

My heartbeat thudded to a stop. "Why?"

She moaned seductively and it went straight to my dick, so I deepened the kiss. I didn't want it to stop, I wanted it to go on and on. Never stop.

"Maddy," she whispered against my lips. "We can't."

I dropped my forehead to hers, knowing she was right. I'd been the one to suggest she stay over in the spare bedroom, and it would be wrong to change my mind. It wouldn't be fair on Maddy and the embarrassment it would cause her. Plus, I wanted to make Maya scream my name, and that wasn't possible with my daughter across the landing.

Groaning, I sighed. "You're right. I know you're right but it's hard."

Maya giggled and pushed her hips forward, her core grazing my hard on, making it even more difficult to let her go. She took the initiative and moved off me and back to her spot on the sofa.

"Maybe we should call it a night," she said, tucking the blanket around her legs, like she needed a barrier.

She was right, we did need to call it a night, and she needed that barrier, otherwise those tights of hers might have been ripped off. She might well have been on her back in seconds.

"You're right. We should." I adjusted myself, trying to loosen the denim around my dick. "I'll show you to your room."

"No need." She rolled her eyes and grinned. "I'm not sure I trust us together in a room with a bed in it."

"You have a point." I stood up and held a hand out for her. She took it and let me pull her to her feet. "Remember, top of the stairs, door on the right hand side of the landing. Not the one that's got the nameplate of Maddy on it."

"Imagine me wandering in while she's whispering sweet nothings to her boyfriend on the phone." No, I didn't want to imagine it, so as Maya kissed my cheek, I pushed everything to the back of mind and wondered how quickly I could book us a night away.

CHAPTER 25
Maddy

"Quick," I hissed at Zak. "Get in."

He paused in the doorway, glancing up the stairs. "I'm not sure this is a good idea."

I shook my head. "I thought you were a man, not a mouse?"

Zak frowned. "I'm not a mouse, but your dad won't be happy."

"No, you're not a mouse, you're a chicken."

Zak gasped and then grinned at me, grabbing my hand and pulling against his chest. "Well, that's rude." His lips found mine and he gave me the softest of kisses.

I could have easily got lost in it, but the cold air from the open door brought me back to my senses. Pulling away, I pushed at his chest and closed the front door. "Get in the lounge before you wake him up."

His eyes darted towards the stairs again and then I zipped into the lounge after Zak who was standing in front of the fireplace. His hands were deep in the pockets of his sweatpants, and he was looking nervous.

"He's fast asleep, Zak."

"How do you know?" he asked, looking up at the ceiling.

"He's snoring. Plus, if he wasn't and had even an inkling that you were in the house, he'd be in here now."

"What about Maya? Is she still here?"

Nodding, I grabbed his hand and pulled him down to the sofa. "Yeah, they went to bed about an hour ago. Separately."

"And you haven't caught him sneaking into her bedroom?" He shrugged his denim jacket off and placed it on the arm of the sofa—folded neatly and placed precisely, making me grin.

"No, I'm pretty sure there was quite a lingering kiss on the landing, but they went to their own rooms and closed the doors firmly behind them. Dad's is next to mine, so I heard him tossing and turning for about half an hour, but now he's definitely snoring." I pointed upwards. "His floorboards squeak, so if he gets out of bed, I'll hear him."

When Zak had agreed to come over after we got back from dinner, I hadn't been sure that he was being serious. When I went to my room and called him, I'd half expected him to laugh and tell me it was a bad idea. He didn't, though. He'd sounded excited and said he would get there as soon as he could. As soon as he'd finished his homework. That excitement seemed to have been replaced with fear.

Zak blew out a breath and sat back against the sofa. He lifted his hand and tugged on the end of my hair plait.

"I like your hair like this."

The braid went from the front, around the side and then to the ends of my hair, with it hanging down my back. I often wore it like that for bed, especially if I wanted it to be wavy the next day.

Smiling, I flopped back next to him. "Finish your homework?"

"Of course, and if I don't get an A then there's something wrong with the world."

"Confident much."

"It's part of my natural charm." He pulled a little harder on my hair, making me topple towards him. I put out a hand to brace myself against the sofa so that I didn't smash my face into his.

"Hiya," he said. His lips were inches from mine and curled up into a cute grin.

"Hey," I said, aware that I sounded extremely breathy.

"How was your dinner?" His finger stroked down my cheek, along my jaw and then dragged slowly along my bottom lip. "Did you enjoy it? Do you like her?"

"Dinner was good, I had a burger. I really enjoyed it and yes, I like her a lot. She seems to really like Dad, and he definitely likes her. He might already be in love with her to be honest."

"Really?" he asked, raising a brow. "That was quick."

"She's gorgeous," I admitted. "Stylish and gorgeous. I think I might be a bit in love with her, too."

Zak chuckled, putting an arm around my waist and pulling me towards him. I knew exactly what he wanted, so I straddled him, aware that I was wearing a thin pair of leggings with a crop top *and* the fact there was a definite bulge in his sweatpants.

"I missed you today," he said, licking his lips and letting his tongue linger on his top one.

"You saw me in maths."

"Yeah, but we didn't really get chance to talk, seeing as Collard set us that shitty test. It was bloody hard."

As he cupped my cheek, his ring felt cool against my heated skin. The hardness in his trousers. His accent. His perfectly straight, perfectly white teeth. It all made me feel like the air had rushed from my lungs. Like I couldn't breathe unless I kissed him, so I smashed my lips against his.

Zak gripped my bum, pulling me towards him so my core was tight against his erection. I rolled my hips enjoying the sensation of the friction, going a little faster when it elicited a groan from the gorgeous boy beneath me.

As his tongue swept erotically against mine, I tasted mint with a tiny hint of cigarette, and I didn't think there was anything better. My hands went to his biceps as I used them to steady myself while I continued to thrust. They bulged beneath the short sleeves of his white t-shirt, my fingers gripping the hard muscle as I gained traction.

"Maddy," he urged, moving his hands to my hips. "Shit."

The way he groaned out the word told me that he was as heated as I was. It also told me that we needed to stop. As much as I knew Zak would be my first, I wasn't ready for it to be while my dad was sleeping upstairs. My dad *and* his new girlfriend.

Zak took control of the situation and lifted me from his lap, placing me onto the seat next to him. We were both panting, and I knew that my face was flushed.

"We need to calm down," he said, pulling my legs so that they were over his lap. He grinned at me and ran a hand down my calf. "I need to calm down."

There was still a bulge showing in his sweatpants, and I could feel myself pulsing, desperate for him to touch me, knowing it would be like pressing a detonator button. Instead, I blew out a long breath and concentrated on bringing myself back down to earth.

"Seems like you missed me today, too," he said with a laugh.

"I might have been staring at your back instead of concentrating on my test." As Zak's hand moved up and down my leg it was hard not to jump him again. When I squeezed my thighs together, Zak must have seen the movement because his hand stopped moving and he gripped my leg instead. It was like he was hanging onto his temptation by his fingertips.

"Looking at my Oddballs undies again were you?"

"No," I scoffed. I absolutely was. Today's were blue and red stripes.

"Liar." He threaded his fingers with mine and sighed. "I really should go."

"You've only been here fifteen minutes."

He grinned. "But so worth it." I rolled my eyes. "I know it's been a flying visit, babe, but I just wanted to see you. Make sure you were okay."

My stomach swooped at him calling me babe. I'd always thought I'd hate for a boy to call me that. That it would be too icky, but Zak saying it was not icky at all.

"If only my dad had gone to bed earlier."

"Yeah, if only. It's almost half twelve and we've got to get up for school."

"Where do your mum and dad think you are by the way?" I asked, twisting the silver ring on his thumb.

"In bed, I suppose. They both go to bed about nine-thirty and get up at six every day."

"Would they worry, though, if they got up and you weren't in bed?"

"I left a note on my pillow to say I'd gone out for a drive."

I blinked. "And they won't worry about that?"

Zak cleared his throat as he shook his head. "Nope, they're used to me going out for a drive. I don't always sleep brilliantly."

I didn't know that about him, but then I wasn't sure how I would. Our sleeping patterns weren't something we'd discussed.

As if on cue, I yawned, and Zak smiled. "Bedtime, I think."

"I think you're right." I dropped my feet to the floor and sat forward, on the edge of the sofa.

Our eyes trained on each other we couldn't help but smile

"I should go," he said, with a hint of disappointment.

"I suppose you should." I was just as frustrated with the fact that he needed to leave. He was right, though, we had school in the morning, and the longer he stayed the more likely we'd get found out. "I'll see you out."

It was at that moment that I heard the floorboards move up above us. Instantly, both our heads swung back to look up.

"Ah fuck," Zak groaned. "He's awake."

Panic stricken, I stood up and pulled at his arm. "Go out through the kitchen. Quick." Snatching up his jacket, I thrust it at him and then pushed him towards the door into the hallway. As I opened it, a light came on at the top of the stairs from the bathroom, so I pushed Zak down the hall into the kitchen, rushing past him to the back door. The key wasn't in it.

"Shit. Where's the key?"

As my eyes scoured the kitchen counter, I heard a tread on the stairs. Dad was coming down.

"Here." Zak pushed past me and shoved a key in the lock, turning it and then yanking the door open.

"Quick."

He practically jumped out and then just as I was about to close the door on him, he leaned back in and kissed me hard on the lips.

"Night, gorgeous. Sleep tight. I'll message you when I get home."

The moment I turned the lock and threw the key on the side, Dad stepped inside the kitchen.

"What are you doing up?" he asked, rubbing at his chest and yawning.

"I just finished reading, so thought I'd get a drink before I go to sleep."

He peered at the clock on the cooker. "It twenty to one, Mads. You should have been asleep ages ago. I don't like you reading this late at night."

"Why are you up?"

"Same. Wanted a drink." He reached up into the cupboard for a glass and passed it to me and then took another one out for himself.

I ran the cold water tap and filled the glass, passed it to Dad and he handed me the other which I also filled. I turned, expecting Dad to be turning to go back upstairs to bed, but he was perched on the edge of the kitchen table.

"What?" I asked.

"Just wondering what you think of Maya."

"Straight to the point, Dad." I giggled and took a sip of the water that I really didn't want. I could still taste Zak and wasn't sure that I wanted to wash it away.

"You know me, sweetheart, I don't like beating around the bush. So?"

I rolled my eyes. "I like her. She's lovely, really lovely and I think she likes you, a lot."

His smile was optimistic. "You think?"

I patted his shoulder. "Yes, Dad, I do. So, stop worrying." He grinned broadly. "You can go back to bed now and sleep soundly."

He narrowed his eyes on me. "You're a little shit, you know that."

"Yep."

He pushed off the table, wrapped an arm around my neck, and kissed the top of my head. "Right, bed. And no more reading."

As he pushed me towards the hallway, I felt a little bit of guilt at having sneaked Zak into the house, but it had been worth it, even for just fifteen minutes.

As we reached the landing, I turned and kissed his cheek. "Night, Dad," I whispered, not wanting to wake Maya.

"Night, sweetheart." He padded towards his room, and I noticed that he paused for a split second outside the door where his girlfriend was sleeping. He gave his head a quick shake and then moved past.

It seemed that both the Newman's had it bad, and I didn't know who I was more excited for—me or Dad.

MAYA'S DIARY ENTRY

Had a lovely night with Will and Maddy. She's such a sweet girl and they clearly adore each other. I think it went okay. I think she likes me. I hope so because I'd really like to keep seeing him but if Maddy says she hates me I don't think it would be an option. After she went to bed we had a great chat and kiss. I practically rode him and could feel the start of an orgasm building, it was that good. His dick feels like it might be quite big!!! Everything with him so easy and comfortable – apart from the throb between my legs every time I look at him. It's like I've known him for ages, yet I've got those constant new relationship butterflies. I bet I won't want to go home tomorrow but we should take it slow. I've rushed into relationships before, and it was the wrong thing to do. Things with Will seem different, though. Bloody hell, who knows what's right and wrong. I just know I like him...a lot. He has the most beautiful smile – I know I keep going on about it, but it is. Loretta said if I don't stop talking about him to her she's going to stop taking my calls haha. I know she doesn't mean it. She's desperate for the gossip. His eyes as well!!! I really need to stop and act like a grown up!

1215: I can't sleep. I keep thinking about Will in the room next door. I'm feeling so horny but I'm trying to be good. Plus, Maddy is in the house, so it doesn't feel right. Although, I think she's just sneaked her boyfriend in. I was about to go to the bathroom and heard them whispering. I didn't want her to think I was spying so stood in the bedroom doorway like a statue, holding my breath! I bet I looked a right idiot.

I need to try and sleep. If I don't I might do something stupid and sneak into Will's room.

ZAK'S WHATSAPP MESSAGES

ZAK
I'm home. Did your dad suspect anything? x

MADDY
That was a close shave. I don't think he noticed. Glad you're home safely x

ZAK
Night gorgeous. I'll pick you up for school in the morning – 8 okay? We can grab some alone time before everyone else gets to school! X

MADDY
Sounds good. Night night xx

DEACON
Hey mate, sorry it's late but guessed you'd be up. Thanks for the offer of staying over. I'll let you know the exact date next week. I'm trying to persuade the rents to both go to Leicester with Sarah instead of Mum coming with me and Dad with her.

ZAK
Whatever mate. Mum says your mum is welcome to stay. I think she'd like to see her but totally get why you don't want her to come 😆. If you come on your own I'll sort a night out. Maybe get my girlfriend and her mates to come.

DEACON

Ozzy said you had a new girlfriend. Does Connie know??? Can I be the one to tell her?!! Is the new gf fit!

ZAK

If you like but it's none of her business. We were over a long time ago. And yeah she's beautiful! Beautiful, funny and cute.

DEACON

Shit! You've got it bad.

ZAK

Whatever, I need to get some sleep. Speak soon mate. Oh and your lot were fucking lucky at the weekend. Another dodgy penalty!

DEACON

Fuck off loser (laughing emoji). Night mate, speak soon.

CHAPTER 26
Will

I'd heard Maddy leave the house much earlier than usual. When I jumped out of bed, worried I'd overslept, I was surprised to see it wasn't even eight. Then looking out of the window, I spotted her walking towards a Mini. Just about to lose it at the idea of her getting into a strange car, Zak got out and ran around to open the door for her. They both burst out laughing, and then he dropped a quick kiss to her lips. I bristled, but it was strictly PG, so I let myself relax.

Moving back to the bed, I flopped down on the edge and ran a hand over my head. I'd got to bed earlier than normal the night before, but I couldn't say I'd got a great night's sleep. The first hour I'd tossed and turned knowing that Maya was in the room next door, yet she might as well have been a thousand miles away. I heard her walking around and then the duvet rustle as she got into bed. Imaging her in a pair of tiny shorty pyjamas made my dick rock hard, but the idea of knocking one off with her so close didn't seem right—especially as I would be thinking about her while I did it.

There wasn't a sound coming from her room, so maybe she was still sleeping. Or maybe she'd already gone.

"Fuck." I shot back to the bedroom window and craned my neck to look down the driveway. My shoulders sagged in relief when I saw her Kia was still parked behind my Range Rover.

As if someone knew I needed help, noise came from the bedroom. A chuckle rolled up from my throat at how pathetic I'd become, and decided I needed to man up. Pushing off the bed, I was determined that I was going to show Maya how good I could be for her.

***

"Nice," Maya said as we pulled up on the bar's car park. "The Jumping Frog? Where did that name come from?"

I smiled, recalling how the name came about. "Maddy was about ten, and I didn't know what to call the place, so I asked her, and she yelled out 'Jumping Frog.' I quite liked the idea—it was quirky—but then she pointed at this bloody big frog that was jumping around the kitchen. She screamed and ran out of the house, leaving me to catch the bloody thing."

"And the name stuck?"

"The name stuck."

Maya smiled on an inhale, her gaze moving back to the outside of the bar, painted in a deep forest green with gold lettering. Funny how it suddenly reminded me of the colours in her eyes. Those deep greens with hints of amber had kept me awake for days.

"Right, let's get inside, but don't expect anything spectacular like those posh bars in Leeds."

"Posh bars! In Leeds!" she cried, incredulous. "If there are any I don't go into them."

"I'm sure you'd look at home in there if you did."

Her brow furrowed as she stared at me. "You didn't really say that, did you?"

I groaned. "Too cheesy?"

"Err, yeah."

We both burst out laughing, and I wondered what the hell she'd done to me. I wasn't cheesy. I was the cool, smart, always-had-a-clever-answer kind of man. Not one who cracked shitty jokes or said lame comments just to try and impress a woman.

"I apologise and swear I will never say anything so puke inducing again."

She shook her head. "No. Never, ever, again."

Shit, I had to kiss her. Immediately, my lips were on hers and my hands were threaded into the thick strands of her hair. My tongue urged her to open her mouth so that I could deepen the kiss. She knew what I wanted and flicked out her tongue to dual with mine. My grip on her hair tightened.

Maya's hands tugged on my jacket, and as she pulled me closer, everything in the world disappeared except for me and her. We weren't in the small confines of my car; we weren't sitting outside my bar that no doubt had a whole load of problems the other side of the door. It was just us in a bubble of hope and expectancy for what might be.

My chest clenched at the amount of feelings that I had running through my body—how much desire I had for the woman in my arms. I'd felt love before. For Mrs Powell, for Sam, Louise, Darcy and Liam. It was nothing like that I had for my daughter. That love was on another level. That was a love I couldn't explain. That was a love that sometimes felt far too big. The swirling in my stomach, the way my heart was catapulting around my chest, the shake in my hands—it made me feel like maybe another big kind of love was on its way. A life defining love. One for a lifetime.

"We need to stop," I eventually said, dropping my forehead against Maya's.

Her chest was heaving heavily underneath the thick jumper that she was wearing with thin leggings. It almost came to her knees, hiding her pert arse and slim thighs, but she looked sexy as hell.

"I think maybe we should take a minute, though, before we go inside." She nodded down at my crotch. There was more than a slight bulge in my jeans.

Her giggle chimed around the inside of the car as we stared at each other, huge grins on both our faces. I knew instantly that we were on the same page as to where we were going, about what we wanted for our future.

"Come on, let's go." I took my phone from the centre console and then opened my door. "Oh, and please ignore Marcus' flirting. He thinks he's irresistible."

"Don't worry," she said, brushing soft fingertips down my cheek, "there's nothing that could sway me."

"Nothing?" I asked tentatively.

She chewed on her bottom lip and with her gaze pinned to mine, shook her head. And suddenly, my heart felt fuller.

***

Showing Maya around the bar, introducing her to Marcus, Robbie, and the regular customers made me feel proud. Incredibly proud of what I'd achieved in my life and for the fact that the woman by my side hadn't stopped smiling. A true, real, huge smile.

Marcus had tried to flirt with her, but like she said, she hadn't been swayed. Her hand had clutched mine the whole time, and if for any reason we had to let go, it was at the small of my back, holding softly onto my t-shirt.

"And you've never thought of doing proper meals?" she asked as Marcus placed a plate of bacon sandwiches in front of us.

"We'd need to update the kitchen," I replied, taking a quick swig of my tea. "And that takes money that I don't have."

"We could do more sandwiches," Marcus offered.

"Yeah, I guess, but people know what they get here—bacon butties and chips. We do alright with that." I was also scared of expanding and it not working out. Losing everything for the sake of wanting more.

"Well, these are perfect," Maya said around a bite of her sandwich.

"Robbie our dishwasher made them." Marcus grinned at me. "I told you he made a good sandwich."

"Maybe we should promote him," I suggested. "Increase that variety of sandwiches like you said."

"Fuck no." His head whipped towards Maya, and he held up a hand. "Sorry for the language, Maya, but I need a dishwasher more than a sandwich maker. He can manage to do both."

"Well let's at least give him a bit more money." I reached for the notepad on my desk and scribbled a note to remind myself to increase Robbie's wages. It wouldn't be much, but if he was doing extra stuff he deserved to be paid for it.

Marcus pulled out the chair from the table that we cashed up on and placed it next to Maya. I knew what he was doing, and he was a little shit, but I wasn't worried. His charm wasn't working on her.

"What do you do again, Maya?" he asked her.

"I'm a software developer. For doctor's surgeries and health authorities. Nothing exciting, I'm afraid."

"I always wanted to work with computers," Marcus said with a sigh. "If only I'd not bunked off school so often." He gave a deep laugh, one that was overly loud. I groaned inwardly, because it was the one he used when he was trying to impress a woman. It rarely worked.

"I think it would take more than a few extra days at school, mate." I reached for one of the sandwiches and took a bite. They *were* good.

"Really? Do you need a degree?"

Maya smiled. "Yes, you do."

"Where did you get yours?" he asked, reaching past her for a sandwich.

"Sheffield, because it was close to home."

"Which is..." He looked at her with one eye closed. "Leeds, right?"

Marcus lifted his ankle to rest on the opposite knee and leaned his head on a curled-up fist. He had a huge grin, and I wanted to punch him on the nose. My stomach felt like it was chewing up my insides and my chest was going to explode. It was Marcus. I had nothing to worry about with him. It was his usual behaviour, and Maya wasn't interested anyway, but I couldn't help it. I was jealous. I'd never been jealous over a woman before, especially with Marcus. He was a good friend and wouldn't overstep, it was how he was, but it was making me angry in a way I'd never felt before. I could even taste the bitterness on my tongue.

"Yes, I live in Leeds. It's a great city," Maya replied. She turned to me.

"Talking of which, fancy showing me around town?"

"Yes, sure." I stood up and reached out a hand for her. "Let's show you the sites of Norford."

"That'll take ten minutes," Marcus quipped.

"Maybe not even that long," I added.

"Lovely to meet you, Marcus," Maya said, getting up and moving to my side. "Hopefully see you again soon."

My heart missed a single beat, and Marcus raised an eyebrow at what I hoped was a promise. If I had anything to do with it, she would definitely be back and maybe for longer next time.

As I led her outside, her fingers still entwined with mine, the late January day was grey and damp, with a coldness that chilled your bones. I didn't feel it, though. I could feel nothing but warmth. Any scars from childhood, the ones beneath my skin, in my head, were slowly being salved with each moment I spent with her. It wasn't like they were deep or had defined me, but I knew my childhood was what had made me wary of relationships. Yet, Maya made me want to change. She had already started to take away the fear.

"Right," I said, pulling her towards the pavement. "First stop, Bennetts for some takeout for dinner. Their food is brilliant, but their hot chocolate is incredible."

Maya responded with a warm smile, and I knew I wanted more of that every day.

CHAPTER 27
Maddy

Sitting on the wall, at the far end of the upper school yard, Zak looked like he didn't have a care in the world. Looking at him, you wouldn't know that we'd just started study sessions for our A-level exams. The rest of my friends, and myself, were all looking pained and stressed.

"It makes it all real," Emma said, pinching a crisp from the bag Liam was scoffing.

"I've got a headache." Liv pressed her forefingers against her temples and groaned dramatically. "I'm sure it's going to be a migraine."

Zak stretched his legs out and hooked them around my hips, pulling me closer. "You okay?" he asked. "You haven't got a headache as well, have you?" He licked his lips and then sucked the bottom one between his teeth.

"No. I do feel sick every time I think about it, though."

"You'll be fine," Ana chimed in from where she was sitting on the grass, leaning against the wall and reading a magazine. "You're a nerd."

"No, I'm not," I said, glaring at her.

Zak laughed and tugged on a strand of my hair, regaining my attention. "You are a bit, babe."

I inhaled, feeling a swoop in my belly. He'd started to call me babe for the last couple of weeks, since he'd sneaked into the house. Not all the time, but when he did, I went all funny, like I was on a rollercoaster. He'd also started to pick me up for school in the morning on a Wednesday and Thursday when his mum didn't need her car to get to work. I loved those days, arriving in the student car park in Zak Hoyland's car. I *loved* that he'd wait at the bonnet of the car with his hand out for me and then he'd link his fingers with mine. I *loved* how we'd then walk hand in hand to whichever class I was in, while all the girls watched with envy.

"Says you who wants to be a vet." I poked him in his hard stomach, only for Zak to capture my hand and pull until my chest was against his.

"You're a sexy nerd, though," he whispered close to my ear.

We hadn't moved on from kissing in the last fortnight, but it had become pretty hot and heavy at times. Strictly PG at school and in public, but on the days he drove us to and from school, we'd go back to my house to study. They just happened to be the nights Dad worked until nine, so for the first hour or so there wasn't much studying going on. We always made sure we were sitting at the kitchen table with our books open when Dad came through the door, though.

"Anyone fancy doing anything tonight?" Liam asked, handing half a chocolate bar to Emma.

"Like what?" Ana asked. "It's not like we can get into any pubs locally. There's only three in town. Maddy's dad owns one of them, one is full of old men and the other always asks for ID. Plus, it's a school night."

"I can get us ID," Liam suggested. "It'll cost about fifteen quid each, but its good."

Liv sighed. "I can't be bothered changing all my socials just in case they cross-reference it. It's too much effort."

"If I got caught my dad would ground me forever," I said, turning to put my back against Zak. "And like Emma said, it's a school night. I don't want to get pissed and have a hangover for maths study group tomorrow."

Zak wrapped an arm across my chest and rested his chin on my head. "You could all come to mine. My mum and dad won't mind."

"In your basement?" Liam asked, excitement lacing his tone.

"Ugh, it's not all damp and smelly is it?" Liv asked.

"No, is it hell." Liam jumped up onto the wall next to Zak. "He's got a dartboard in there, two sofas and a huge TV."

I hadn't seen it the day I'd gone to Zak's house, but he'd told me about it since. I looked up at him and saw that he was grinning.

"Are you sure they won't mind?" I asked.

"Nah. As long as we don't make a noise and it's only us lot." He fished his phone out of his pocket. "Let me double check." He quickly tapped out a message and then wrapped his arm back around me. "Your dad will let you, won't he?" he asked close to my ear.

"Yeah," I replied without hesitation. "He won't mind."

Zak's tongue flicked against the shell of my ear and then he said quietly, "Even if you're in a dark place with me?"

A shiver rolled through my body, and my stomach clenched. "We won't be alone, though, will we?"

"Yeah, and that's disappointing." His voice was low, and as his words whispered against my skin, I felt desperate for him.

"Ugh," Ana groaned. "Can you two get a bloody room or something. Some of us are having a huge dry spell."

"PDA's aren't pleasant anyway," Liv complained, checking her phone for about the tenth time in five minutes.

"Funny that, because I bet if Harry Mayhew wanted to suck your tits in public, you'd let him."

"Ana!" Emma and I exclaimed united in shock.

"That's rude," Liv responded.

Ana, who was particularly snarky today, tutted loudly and pushed up from the grass. "Oh, whatever, I'm going to the library."

"Want me to come with you?" I asked, wondering what was wrong with her. She could be moody from time to time, but it rarely lasted more than a couple of hours. Yet this one had been going on since the previous day.

"No. Stay here and continue duelling tongues with your bf." She stormed off across the yard without a backward glance, a determined stomp in her stride.

"What's upsetting her?" Zak asked just as his phone chimed with an incoming message.

I shrugged. "I have no idea. She's been in a mood since yesterday."

"She didn't even speak to me on the bus this morning," Emma said. "Sat with her earbuds in and totally ignored me."

"You should have come and sat with me." Liam grinned at her, and when I spotted Emma's cheeks pink, I wondered if they'd finally admit to liking each other.

All the flirting, sharing of food and sitting next to each other had ramped up over the last week so perhaps there was about to be another new couple in our circle. Admittedly, it had only become a circle since Emma's sleepover, since Zak and I had got together. It was only natural I supposed, seeing as me, Emma, Ana and Liv were always together, with the occasional infiltration from Liam and maybe one of his gross mates. Now we both had Zak, and so were one big happy group. Or maybe not where Ana was concerned.

"Mum says that's fine by the way," Zak announced, dropping his phone back into his jacket pocket. "As long as we don't make a noise and leave a load of rubbish down there."

Excitement rumbled through my veins at the thought of what a good night it was going to be.

"Want me to bring booze?" Liam asked.

Zak thought about it and then shook his head. "Not for me. I'll be driving."

"Driving? It's your house, mate." Liam looked confused.

"Yeah but I'll be driving Mads home after."

My stomach swooped again.

"What about the rest of us?" Liv asked. "Are you taking us home, too?"

He thought about that too and shook his head again. "Nah, Liam can make sure you get home." He then leaned down and nipped my ear and whispered. "Want to go for a walk around the back of the science block?"

Code for 'want to go and neck on where no one can see us?'. I nodded and when Zak jumped off the wall, I took his hand and followed him, ignoring Liam and Emma making stupid kissy noises.

"You sure your dad won't mind you coming to mine?" Zak asked. He put his arm around me and reached for my hand.

I took it, linking our fingers and resting my head on his shoulder, surprising myself at how easy I felt with him. How much I always wanted to be with him. My stomach might have been constantly clutching in on itself, but I still relished every single moment.

"He'll be fine. Honestly. He won't mind." I looked up at him and grinned. "So nothing to be scared of."

"Yeah, well, he does." Zak groaned. "In fact, he fucking petrifies me."

"Why? He's the least aggressive person that I know." I narrowed my eyes. "Well, he did threaten this boy who bullied me the first year here."

"Seriously?"

"Yep. Told him if he touched me again he'd cut his balls off."

"What did he do to you? The boy. Does he still go here?" His arm tightened around me, and his fingers curled into mine.

"Called me fat, pushed me off the stage during a rehearsal for the school play, and snapped my favourite rainbow pen in half and then laughed in my face."

"Fucker," he snarled. "So, is he still at this school?"

I wasn't sure I dared tell him but hoped he was sensible enough to leave it. "Yes. It's Christian Daniels."

Zak stopped walking and looked down at me, blinking slowly. "The kid from the football team?"

"Yep. That's the one."

"The kid who walks around with his sleeves rolled up all the time?"

"Yep. That's the one."

"I'll kill him." His whole body stiffened, and his chest rose and fell with heavy breaths.

"It was six years ago, Zak. He hasn't spoken to me since. Dad really scared him off."

"I'm going to talk to him."

He tried to pull away from me, but I hooked my fingers in the belt loops of his jeans. "No." I pleaded with him, giving him my best puppy dog eyes. "It was so long ago that I don't even think about it."

"Did he hurt you?" His eyes grazed over my face, like he was searching for something. Desperate for a sign. When there clearly wasn't one, he exhaled slowly and pulled me against his chest.

"Honestly, once Dad spoke to him he stayed well clear of me."

"Good. And I promise your dad will never have to threaten my bollocks. Ever."

"Good to know."

As we rounded the corner of the science block, I was happy to see there was no one around. We had the place to ourselves. Zak led us to a bench that was underneath the Biology room window. As the window was six feet higher than the ground we couldn't be seen, and it had become our favourite spot to have time alone.

"We should do a two-man soon, with Liam and Emma," Zak suggested, pulling a cigarette out of the packet in his pocket.

"If they ever admit to liking each other."

"That's why we do a two-man," he replied. "You bring your friend on a date, and I bring mine, and we hope they get on. It'll be a true definition of one."

I shook my head and smirked. "I suppose it will." I watched as Zak put the cigarette in his mouth but didn't light it.

"No one will see you smoking around here," I told him.

"I'm not lighting it."

"Why not."

He grinned around it. "I fancied one, but I've only got three left and once they've gone, that's it, remember, so I don't want to taste of it." He wiggled his eyebrows. "Plus, I don't want to taste of it when I kiss you."

"Oh, you think you're going to kiss me, do you?"

He exhaled and tilted his head on one side and looking at me, he smiled. "Yeah, I do." He put his cigarette behind his ear and then leaned in to place his lips on mine.

This boy made me feel alive. He made me smile. He made my heart race. Gave me butterflies. Made me nervous yet confident. Made me shy yet bold.

"I really like you," I whispered as his mouth went to my neck.

I felt his lips smile against my skin. "I really like you, too."

My chest felt full. My life felt full. I was happy.

CHAPTER 28
Will

Louise chewed on her bottom lip and narrowed her eyes on me. She and Sam had been questioning and scrutinising me for over half an hour, wanting to know everything about Maya and the dates that we'd had. Since she'd stayed over two weeks before, we'd met up in Manchester for dinner one night and then I'd gone to Leeds just to spend her lunch hour with her, but otherwise we'd only spoken on the phone, seeing as the weekend in between she'd been on her future sister-in-law's hen weekend. When we had spoken, though, it had been every night for at least two hours, but it wasn't the same as seeing her in person. The coming weekend was changing that, though—she was coming to stay for the whole weekend, through to Monday. I hoped that we were going to take the next step, because I had to be honest, my balls were fucking blue. I was sick of throwing one out every night, it didn't replace the real thing, and I'd dreamed about what she was going to feel like beneath me.

"You hardly ever introduce anyone to Maddy," Louise said, sitting back in her chair at their dining room table.

"I know." I grinned. It was the same one that I'd had for the last two weeks.

"And he left you all night?" she asked her husband.

"Almost all night. Think he stayed with us for about an hour. Until he spotted her. Then that was it." Sam rolled his eyes and reached for a biscuit from the plate in the middle of the table, earning a raised eyebrow from Louise. "It's one flipping biscuit, Lou."

"One to add to the other three." She then turned sharply back to me. "And does Maddy like her?"

Louise and Sam loved my daughter as if she was their actual niece and had always been protective of her. I loved that they were, that they always wanted the best for her. To be honest, I doubted I'd be a half decent parent without their help, particularly Lou's. Her advice about female issues had been invaluable, and it meant I was prepared for every eventuality as Maddy grew up.

"Yes," I replied. "Maddy likes her. At least she told me she did."

"She told Liam the same," Sam added. "He told me that Maddy told him that she thought Maya was lovely."

"When did he tell you that?" Louise asked, pulling her shoulders back. "He normally tells me everything and he hasn't told me anything."

"It was on the way to football practice. I asked him if Maddy liked Will's new girlfriend."

"Well, I'd have asked him if I'd known about her." Louise pouted and stole Sam's half eaten biscuit from his fingers. "It would have been nice if you'd told me so I could have asked Liam."

"I didn't know if it was just one of his usual one night shags or not. What would be the point of telling you about that?"

"Please don't call women 'one night shags,'" she complained, throwing him a look of disappointment.

Looking suitably reprimanded, Sam sighed. "Sorry. I just thought it was a *lady* who he'd never be seeing again."

I hid a snort of laughter knowing that he probably hadn't learned a damn thing. "The point is she wasn't a one night thing. I like her, a lot. Enough to want to introduce her to Mads. You know I wouldn't do that if I wasn't sure about her."

Louise patted my hand. "We know that love. But, even though Maddy is seventeen, it could still affect her if this doesn't work out."

I had a feeling in my chest, in my heart, in my bones. "It's going to be fine. Nothing is going to go wrong."

"You sound pretty sure," Sam said, looking surprised. I wasn't, seeing as he knew about every single one of my one night stands, most of them in graphic detail. He knew that someone permanent had never been my plan—until I met Maya. Maddy had always been my priority, still was, but if I could also have Maya in my life then I'd go for it. I'd try as hard as I could to make sure both sides of my life, both women, worked alongside the other.

"Maddy will always come first, but that doesn't mean I can't be with Maya as well." I sat up straighter. "However, if at any time I think my relationship is affecting my daughter adversely, well, then I'll have to reconsider whether it's the right thing."

"Christ, Will," Louise cried, "Liam and Darcy both think Sam is a knob head, but I wouldn't swap him for the world."

"Oi." Sam's eyes went as wide as saucers. "That's my kids you're talking about."

She narrowed her eyes on him. "But are they?"

I burst out laughing, and when Sam's mouth dropped open, Louise joined in.

"You stupid bugger," she said, giggling. "As if. Those kids adore you, for some reason I can't fathom."

Sam turned to me. "Ignore my stupid wife. It's her they think is a knob head."

The laughter around the table was loud, and it just added to the warmth

I'd been feeling for weeks. I had an incredible daughter, fantastic friends and a gorgeous woman who seemed to think I was worth the effort.

As if thinking about Maya conjured her up, my phone shrilled out with her name flashing.

Louise almost dived across the table to get a look at my phone, while Sam bounced in his seat.

"It's her," he gasped, pointing at my phone. "Louise, it's her."

"Answer it, answer it."

I shook my head, picked up my phone and stood up. "You two are fucking weird. I'll be back in a minute."

Trying not to look like I was rushing, I walked into the hallway and answered the call.

"Hey, gorgeous."

"Hiya," she sounded breathless and happy. At least, I hoped she did, and I hoped it was because she was talking to me.

"I wasn't expecting you to call me." I glanced at clock on the wall, next to a large family photograph, where they were all dressed in white and laughing.

"I have ten minutes before a meeting, so what better way to spend it than speaking to you."

I blew out a breath, wondering how the hell I'd been so lucky. If I'd have skipped the stag do, or we'd left that bar a few minutes earlier... I didn't even want to think about it.

"I'm glad you did." I leaned against the wall. "I've missed you."

"I spoke to you last night." She giggled, and I loved the sound of it, loved the warmth it spread through me.

"Still missed you." I sighed, knowing I probably sounded like a stupid idiot, but I didn't care. "So how can I help you, Miss Mackenzie?"

"How do you know I want something?"

"I don't, just guessing. So, do you? Want something?"

She paused and let out a shaky breath. "Yes, but that's not something I think we should talk about now. Maybe leave that until the weekend."

Instantly my dick went hard at the prospect, at the idea of what the possibilities were. "Yeah, perhaps we should." I readjusted myself and leaned forward to look through the doorway to check that Louise and Sam weren't listening. I heard her hiss at him to be quiet, so I moved further down the hall towards the kitchen, where I could be alone, except for their cat, Dennis. "How's your day been so far?"

"Great. We got a new contract, but that wasn't why I called you."

"Why did you, then? And please don't say for phone sex because I'm currently in my best friend's kitchen, watching their cat lick its own arse."

She laughed again and then whispered, "It wasn't for that, seeing as I'm in the office kitchen, currently watching Jamie from accounts shovel a huge plate of noodles into his mouth."

"Wow, sounds delightful."

"It is. Very sloppy and extremely nauseating." She giggled. "What I really called you for is to ask you something."

If she asked me to marry her, I knew I'd actually think about it. When I thought about *that,* I blinked, wondering what the hell was going on in my head.

"Go on, then."

She took a breath and then said, "You know it's Charlie's wedding next Friday?"

"Yeah. It's a pretty fancy do from what you told me."

"It is. No expense spared. Anyway, I was wondering if you'd like to come. At night. We're staying over at the hotel so thought maybe you could stay... in my room, with me."

My heart seized and then jumped into over drive. "Yeah, that sounds good." I tried to sound casual but not sure I really managed it. "I'll look forward to it."

"Good, me too." She sounded relieved, and it struck me how much like a pair of teenagers we were. "Maddy will be okay on her own for the night?"

"Yeah, I can ask Louise and Sam if she can stay here."

Maya laughed. "Will, she's seventeen. I'm sure she'd like a night home alone."

"I'm sure she would, but I'm also sure her bloody boyfriend would like it, too." I rubbed a hand down my face and groaned. "I know I need to let her grow up."

"She seems like a sensible girl, Will, but you have to do whatever you think is best. She's your daughter."

She was spot-on. What was right was to let Maddy grow up and be a normal teenager. If that meant… fuck, I didn't want to think about it.

"I'd love to come the wedding," I told Maya. "Are you sure it's okay?"

"Yes." She made a little squeaking noise. "All the family are desperate to meet you. Shit, I'm so sorry."

I laughed, amused by the fact that she was sure I'd be upset, but I wasn't. I loved that her family wanted to meet me. It meant that she'd talked about me. That she'd shared. That had to mean something, didn't it?

"And I'm desperate to meet them, too. I can't wait to hear all their stories about you.' The smile that stretched across my face made my cheeks ache, and I wondered what the hell I was turning into?

"Don't believe a word of whatever they tell you. It'll all be lies." She giggled, and my dick stirred again.

"Maya," I groaned.

She didn't speak, and all I could hear was her breathing. Electricity crackled down the line as we both struggled to find the words big enough. I didn't know what I wanted to say to her, but I knew I wanted it to be important.

"I know," she croaked. "The weekend can't come quickly enough."

Those words told me a lot. They told me that she was as desperate as I was. That maybe she had the same hope in her heart that I did.

"I'll be counting the days," I whispered.

"Speak to you later?"

"You definitely will, gorgeous."

As we said our goodbyes, I was already desperate for it to be time to call her back. Desperate for the weekend and desperate for the future.

Yep, I was turning into a fucking love sick moron!

CHAPTER 29
Maddy

DAD

Have a good time. Be good. Call the bar if you need anything in case I can't hear my phone. If you walk home DO NOT take the short cut across the railway line. DO NOT WALK HOME ALONE in fact make sure Zak walks you home.

"Your dad again?" Emma asked as we walked towards Zak's house, carrying bags of snacks and some beers from the previous Christmas that I'd found in the cupboard under the stairs.

TAKE MY HAND

I dropped my phone into my jacket pocket. "Yeah. Last-minute check in that I'm going to be good."

Emma giggled and poked me in the side. "And do you think you will be?"

"Of course." I frowned at her. "I'm always good."

"Yes, but you haven't had a hot boyfriend before."

My stomach swooped as I thought about Zak and the fact that we would be spending the evening together. Admittedly with our friends, but there would be no adults which meant we would have a certain amount of freedom. Which meant that there would be a lot of necking on. At least I hoped so. The more time I spent with the Zak, the further that I wanted to go. I knew it wouldn't be long before we moved past him feeling my boobs and putting our hands inside each other's jeans.

"Not denying it, are you?" she laughed.

"You can talk. I saw you and Liam getting cosy at lunchtime."

"Don't know how, seeing as you two sneaked off behind the science block."

"Stop changing the subject." I nudged her. "So, do you like him?"

"I'm a bit surprised, seeing as we've known each other since we were little. He's got kind of hot over the last year."

I screwed up my face. "Ugh, no way."

"You just think that because you're practically family. You really should look carefully."

"No thanks." I jumped a puddle, the bag of goodies swinging, and I couldn't resist the urge to smile. The idea of the next few hours was exciting like this was some of the best times of our lives, but we would never realise how much until we were older. "Is Ana coming or not?"

"If you don't know, how am I supposed to?" Emma said, catching me up.

Everybody knew Ana and I were close, just like Emma was closer to Liv. It seemed to have become the natural order of things after our first year at school. Liam was an unofficial member of our little gang because we spent so much time together. He'd spent many hours suffering Twilight marathons and make-up tutorials on YouTube. Sometimes Dad would rescue him to watch football or play Xbox with him, but often he had his toenails painted pink and cheered for Team Edward.

"She didn't mention anything to me about whether she was coming or not. She's been in a bad mood today." I was worried about her. Hated when she was down, especially as she didn't seem to be snapping out of it. "Maybe she'll come with Liv later."

"Honestly, she's been proper miserable," Emma grumbled. "Bit my head off earlier when I asked if she wanted a lift home."

"She walked home then?"

"Yeah," Emma sighed. "Said she wanted to be on her own."

I pulled my phone back out and clicked on her name. "I'm going to call her." As we carried on walking, I listened to the line ringing out without anyone answering.

"She must still be in a mood," Emma said as we reached the gate to the path leading up to Zak's house.

"Hmm, maybe." Ending the call, my nerves suddenly kicked in. We'd arrived.

"Nice house," Emma commented, looking up at the large detached Victorian property with its bright red front door. The pebbled driveway ran across the front of the house, with the path alongside it, and there were three cars parked up. I recognised the third one as Liam's Corsa that his grandparents had bought for him.

"I thought his mum and dad were out," Em said, grabbing my forearm. "I'm scared. What do I call his dad? Sir or doctor?"

"Mr Hoyland." I didn't tell her he'd told me to call him Jim as we ate pizza. "And Mrs Hoyland." Again, no point in mentioning I'd been invited to call her Lisa.

We didn't have any more time to worry about it, because the door swung open, and standing there were the Hoylands and Amelia.

"Maddy," Lisa cried. "How are you?"

"Hi." I gave them all a shy smile and a small wave.

"Hi, Maddy." Amelia beamed at me as Jim ran a hand down her hair.

"Hi, Amelia. You look pretty."

She looked down at her jeans, sparkly pink jumper and matching pumps and then up at her dad. "Dad wanted me to wear a dress, but I didn't want to."

"I was never going to win that argument." He laughed and shook his head. "Nice to see you again, Maddy."

"You, too. Are you all going somewhere nice?" I asked.

"Cinema and then Nando's," Lisa told me with a roll of her eyes. "Anyway, we need to go otherwise we'll miss the start of the film."

"Yes, let's get going." Jim gave us a wide smile. "So, the boys are downstairs. Go towards the kitchen, and the door to the basement is just before it on the right."

"Okay, thank you and enjoy the film," I told them as we stood aside for them to pass.

"Wow," Emma whispered as they got into the car. "Zak's dad is hot."

"Come on," I groaned, "let's get inside."

As we made our way down the stairs to the basement it was obvious that it wasn't going to be dank, dark, and smelly. The walls were painted white with framed gig posters, and there was a shiny steel banister. The smell of cinnamon and the sound of laughter floated up the stairs, and as I looked down I could see the floor was a rich dark wood. On it was a huge rug of every colour you could think of, and on a unit, the same wood as the floor, which took up the whole of one wall was a massive TV. It was not like any basement that I'd imagined.

"Hey," I said as I reached the bottom stair.

Zak was sprawled on one end of a large corner sofa, a huge cushion behind his head, while Liam echoed his position at the opposite end. As soon as he saw me, he sat and grinned, dropping his feet to the floor.

"Hello gorgeous."

I felt the usual reaction of nerves, butterflies, excitement.

"Oh God," Emma groaned behind me. "You two have it really bad."

I nudged my elbow back into her stomach and flashed a smile at Zak. "Hiya."

Zak got up and sauntered over, meeting me halfway. He dipped his head and kissed me softly, his hands going to my hips. I leaned into him, relishing in his taste and the feel of the cool steel of his rings on my skin as he slipped his hands inside my coat and under my t-shirt. I was about to open my mouth to allow him in when we were pushed from behind.

"Please," Emma groaned. "Liam, why are you driving?"

I pulled away from Zak and looked over as she flopped down next to Liam, leaning into him. "There has to be something going on with them," I muttered.

"Well seeing as he's been talking about her for ages and wondering what time you'll be here, I think you're right." Zak slipped his hands into the back pockets of my jeans. "No Ana or Liv?"

"No idea about Ana but Liv is going to be late. She's gone shopping with her dad to get something for her mum's birthday."

He frowned. "Ana didn't call or anything?"

"Nope. I'm worried about her. She never takes this long to snap out of it."

"I'm sure she'll be fine." He dropped a kiss to my forehead. "We can call her later if she doesn't turn up. Even stop by her house if you want."

I shook my head. "No, let's see how she is tomorrow."

He looked down at the carrier bag in my hand. "Supplies?"

"Chocolate, popcorn and bottles of beer courtesy of a stash that my dad's forgotten about." I held up the bag and opened it out for him to look inside. "I found them in the cupboard under the stairs, but I'm sure he'd have said yes anyway." I rolled my eyes. "Seeing as he obviously likes you."

"I don't know about that." He leaned in closer. "Especially not if he knew what I wanted to do to you."

My breath stalled and instinctively my hips jerked forward. He wasn't fully hard but was *definitely* on his way to it. When I shifted my hips again, he groaned quietly and pushed himself up against me. He was *definitely* fully hard now.

"Maybe we shouldn't tell him," I replied, close to his ear.

His breath was ragged. "Perhaps you're right."

The air was electric as we stared at each other, both of us knowing that things were going to change even more than they already had. Our feelings for each other were about to take another shift. The ground beneath our feet was about to flip and we were about to become something more. I was ready to give him something that I'd never wanted to give to anyone before.

"Oi," Liam yelled. "Are we watching this film or not?"

"Yeah," Zak said, his lips against my forehead. "We're coming."

***

We were alone. Liam had taken Emma and Liv home about half an hour before. Liv had had turned up halfway through the film, moaning that her parents wanted her home by half nine. That meant that it was just the two of us snuggled up on the sofa with a large, brown, furry throw over us and we were dangerously close to taking the next step.

"Zak," I groaned as he ran a hand over my bum, his fingers playing with the elastic on my knickers. He was inches away from my wetness after already giving me an orgasm with his fingers. "What if your mum and dad come back?"

"They won't come down here." He nibbled at my ear lobe, pushing his hard on between the apex of my thighs. "I locked the door when the others left."

Our jeans and t-shirts were on the floor down the side of the sofa, and Spotify was on the huge TV, quietly playing Made for Me by Muni Long. I was running my fingers along the ridges of his abs in a rhythm he clearly liked, if the soft moans were anything to go by.

"Won't they wonder why it's locked?" As Zak's tongue slithered down my neck, I arched my back and let out a soft breath. My nipples were so hard they hurt.

"They'll know I want some privacy, but they won't even try it. I promise."

Any nerves I had disappeared. Any worries that he wouldn't be the boy I thought he was, seemed unfounded. But I didn't care if nothing came of it, of us, because I was ready. It was what I wanted even if our time together was brief.

Everything about this boy made me feel. My blood thrummed rapidly through my veins. I had constant butterflies in my stomach. I jumped out of bed in a morning, desperate to start a new day with him. He made me want to laugh and smile all the time. Maybe those feelings wouldn't last forever but they were there now, and I was going to embrace them.

"Do you have a condom?" I asked, closing my eyes to avoid watching his expression. Scared that he might reject me, and not wanting to see it if he did.

"Open your eyes," he whispered, kissing my forehead. "Mads, please, open them."

Slowly I did as he asked and peeked up at him through my lashes. He was smiling softly as he pushed the hair from my eyes.

"Are you sure this is what you want?" he asked, "because I swear, we don't have to."

My heart was thudding so fast, I wondered if it was what a heart attack felt like. The anticipation of what we were about to do sending an electric current through ever nerve ending but I knew what I wanted.

Nodding, I reached up to run a finger down his cheek. "I do. I do want to."

"Okay, if you're sure," he said softly, "then yes, I have a condom."

I pushed the breath of nervous energy from my lungs and allowed myself to relax into the sofa, letting my limbs soften and soak up the attention that Zak was giving to me.

"Would you prefer to go upstairs?" he asked, linking our fingers together. "To my bedroom?"

"Here is good." Here was perfect. Moving might change that.

After pecking a kiss to my lips, Zak slipped from under the throw and padded over to the unit against the wall. As he opened up one of the drawers, he took out a box and turned to me.

"I put them in here earlier."

I burst out laughing. "You thought I'd be a sure thing, did you?"

His eyes went wide, and he ran a hand over his head, shaking it fiercely. "Shit, no. I swear. I just thought that… honestly, Maddie, I didn't… I thought that maybe—"

"Zak, it's fine." Giggling, I sat up letting the throw drop to my waist. I was wearing a bright pink bra with electric blue lace and my nipples were hard and pushing against the jersey material—instantly his eyes were drawn to them.

"Shit, Mads." He rubbed a hand down his face and groaned. "Anyway, if you think I'm a twat then I understand, but I swear I didn't—"

"Zak." I rolled my eyes. "Just get back over here."

"Are you sure?" He put the box back in the drawer and took a tentative step back to me.

"I am, but please don't forget the condoms. We're going to need them."

He exhaled and turning quickly, reached for them, and then almost ran back to me, launching himself on the sofa on top of me, dropping the condoms behind my head. I let out an explosion of air and laughter, relishing in the warmth he brought to me, not just from his body against mine.

His hands moved to either side of my face, pushing all my hair away from it and his beautiful chocolate pools studied me. "I really like you, Maddy. A lot."

I swallowed. "I like you, too. A lot."

"This means something to me, you know." He licked his lips. "What we're about to do. I know we haven't been together long, but I think you're incredible, and I don't think I've ever wanted to spend as much time with a girl as I want to spend with you. I've never *liked* anyone as much as I do you."

My face flushed hot as his words hit me in the chest. "The same," I whispered. "You're not like any other boy I've ever met before. You're," I dropped my gaze feeling shy, "lovely."

Zak ran a finger along the apple of my cheek and sighed reverently. "Look at me, babe." I did as he asked. "I think you're lovely too."

The kiss that followed was gentle and full of promises. It was sweet. It was sexy. It was everything. It quickly moved to feverish as Zak's fingers tangled in my hair and mine grabbed at the hard muscles of his back. He squeezed one boob, while his mouth sucked the nipple of my other over my bra. Not even the fabric of my bra stopped the sensation making me arch and keen with the pleasure. Slowly and tenderly, we removed each other's underwear and explored. Zak was bold and confident, whereas I touched him with a little shyness and hesitancy, but when he kicked the throw off us, I felt bolder. It was because of him and the care and devotion that he was giving to me. My heart raced as joy flowed through me, heating my blood and igniting a fire.

As my legs parted, Zak groaned. "I need to put the condom on." He got to his knees and reached behind me for the box.

"I have the implant," I told him, suddenly too impatient.

"Okay, but I want to be sure we're totally safe. I mean I don't have—"

"Zak it's fine, put the condom on. I like that you care."

His smile was dazzling as he ripped open the packet, his stomach muscles taut as his dick bobbed against it. I swallowed wondering whether it would fit but determined that it would.

"Can I help?" I asked, desperate to touch him.

He licked his lips and then reached a hand out for me and pulled me up. We were eye to eye, his dark with desire as he watched me.

"You're gorgeous, you know," he whispered, tracing a finger along the curve of my nose.

"So, are you, but that didn't answer my question."

His grin matched mine as he held the condom up. "You still want to do this?" he asked.

I nodded and tentatively took it from him. "I've only ever put one on a banana."

Zak laughed quietly, and guiding my hand, we put the condom on together, and I knew that we would always be connected, even if we were apart.

"You sure?" he asked me again as he gently lowered me back to the sofa.

His necklace dangled as he looked down at me, and I hooked my finger in it, pulling his mouth closer to mine. "Definitely."

Nothing after that moment mattered and as he pushed into me, my fingertips pressed into the muscles of his hard, toned back. In that moment I was lost letting myself fall in love.

CHAPTER 30
Maddy

"You sure you're okay?" Zak asked, wrapping an arm around me.

We were fully dressed after the most incredible experience of my life. I knew people always said your first time was terrible, but mine hadn't been. I had an idea of what to do; I wasn't totally inept or naïve. I had read a few dirty books and Zak wasn't the first boy to have his hands in my knickers. I just wasn't sure that I'd done the whole sex thing right.

"I'm fine." I cleared the nerves from my throat. "Was I okay?"

"You were incredible," he whispered. "Amazing."

I couldn't shake the insecurity. The fact that maybe I hadn't been anywhere near as good as he'd hoped.

"You don't have to say that, not if you don't mean it."

"I mean it." His eyes searched mine as he pulled me closer. His hold on me tight and protective. Tender. "I didn't hurt you, did I?"

I shook my head. It hadn't, not like some people said to expect. I'd been surprised by how good it felt. How easily he'd made me orgasm.

"You do know I care about you, don't you?"

I frowned. "Is this you about to dump me?" I asked.

"God no." He laughed and then kissed me. "You're stuck with me now."

"So why so serious?" I snuggled closer to him, resting my head on his chest, feeling the beat of his heart against my cheek.

"I just want you to know. It was special, what we did, what you gave to me." He looked unsure of himself. Like he'd been the inexperienced virgin. He was chewing on the side of his bottom lip and swallowing hard. I knew he wasn't, though, because of the game of Never Have I Ever. And because in the moment he'd been so confident.

"I know. I trusted you. I still trust you."

"Good." He held his hand up and cocked his head to one side, listening. "I think they're back. One minute." He got up and bounded up the stairs. I heard the click of the lock and then he came back down, grabbed the remote and turned the TV to the adverts that were showing.

"I though you said they wouldn't come in," I cried, realising that we'd been close to being discovered bloody shagging on his mum and dad's sofa.

"They wouldn't, but now it looks entirely innocent if by any chance they do." He smirked and nodded at the TV as the film came back on. "The film is *Fast & The Furious* if they come in."

I stared at the screen. "I know that, but how am I supposed to pretend we've been watching films and doing nothing else?"

Zak chuckled. "Just don't look my mum in the eye; she can spot a lie a mile away."

I nudged him hard in the ribs. "You're not funny."

"I think I'm hilarious, love."

His accent made me shiver with anticipation, wondering whether it was too trashy to ask him for sex in the back of his mum's car on the way home.

"I think you'll find you're not."

There was thundering up above us, and I tensed, wondering whether the door at the top of the stairs would open. I held my breath, but no one came down.

"Told you." Zak tugged the throw up to our necks. "Now you want to watch the end of this film or fancy some more fun."

"I think we've reached our limit of luck for one night."

"Okay, film it is." His hand went to my head, and that's how we watched the film, snuggled together with Zak gently combing his fingers through my hair.

***

Zak walked backwards down the path, watching me as I stood in the open front door way.

"See you tomorrow."

I nodded. "Yeah, okay," I breathed out, giving him a little wave. "See you tomorrow."

He stopped walking and then ran back to me. His arm went around my waist, his hand on my bum and he kissed me.

"I'll message you when I get home," he said against my mouth. "We can talk until we go to sleep."

Giggling, I reached up on my tiptoes and cupped the back of his head, pushing his lips closer to mine. I didn't think I'd ever get enough of the taste of him. He would always be my addiction.

"I should go," he eventually said.

"Yeah, you bloody should." Dad's voice boomed behind us. "You're letting all the cold in."

Zak's shoulders stiffened and he pulled away from me. "Shit," he hissed. "I'd better go."

"Good idea."

Oh, shut up, William.

I turned to see Dad hovering in the doorway, his hand on the door and one eyebrow raised.

"Hey Mr Newm—sorry, Will."

"Hey, Zak." He cleared his throat. "It's getting late, and you two have school in the morning."

"Dad," I whined.

"Maddy, it's gone half eleven. I'm going to bed; you've got you five minutes."

I could have killed him, embarrassing me like that. "Okay, Dad," I said full of frustration.

"Good night," he replied with a heavy sigh.

"I should go." Zak winced and looked over my shoulder. "I don't want him coming back out."

"You're such a chicken." I gave him one last kiss and then took a step back. "Okay, I'll speak to you in about fifteen minutes."

His smile was beautiful and lit up the night sky. "You certainly will."

He leaned in for another kiss but pulled back when we heard, "Say goodnight, Zak."

He was down the path faster than if he was being chased by a wild animal, with me gazing after him like a lovesick idiot.

ZAK'S WHATSAPP MESSAGES

LIAM
Did you have fun after we left?

ZAK
A fucking gentleman never tells!!

LIAM
Shit you did it didn't you! I hope her dad doesn't find out 👊

ZAK
Don't even joke about it. He scares the shit out of me. He's already had a dig at me tonight for kissing her at the front door. Basically, told me to fuck off!

LIAM
You dick! Fancy necking on under his nose! Honestly he's okay really. He's just protective of her. Seriously though don't break her heart mate because I might have to have a word too.

ZAK
I know I'm an idiot. I have no intention. I really like her. More than I've liked anyone. It's just shit that we're going to uni soon.

LIAM
It is shit about uni but you never know...

ZAK

Yeah, I think we just need to enjoy it until we go and then hopefully she'll think about going to uni in Edinburgh or close by 😏. Talking of girls, what's happening with you and Em?

LIAM

Fucked if I know. I think she's into me but then she goes cold. After we dropped Liv off we necked on in the car for ages. Then when I suggested we do a two man with you and Maddy she said she wasn't sure when she'd have time 🙄.

ZAK

😂😂😂 She's playing you mate. She likes you but I'll speak to Mads see if she can find out more. Right I'm off to bed. See you at school in the morning.

LIAM

Night mate. Don't forget to bring that Xbox game.

ZAK

👍

CHAPTER 31
Will

The lights from the country house shone out brightly into the dark, casting a glow on the ivy covering the frontage. It was huge and looked luxurious, and I was glad I'd worn a suit instead of just trousers and a shirt. Maya had said no expense had been spared, but that everyone there was relaxed and, in her words, 'not up their own arses', but I was still glad I'd gone smart. I wanted to make a good impression with her family, because she mattered.

With a deep breath, I ran up the stone steps to the huge double front door that was open to the cool evening air. Inside the grand entrance, which had a tiled floor and wood-panelled walls, people milled around chatting and drinking. On the far side was another set of double doors open to what looked like a ballroom. I could see tables with white cloths and gold and purple chairs, and loads of candles around the room, light was reflecting off the glasses, and it looked exactly like Maya had said; no expense had been spared.

I looked around, over the tops of people's heads, searching for her. She'd said she'd meet me at the door, but I was a little early and I knew what weddings were like. You started to do something, go somewhere, and got side tracked by some relative you hadn't seen in ten years.

"Can I help you?" A tall guy dressed like a butler asked.

"Oh, yeah. I'm looking for my girlf—erm, my friend. It's her brother's wedding. Maya Mackenzie."

He nodded once. "Yes, sir, she did ask me to keep a look out for you. If you'd like to come this way." He took a step forward and then looked back over his shoulder. "She got waylaid helping the bride's mother in the bathroom."

I raised an eyebrow, only able to imagine what that meant. "No problem."

He led a path through the tables and past the already packed area to a table at the head of the room. It had a tall candle in the middle with an array of smaller ones of varying sizes placed around it. And there, leaning over a woman who looked like she'd had far too many champagnes, was Maya. She looked beautiful. Wearing a tight, emerald green dress, a shade darker than her eyes, that hugged every single one of her curves, her long hair hung down her back in soft waves. Her arms were bare, and her skin practically glowed in the candlelight. She had gold hoops at her ears and gold bangles on her wrists, and when my gaze travelled down her long legs, my dick stirred. I imagined them wrapped around me while she still wore the high, pointed, bronze coloured shoes that she had on. I just knew she smelled good, too.

"Here you are, sir." He waved a hand towards the table. "Miss Mackenzie."

As he walked away, I took a step closer to the woman who had been filling my head twenty-four hours a day. As if she'd felt me close, her head whipped around, and her eyes locked with mine. The glorious smile that broke out sent my dick fully hard, and I was glad I'd worn boxer briefs to at least keep it under some control.

"Will," my name came out as a gasp as she moved towards me.

As soon as she reached me, she walked into my arms, wrapping hers around my neck and standing on tiptoe to kiss me.

"You look gorgeous," I told her. "Absolutely stunning." I ran a hand down her arm until our hands met, and I linked them together. With her in my arms, my heart expanded, filling my chest until it felt too tight. Everything about her made me want more. I knew that she was what I wanted for my future, for however long that would be, because the idea of a moment without her was too hard to think about. She'd become my reason.

"You don't look too bad yourself." She drew back to look me up and down. "Very handsome."

"Didn't want to disappoint you."

She licked her bottom lip and sighed. "I don't think you could ever disappoint me, Will."

I couldn't resist her pouty lips and kissed her softly. My hand went to the small of her back and pulled her closer. As we got lost in the kiss, there was a danger that I might take it further, and we were at a family wedding.

"We need to stop," I groaned. "Your whole family are watching."

Maya swung her gaze over her shoulder, to the table behind her. Everyone sitting around it was watching us with their mouths hanging open, apart from the drunk woman, whose head was down on the white cloth. It was also clear that they were one family. They all had the same shade of dark hair and the two men staring back at me with huge grins, had the gap between their top front teeth, just like Maya.

Maya sighed. "Okay. I suppose we should do introductions. Will, meet my family. My brothers Jack and Charlie," they both waved, "Jack's wife, Heather, my mum Debra, my dad, Ian and my new sister in law Laura's mum, Paula." She leaned closer. "She's the one asleep on the table." She looked around and pointed to the dancefloor. "And the woman in the gorgeous cream lace dress is Laura and the three kids dancing with her belong to Jack. They are Daisy, George and Claudia."

I looked back to the table. "Hey everyone." I gave them a chin lift and what I hoped was a winning smile. "Nice to meet you all."

"Come and sit next to me," Debra patted the chair next to her, mischief in her eyes.

"Mother," Maya chastised her. "Stop flirting."

"I'm not." She fluttered her eyelashes and pulled the chair out.

"Can he at least get a drink from the bar first?"

Ian stood up and held out his hand. "Please to meet you, Will. What can I get you to drink?"

"No let me."

"I'll be offended, lad," he said sternly but with a smile.

I nodded. "Okay, thanks. Any bottled lager, please."

He asked around the table and everyone gave him their order, before trailing off to the bar. Maya led me to a seat, two away from her mum, and then plonked herself down in the one next to it.

"Great to finally meet you, Will," Jack said, giving me a nod. "We've heard a lot about you."

Maya groaned. "I think I hate you, Jack."

"What. You don't stop talking about him. It's Will this, Will that, Will she ever shut up about him?"

When she narrowed her eyes on him I laughed. The love between them was clear to see, and it hit me how much I'd missed that kind of relationship you got with a sibling. I doubted that there was one like it.

"Leave her alone," Charlie replied, nudging his brother in the ribs. "It's not all the time, just twenty of the twenty four hours in a day."

Heather rolled her eyes and reached a hand across the table. "Nice to meet you, Will. And please ignore the Chuckle brothers."

"It's fine. Great to meet all of you, too. And I *have* heard a lot about all of you. Most of it good."

"Whatever she said is a lie," Jack added.

"Funny, Maya said exactly the same thing."

"And she's right," Debra said wryly. "These two are always making up stuff about her. In fact, they lie about everything. Have done since they were little. Anyway, Will, tell us all about that lovely daughter of yours. Maya says she's beautiful and very funny."

"I don't know about funny—sarcastic and stubborn more like." I glanced at Maya who was looking at me with her head resting in her hand. I wanted to grab her, pull her across the table and kiss the life out of her. Kiss off all her bronze lipstick and push my hand up her dress and get a handful of her incredible, voluptuous arse.

"She's hilarious," she said, reaching for my hand. "Don't believe him."

"She is funny." I raised an eyebrow. "But she's still sarcastic and stubborn, but she's beautiful, too. I'm very lucky and very proud."

When I looked at Debra, she was staring at me like she was in a trance and then when my gaze moved on to Heather and Maya they had the same look in their eyes. Christ, it was the Maddy effect again. Just me mentioning her got women looking all dreamy.

"You okay?" I whispered to Maya. "Your eyes have gone a bit glazed."

She gave a happy sigh. "Yes, just the way you talk about her. It's so swoony."

I burst out laughing. "Swoony?"

"That's the word," Debra chipped in, pointing a finger at Maya. "Swoony. Very swoony."

"Very," Heather added and then nudged Jack. "Why can't you be swoony?"

"I'm swoony," he protested. "I swooned you easily enough this morning before the kids woke up."

"I swooned Laura after the ceremony," Charlie added, wiggling his eyebrows. "Just before the photos."

Everyone burst out laughing, while his mum threw a napkin at him, cursing him for being the crudest, most annoying of her children. Ian then appeared back with a tray of drinks.

"What's going on here then?" he asked. "What's all the laughing about?"

"Your son," Maya told him. "The one who is such a disappointment to you and Mum."

Ian didn't even look up but shook his head and said, "For feck's sake, Charlie, what have you been up to now?"

***

As soon as Maya opened the bedroom door, we stumbled into the room, lips locked as she grabbed at my clothes.

"Fuck, Maya, I've been wanting to get this dress off you all night."

"I've been wanting to take it off for you all night." She threw my jacket onto the floor. "I didn't think Charlie and Laura would ever leave."

"That was the longest last dance of last dances," I said, in between kissing her pouty lips.

"I'm so wet for you, Will." She gasped as I pushed my hand up her dress and ran my thumb over the top of her knickers. "We need to be naked."

I pulled the zip down and then shoved it off her shoulders. She wiggled out of it, and I felt my dick go steel hard. She was a vision.

"Shit, Maya, you're incredible."

Her bra was the same green as her dress, as was the tiny scrap of lace covering what I was sure would be a perfect pussy, seeing as the weekend before her period had stopped me getting a look at it. Her tits were high and full, and she had a gentle curve to her hips, and I was entranced by a small heart tattooed just above her right one.

Maya didn't speak but reached for me and pulled at the buttons on my shirt, tugging them open as quickly as her fingers would allow. I shrugged it off, pulling it over my wrists without opening the cuffs. As soon as I was rid of it, I went for the belt on my trousers. Maya shoved my hands out of the way and grabbed at it.

"Will, you need to hurry and get your clothes off," she cried, going for the button on my trousers.

Within seconds they were undone, so I toed off my shoes and socks and then let them drop to the floor. I stepped out of them and kicked them to the side with my jacket and shirt.

"Oh my God," Maya put her hand to the back of my head and pulled me to her.

The kiss was fervent. Our limbs tangled as desperation overpowered us, anxious to be inside her but panicked about it being over. I had never wanted something or someone so much in all my life and as her delicate fingers scorched a path over my skin, I thought my heart might explode with the speed it was drumming.

"Your body," she gasped. "It's…" She ran her fingers down my flat stomach, along the ridges of muscle I earned through lugging beer barrels around.

I put my fingertips in the elastic of her knickers and, dropping to my knees, pulled them down her long, legs, still lightly tanned. As she stepped out of them, I lifted my face to her pussy with the thin strip of hair, and grabbing her hips pulled her to me. Inhaling her the sweet smell of her desire mixed with whatever perfume or cream she rubbed into her skin, gave me a rush like I was sure no drug could.

"Open your legs," I groaned. "I need to taste you."

She did as I asked, and I felt the ground beneath me shift. With one long sweep of my tongue, I savoured her, eliciting a deep moan of pleasure from her. She was sweet and warm, and I wanted to lick her dry and then get her wet all over again.

"Oh my…" Maya threw her head back, pushing her pelvis forward, eager for more. "Will, I think I need you to fuck me now."

"I think that would be a great idea."

Standing, I put my shoulder against her stomach and lifted her up, marching us to the bed. Dropping her down to the mattress, I yanked my boxer briefs down and stood tall, looking over her.

"Get that bra off," I demanded. "Now."

Fisting my dick, I watched her as she reached behind and unhooked it, letting her full breasts spill free. Her nipples were brown, perfectly round and totally suckable. Bending down, I took one into my mouth, licking my tongue around and around the tight bud, as Maya writhed in pleasure beneath me.

"So damn gorgeous and sexy." I moved from one nipple to the next, giving it the same attention as the first. "So fuckable."

"Do it then," she groaned, gripping my short hair, "fuck me."

I looked around for my jacket and reached into the inside pocket, pulling out the single condom. "The rest are in my bag, which is in my car," I told her. "I'll go and get them later."

She gave me a smirk. "You think you'll need more do you?"

"Fucking too right," I growled. "You won't be getting much sleep tonight."

Her mouth dropped open and she bit down on her lip, making my dick bob with the anticipation.

"When you say not much, how little is that?" she asked, gripping the duvet cover.

I looked her up and down, giving myself another pump. "Maybe five minutes here and there." I threw the condom onto the bed and then crawled to her, pushing her legs open. "But before then I'm going to…" I leaned in close to her ear and whispered, "fuck you hard."

Maya's hand came to my cheek and electricity zapped around my body, like she'd lit the touch paper of a firework. I reached for the condom and ripped the packet open with my teeth. As I rolled it on in record time, Maya watched me, emerald greens boring into my soul. So intense, like she could read every thought in my head, knew every single dream I'd had about her.

"Will, please."

With a hand on each knee, I pushed her legs further apart and pushed inside her. She was so wet I didn't need to wait, and I couldn't even if I wanted to. I was desperate for her. In fact, desperate wasn't a big enough word for the need that consumed me.

The feeling of her clenched around me was like no other sensation I'd ever experienced before. It was pleasure and joy. It was ecstasy. It was everything. When her fingers clung to me and her hips matched the rhythm of mine, I knew I would never not want the beautiful woman I was growing huge, mountainous feelings for.

The heels of her shoes dug into my backside, urging me on, making me go quicker, as she raced for her climax. Yet, I wanted to keep going and never stop. I wanted to stay inside her for as long as I had a breath in my body. I knew I would just have to do it again and again until we were both exhausted to the point of being unable to move.

"I'm going to come," she gasped, her nipples rubbing against my chest. "Oh my God. Will."

The pinch from her fingertips stung as they dug into my back, but I loved it because it meant she was there with me. Loving it as much as I did. We were in the same moment.

I straightened my arm, leaning on one hand while gripping her knee with the other, and increased the speed of my hips as they pistoned back and forth. Sweat was beading on my forehead and there was a sheen on Maya's gorgeous skin. A mist from our exertions.

"Fuck, Maya," I groaned as the familiar feeling of an orgasm began to take hold. It started in the pit of my stomach and wound its way around my body. Touching every nerve ending, every inch of skin, emanating from every pore, until I felt like I might black out.

I wanted us to fall together so I reached between us and ran my fingers over her clit. It only took two strokes before I felt her muscles clench. Her thighs squeezed tight, and hands gripped harder.

Then we both fell. Into the abys of pleasure.

I roared out her name. She yelled mine. We came hard, panting, and breathless and as we clung to each other, and I felt like I wanted to crawl inside her.

"Wow," Maya whispered. "That was…" She let her arms drop back against the bed, her chest heaving.

"I know," I replied. "It was, but that was just the beginning, gorgeous. There's going to be much more of that tonight."

Maya's smile was brilliant, and I couldn't wait to make her come again, and again and again. I was going to love her all night, just like I'd promised.

CHAPTER 32
Will

Watching Maya sleep was the deepest kind of serenity I'd ever felt. She was giving tiny little breaths, and every so often, her nose would scrunch up and she'd rub at it with her hand. Then she'd go back to a peaceful, blissful slumber while I watched her, enraptured with just how fucking beautiful she was.

Beautiful and astonishing.

The sex had been mind-blowing, and I kept my promise to keep going most of the night. We'd finally exhausted ourselves at around five-thirty, only for her to reach for me an hour later and ride us both to more oblivion. Then, and only then, had we slept with me waking three hours later. We'd missed breakfast, but I didn't care. I'd take her somewhere if that was what she wanted, but I'd be more than happy to feast on her. I probably owed her that much, seeing as she'd given me an amazing blow job just before the first time we'd fallen asleep.

As my dick went hard at the thought of it, Maya stirred and turned over towards me. The duvet shifted and she gave me a great view of her tits. Resisting the temptation to suck a nipple into my mouth, I gently brushed hair from her face. Her tongue flicked out to lick across her kiss swollen bottom lip, and her eyelashes fluttered open.

She rubbed her nose and looked up at me, sleep threatening to drag her back under. "Morning."

"Good morning," I replied, running a finger across her cheek. "Did you sleep well?"

A slow, sexy smile accompanied a nod as she stretched her arms above her head. "Hmm. Really well. Did you?"

"Yeah, but I was exhausted."

We shared a smirk, but when Maya wrapped an arm across my stomach and laid her head against my chest, mine turned to a full on beam.

"Last night was just..." Maya trailed off, her eyes searching mine.

"I know," I whispered, giving her my truth. "The best of my life."

Huge emerald eyes blinked and her mouth fell into a perfect o shape. "Really," she finally said.

"Really." My throat bobbed as I swallowed back the emotion being with her made me feel.

Pride. Joy. Hope.

Maybe even love. If not now then soon, that much I knew.

"You are incredible, Maya."

She reached up and cupped my face, rubbing her thumb backwards and forwards across my stubbled cheek.

"I think you might have broken my vagina, though."

I burst out laughing. "I have?"

"Hmm, definitely." She stretched again, with a yawn. "In the best way, though. How is that awesome cock of yours?"

I lifted the duvet and looked down. "Hard. Still awesome."

Maya gasped and looked under the cover. "Looks okay to me, although," she said reappearing, "I can't believe it's hard again."

"Not sure it's been anything but all night."

Her soft giggle made said dick twitch, but seeing as I'd broken her vagina, I kissed her forehead instead.

"I think we've missed breakfast," I said, resting my head back against the pillow.

"Why, what time is it?" She reached for her phone and looking at the screen groaned. "Christ, I've got seven missed calls from my mum, three from Jack and two from my niece Daisy." She peered at the screen again. "Even Charlie has sent me a message."

I chuckled. "What does is say?"

"He's a dickhead." She sighed. "'Hope your fanny doesn't catch fire. See you at breakfast.' Yeah, well, he's got that wrong." Throwing her phone back on the bedside table, she snuggled back down against my chest. "I suppose we should get up. I think we have to check out by eleven."

"We could and then I could take you out for breakfast. I checked the area out, and there's a farm shop about a mile away with a really good café, apparently."

Maya rubbed her stomach. "Ooh, I could eat a full English. With a nice mug of tea."

"That's what we'll do then." I pulled her closer and whispered my fingertips up and down her arm. "I need to call Maddy first, though."

"What did she do last night? Did you let her stay on her own?"

My stomach did a little jump, and suddenly I was desperate to call my daughter. "Yeah, yeah I did, although, I think her friend Emma was going to stay with her."

Maya frowned at me. "You know, if you're worried about her, we can skip breakfast."

"I'm not worried about her. She'd have called me if she needed me. I gave her the warning, no boys, but I'll bet that bloody boyfriend of hers has been round."

"He wouldn't have stayed the night, though, would he?" She didn't sound any more convinced than I felt.

I scrubbed a hand down my face. "I don't know. Maybe. He better have bloody not, but who knows."

Maya brushed the hair from my face and placed a soft kiss on my chest. "You have to trust her, Will. And if he did stay, at least you know she'll have been safe—not scared or worried about being on her own."

I knew she was right, but it didn't make it any easier to swallow. "I know that at some point she's going to have sex and I'm pretty sure it'll be with Zak, but…"

"But you're just not ready for her to become a woman."

I nodded in agreement. "He's a nice kid. I like him, and if it's going to be anyone, then I'm glad it's Zak. I don't know, Maya, it's just it's a scary prospect, her growing up."

"I know," she said, her tone soft and soothing. "But you can't stop time, and if you like Zak, then you need to trust him to take care of her. *And* trust Maddy's judgement."

"You're very wise for a woman who doesn't have a teenage daughter."

She shrugged. "It's just common sense."

"Which I apparently don't have any of." I raised an eyebrow.

"Maybe not," she said, grinning. "But you do have an amazing tongue and penis."

"I won't refuse that compliment." I kissed her quickly, a short peck, because I knew anything else would distract me. "Now, let me call her, and then we'll go and get that breakfast."

"And then what?" she asked.

"Then, I'll follow you home, and I'm going to spend the rest of the weekend with you."

Her eyebrows raised. "Really?"

"Yeah, really. I'll tell Maddy I'll be home tomorrow night."

Reaching for my phone, I took a deep breath, knowing that it was more than my love life that was about to change.

CHAPTER 33
Maddy

When I woke, the first thing I felt was the molten heat of Zak's body against mine. The next thing was his dick, hard and persistent in my back. And then there was his big hand on my stomach, underneath my vest top, his rings cool against my blazing skin.

He wasn't the only who had stayed over at my house, but he was the only one who had sneaked into my bed after everyone had fallen asleep. We hadn't done anything, except snuggle because Zak had said it would be disrespectful to Dad for us to have sex in his house while he was away for the night. Maybe if I hadn't been so exhausted and woozy from vodka, I might have argued, but to be honest, drifting off in his arms was perfect.

Sleep had been that broken, alcohol-induced one, but each time I stirred Zak pulled me closer, kissed the back of my head and lulled me back into unconsciousness. It was blissful, and I could have stayed there all day. Warm and comfortable in Zak's arms. Happy and safe.

It had just been me and Emma on Friday night, but when Dad called me to say he was staying another night with Maya, I knew it would be a waste not to take advantage of it. Liv had tried to encourage me to have a full-blown party, but I knew I'd be grounded for months if I did. He would have let me if I'd asked, but I knew he would have wanted to be close by, not over an hour and a half away at some Yorkshire Manor house. That was why just the six of us, because Ana had finally come out of her bad mood. In fact, she'd been happier than I'd seen her in ages as she bounced in with a litre bottle of rum and a carrier bag of chocolate and crisps.

"Don't move," Zak groaned, pulling me closer. "I'm too comfy and my undies are a bit stretched."

I chuckled and looked at him over my shoulder. "I know. I can feel it in the crack of my arse."

He groaned and shifted up a little, so his dick was no longer nestled between my bum cheeks and buried his nose in my hair.

"You smell of sleep and strawberries."

With my hand over the top of Zak's at my stomach, I savoured the moment. Basked in the attention and protection I felt with him wrapped around me.

"What time is your dad back?" He asked sleepily.

"He said he'd be home for six, so we can watch Match of The Day from last night."

Zak laughed and cuddled closer. "Makes me laugh how much you like footy. Wrong team, though. Flipping City," he complained.

"I had no choice. As the only child of a single dad who is obsessed."

"I suppose. If you and I ever got married and had kids, though, they wouldn't be City fans. Hammers through and through. My dad is from the East End originally so we're four-generation West Ham fans. Five with our kids," he said with a chuckle.

I knew that he was just making a flippant comment, but it still made my heart thud and my stomach do a loop-the-loop.

Clearing my throat, I stroked his hand. "We'll see." It wasn't the most eloquent of comebacks, but I didn't have anything else. My head was mashed. I was seventeen it shouldn't have even been on my radar, or his, yet it made me feel warm and squishy inside. I knew how lucky Dad had been with my mum's auntie Miriam. Things could have been so different. We could have been different. Our lives could have been different.

"Want to stay in bed until five fifty-five then?"

Giggling, I wiggled my bum against him. "That would be cutting it fine, plus there are four of our friends in the spare bedroom all probably hanging out of their arses. All wanting a bacon butty and a strong mug of tea."

"Coke and a Mars Bar," Zak said around a yawn. "They are the best things for a hangover. I promise you."

"We'll see." It was then my turn to yawn. "But another half hour snuggling first."

I felt his smile against the back of my neck, and my insides quivered with excitement, nerves, and happiness.

In the first throes of dozing, I jerked awake when the bedroom door swung open, and a body landed on top of us with a groan. Deep blue eyes with smudged mascara looked at me from under a black choppy fringe.

"Everything hurts," Ana groaned. "And I'm knackered."

"So go back to bed then," I suggested, desperately trying to push her off before she smothered me.

"Yeah," Zak agreed. "Go back to bed. We're snuggling."

I giggled and Ana groaned. "I can't sleep, fucking Liam is snoring and Emma keeps smacking me in the face, and Liv's farting is horrendous."

Zak laughed and shifted us both to the other side of the bed so that Ana dropped beside me. "You can snuggle with us," he said, "but no talking."

"Can I get in the middle?"

"No," we chorused.

"Can I snuggle you Zak, or are you naked?"

"No, he isn't and no you can't," I muttered. "Now get in next to me or go."

She groaned and pulled at the duvet beneath her, kicking her feet and tugging at it to try and get underneath.

"Ana," I snapped. "Get inside the bloody bed or piss off. We're trying to snuggle here."

"I know, so you said." She dug me hard with her elbow and then finally pulled the duvet over the top of her. She wriggled around, getting herself comfy, eventually sighing and turning on her side. "Okay, let's snuggle."

Zak chuckled and stroked his hand up and down my stomach, his fingers stopping just below my boobs. Instantly my nipples hardened, and I wondered if Ana could feel them in her back. I expected him to rub his thumb across the tight peak, but he stopped, and kissing my shoulder, said, "Half an hour starts again from now."

"Okay." And within seconds all three of us were fell fast asleep for another two hours.

***

"I think we should all go to the same uni and move in together," Emma said, resting her feet in Liam's lap and nudging him with her foot "And you could find somewhere else to do your business apprenticeship instead of Bentley. Then we could do this *every* weekend."

"I don't want to do it with anyone else," he retorted, clasping her foot in his hands. "I'll get a car with them. Not a Bentley obviously, but I'll still get one."

Emma pouted, clearly upset her boyfriend, or whatever he was, valued a car over us all moving in together in some other part of the country.

"Imagine it, though," Zak said. "Us all living together just so we can get pissed and then feel hanging all the next day?"

"You're not, though," Liv replied. "How the hell do you do that?"

"Yeah," I added. "How come you aren't hungover?"

Zak shrugged. "I didn't really drink that much." He lifted his hand to comb his fingers through my hair.

"Really." Liam groaned. "Every time I looked at you there was vodka and coke in your hand."

"I'm just hard as nails." He grinned and stealing the mug of tea from my hand took a swig. He then passed it back, dropping a quick kiss to my temple. "Anyway, how can we all live together when Maddy is staying here."

"Oh, don't you start." I rolled my eyes. "Has my dad asked you to bring this up?"

"No, but he's got a point. You'd have a much better time doing your uni experience away from home."

"He has said something, hasn't he?" I smarted, nudging him in the ribs.

"Ow, and no, he hasn't. I just think you should go away." He pulled on my hair. "I hear Edinburgh is good."

"That's where you're going isn't it?" Liam laughed loudly. "You soppy dick."

"Exactly." Zak's voice was low and full of innuendo, and there was that warm feeling again. Quickly followed by a cold snap of dread because I had no idea whether he meant it or was he just being nice, or worse, playing to the audience.

"You don't want me there spoiling your rep," I joked, holding my breath because I still didn't know where we stood once he went away to university. We hadn't talked about it—whether we would do the long distance thing or not. The problem was I didn't want to talk about it, only because I was scared what he would say. In case he decided it wasn't what he wanted.

"Babe, I wouldn't want you anywhere else," he whispered, and all my fears disappeared. "And besides, I have no rep for you to spoil."

"Right," Ana said, jumping to her feet. "I'll wash the dishes why you all decide which film we're going to watch."

Everyone passed her their plates and mugs, and we watched as she practically skipped from the room.

"She's in a better mood," Liv whispered, thumbing over her shoulder.

"I know," Emma added. "She won't say what was wrong, though."

"She'll tell us if she wants to." I sighed and looked towards the door that Ana had disappeared through. "As long as she's okay, now."

Zak took my hand in his and linked our fingers. "She'll be fine, babe."

I nodded. "Yeah, I know."

"Right," Zak announced. "Ana said we had to pick a film, so what are we watching?"

Everyone shouted out suggestions, arguing about the best thing to watch. We still hadn't decided when Ana came back and demanded that we watch a romantic comedy. We all groaned, but deep down, were glad that she was feeling okay again. Grumpy Ana was not my favourite Ana.

As we settled down to watch it, I moved in closer to Zak, the arms of his hoody that I was wearing covering my hands and my knees. I lowered my head and inhaled the smell of his aftershave and when he kissed my cheek and whispered, 'Okay, babe?' I nodded and knew that I didn't want to let him go without me. I just wasn't sure whether he really wanted the same.

MAYA'S DIARY ENTRY

I feel free and joyful like a teenager. Like I have no responsibilities. I feel amazing. I think I'm in love. I know I'm in love. Will left earlier after staying here since yesterday afternoon. He came to the wedding on Friday night, and my family loved him. They thought he was hilarious, especially my mum. She was flirting with him all night. Even the kids loved him and had him on the dance floor for ages. Daisy even said she wanted to marry him when she's older. It was cute, and Will told her he was sure she'd meet someone much better for her.

It had to be the best night of my life. We had sex all night—almost. I think we fell asleep about half five, but I woke him up again because I was desperate for him. Couldn't get enough. He is the best sex I ever had. EVER. Amazing. Perfect. Sexy. Hot. There are too many words to express what Will is like, or how he makes me feel.

I don't think I ever felt like this for anyone before. He makes me happy. He makes me feel excited and nervous. He makes me feel everything. I just want to be with him all the time. I just hope we can do this. I just hope this is it. I really want it to work. I just hope I'm not getting ahead of myself.

He's so amazing!

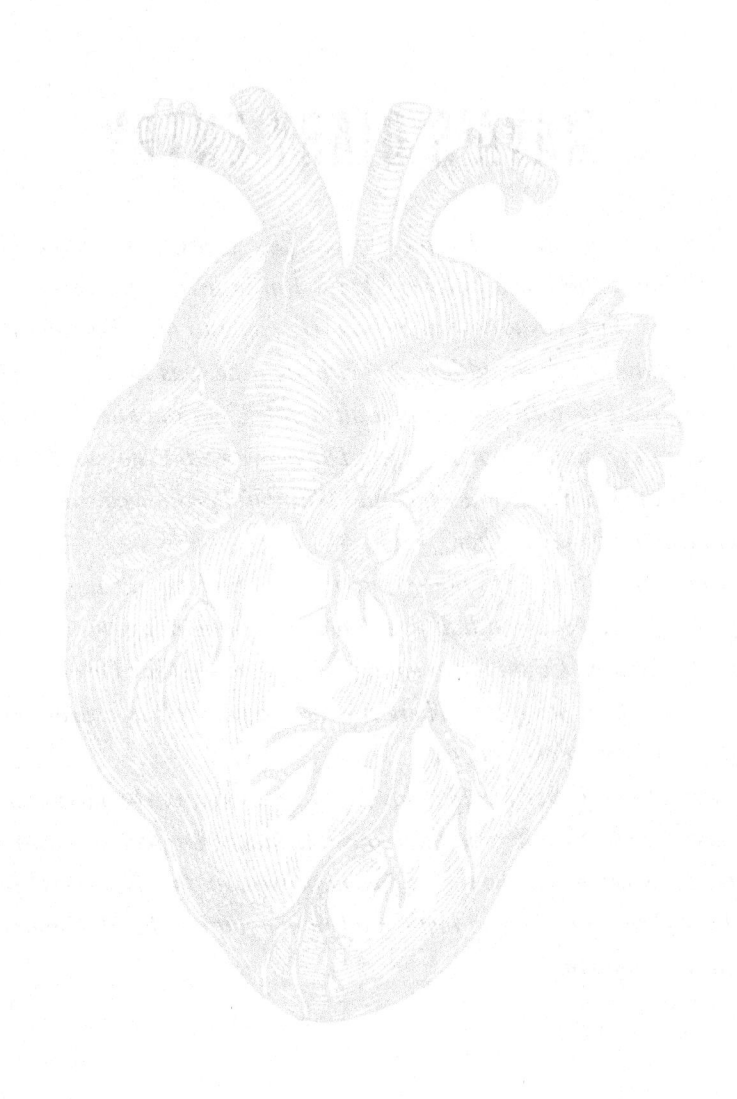

CHANGES

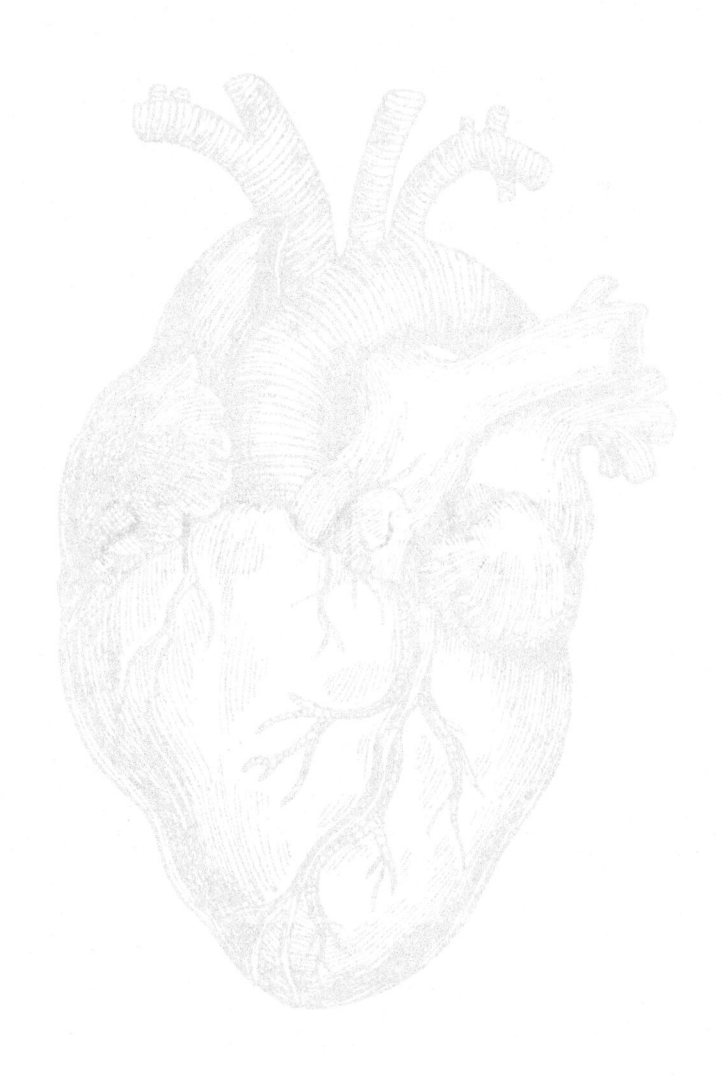

CHAPTER 34
Will

Teenage boys. They'd been in my house while I'd been away. I could smell it. It was a mixture of aftershave, farts, and sweaty armpits.

Maddy had at least told me that they'd been there, but I was sure there was more to it than that. She wasn't spilling, though, no matter how much I questioned her. That had pissed me off because Maddy never lied to me. At least I didn't think she did—how the fuck did I know? She was a bloody teenager; it was part of their DNA.

"What's wrong with your face?" Marcus asked, as he passed me a mug of tea while we took ten minutes before we got ready for opening. "I thought a weekend with the new girlfriend would have put a smile on that ugly jib of yours."

Girlfriend! We hadn't had that conversation but after the weekend, it was probably long overdue. As far as I was concerned, she was, but I needed to at least ask Maya.

"Yeah, the weekend was good. It's what went on at home that bothers me."

"Maddy been up to no good?"

I shrugged. "Says not, but I'm sure she had boys staying over. Specifically, her new boyfriend and Sam's lad, Liam."

Marcus' eyes bugged out. "Maddy and two boys?"

"Fuck off," I snapped, punching him in the arm. "There were other girls there, too. My Maddy isn't like that."

"Well, you clearly think she is, otherwise you wouldn't have a gob on you."

"I don't. I think maybe he's a bad influence." I didn't. Not really, but it was better than thinking him staying over might have been her idea.

Marcus knew me too well. "No, you don't. You told me that you liked him. Said he was a nice lad."

Sighing heavily, I pulled out a bar stool and placed my mug on the bar. "He is. I'm just having a hard time accepting that she's growing up. She told me he didn't stay over, but I'm not sure I believe her. I want to but I don't."

Taking the stool next to me, he shrugged. "And? She's seventeen."

"Exactly, Marcus! I don't doubt that she's done stuff, but I just hope she's been careful." I pinched the bridge of my nose and took a deep breath. "Look, I'm excited for her and all the new things she's going to start to experience," I shuddered, "even falling in love for the first time, but that doesn't mean I'm not going to worry."

"So trust her *and* him."

"I'll have to because at thirty-seven, I'm not ready to be a grandad." I felt the blood drain from my face. "I was fucking lucky that I had Miriam and as much as I would be there for her, I don't want her to have to make sacrifices. She's much brighter, more driven and would be giving up much more than I had to. Because let's be honest Marcus, I gained a hell of a lot when she was born. More than I deserved."

"I know mate," he replied, squeezing my shoulder. "But times are different now old man and maybe she could have both; a child and a career."

My eyes almost popped out of my head as I took a step back from him. "Doesn't mean she should. Zak's a great kid but it doesn't mean I want him impregnating my seventeen year old daughter."

Marcus laughed loudly. "You dick. You don't know for sure they're having sex, although." He tilted his head to one side and screwed up one eye. "It's probably a given."

"Why don't you fuck off." I shook my head and groaned. "Thinking it and knowing it are two different things."

"Listen, Will, if they've had sex then Maddy is sensible enough to take precautions. In fact, she's got the implant."

I blinked and leaned forward. "How the fuck do you know that?"

"Because you researched it for weeks and then asked me to cover an afternoon shift so you could take her to the doctors. Maddy had it because she had painful periods, and she wanted to have it rather than the pill because she thought she might forget to take it."

"Christ, you took notice, didn't you?"

"The point is, she's already being safe, and if Zak is the sort of boy you seem to think he is, well I'm betting he treated her with respect. Whether they had sex or not."

"I know, I know, I'm just being over protective. I get it." I shook my head. "For fuck's sake, I can't believe I'm taking advice from you, Norford's biggest Fuck Boy."

He winked at me and clinked his mug with mine. "My pleasure."

Deciding my daughter's potential sex life was a subject I no longer wanted to discuss, I took a long drink of my tea. When the bar door swung open, I was just finishing it off, enjoying the companable silence that had fallen.

A tall, dark haired man, dressed in a navy blue suit and white open-necked shirt wandered in. He looked around, his chin had a confident jut, which reminded me of Maddy's when she was trying to get her own way.

"Shit, I forgot to lock the door after the bread was delivered." I groaned and put my mug down on the bar and turned to the visitor. "Can I help you?"

The man's gaze whipped to me, and he smoothed a hand down his shirt. "I'm looking for William Newman."

I sighed; sales reps were my worst nightmare. They knew I insisted on an appointment. I hadn't seen him before, though, so I'd cut him some slack.

"That's me, but if you want to try and sell me your beer or spirits then I operate on appointment only."

Marcus stood up and grabbed both the mugs. "I'll leave you to it." He grinned because he hated sales reps as much as I did.

The man wandered over, and as he got closer, I felt like I knew him. Like I recognised him from somewhere. His eyes were familiar.

"It's not about beer," he said, coming closer, and I got a whiff of aftershave. I frowned because it dragged a memory right from the back of my mind. I had no idea *what* I was remembering, just something.

"Well, we don't do much in the way of food, so not sure I can help you with much else. Sorry."

He put his hands on the back of the stool that Marcus had vacated, his fingers digging into the leather. Narrowing his eyes on me, he cleared his throat, and the confidence of a few minutes earlier seemed to have disappeared.

"It's nothing to do with the bar at all," he told me in a deep baritone.

I swung my legs around, away from the bar, ready to stand up and invite him to leave, if necessary. There was something about his demeanour that was edgy. Like he was looking for an argument, or he was at least ready for one. His tongue flicked along his bottom lip, backwards and forwards, like he was playing for time.

"Listen, mate," I sighed. "Do you want to tell me why you're in my bar. I really need to get ready for lunchtime opening in," I glanced at the clock on the wall, "an hour."

"Yeah, sorry," he replied and pulled his shoulders back. "You're William Newman, right?"

"Yes. I told you that."

With a quick nod, he held out his hand, like he wanted me to shake it.

"Nice to meet you, William. I'm Steven Brownlow. I'm your dad."

My mouth instantly went dry, and all I could hear was my heart pounding in my ears. The earth tilted a little beneath me as I stared at the eyes I suddenly recognised. They were mine. *Maddy's*. The tilt of his chin was Maddy's.

I shook my head. "No. Not a chance."

He inhaled slowly and then let it out even slower, like he was the most relaxed man in the world. A small smile at his lips and the straightening of his spine brought back his air of confidence. Like he was a man who was never told no, never questioned.

"I can assure you I am." He reached inside his jacket pocket and pulled out a photograph. "Your mum and me in Blackpool where we met. She was on holiday with her friend, Helen. She was twenty-two when she had you and her name is Marie."

"Was," I croaked out. "Her name *was*, Marie."

If it was shock that made his smile drop and his shoulders stoop, it was only for a split second. In a snap his poise was back.

"I'm really sorry for your loss. When did she die?"

If I expected any emotion from him, I wasn't getting any. Platitudes from the man who'd suddenly announced we were blood related.

Gripping the brass rail in front of the bar I pulled myself to standing. "Listen, I know who you say you are, but I'm not sure I want you here."

"I understand. It's a shock. Not what you were expecting when you got out of bed this morning."

"Not what I expected for the last thirty-seven years," I said through gritted teeth. "A bit late, if I'm honest. And don't tell me you didn't know about me because I know Mum told you."

I was aware I was the product of a summer fling, but I also knew she'd told him, and he wasn't interested. When I was eighteen, a box of Mum's papers found their way to me. In it was the usual stuff like my birth certificate, Mum's death certificate and a letter from my father stating he couldn't be involved with me because he was about to get married to his long-term girlfriend. He signed it with an S, couldn't even be arsed to put his full name. For years, I'd told myself it stood for shit bag.

"Circumstances made it difficult for me to be involved," he retorted, flatly, like I should accept it as being okay.

"Yeah, how is your wife? I assume you married her despite getting my mum pregnant."

"She passed away a couple of months ago," he stated, still showing no real emotion.

"Oh right, so you thought I know I'll go and find my long lost son." Shaking my head, I pushed past him, nudging him with my shoulder. He was tall, yet I still had a couple of inches on him and few pounds of muscle, and he took a stumbling step backwards.

"William, please."

"It's Will and I'm not fucking interested."

My heart felt like it was about to jump up out of my throat and throw itself onto the floor in front of me. It was beating so hard as I walked away from him, an act that didn't distress me in any way. I'd never been the sort of kid who had an idealistic view of what his dad might be like, or that he might come riding in on a white horse to rescue me from my shitty childhood in foster homes. For one, he'd made it clear he didn't want me, and for two, I'd lived with foster families and in the main they were okay until Mrs P and she was incredible. I couldn't have wanted for a better home if I couldn't be with my mum. In fact, Mrs P probably gave me more support and home comforts than Mum ever did or could have. How could she when she worked two jobs? It didn't make her a bad mother, if anything, it was what made her a great mother. Mrs P just gave me something different that I needed at that time in my life. That was why Steven Brownlow could fuck off.

"I can understand why you're angry," he called to my retreating back. "Things were different then. I was different then. I was just a stupid young man who had no backbone. If I had, I'd have told my wife the truth."

I swung around my chest burning with anger. "But you weren't, and you didn't. I've had thirty-seven years without you and not missed you one little bit, so I don't really see the need to have you in my life now." I lifted up the bar flap and walked through. "Now if you'd like to leave through the front door, I'd appreciate it."

"William," he snapped like he was my dad and could tell me what to do. "I thin—"

"I don't care what you think, now piss off out of my bar."

As his footsteps sounded on the wooden floor, I waited, my spine stiff until I heard the front door open and then close. As soon as it banged shut, my whole body relaxed, and I grabbed the door handle to stop myself from stumbling. I'd never missed him. Never thought about him, and yet I knew now my head would be full of him and what might have been, and I hated it.

CHAPTER 35
Maddy

I was stirring the chilli I'd made for tea when I heard the front door slam. Heavy boots stamped along the hall, and my dad appeared looking like he was ready to kill. The veins in his neck were bulging and his nostrils were flared.

Turning the heat off, I turned to him. "What's wrong? Who's upset you?"

He threw his phone down onto the table and, with one hand on his hip, pinched the bridge of his nose. "You wouldn't believe it if I told you."

Moving over to him, I pulled out a chair. "Sit down and tell me."

He shook his head. "It's nothing for you to worry about."

"Obviously it is because you're fuming about something." I sat down and looked up at him. "Dad, what's wrong?"

He sighed and sat down heavily. He picked up his phone, looked at the screen, and then threw it down again. Scrubbed a hand down his face and then slammed his palms down on the table.

"A man came into the bar today."

I frowned. "Are you about to tell me a joke, because if you are, your delivery is rubbish?"

"I wish it was a bloody joke, sweetheart."

"Take my hand, Dad." He wrapped his fingers around mine. "Tell me all about the man who came into the bar."

He blew out his cheeks. "He said he was my dad. Your grandad."

As Dad's fingers squeezed mine, my other hand slapped against my chest, and I let out a shocked gasp. "No way."

He nodded slowly, his eyes searching mine for something. Searching for what I didn't know, but I had the feeling he was battling with his emotions.

"H-how did you feel when you met him?" I asked. "How did he even find you? Did you know he was looking for you?"

"No idea, he just turned up. Wandered into the bar and did his best impression of Darth Vader and told me he was my dad." I frowned. "Bloody hell, Maddy, when are you going to watch it. I keep telling you that you need to."

"Not happening, Dad, but I'm guessing it has something to do with Star Wars."

"Yes, it's what... you know what, it doesn't matter. The point is he turned up today and I don't know how to feel about it."

"Angry, by the look of your face." I studied him and could see that the hurt was slowly dissolving, and he was now more annoyed than anything else. "What did you say to him? Do you look like him? Did he say what happened? Why did he—"

"Mads." Dad curled his hand around ours that were already joined and dipped his head to look me directly in the eye. "Slow down. I'll tell you everything. As much as I know anyway."

"Sorry. It's just I can't believe it. I can't believe after all this time he's come to find you."

"Yeah, well, it wasn't what I was expecting either." Letting my hand go, he sat back in his chair and rubbed his on his jean covered thighs. "I'm so angry, Maddy. Wondering how he dare walk into my bloody bar and just tell me like that. Like it wasn't anything big."

"Did you talk to him for long?"

"No, I pretty much threw him out. I didn't want to hear what he had to say."

I looked at the downturn of his mouth and the slope of his normally straight shoulders. "And now you're wondering if you should have listened to him?"

"Shit!"

When he scrubbed a hand down his face, my heart hurt for him. He'd always said he hadn't missed having a dad, that he didn't need one, but it had to have affected him. If not that, then being brought up for years by different foster parents surely had. There'd been times in my life when I'd thrown it back in Dad's face that he hadn't been there when I was born. Of course, I was just being a silly, spoiled brat, but I had thought it. I had felt like it had to be the answer when things weren't going my way, and my Dad was the best. He'd only been out of my life for the first five months; his had been missing for all his. No wonder he was angry, sad, and inquisitive all at the same time.

"Do you have his number?" I asked. "Can you call him and ask him to come back?"

He shook his head. "I just threw him out. Told him that I didn't want him in my life and to leave."

His eyes closed and his head dropped. Dejected and saddened.

"Oh, Dad." I shuffled my chair closer and pulled him into a hug. "I'm so sorry."

We stayed that like for a few minutes, until he sighed heavily and extracted himself from me.

"What's for tea? It smells good."

"Chilli and tacos. I was going to do rice, but we've had them in the cupboard for ages, so I thought we should eat them."

"That's fine by me. Sounds good."

He didn't look like it sounded good. He looked like nothing in the world would cheer him up. I hated that for him because he did everything he could to make my life happy.

"Why don't you grab a shower and I'll sort tea out."

He looked over at the pan on the stove and then back to me. "Okay. I'll be five minutes." His chair scraped on the floor when he pushed it back and dragged himself to his feet. "I'll have loads, please. I'm starving."

I went back to organising everything and had turned the oven on to warm the tacos when Dad's phone rang out. It was still on the table, surprising me because he never usually let it out of his sight. When I went over and peeked at the screen, it was flashing with a gorgeous picture of Maya laughing. I could hear the shower still going upstairs so picked it up and answered it.

"Hi, Maya, it's me, Dad's in the shower."

"Oh hiya, Maddy. How are you?"

"Good, thanks. How was your brother's wedding? Dad said it was great." After he'd asked me a thousand questions about who'd stayed over.

"It was. We had a lovely time, and your dad has some moves on the dancefloor." She giggled, and in it, I could hear that she was already falling hard for him. It was soft and light, like it had a heartfelt sigh in it.

"Yuk, I don't even want to think about it." I shuddered but had a smile on my face imaging him busting out his dad dancing. Even though he thought he was good.

"My family think he's incredible. In fact, I think my brother, Charlie, the one who got married, might fancy him more than I do."

We both giggled, and I felt happy that he had finally met someone he seemed to care about. She was lovely, and he deserved lovely.

"Maya," I said, tentatively, "can I tell you something?"

"Oh dear, that sounds serious. It's not is it? It's not something I'm going to have to keep from your dad, is it?"

"No, honestly no." I listened to check if Dad was finished, but I could hear him moving around his bedroom. "It's just he's had a bit of a crap day today, so well, say if you can't, but would you be able to come over?" I glanced at the clock on the cooker. It was almost six, so it'd probably be near to nine by the time she got here. "If you can't, then that's fine, but I think he'd love to see you."

"Are you going out?"

"No. No, I've got a fair amount of homework to do." I would be calling Zak later, but we'd agreed we both had too much homework to do to meet up. "I just think that it's you he needs more tonight."

"Oh, Maddy," she whispered, with a little crack of emotion. "Thank you."

"Are you okay? Have I overstepped the mark?"

"Of course not," she gushed. "Absolutely not. Of course I'll come over. Let's surprise him." She gasped. "You don't think he'll mind do you?"

"Not at all." I grinned. "I think he'll love it."

"Delete my call then and I'll be with you as soon as I can. I'll message him to say I'm busy and that I'll call him later."

I heard his bedroom door open. "He's coming," I hissed. "I'll see you later."

"Yep. Bye, Maddy."

As soon as the line went dead, I quickly deleted the call record and then put dad's phone back. By the time he was coming through the door, I was dishing up chilli and tacos, and he was none the wiser. As we sat down to eat he looked a little lighter, but I could still the sadness in his eyes. Until he got a message from Maya and then they lit up and I knew I'd done the right thing.

CHAPTER 36
Will

As soon as Maya had walked through my door, I'd felt a sense of calm. Her surprise visit was just what I needed, especially as she'd messaged earlier to say she was busy and would call me when she could. I had no idea it was because she was on her way to see me. Maddy had stayed to chat for a few minutes, but soon disappeared up to her room to leave us alone.

"And he just walked in?" Maya asked, shaking her head, surprise written all over her face. "Told you he was your dad and that was it?"

"Yeah." I scrubbed a hand down my face. "It's a total mind fuck."

"How did he find you? Did he say?"

Shaking my head, I reached for her hand, stroking the soft skin of her palm. "I have no idea. He knew my name because my mum wrote to him when I was born. We didn't even live around here, so not sure how he tracked me down. There must be millions of William Newman's in this world."

"It probably only took an investigator to find your birth certificate."

When she kissed my cheek, more warmth and calm enveloped me. Quickly, she had become my anchor in a storm—not that I'd had many since we'd been together. It had been one steady, but exciting, incredible ride, so far. I was determined that the thing with my dad was going to be a gentle speed bump, a little pot hole. I wasn't going to let it make us veer off the road we were on, because I wouldn't be letting Maya go. It would never be my choice if it ended, I could feel it in my chest. She was my person, the one who I wanted to always be with, and I was sure she was feeling the same way. I *hoped* that she was feeling the same way.

"What now?" Maya dragged my attention back the one thing that I wasn't sure about.

"He left. I told him to leave, and he went." Maya's eyes filled with tears, and she drew in a breath. "Hey," I soothed, squeezing her fingers gently. "What's wrong? I'm fine you know."

Her green eyes looked uncertain as they scrutinised me. "Are you sure because this is a huge thing, Will. All your life without a dad and then he walks in and out of your life within a matter of minutes." She cleared her throat of emotion. "I can't envisage not having my dad in my life, and for you not to have one, well…" She blew out her breath. "I just can't comprehend how that must feel. Wouldn't ever want to. Then to see what a great dad you are to Maddy without a role model, it's just incredible."

I laughed softly. "Clearly not that good because she's lied to me about boys staying over at the weekend. I know she has."

"How do you know?" Maya raised a sceptical eyebrow.

"I know." Exhaling, I looked up at the ceiling to the floor of her bedroom. "I could smell them the moment I walked through the door."

A rich giggle sounded out as Maya dropped her head to our joined hands. Her shoulders were shaking as she found what I'd said amusing.

"What?" I asked. "What's so funny?"

Her eyes lifted to mine, humour replacing the tears of a few minutes before. "You could smell them?"

"Yeah! Don't tell me you don't know what teenage boys smell like. You've got brothers."

"Can't say that I recall a specific smell."

"It's distinctive," I cried. "How can you not know it? And it was in my bloody house when I got home from yours."

Cool fingers cupped my cheek. "Oh baby, don't stress about it."

"She's seventeen, Maya."

"I know and in a few months she'll be eighteen, an adult, possibly living away from home. You're not going to know what's she doing. If she doesn't go away, you can't keep her locked up in the house. Besides," she said with a shrug, "you're the one trying to persuade her to leave home."

"Don't remind me." I groaned, turning my head so that I could kiss her palm at the side of my face.

She tickled my stubble with her fingertips and giggled. "Poor baby."

"It is poor bloody baby, so don't make fun of me." Christ, my heart felt full, stinky teenage boys aside. Maddy was my world, and now Maya was joining it, and she'd done nothing but enhance it. She and my daughter seemed to like each other and that was a huge weight off my shoulders, but it was getting that I couldn't imagine how I'd traverse it if they didn't.

"Seriously, Will, she's a fantastic young woman and she's bright and sensible and she's happy and that's because of you. She would never want to upset or disappoint you, so whatever she does it will be with the best of intention, so trust her."

I let out a short breath. "How did you get so wise about teenagers?"

"Well, I was a teenage girl, and my mum and dad were pretty cool when I was."

I hadn't realised how hard it was being a single parent; I'd always just got on with things. Sam and Louise had always helped, but big decisions had always been down to me. Now with Maya in my life, I'd at least have someone to check in with. And the idea of that made me equal parts scared and excited. Was I going too fast? Thinking too far ahead? I had no idea, but it felt right.

"Can I let you into a little secret," Maya said, tilting her head on one side.

My heart squeezed involuntarily, scared because of the furrow of her brow. "What?"

Worry flashed over her beautiful features, and I gritted my teeth, waiting for something bad.

"Don't be angry with her, because she did a good thing."

"Fucking hell. Tell me." My pulse began to race. "What is it?"

"I called earlier, and Maddy answered your phone. She asked me to come over. She said that you'd had a bad day." Her shoulders heaved, like she was relieved to have got it out. "She did that for you because she loves you, Will. Because you're a good dad and she's an amazing young woman, so don't worry about her too much."

I wasn't sure my heart could get any fuller, but in that moment it did. There was nothing more I wanted or needed to feel fulfilled.

"She did?" I whispered.

Maya nodded. "She did."

"And you didn't mind coming over here? You didn't feel pressured?" They weren't really questions because I knew the answers. They were statements of fact.

"Not at all. In fact," she said with a giggle, "I was glad of the excuse."

"She certainly understands me." I let a smile hitch at the corner of my lips. "She knows exactly what I needed."

As we watched each other, an intense energy crackled, sending a shiver over my skin. Maya's eyes were bright, and when she licked her lips, need and want twisted together in my stomach.

"I don't know if you realise this," I said, quietly as my hand moved up her arm, "but I really, *really*, like you."

Maya's gasp was quiet, more like a small inhale but combined with the tremble of her hand, I knew what it meant. She was feeling it too. The connection we had so soon. The desire to be together. The need to share the same space.

"I know," she admitted. "I really, *really* like you, too."

Euphoria was probably the word to describe the emotion I had bubbling inside of me. Excitement and happiness were overpowering any sensible thoughts that I should have. Yet, I held back from saying the words that were on the tip of my tongue. They didn't scare me, but I didn't want Maya frightened into making a decision that might damage my heart.

"Are you staying all night?" I asked, taking a lock of her hair and winding it around my finger, my gaze intent on hers.

"If that's okay. Maddy won't mind, will she?"

I shook my head. "We've had a conversation about it and she's more than happy. Besides, she wouldn't have asked you if she was."

Maya's smile was beaming as she gave a contented sigh. "Then I'd love to stay."

I knew then that if she'd have added the word *forever* to the end of that sentence, I really wouldn't have minded. Not one little bit.

CHAPTER 37
Maddy

Dad was clearly troubled by the sudden appearance of his own father. He was trying to act like he didn't care, but I knew he did. He'd taken time off from the bar, saying it was to spend the day with Maya, but I was sure it was in case his dad turned up again.

When I got home, they were both sitting on the sofa, Maya pushed up against his side, reading something on his laptop."

"Hi," I said, flopping down in the armchair.

"Hey." Dad looked up and frowned. "You're early. I thought you and

Zak were going out for tea after school."

I shrugged. "I thought you probably needed me more."

Maya's hand went to her chest as a smile lit up her face. Dad exhaled and shook his head.

"Sweetheart, I'm fine. You didn't need to worry about me."

"I do, though, Dad. It's a big thing. What are you looking at anyway?" I pointed at the laptop.

He glanced at the screen, then Maya, and then brought his gaze back to me. "Research."

"Research for what?" I frowned, pulling my legs under me and getting comfy.

"Trying to find out more about Steven Brownlow."

"I thought maybe your dad should know more about him," Maya said, pulling the sleeves of her jumper down over her hands. "What do you think?"

"I think it's a good idea." We'd only had a handful of chats about his father over the years, but they had always been the same vein. Dad didn't care about him because he clearly didn't care about Dad. He had a preconceived idea that he wasn't a good man, seeing as he was about to get married when he'd got my grandma pregnant, but that didn't mean he wasn't curious to find out what his father was truly like. "What have you found out?"

"He's a car salesman," Dad scoffed. "Or at least he was. He recently sold his business to some big franchise."

"A car salesman," I repeated. "Nothing exciting like a spy or a forensic scientist then?"

"No." Dad rolled his eyes. "Probably explains how he talked my mum into getting into bed with him."

"Also explains your silver tongue," I offered, and it didn't go unnoticed that Maya blushed and shifted in her seat. I shuddered, really not wanting to think about what that meant—because I could guess.

Dad coughed and nodded. "Yeah, I guess I am pretty good at getting a good deal from suppliers."

"Yeah, exactly." I resisted the urge to roll my eyes. "Anyway, apart from him selling cars, what else have you found out?"

"He has a wife—or did. She died. Breast cancer."

"He has a Facebook profile, believe it or not," Maya added. "Open to everyone."

"Maybe he thought you might do this." I nodded at the laptop on Dad's knee. "Go snooping."

"Research," he corrected with a raised eyebrow. "Maybe." He sighed heavily. "And I have a brother."

Gasping, I leaned forward at the waist. "A brother!"

A shadow passed over his face, but he soon replaced it with a tight smile. That had to hurt, knowing that his dad had an active part in his sibling's life.

"He's the same age as me. Three months younger."

Shit, that had to hurt more. "Just three months."

"Hmm. Seems he got Mrs Brownlow up the duffer on their honeymoon."

"Dad," I groaned. "You can't say up the duffer."

"No," Maya agreed, nudging him. "That is so wrong."

"Okay, okay. He impregnated her on their honeymoon and produced Cameron Brownlow, my brother, who is also a car salesman."

"Does this make us Brownlows?" I asked. "Maddy Brownlow." It sounded strange. Felt strange on my tongue. "Nah, I prefer Maddy Newman."

"Yeah, well," Dad scoffed. "Me, too. We won't be changing our surname. I'm very happy with Newman, thank you very much. I vaguely remember your grandma telling me that her dad Bill Newman, was a great man, which is why she called me William. After him."

"He died when she was ten, didn't he?" I asked.

"Yeah. It was him she inherited the heart condition from."

"Do you know what happened to her mum?" Maya asked, turning her body to dad's. "I know she kicked your mum out at sixteen."

Dad shrugged. "No idea. She might be alive, but I have no idea. Don't want to know either." He flashed Maya a smile, and I gave a little sigh. He really liked her, and I was so happy for him. "Neither of her parents had siblings, and neither did Mum, so that's why it was just me and her and I ended up in care."

I hated when he talked about his childhood. It was awful thinking about him being all alone. Having to live with people he didn't know and who rarely wanted him, must have awful. He'd never hidden his time as a child from me, but had only gone into detail once I hit thirteen. I'd cried for ages. Sobbed, in fact. I hated to think of my dad being lonely or sad. I loved him so much, and the idea that he would have to live like that broke my heart. He didn't deserve a life like that. He was lovely. He was my daddy.

As I looked at Maya, it was obvious it hurt her heart, too. She was worrying her bottom lip, and her eyes were fixed on Dad. She opened her mouth and I thought that she was about to say something, but she quickly closed it and grabbed his hand. Dad glanced at her and smiled and then shrugged his shoulders.

"It is what it is, and nothing is going to change the past." A thin lipped smile acted as a full stop to the conversation, and he slammed the laptop shut. "Right, who fancies a takeaway."

"Are you staying another night, Maya?" I asked, just about stopping myself from bouncing in my seat due to the excitement.

"Is that okay?" she asked.

"Of course. No problem at all." I mean, I knew they'd had sex the night before, but at least they'd tried to be quiet. The gentle thud, thud, thud of the headboard had told me enough. "What takeaway are we having?"

"You choose," Dad said and then sighed. "And you can get Zak over if you like. Seeing as you were supposed to be with him."

My heart leapt. I had wanted desperately to spend more time with him after school, but I just thought I should go home. "Are you sure that's okay?"

He shook his head. "I wouldn't have said if it wasn't. I'll order a few dishes. The Chinese is always quicker, so tell him to hurry up." Dad stood up and fished his phone out of his pocket. "He's not a veggie, is he?"

"No. He doesn't like fish, though."

"No king prawn then." He bent down and kissed Maya's cheek. "And no mushrooms for you."

The way she looked at him, just because he remembered she didn't like mushrooms, made my insides feel all squidgy. Anyone would think he'd just told her she was the most beautiful woman in the world, which, as an aside, I think he thought was true. She was gorgeous, though. Gorgeous and stylish, and I really wouldn't have minded her as a step-mum, but that was jumping way ahead.

"I'll go and call Zak." I jumped up out of my seat. "I'll get him to get here as quick as he can."

Leaving my Dad on the phone ordering food, while Maya gazed up at him, I ran up to my room and bounced on the bed. My blinds were still closed, and my bed still unmade and there was a wet towel on the floor. It wasn't like me, but I'd been in a rush to leave the house that morning. My hot boyfriend was waiting outside in his mum's car to take me to school. As his number rang out I made a mental note to tidy it all up before Zak came over.

"Hello gorgeous. Missing me already?"

God, yes. I missed him even if I'd only seen him a few of minutes before.

"Nah, not really. My dad is, though. He wants to know if you want to come over for takeaway, seeing as we didn't get to go out after school." I heard something bang in the background and the clinking of a glass. My heart dropped. "Oh, are you already eating?"

"Just a snack, babe. I can eat don't you worry about that."

"So, you'll come over then?"

"On my way."

He laughed, and the richness of it warmed my blood. "See you soon."

"See you soon." I sighed and quickly set about tidying my bedroom just in case Dad let me bring Zak up there. Like that would happen!

***

"I hear you want to be a vet, is that right, Zak?" Maya asked, forking a piece of chicken.

Zak nodded, chewing the food in his mouth. After swallowing he said, "Yeah. Hopefully I'm going to Edinburgh. If I get the A-level grades I need."

"You never wanted to be a doctor or dentist like your parents?" Dad snagged a prawn cracker from the dish in the middle of the table and popped it whole into his mouth.

"Dad!"

He shrugged and turned back to Zak, waiting for his reply.

"Not really," Zak replied. "I don't ever want to be compared to either of them. I'd rather make my own path."

I could see that Dad was impressed by his raised eyebrow and slight nod of his head. The fact that he was, and that he seemed to like Zak, was the best feeling. I remember Ana having a boyfriend, Alfie, in year ten, and her parents hated him. It wasn't anything particularly serious because we were only fifteen, but they still made it difficult for her. In the end, he finished with her because she was never allowed out and when she was had to be home by eight-thirty. She was so sad most of the time when she should have been enjoying it.

"I can't imagine doing anything so academic," Maya said.

"Yeah, but software development isn't easy," I told her. "I'd never be able to write code."

She screwed up her nose. "It's easy once you know how." She looked at Dad. "I certainly couldn't run a bar or a pub. How on earth do you act pleasant all the time as well as making sure you have the right amounts of everything you need?"

"Same, the more you do the easier it is. As for being nice to people all the time, I'm not sure I am."

"He's right." I laughed. "You should hear him talking to some of the reps. He's really rude."

"Yeah, because they deserve it," he grumbled. "They're a bunch of pushy tossers half the time."

Zak chuckled and shoved more food into his mouth. Whether he'd had a snack or not earlier, he could seriously eat. He was on his second plateful of food, and I was glad Dad had ordered too much, as usual.

"What are your plans after we've eaten?" Dad asked. "Homework?"

I looked at Zak, knowing full well he hadn't brought any books with him. "Maybe listen to some music or watch TV in my room, if that's okay."

Dad contemplated it while he chewed his food and, after glancing at Maya, nodded. "Yeah, no problem."

Beaming at him I was startled when my phone pinged with a message. I looked down at it to see it was Ana's mum.

I frowned at Zak. "It's Ana's mum."

"Her *mum*?"

"Yeah." Fear spiked because my friend's parents only ever messaged any of us if we were in trouble, or they wanted to know ideas for Christmas presents.

I opened up the message and frowned as I read it.

Susan (Ana's Mum)
Hi Maddy. Sorry to bother you but can I ask if Ana was at school today?

I read the message out, wondering why on earth she was asking.

"Was she?" Dad asked, pouring more wine into Maya's glass.

"Yes. She was with you last lesson, wasn't she?" I asked Zak.

"Yep. Definitely. She sat in front of me." He peered at the text. "I wonder why she's asking?"

I typed out a reply to say she was. "Should I call Ana?" I asked the three people watching me.

"Maybe wait until her mum replies," Dad said.

"You don't want to cause trouble between them." Zak stroked a hand down my back. "Or is it normal for her to ask?"

I shook my head. "We only have each other's parents numbers for emergencies, and they have ours for the same reason."

"And when I need to know what size bra to buy you for Christmas," Dad quipped.

I slapped at his arm. "Dad!"

Zak laughed, but Maya bit back her smile. We were quite the happy little circle around the dining table.

"The point is," I stressed, "it's not usual for her to ask something like that."

As soon as the message went, I quickly got a thank you back, but I couldn't shake the worry that something was wrong.

"Maybe I'll call Ana and say it's about school or something."

Zak nodded, leaned in, and kissed my cheek. "Good idea."

I loved that he wasn't embarrassed or too scared to show me affection in front of my dad, despite claiming Dad petrified him. He was respectful of him. He was respectful of me.

When Zak and Dad then started to discuss football, Maya and I rolled our eyes and my concern about Ana was forgotten..

CHAPTER 38
Maddy

Walking through the school gates, Zak's fingers curled around mine as I looked out for my friends. Emma, Liv and Liam were waiting in what had become our usual spot before classes, on the bench under the Library window.

"No Ana," I whispered, glancing up at Zak.

He didn't reply verbally, but he tugged on my hand giving me a silent sign of support.

"I should have called her," I echoed the thoughts running around in my head. "I should have tried to find out why her mum messaged me."

"Maybe the others will know," Zak said as we approached our friends.

"Hiya." Liv held her hands out for me. "Come and sit next to me. We need to talk Harry Mayhew."

As I was pulled onto the bench between her and Emma, Zak bumped fists with Liam, who immediately struck up a conversation with him.

"Before we do." I patted their thighs. "We need to talk about Ana."

"Did you get the weird message from her mum as well?" Emma asked.

My gaze whipped to hers. "Yes. What did you make of it?"

She shrugged. "No idea really."

"Did you call Ana afterwards?"

Emma's eyes flicked to Liam so quickly I almost missed it. "No. You?"

I shook my head. "I wish I had, though. I feel bad now."

"Have you seen her this morning?" Emma asked.

"She'll be here soon," Liv said with a sigh. "You know how she likes the drama."

I blinked my eyes slowly, and Emma almost choked. There was only one drama queen amongst us, and she was sitting on the bench, and it wasn't me or Emma.

"I think Maddy is worried because of the mood Ana has been in." Zak shifted his bag on his shoulder and shoved his hands under his armpits. "And we usually see her on the way in, but there was no sign this morning."

Liv thrust her hand into the pocket of her pink wool coat and pulled out her phone. "I'll call her now and then can we talk about Harry?"

Zak pulled a cigarette from the top pocket of his padded denim jacket, and put it, unlit, into his mouth.

"You better not be about to light that, Mr Hoyland."

We swung our gazes to see Mr Barber, our head of History, strolling past us with his stare aimed at Zak.

"No, sir." Zak gave him one of his best smiles. "I would never smoke on school property."

"No point in putting that disgusting thing in your mouth then." He took a step towards us and held out his hand, palm up. "I'll take that."

Zak reached for the cigarette and taking it from his mouth, dropped it into Mr Barber's hand. "Sorry, it's a bit wet, sir."

Liam snorted, earning him a poke in the back of his leg with the toe of Emma's boot. Liv tutted with her phone to her ear, and I guessed it was because we were wasting Harry time. Mr Barber pocketed the cigarette and marched on, wiping his hand on his jacket.

After we watched him disappear inside school, Liv dropped her phone back into her pocket. "Straight to voicemail. Now can we actually talk about Harry," she demanded. "I need to come up with a plan on how to get him to notice me, seeing as no one really wanted to help the other day. And he was a no show at that lame party of Jack's."

I opened my mouth to speak, but the sight of Ana walking towards us stopped me. It wasn't just the message from her mum the night before, or that she was running late, which was unusual for her. It was the fact that she looked dishevelled. Her short black bob was messed up like a bird's nest, and her jeans were the one she'd worn the day before—the ones that she'd spilled tomato ketchup on the day before. Even her coat was buttoned incorrectly.

"Ana," I whispered. "Ana's here."

"What the hell is wrong with her?" Liv asked. "She looks terrible."

As she got closer, it was clear how terrible she looked. Makeup was smudged under her eyes, and her face was pale.

"Wow." Liam blinked a couple of times as we all watched Ana stumble over her own feet. "Is she drunk?"

Her bag dropped from her shoulder, down her arm, and the change of weight unbalanced her. She listed to the right and grabbed for fresh air, I guessed to hopefully hold her upright. It didn't work because her legs went from under her, and she landed in a heap on the ground. Her bag softened the blow a little, but when her shoulder hit the concrete she let out a yelp.

We all ran towards her, yelling and calling her name. Liam reached her first and crouched down next to her, placing a hand on her arm.

"Ana, are you okay? Does it hurt anywhere?"

"My fucking arm. What do you think?" Her words slurred a little leaving her mouth. "Shit."

Liam and Zak put their hands under her arms and tried to help her to her feet, but her legs were like spaghetti and didn't want to hold her up. She kept bending at the knees and giggling.

"She's shitfaced," Emma hissed from the corner of her mouth. "How the hell is she like this? It's only half eight."

I shrugged. "No idea." Stepping forward, I stooped down to look Ana in the face. "What have you been drinking?"

She gave me a slow grin. "Alcohol."

"I know that. What sort of alcohol and how much?"

"Rum. Lots."

"We should get her out of here," Zak said, gaining my attention. "We need to take her home, babe."

"Yeah, I know." I looked over my shoulder to Emma. "Is your mum home today?"

She shook her head. "No, visiting a client in York. She won't be home until seven. Why?"

I grimaced. "My dad is home, he's on the evening shift at the bar. Liv's gran lives with them, so…" I pointed at Ana.

Emma rolled her eyes. "Okay, but she better not puke everywhere."

"I have to go to German," Liv griped. "If I'm not there Miss Wright will go straight to the office and tell my mum."

She had a point. While having your mum work at school had some benefits, it meant that she knew Liv's every move.

"We can take her," Zak offered. "I have mum's car."

I straightened up and smiled at him. "Are you sure?"

"Yeah, I have a double study period." He turned to Liam. "Can you come? I'm not sure I can manage her on my own."

As if to prove a point, Ana flopped forward, almost headbutting me. "Woah, careful." Pushing a hand against her chest, I noticed that as more people arrived at school, more were gawking at us.

"We need to get her out of her quick before someone tells a teacher."

Zak nodded. "Come on, Ana," he said softly, "work with us here."

Ana giggled and grinned at him. "Okay, Zakky."

"Oh fuck," Liam groaned, hoisting her higher. "She's more than shitfaced. And she's heavier than she looks."

"Liam," she snapped, looking affronted with her brows screwed together. "That's not a nice thing to say." She tried to slap at his arm, but it sent her off balance again.

"Teacher on the way," Emma hissed. "Hurry up!"

"Ana," I snapped, grabbing her chin, forcing her to look at me. "Just help Zak and Liam, stop being a dick. Okay!"

Ana inhaled, her eyes closing like they were too heavy, as she gave me a slow nod.

"Let's go." Zak said, giving Liam a nod. They lifted her up and started to drag her away. As they did, she dropped her bag, so I snatched it up while Emma took Zak and Liam's, passing one off to Liv. She shook her head and sighed but took the bag anyway. I gave one last look to the bench to check we hadn't left anything behind, and then followed them as they practically dragged our friend to Zak's car.

As they bundled her into the back seat, buckling her in, I turned to Liv and Emma. "Are you staying here, Liv?"

"Yeah. I can't risk my mum finding out I skipped. If anyone asks, I'll tell them you all had the shits yesterday." She dropped Zak's bag at my feet. "Are you coming back?"

I looked at Ana, her head lolling as she fell to one side. "I doubt it. Not by the look of her. Maybe the boys will."

Zak straightened. "I'll stay with you. Just in case." His eyes were full of worry, and I knew he meant in case we needed transport.

"Okay." Liv smoothed down her coat and leaned forward to look at Ana. "I think she may puke, by the way."

Ana's chest heaved, but instead of throwing up, she collapsed with a groan.

"We need to get going," Zak said. "Liam, can you and Em get in either side of her. I know it's a tight fit." He looked disdainfully at his mum's Mini. "If I'd known we were transporting a pissed mate, I'd have begged my dad's car."

I placed a hand on his back. "I'm sorry, Zak."

He whizzed around to look at me. "Hey, it's alright. I don't mind. As long as she doesn't puke. My mum will freak if she does."

"Let's go then." I pulled open the passenger door. "I'll message you Liv."

"Here have this." She thrust a carrier bag at me. "She can be sick in that. It's had my brother's trainers in it, so it probably stinks."

I threw it into the back to Emma. "I doubt she'll notice." After giving Liv a quick hug, I got inside the car and buckled up as Zak sped off.

***

"She's finally stopped," Emma sighed as she flopped down onto the sofa next to me. "And she's asleep."

"Did you put her on her side?" Zak asked, grabbing my ankle and pulling my legs over his thighs. "If she pukes in her sleep, she might choke."

"Yes, thank you, Zak," she snapped. "I put her on her side."

As Liam walked in with his head in a bag of crisps, we all turned to look at him. He hadn't stopped raiding Emma's mum's food cupboard since we'd got there an hour before.

"I've never had chicken and stuffing flavour before," he said, shoving another handful into his mouth. "They're nice. I might ask my mum to get some."

"Liam! They're my mum's favourites." Emma jumped up and tried to snatch the family-sized bag from his hand. Too quick for her, Liam lifted his hand in the air, leaving her jumping to try and grab it.

"Liam. Give me the crisps," she cried, giggling as he moved his hand further away and tickled her side. "No, Stop it. I want the crisps."

"You do, do you?" He smirked and took a step back. "Is that all you want?"

My eyes widened and I nudged Zak. "He's flirting with her," I whispered.

"I know," he whispered back. "He finally found his bollocks."

Our heads craned forward as we watched Liam pull Emma to him with an arm around her waist. He then dipped his head and smacked a kiss against her smiling lips. Emma's arm went around his neck, and Liam walked them backwards, out of the lounge, leaving Zak and I staring after them.

"Well." Zak looked at me and grinned. "I knew he liked her, but I didn't think he'd do anything about it."

"You knew he liked her." I poked at his hard stomach. "Why didn't you tell me?"

"He asked me not to tell anyone." He shrugged.

"Yeah, but that doesn't include me."

He grinned before stealing a kiss. "Babe, I'm sorry but it does. In fact, he asked me especially not to tell you."

"What?" I whipped my head around towards the door that Liam and Emma had disappeared through. "I'm practically family. How could he. How could you, Liam?" I yelled.

Zak laughed loudly and tugged on my hand, pulling me fully into his lap, so that I was straddling him. He was smiling broadly as his hands went to my bum, pulling me closer to the hard on already growing behind his jeans.

"You know," he said, "this is a much better way of spending the morning than studying."

I leaned in for a kiss, loving how our tongues slowly danced with each other. When he groaned against my mouth, I thrust my hips forward, and rocked against him, relishing in the feel of him against my core. Waves of pleasure were already starting to roll through my body as Zak's hips met mine in a perfect rhythm.

"Fuck, Maddy, you're so fucking perfect," he moaned against my mouth, his fingertips digging into the denim covering my backside.

"I wish we could go somewhere," I whispered, feeling everything build within me.

"We have to take care of Ana." His hand moved to my boob and his thumb brushed over my nipple. "But maybe afterwards…" His words trailed off as he kissed me again.

The feelings I had for this boy were nothing short of intense. He was the sun who brightened my day, and the fire who warmed me from within. We had so many years ahead of us, so many things that we needed to do, yet already I wanted all of that with him. I couldn't explain to anyone how he made me feel. What he made me want. I was afraid that people would laugh. That my friends would say I was stupid. That my dad would say I was too young. Keeping it a secret was safer, because while it was, I could still believe in it happening.

"Hey," Liam's voice interrupted us ten minutes later. "Ana is still sleeping, so me and Em are going to go and get us something to eat."

We looked over to see him standing in the doorway, his arm draped over my friend's shoulder. She was grinning, looking relaxed and thoroughly satisfied.

"What did you do?" I gasped.

She cleared her throat before straightening her shirt. "Do you want anything?" she asked us.

Zak chuckled, kissed my forehead, and then lifted me from his lap. "I'll go with you, mate. I think Mads has questions." He stood up, furtively adjusting his jeans. "Chicken nuggets, babe?"

I nodded. "And chocolate milkshake."

As the boys left, Emma sank down next to me, her grin a mile wide. "Fancy a two man?" she asked.

"You're together then?" I asked, unable to hide the excitement it made me feel. My friend with my boyfriend's friend. It was just perfect.

"I hope so," she said, raising an eyebrow. "Seeing as he's just had his hand in my knickers."

We both burst out laughing, clinging together as we embraced the joy we were finding in life. We were so engrossed neither of us heard Ana enter the room until she spoke.

"Fucking great," she snapped. "More smug couples to deal with."

Then, as we both turned to look at her, she puked all over the carpet.

ZAK'S WHATSAPP MESSAGES

DEACON
Hey mate. There's been a change of plan. Thanks for the offer but I won't need to stay at yours. Mum and Dad want to make a bit of a road trip of it so we're going direct to York after visiting Manchester. I tried to persuade them, but they think it'll be good 'family time'.

ZAK
Don't worry about it Deac. We can catch up some other time. Would have been great to see you, though.

DEACON
Why don't you come here for Nick's 18th on the 6th. He's having a big party. Bring your new gf. You can both stay here.

ZAK
Yeah? Might be a plan. Let me speak to her and see if she can make it. Think maybe he'd mind if we brought a couple of mates?

DEACON
Doubt it. You know how big his house is. His parents are throwing money at the party and he'll prob have no idea who is there. Let me know but would be good to see you and meet Maggy.

ZAK
Maddy!!!

DEACON
Shit! Sorry mate. How's it going anyway? Still in lurrrvvve!!!!

ZAK
… (Zak is typing)

ZAK
... (Zak is typing)

ZAK
It's going good. She's pretty special but I'm saying nothing else cos you'll just take the piss out of me if I do. Hopefully see you soon.

ZAK
Hey gorgeous, think you'd be allowed to go to London with me next month? My mate is having an 18th birthday party. Thought we could ask the others if they want to come too. Or at least Liam and Emma. Have you spoken to Ana since we took her home btw?

MADDY
I don't see why not. I'd have to ask Dad and he's at the bar atm. Sounds good though. I called her but she didn't answer. She texted me back to say she was going to bed. You'd think sleeping all day would have been enough. I am worried about her. Don't know why she wouldn't speak to us about why she was drunk.

ZAK
She will when she's ready. Just be there for her. Funny she wouldn't let you go in with her, though.

MADDY
I know. She's my best friend Zak. We tell each other everything usually.

ZAK
Like I said, give her time. Anyway, better go and do some studying. Can't pick you up in the morning, Mum needs her car. See you at the gate usual time?

MADDY
Yes. Night Zakky 😆.

ZAK:

Fuck is that my new name now!!!

MADDY

🤐.

ZAK

Night gorgeous girl. See you in the morning.

MADDY

XOXOXO

MAYA'S DIARY ENTRY

Poor Will. His long lost dad has appeared, and he has no idea how to deal with it. I've stayed at his place the last couple of days, but I have to go into the office tomorrow. I really didn't want to leave him, though. He's acting like he's fine about it, but he isn't. Especially finding out he has a brother. He says he's going to think things over for a while before deciding what to do about him. As much as he says he hates the man, I think he's also curious. Who wouldn't be?

I'm honoured that he's shared it all with me. I know Maddy was the one who asked me to go over there, but he was so glad to see me. We seem to be moving at warp speed, but I don't care. I really, really, like him, and I honestly think he might be the one. I feel like a giggly teenager just thinking that, but I can't help it.

Staying at his house for the last couple of days felt normal. Like it had always been like that. Maddy is gorgeous and sweet, so nice to me, and I think it's genuine. She asked me after all. Having sex with her across the landing was difficult, but I think we managed to keep quiet! I hope we did. She's really happy with her new boyfriend, and he seems like a nice boy. Will seems to like him, which says a lot. I wouldn't want to be him if he ever hurt Maddy, though. Not so sure Will would be as pleasant to him if he did.

When I go into the office tomorrow, I'm going to ask about home working. That way I could stay at Will's more. I've got my laptop and all I need is a good internet connection and maybe an extra screen. I could see him more often then. Shit. He might not even want to. HAHAHA who am I kidding, he's mad on me – at least I hope he is. I think he is.

God, I need to stop acting like I'm sixteen. Maddy is more grown up than I am!!!

CHAPTER 39
Will

Moving along the aisles of the supermarket, my head was definitely not on my weekly shopping list. It was split into three.

First there was my dad and whether I wanted to see him again. Whether I even wanted to *think* about him again. I had to admit I was curious about him, but was that enough to give him a chance when he didn't deserve one.

Second there was my daughter. She'd landed it on me that she wanted to go to London for the weekend. To go to a fucking party! With her boyfriend and their friends. I knew I should let her go. That I should encourage her, because if she enjoyed it, well then maybe she'd seriously consider going away to university. It still didn't mean I wasn't shit scared about her going partying *with her boyfriend.*

Third, there was Maya. No problems there, other than I didn't see her often enough. While two hours distance wasn't massive, it was still too far. It wasn't a nip around to see her for a quick coffee and chat, distance. Or even a stay overnight and then go to work after morning sex, distance. It was just too bloody far. Especially after having her stay over for a couple of nights. I'd got used to her being there. That had been all it had taken—two nights of her being in my arms and I was lost without her.

All that was why it was difficult to decide between fresh orange with bits or without bits. It was bloody confusing. As for cereal I thought my head might pop. Maddy was obsessed with the amber, green and red symbols on boxes and the cereal that I liked had more red symbols than anything else. The ones with green looked like they'd taste like cardboard.

Moving on to the bread aisle, I was surprised to see Ana, Maddy's friend pushing a trolley around. I knew that since they'd gone into the sixth form they had a lot of free periods, but Ana did the same subjects as Maddy, and she was at school all day. Looking at her, I could see that she didn't look well. Maybe that was why she wasn't at school. Shuffling around and leaning on the trolley, she lingered in front of the bagels, then after a few seconds grabbed some and threw them on top of the rest of her shopping. She hadn't even glanced at the packaging, so much for red, amber and green.

Manoeuvring my own trolley towards her, I moved up beside her. "Hi, Ana."

Her head whipped around, and sad grey eyes looked up at me. "Mr Newman."

"No school today?"

She shook her head, and I noticed how pale she was. Usually, she was made up with her thick eyeliner, mascara and blood red lips, but none of that was present. Instead, I could see her freckles and her youthful complexion. It reminded me how young my daughter and her friends were, trying to take tentative steps into adulthood.

"I-I should go," Ana said. "I need to finish this. Mum is waiting for it."

"How are your mum and dad?" I didn't know her parents well, but enough that we called each other about sleepovers and pick-ups from parties.

She tucked her hair behind her ears and gave me a tight smile. "They're fine."

"And the Martial Arts school, how's that doing? Busy?"

She nodded slowly. "Yeah, yep. It's busy."

It was obvious she didn't want to talk to me, and seeing as I was always tuned in to teenagers, I decided to call it quits, and patted her shoulder. "Well, good to see you. Say hello to your mum and dad for me."

She swallowed hard and, with another nod, she walked away and headed straight for the checkout. As I watched her, I wondered what was troubling her, because something definitely was. Following her, I watched her load her shopping onto the conveyor belt and noted the stoop of her shoulders. She barely acknowledged the till assistant, who was clearly chatting to her, which was unlike her. Ana was Maddy's most exuberant friend, the most confident one who had never been shy in front of me, so I knew that I needed to talk to Maddy when she got home.

***

I'd just put enchilada's into the oven when I heard the front door bang, a bag being flung to the floor, and then a pair of shoes skidding along the hallway as Maddy kicked them off.

"Cupboard," I yelled. A grumble was followed by the understairs cupboard being opened and then slammed shut after a few more seconds. "Thank you."

"I'm starving," said the voice at the kitchen doorway. "What's for tea?"

Turning to Maddy, I raised an eyebrow. "Hello to you, too."

"Hi, Dad." She grabbed her hair, took a scrunchie off her wrist, and then created what looked like a bird's nest on top of her head. "So? What is it?"

"Enchilada's and salad. Can you lay the table."

"Two or three?" she asked, opening up the cutlery drawer.

"Two. Maya is out with her friends tonight and has to work in the office the rest of the week."

"You know you can stay over there, don't you. I wouldn't mind."

With a half turn of my head, I watched how her lips twitched for a second before she schooled her face and narrowed her eyes on me.

"I'm old enough to look after myself."

"I know. And you also have a boyfriend."

She just about resisted an eye roll. "Dad, I am seventeen. Did you forget that?"

"Nope." I grabbed the salad tongues and stuck them in the bowl. "I also remember being seventeen, which means I know it's an opportunity for unofficial sleepovers and what happens at those sleepovers."

"I wouldn't if you said no," she snapped.

I wasn't so sure, but then I never stuck to the rules at that age either. "I'm not saying you can't have friends to stay with you but it's just a bit weird for me to think that friend might be male." I swallowed, preparing for the words I was about to say. "So, if you did ever find yourself home alone and had him stay just be sensible and safe."

Maddy flashed a grin, it was quick, but I saw it, before she protested, "*Dad*, how stupid do you think I am?"

I shrugged. "Not at all, but sometimes sensibility goes out of the window when you're in a moment."

She fake gagged. "I don't want you to ever say that again. I've just been sick in my mouth."

"Can't promise that, sorry, Madeline."

My daughter's emotions often showed on her face, and the by the look of her pinched lips and raised eyebrows, I'd say she was feeling nauseous. Probably time to change the subject.

"I saw Ana today," I said, placing the salad on the table. "Is she okay?"

Maddy's eyes went wide. Her expression changed from anger to worry. Something was going on; this wasn't the first time she'd heard about her friend not being okay.

"Why do you ask?" She tucked a loose strand of hair behind her ears.

There was no question of where I'd seen her, or what was wrong. I might not know much, but I knew my daughter.

"Sit down," I said, pointing to one of the chairs at the table. "And tell me what's going on."

"Nothing is going on." She looked anywhere but at me, so I knew that was a lie.

"Now tell me the truth." I was ready to wait for as long as it took. Thankfully, Maddy's worry for her friend must have been foremost in her mind, because she confessed straight away.

"You know her mum messaged to ask if she'd been to school?" I nodded. "Well, the next day she came to school drunk off her face, Dad."

"What?" I leaned forward, unsure if I'd heard her properly. "Say that again."

As she bit on her bottom lip, I reached for her. "Take my hand, sweetheart, and tell me everything."

"She's been moody for a couple of weeks but seemed to have pulled out of it. Then yesterday, she turned up at school absolutely legless. And I mean literally legless, Dad. She couldn't stand up. Zak and Liam had to help her walk to Zak's mum's car."

"So, the boys took her home?"

"We all took her to Emma's house and stayed the day there with her."

"You all took the day off school?"

She winced. "I know, and I'm sorry, Dad, but she was in a real state, and we didn't want her to get in trouble with her parents. Please don't tell them. I've only told you in case we need your help."

The trepidation in her eyes was justified, but Ana was more import than Maddy missing a day of school. I was just glad she felt she could come to me for help.

"What happened at the house? Was she okay?"

"She puked a few times, and we put her to bed, checking on her. After a while, she got up, but then puked again." She sighed heavily. "So, we put her back to bed and then eventually took her home. We haven't seen or heard from her since."

I squeezed her hand. "I saw her in the supermarket, doing her mum's shopping."

"Did she look okay?" Maddy's bottom lip trembled slightly as big brown eyes almost pleaded with me.

"A bit pale, none of her usual makeup, which is understandable if she was hungover." As Maddy's fingers gripped mine, I scrubbed my other hand down my face. "Do you have any idea why she was drunk? Why she's been moody lately? Because I'm guessing the two are connected."

"We just thought she was in a bad mood," she replied with a shrug. "Then when she stayed here, when you went to the wedding, she was fine. She was laughing and joking and…" Her words trailed off and her shoulders dropped. "How did we not notice, Dad? We should have known something was wrong."

"Don't beat yourself up about it, Mads. The main thing is that you're there to help her."

"How do we do that? I know her, and she won't tell us what's wrong; I know she won't."

"Maybe speak to her parents?" I suggested.

Maddy gasped. "No way. She'd never speak to me again."

I shook my head, wishing my daughter had already had the benefit of experience and hindsight. "She might not speak to you for a while, but at least she'll have people—*her parents*—looking out for her."

"Dad," she groaned. "I can't speak to them. Honestly, she'll go mad, and what if she gets into trouble for drinking?"

"Then she gets into trouble for it, sweetheart. But you have to know her drinking at eight-thirty in the morning isn't a good thing. It's a bad thing, and she's clearly got something troubling her."

She nodded solemnly. "I know. Can I speak to her first, though. See if she'll tell me."

"I think that's reasonable, but if she won't tell you, then her mum and dad have to be told. Okay?"

With an inhalation, she nodded. "Okay."

Letting go of her hand, I slapped the table, leaned in to kiss her forehead, and then stood up. "Right, let's get something to eat."

Placing the plates on the table, I turned back to the oven when the front doorbell rang. "That better not be one of your mates," I said over my shoulder. "You've got revision to do."

"It won't be," Maddy argued. "It'll be for you."

The bell shrilled again. "You could answer it."

"I've told you it'll be for you. You go and I'll dish the food out."

When she pushed me out of the way with a hip bump, it was clear I had no choice, so I wandered off down the hall. When I pulled the door open, I took a step back.

"How the hell did you find me?" I asked.

The man in front of me smiled, not looking one bit embarrassed at turning up on my doorstep unannounced.

"I know you told me to fuck off, but—" He shrugged. "You're my son, so…"

As I stared at him, I felt a presence behind me and glanced over my shoulder at Maddy.

"Dad?"

"Maddy," I groaned, looking up at the ceiling. "This is your grandfather, Steven."

Her hand came to the small of my back, offering me support as she silently watched my father from by my side. When I looked back at him, his eyes were expectant and with one foot on my doorstep, it was clear he wasn't going to leave without a fight. When Maddy's hand pulled on my t-shirt, I was urged back to life.

"You'd better come in," I told him. "You have ten minutes and that's all."

He gave me a single nod of the head and stepped inside my house, as if he belonged there.

CHAPTER 40
Will

"Dad," Maddy hissed, "shall I turn the oven off?"

I nodded. "Please."

"Shall I put the kettle on?"

I glanced over at Steven, who was bent at the waist peering at some framed photos that I had on a shelf in the lounge. "No. He won't be staying long. Turn the oven off and then come back in here."

I didn't want to be alone with him because I was scared.

He'd been a mythical man in my childhood, a character from a story that my mum had made up, not a real person who had the ability to crush me. Yet he had. Without even trying, he'd smashed it to pieces, leaving me with an empty husk of a childhood once Mum passed away. If he hadn't rejected us, I would never have had to endure Christmas' with families who tried not to treat me like an outsider, or the embarrassment of having no one to attend a parent's evening at school, or hide when family photos were taken because I didn't look like everyone else. The only way I'd got through all of that was by building a hard shell around myself, and creating the boy who didn't care. But, with him standing in front of me again, for only the second time in my life, I had a strange sensation overwhelm me, as if my heart and lungs were arguing with each other, trying to decide which one hurt the most.

He was my dad, the man who'd biologically given me life, yet I'd never had any feelings for him. Now, though, I had a nervous sweat trickling down my temples and pricking at the back of my neck. As if he mattered, and it was unsettling.

"What do you want?" I asked, pushing my hands into my jeans' pockets. If I feigned indifference, maybe I'd feel it. Maybe I'd *feel* detached from my gene pool.

He turned from looking at the photographs and studied me, like he didn't understand the question. Like I was stupid for asking such a thing. Well, Mrs P had taught me never let anyone make me inadequate.

"I told you," I stated, keeping my voice as even as I could, "I didn't want to see you again. I asked you to leave my bar and not come back, so tell me, what the hell are you doing here? Why did the message not get through?"

"William—"

"For fuck's sake, if you knew me at all, you'd know it's Will. No one ever calls me William, except my mum, and she's fucking dead."

He jaw tightened, a gesture I recognised because I did the same when I was frustrated. Well, he could be as frustrated as he liked. There was no way I was going to make things easy for him. It wasn't like he didn't know that I existed. It was his choice to wait thirty-seven years to come and find me.

"So?"

His stance copied mine, with his hands deep inside the pockets of his grey tailored trousers, which he wore with a maroon jumper. I made a mental note to ask Maddy to shoot me if I ever started to dress like that.

"I want to get to know you. Make up for lost time," he explained without, what sounded like, an ounce of regret.

"And you just decided that would be now? No reason other than it suddenly hit you that you have another son."

His left eye twitched, leaving me wondering if it was because of my revelation that I knew I had a brother.

"Yeah, I can do research as well." My tone was snarky because that was how I was feeling. Irritated to the point my skin itched. Him being in my home felt wrong, like he was an extra piece on chess board with no space for him. Like he didn't belong. "There's no reason that you need to be here," I continued, "I asked you to leave. I didn't ask you to come back a few days later and come to my home—a home, I should add, that I never gave you the address of."

He shrugged. "Like you said, research."

Irritation was turning to anger and frustration. "I'd like you to leave."

Moving his gaze from me to Maddy, he gave her a smile. I saw myself in him, and that infuriated me even more. I didn't want him looking at my daughter or even being in the same air space as her.

"Hey, love," he said to her. "Nice to meet you."

Maddy stiffened at my side, and because she'd been taught to have manners, she replied. "Hi. Pleased to... erm, hello."

"I'm your grandfather, Steven."

Bristling, I took a step closer to him, holding my hands up as if in surrender.

"You're not," I told him. "You just happen to be the man who provided the means for my mum to give birth to me. You're not my father, and you are not my daughter's grandfather. *You* are not important to me. Now if you'd like to leave."

"Please, Will."

Shaking my head, I moved towards the door and pulled it open wider. "If you'd leave now, I'd appreciate it."

"If I can just talk to you." His hands went to his hips, his stance far too aggressive for a man trying to make up for things. "If you'd just listen."

"No. I don't want to listen. I have nothing I want to say to you or hear from you." My voice broke, and instantly Maddy's hand slipped into mine, her small fingers holding on tight.

"There are things you need to know," he continued like he hadn't heard a fucking word I'd said.

"No, there aren't." My heart thudded against my ribcage as I stared at him, aware that I was probably wild eyed. "There is nothing at all that I need to know."

"Dad," Maddy whispered, sounding anxious.

Turning to her, I put a comforting hand on her shoulder. "It's okay, sweetheart. I'm okay."

She looked around me. "I think you should go. Dad made it clear he doesn't want to speak to you."

Steven didn't say anything, probably because he knew if he said anything to my daughter, I'd punch his fucking lights out.

"I asked to see you when you were five years old," he suddenly blurted. "But your mum said no."

You know when people talk about tumbleweed moments, well that was the first time I'd ever experienced a real one. The air thinned as we all watched each other, waiting for one of us to break the interminable silence. All you could hear was the gentle hum of the electricity buzzing around the house. My heart had jumped to my throat and the noise of its deep thrum started pounding in my ears.

"What?" I finally asked.

Steven swallowed. "I wanted to see you when you were about five, but your mum said no. She said that it would be too difficult for you to understand." He dropped his gaze to the floor and shook his head. "I think she was worried that I'd take you from her."

"I don't believe you," I whispered, barely able to hear the words myself.

"Dad, are you okay?" Maddy's arm went around my waist, and she lifted mine to go around her shoulder.

"I'm fine, sweetheart." My lips went to her hair, and I breathed her in, using her as my support to stop me from falling to my knees. "I'm okay."

"I'm sorry, Will. I really am. I didn't want to have to tell you, especially as…"

His gaze finally showed me an emotion. It was pain. He truly felt sorry for the life I'd led. There wasn't just pain in his eyes, but truth, too.

"I argued with her until I was blue in the face," he continued. "But she said it wouldn't be fair on you, especially if I disappeared out of your life again." He inhaled slowly and then just as slowly let it out. "And she was right. I'd left my wife and son twice at that point. Had an affair with another woman and was barely holding down my business. She made the right choice, Will. You were her priority, and she made entirely the right choice."

Somehow that didn't make it any better. It didn't make the years of loneliness, sadness and insecurity go away. Only one person had done that, and she was currently hugging me tight. It wasn't the words of a man who should never have waited for five years to decide to be my dad, and then another thirty-two to try again.

"How many times did you ask her?" Nausea enveloped me. I already knew the answer.

"Well, erm, the one time. Like I said, I argued with her, but she was adamant." He shrugged his shoulders like he didn't understand the question.

Pinching the bridge of my nose, I wondered if I should let the past go. Was holding onto it stopping me from moving on properly? Had I pushed relationships to one side just because my childhood was clogging up the cracks that would let the light in. What if I could have been settled a long time ago? But then I wouldn't have met Maya, and life without her was incomprehensible.

"I commend you for your one attempt at being in my life, well two if you count this time, but it changes nothing." My tone was steady. I was determined not to show how much his admission had affected me. "I have nothing to say to you."

Finally, his shoulders dropped in defeat, and he nodded. "Okay, I can't say I understand, but I accept your decision..." Relief flooded me until he said, "For now. But I did try, and I've regretted leaving you behind all of your life."

"Good to know." I stood to one side, letting him walk past me, trying to ignore the pull of wanting to grab his arm. It wasn't a real reaction it was just a by-product of my empty days of childhood.

"I'll be back, William," he said as he reached the front door, using my full name his final act of defiance.

As the door closed behind him, I exhaled like a week old balloon, sagging at my knees. Maddy was there, though, holding me up.

"Are you okay, Dad?" she asked softly.

"I think so." Resting my cheek on the top of her head, I watched through the glass panel of the front door. We stayed there until way after the red rear lights of the car disappeared out of sight. "I don't know what to do," I finally whispered.

Maddy gave me a squeeze and said quietly. "You'll do the right thing, Dad, but in the meantime call Maya. She'll help you."

"Why not you?" I questioned, curious.

She blew out a breath and said, "Because what I want isn't important."

As I wrapped my arms tighter around her, I knew I'd done a good job. With or without a father to guide me, I'd created a bloody amazing child.

CHAPTER 41
Maddy

"She's not going to tell us anything, you know," Emma grumbled as we walked towards Ana's house. "She's just going to tell us to fuck off."

"Maybe, but Dad said we need to talk to her."

"And he said she was doing the *food* shopping?"

"Yes, Emma," I replied, exasperated that she'd asked me the same question about a million and ten times. Shaking my head in frustration, I glanced over my shoulder at her. "Can you go any slower?"

"Yes, sure if you want me to."

She would as well, if I let her. "Come on, hurry up, we need to talk to her before her mum and dad get home."

Ana's parents ran a martial arts school but always took Saturday afternoon's off. It was the only time they were off together and so we had a window of about an hour to talk to Ana. All because Emma took ages to decide what to wear to talk to our friend about her recent hammered state at school.

A few minutes later, we approached Ana's house, and we both pulled up and stared.

"What the hell!"

Emma looked at me and then back to the bags of rubbish and overflowing bins in front of the garage, along with a black bin liner overflowing with wet clothes.

"That's not like her dad to let it get like this," I replied, frowning. "He's really particular about the appearance of the house."

"Do you think they've given Ana and Theo jobs to do and they're not doing them?" Her gaze whipped to mine. "Maybe that was why she was doing the shopping. Perhaps the garden is Theo's job."

I shrugged. "I have no clue." I took her hand in mine. "Come on let's go."

She pulled me to a stop. "Do you think Theo is home?" Whipping her lip gloss out of her jeans' pocket, she slicked it on.

Ana's older brother, Theo, was twenty and still lived at home after dropping out of uni after just a year. He was also extremely pretty. A much softer version of Ana, but taller and with muscles.

"He's probably at his girlfriend's house," I said. "Whichever one he's seeing at the moment."

"I don't believe everything that Ana says about his sex life."

She didn't want to believe her. We'd all had a crush on Theo, right from the age of eleven when he grew five inches just after his fourteenth birthday. Emma, however, had always taken it a step further believing she was in with a chance. She wasn't.

Once she felt she was 'Theo ready' we continued on up the drive to the front door. Before we could talk ourselves out of it, I rang the doorbell. It took a few minutes, but eventually the door was pulled open by Ana.

I held back my gasp, but Emma didn't. Ana looked terrible. Her bobbed hair was scraped back in a short stubby ponytail, her clothes were grubby, and there were dark grey circles under her eyes.

"What are you doing here?" she snapped, stepping out of the house and pulling the door closed behind her. "Why didn't you tell me?"

If I didn't think before something was wrong, I did then, seeing my friend who was part angry, part scared that we, her best friends, had shown up at her house. That hurt my heart because Ana and I had always been the best of friends. I loved Liv and Emma, but Ana was my person.

"What's going on?" Emma was right in there. "Why do you look like that? Why were you pissed at school?"

Ana's eyes widened. "Bloody hell, Emma," she said, glancing behind her, "shout it why don't you? My mum will hear you."

"Your mum is home?" I questioned. "Why isn't she at work?"

"She just isn't, okay. Now just go." Ana's eyes were suddenly wild, darting between Emma and me, then down towards the end of the drive. "You should have called me."

There was something serious going on, and it was obvious that Ana wasn't coping with it. Her appearance, the state of the garden and the drive, her being drunk and her mum not being at work—it all added up to something that we, as her friends we, shouldn't ignore.

I thought about what Dad had said, that we should help her with whatever it was troubling her. I knew that she probably would never speak to me again, but I wasn't prepared to let her fall deeper into the pit of hell that she was clearly in.

Without giving her any warning, I pushed past her, shoved the door open and strode inside.

"Maddy, no!" Ana yelled—screamed, in fact—making a grab for my arm.

"Ana, we just want to help you," Emma said behind me, her voice strained like she was struggling with something.

The door to the lounge was immediately off the small hallway, so I opened it, going in search of Susan, Ana's mum. Straight away, it was obvious what part of the issue was, because she was lying on the sofa, passed out with a bottle of vodka clutched to her chest. The room was a mess, it stunk of bleach, though—I assumed from cleaning up puke, since it was the same odour as Emma's house after we'd taken care of Ana. The curtains at the patio doors to the garden were closed, so the dining room end of the room was in a half-light. There was piles of clothes on the dining table, and the vacuum was standing next to it, the cord plugged in.

I swung around to Ana who was standing with her face in her hands, Emma's arm around her shoulder.

"Ana, what the hell has happened?" I moved quickly and pulled them both into a group hug, wanting to cry as I heard my friend's muffled sobs. "It's okay, we're here to help you."

"You shouldn't have come. You weren't supposed to find out."

Pulling away from her, I cupped her head and forced her to look at me. "What's going on?"

Behind us, Susan stirred, and Ana held her breath, only letting it go once her mum settled again.

"How long has she been like this?" Emma asked.

Ana drew in a shaky breath, swiping at tears on her cheeks. "Since Dad left."

Emma and I both gasped, exchanging a shocked glance.

"Mike's gone?" I looked at Susan who was still passed out. "When?"

"About three weeks. He left us for some fucking slag who he met at a competition." The hate in her tone for her dad felt like it scored my chest; it was so sharp. "And she started drinking and hasn't stopped since."

"Where's Theo?" Emma asked, worry thickly lacing her voice. "Why isn't he taking care of you both?"

"He's got a job in Milton Keynes. He doesn't know how bad it is." Ana's eyes swam with tears as she looked at the family picture on the mantlepiece. "He knows Dad has gone and that Mum isn't coping, but he—"

"He doesn't know you're not coping either," I said over her, feeling a mixture of pure anger and sadness for my best friend. "You have to tell him, Ana."

"I can't. He's just started his job; it's taken him ages to find one he likes." Her shoulders shuddered, and it struck me how thin she'd become.

"How did we miss all of this?" I asked Emma.

She shook her head and looked as guilty as I felt. "I don't know."

"I just thought getting drunk like her might help," Ana offered. "That day at school. I thought if she was getting pissed all the time, then maybe it made things easier."

"Did it?" I asked, knowing the answer.

She shook her head and let out another quiet sob. I hugged her again, wondering again how we hadn't seen that she was suffering, why we'd thought she was just being moody.

"You should have told us," I whispered against her hair. "We're your friends. We would have helped you."

"I couldn't. I felt ashamed."

"Why?" Emma exclaimed. "You've got nothing to feel ashamed about. There's only one person who needs to feel like that."

I thought that both her parents should feel like that. Her dad might have left, but Susan should have been there for her daughter, not expecting Ana to be the one to keep everything together.

"How has the place got like this in three weeks?" Emma moved away from us and picked up an empty wine bottle.

"It hasn't. She's been working so much she hasn't done any cleaning for ages, and it was gradually getting worse. At first I didn't do anything," Ana informed us. "I didn't think it was up to me, so I just kept my room tidy and did my own washing. Since Dad left, though, she's given up totally, and I've been trying to take care of her and the house."

"Which is why Dad saw you in the supermarket?"

Ana nodded solemnly. "Yeah, we've had no proper food for weeks, even before it all kicked off. That was what they started arguing about. Dad was a typical twatty man expecting Mum to work full time and keep the house tidy and the fridge full."

It made me realise how good my Dad was. He expected me to do chores and help around the house, but he had everything under control as well as running the bar. I knew there were only the two of us, but even so, I couldn't imagine him expecting his wife to work and look after the house.

"But he's met someone else?" Emma asked.

Ana's expression turned angry. "Yeah. Slag. And he's a bastard."

Emma and I exchanged a worried glance as our friend's hands fisted at her side.

"Okay," I said with a resigned sigh. "What about food? Did you manage to get everything you needed from the supermarket?"

She nodded. "Dad at least remembered to transfer my allowance into my bank account, so I used it to buy food." She gave her mum an accusatory glare. "She's too fucking out of it to know where she's put her bank card for me to use that."

"Ana, you need to tell your dad," I replied. "He needs to know exactly what state she's in—what you're having to deal with."

She shook her head. "No. I don't want him to know. *She* wouldn't want him to know."

"But you need help," I stressed.

"I just need a couple of weeks off school, so I can get on top of everything. Then, when I have, I'll call him and ask him to come back. If the house is clean, the fridge full, and she's sober, then maybe he will."

My heart sank, because by the look of her mum I wondered if she was too far gone to get better without professional help. Then I remembered something.

"She messaged me the other day," I told her. "Asking if you'd been to school. It didn't seem like she was drunk."

"Some days she's worse than others." Ana shrugged. "She thought I was sneaking off to see Dad instead of going to school. We had a huge row about it, and she downed a bottle of wine."

Emma thrust her hands to her hips. "Okay let's get to work."

"Doing what?" Ana asked petulantly, like she'd tried everything that she could beforehand.

"Cleaning up for starters." Emma raised an eyebrow, daring her to argue. "Maybe you could get your mum in the shower, and then we'll make her some food and coffee."

I admired Emma's determination, but I couldn't help thinking that all of it was too much for us—too big a situation for three teenagers to resolve.

"Ana," I said tentatively, "if you won't call your dad or Theo, can I please get my dad to help?"

She shook her head vigorously, giving me her back as she walked away. "No. Not happening."

"Please, Ana," I begged.

When Susan stirred again on the sofa, all three of our gazes whipped in her direction. She opened one eye and licked her lips, clearly unsure of her surroundings despite being in her own home.

"Mike?"

Ana groaned and stepped back in her mum's eyeline. "He's not here. He left, remember."

Letting out a pained groan, Susan rolled onto her side to go back to sleep.

"Ana, let me call my dad." I grabbed her hand. "He knows how to deal with this sort of thing."

"Drunks, you mean." Ana, reached for the empty drink bottle and snatched it from her mum's arms.

The atmosphere became super awkward as Ana refused to give me eye contact. I wasn't letting it go easily, though. A responsible adult needed to know what was happening and if she didn't want her own dad to know then mine would.

"I mean it, Ana. You can't be dealing with all of this. Your mum is clearly not coping, you won't tell your dad or Theo and you have A-levels to think about." Her fingers curled around mine, and I felt like maybe I was getting through. "So, please let me call him."

When she opened her mouth, I had a feeling she was going to say no again. Instead, she slammed her lips shut and gave me a sharp nod.

Breathing a sigh of relief, I pulled my phone out and called his number. It only took a couple of rings and instantly he asked, "Hey, sweetheart, what do you need?"

He asked because I rarely called him when he was working, unless it was an emergency. And each and every time I asked, he said yes.

"Dad, I'm with Ana."

"Okay..."

"We need your help."

"Right, give me half an hour to sort some cover out to help Marcus, and I'll be with you."

And that was my incredible Dad. Always there when I needed him.

CHAPTER 42
Will

Susan hugged the mug of coffee to her chest as she sat opposite me at the breakfast bar in their huge kitchen. It smelled of lemon after Maddy had mopped the floor and cleaned all the work surfaces. There were two black bin bags at the back door waiting to be taken out, one of which included numerous empty booze bottles.

"You have to get it together, Susan," I said, turning my attention back to her. "Ana needs you to be her support."

"I know." Her gaze dropped to the marble work top. "It's just been so difficult. We've been drifting apart for years, but him leaving me for someone else was just… difficult."

"A blow to your confidence?" I asked.

"Definitely." She gave me a small smile, the first in the couple of hours I'd been there. "She's a little younger as well, so…" She shrugged. "I thought he only cared about the business, but it seems I was wrong. Knowing that it was just me he didn't care about sent me over the edge, and it only went away when I got drunk." Her shoulders went back. "But I know that isn't going to help for long, and I'm finished with it before it gets to be a real problem."

Her bottom lip trembled, and I felt for her. The situation must have been hard, but she was the adult. "I hope so, because she's just a kid, Susan, and she's supposed to be enjoying the best time of her life. Apart from the fact she's got exams to study for."

"How did you do it, Will?" she asked, putting her mug down and looking at me with sad eyes. "Bring Maddy up on your own all these years. How do you be both Mum and Dad?"

"I never knew any different, and you're not on your own. Mike left you, but he didn't give up responsibility for his kids. Besides which, Theo has left home, and Ana will be going to uni soon. So, until then, it's up to you to hold it together. Now," I said, tapping the top of her hand, "call Mike and tell him you need to sort out money, the business and whatever is best for Ana."

She gave me a nod and when she pulled her phone from her hoody pocket, I stood up and left her to it and went to join the girls in the lounge.

Looking around, I felt proud of them and the work they'd put in to getting it tidied. When I'd arrived, Maddy and Emma were trying to persuade Susan to get a shower while Ana looked on scowling. Taking charge, I told the girls to start cleaning while I spoke to Susan, and I gave it to her straight. Told her that if she didn't pull herself together, then she'd lose her kids as well as her husband. They were too old to be taken into care, but it didn't mean they wouldn't cut her out of their lives if she carried on drinking.

As I watched the girls finish up, Ana approached me, her feet dragging, and her shoulders rounded.

"Thank you so much, Mr Newman," she said in a quiet voice, pulling the arms of her jumper down over her hands. "I don't know what you said to her, but at least she's showered and dressed."

I placed a hand on her shoulder, hoping it gave her some comfort. The poor kid didn't know what had hit her recently. She was finding it hard enough with her dad leaving, then her mum checked out on life. I knew what it was like to have no one, and I hated the idea of that for her.

"I think she just needed to be reminded of the fact that life needs to carry on." She gave me a watery smile. "She might take a few steps back at times, but she's made a start. And *you* don't forget to call, Theo."

Frowning, she nodded. "If I must."

"Yes, you do," I chastised her gently. "He needs to know what you're dealing with and take some of the strain. This might not be a magical recovery, you know."

Her shoulders dropped in defeat. "Okay. I'll call him later." She looked over her shoulder, at Maddy and Emma, who were giggling about something as they flicked dusters at each other. "I'm still mad at her for calling you, but she was right—we needed help."

"Well, it should never have got to this, Ana, so, if there's any hint of it happening again, you tell Mads, okay?" I peered into her eyes. "Promise me."

With a single nod, she said, "Yeah."

She didn't sound very convincing, but I'd have to take her at her word. "Right," I said, "we'll go and let you have some peace. Pizza is on its way for you and your mum."

Her eyes went wide with surprise. "You didn't have to do that."

"I did, love, I saw what you had in your trolley at the supermarket. Pasta is boring without anything to put with it."

We both grinned, and then she flung her arms around me and gave me a tight squeeze with a whispered, "Thank you." As she moved away, her mum shuffled into the room with her arms wrapped around her body.

"Okay?" I asked.

She nodded and came over to us, placing an arm around Ana's shoulder. "Your dad is coming over tomorrow, and we're going to sort a few things out."

The optimism in Ana's eyes was brighter than the lamp shining next to the TV, but I had a feeling it was about to be dimmed. Susan had clearly been crying and they were threatening again. She must have noticed her daughter's excitement because she pulled her closer and said, "He's not coming home, love. We're just going to talk about a few things, like the house and you and Theo, because you might both be grown up, but you're still our kids. He also wants to spend some time with you."

"I might not want to spend time with him," Ana said sulkily.

"Ana," Susan sighed. "This wasn't all down to your dad."

"He was the one who—"

"Enough." Susan stopped her. "You're not privy to everything that went on with me and Dad, so just give him a chance."

"And what about *her*?" Ana spat out. "Is she coming with him?"

Susan swallowed and shook her head. "No. Just your dad."

That seemed to satisfy Ana because she visibly relaxed, even giving her mum a small smile.

"Okay, girls," I announced, clapping my hands together once, "let's go and leave Susan and Ana to it."

As I bundled the girls into my Range Rover, I hoped that they'd be okay, aware that it would take much more than pizza and a quick clean of the house to sort them out. At least it was a start.

"Fancy something to eat girls?" I asked as I drove away from the house. "We've got burger night on at the bar tonight."

As I glanced over at Maddy, she looked hesitant, and my heart sank. It was starting to happen. The day I'd dreaded since she was a tiny baby. The time when there was someone else she'd rather spend her time with. The idea of it was more painful than I'd ever imagined, and that look on her face was just the very start of it, and it had only been for a second. Soon, it would get the point that she couldn't even hide it from me. She would look at me with disdain and surprise that I would even think for one minute that she'd want to spend time with me. Then it would come to the point where I'd have to beg her to come home and visit me and... shit, I needed to sort my head out, I was going to drive myself crazy.

"Could I ask Zak to come, Dad?" she asked. "Only we were supposed to be going to Maccies for tea."

I gripped the gear stick, my fingers clenching around it, knowing that I needed to be the grown up. "You go off to Maccies if you want, sweetheart."

"No way," she gasped, "I want to come with you. Plus, I've heard that Robbie's burgers are amazing."

"Yeah," Emma added from the back seat. "My mum said it was the best burger she's ever had on the last burger night you had."

The relief that seeped through me was ridiculous. It didn't matter that it was my burgers she was interested in as well; it was those words, 'I want to come with you'. They'd made me feel happier than I thought possible, happier than was necessary. She wasn't going anywhere, she was my little girl, and she loved me, but life was moving on. This was what I'd wanted for her, to spread her wings and be independent, so I had to accept that her need for me would lessen with time.

"What about Liam?" I asked, cocking an eyebrow at Emma in the mirror. "Do you want to ask him as well?"

She leaned forward and poked Maddy in the shoulder. "You told him."

Maddy and I both burst out laughing, and once again my chest filled with joy. Maddy was still confiding in me and that was a win.

"I know everything," I told her. "So, do you want him to come?"

"Is that okay?" she asked, her irritation quickly forgotten.

"Yes, it's fine." I sighed, like I was agreeing under sufferance, when really I loved the idea.

"You're still going to sit with us, though, aren't you, Dad?" Maddy said while tapping at her phone screen.

There was that pinch in my chest again.

"Sure, if you don't mind me cramping your style." Hiding my grin was hard, but I managed to keep it to a small smile.

Emma giggled and when she did Maddy shushed her. "Don't even say it. His head is big enough as it is."

"What?" I asked.

"You know exactly what she's *not* saying," my daughter grumbled. "All the bloody women in this town fancy you. As if you could cramp our style."

Chuckling, I continued the drive to the bar with only had one wish—that

Maya was there, too.

CHAPTER 43
Maddy

"So, how did you leave things with her?" Zak asked, playing with my fingers across the table.

"Dad ordered them pizza, but I reckon she's still mad at me."

"You did the right thing," Emma offered, leaning into my side. "She couldn't have carried on like that."

"Em's right, babe. You did exactly the right thing." Zak leaned across the table and pecked me on the lips. "You're a good friend."

When I sighed heavily, Liam rolled his eyes. "Seriously, if she's got a mood on about it, just leave her to it. Did you order chips as well, Em?"

Emma groaned. "Yes, I did and yes you can have them."

As I watched them making eyes at each other across the table, I couldn't help but giggle. Since their little session at Emma's house, they seemed to have gone back to being flirtatious friends. That seemed stupid to me. It was clear that they liked each other, *and* he'd had his hands in her knickers, so why waste time? I knew I didn't want to waste any with Zak. Who knew how far apart we'd be in a year's time. Or even if we'd be together.

"Is your dad eating with us?" Zak asked, glancing over at the bar where Dad was talking to Sam, Liam's dad, who'd brought the boys to the bar.

"He said he was." I frowned and followed Zak's gaze, concerned that Dad would think he wasn't welcome.

"You know we haven't got any parties lined up for the next month." Emma said, drawing my attention.

"I wanted to talk to you about that," Zak said, bouncing in his seat. "We've had an invite to a party on the sixth."

"Who do you know that we don't," Liam asked with a laugh.

Zak rolled his eyes. "A few people." He grinned. "I do speak to more people than you lot."

"And where is this party?"

"London, Liam, good old London." He looked at each of us in turn, his gaze stopping on me. "Did you ask your dad?"

"I did and he said he'd think about it, but I forgot to remind him." I felt awful because I knew that he was excited about going. "It's just everything going on with Ana…"

"It's fine, honestly. Can you ask him tonight?" he asked eagerly.

"I'll definitely ask him tonight," I promised. "I'm sure he'll say it's fine."

"If he knows Zak is taking care of you, he'll say yes," Liam winked.

My cheeks flamed, and I felt Zak's knee nudge mine under the table, when I looked at him, he was grinning. Like we had a secret. I mean we kind of did because we'd sneaked out of school at lunch the day before and gone back to his house. His empty house. For sex. Thankfully our first period in the afternoon was a study one and no one noticed us sneaking in half an hour late. Thinking about it and watching him, just made me want him there and then. I might have been new to sex, but having a taste with Zak, had made me insatiable. Who wouldn't be with a boyfriend like him, though. There were a whole host of feelings that I had about him whirring around my body. Some were new, like how my heart felt like it might burst at times and my constant need to be near him, those I could cope with. Those I enjoyed. The incessant desire to have sex with him, though, was distracting. Hence why we'd sneaked home for 'lunch', and why at that very moment, I was considering how much time we might have.

I glanced over at Dad who was laughing loudly at something with Sam. The burgers had only been on order for about ten minutes, so maybe we had a little time.

I pushed up from my chair and grabbed Zak's hand. "Did you say you wanted a smoke? I'll come with you."

"No, I—"

"Yes, Zak." I widened my eyes and stared at him, trying to tell him telepathically what I wanted—needed.

Suddenly he understand. "Fuck. Yeah, yeah, I need a cigarette. Be back soon."

Emma grinned, but Liam just picked at a scab on his elbow as Zak's hand curled around mine and he pulled me past the bar.

"Zak's just going out for a smoke," I yelled towards Dad as he watched us.

"Don't be long. Burgers will be ten minutes." He narrowed his eyes directly on Zak in warning.

"It's a quick smoke, Dad," I scoffed, hoping he heard, *'how much trouble can we get into in ten minutes, William?'* instead.

He didn't say anything else, but I felt his stare boring into the back of my head all the way to the door. Once we got outside, Zak wasted no time in dragging me around the corner to the entrance of an old storeroom where deliveries were made to the pet shop. Since Dad had opened the building up into one big space and added the kitchen on the back, the door had been blocked up, but the porch was still there.

Once we were inside, our hands were all over each other, grabbing at jackets and pushing up jumpers and t-shirts, our breaths fogging in the cold night air, not that I felt the cold, not one bit, not with Zak's hands heating my skin.

He pushed his hips forward, and I could feel his bulge in exactly the right place. The one that gave me some relief. I was desperate for more but couldn't risk Dad coming out and finding us. That didn't mean we couldn't get each other off in other ways, *quicker* ways. Moving my hand to the zip of his jeans, I yanked it down loving the groan that he gave. When I moved my hand inside his boxers, he whispered, "Fuck," in my ear, which only excited me even more.

As I took him in my hand, pumping slowly, it was Zak's turn to undo my jeans. As soon as he ran his fingers over my knickers, I felt the threads of an orgasm already knotting together into a long rope, wrapping itself around my body. The waves of pleasure started to build with each flick of Zak's finger, and when he pushed them inside me, I reached up onto my tiptoes, urging him for more. As I begged him with the thrust of my hips, I moved my hand quicker up and down his shaft as we both raced to finish. We were both aware of the jeopardy, but the addiction to the excitement overshadowed it.

"Shit, Mads," Zak said on a gasp as I did a corkscrew motion with my hand and then rubbed my thumb over the tip. Praise be for sexy romance books.

"Zak, I think I'm going to c—"

I didn't even have time to finish the word because I came without warning. Too engrossed in my own orgasm, I was barely concentrating on Zak, but when his hips moved, he regained my attention. Clearly I hadn't abandoned him for too long because, with his mouth at my ear, Zak came with just two more pumps.

"Oh shit," he moaned. "Maddy."

Burying my face against his chest, I started to giggle, high on the orgasm I'd just had. Not to mention the exhilaration at the risk we were taking. If my dad decided to come looking for us, he'd have no doubts about what we'd been doing. Zak's stomach was sticky with cum for a start.

"I don't have any tissue," I told him.

He shrugged and pulled his t-shirt down and used it to clean up.

"Zak!"

"You said you didn't have a tissue. I'll just tuck it in. No one will know."

"My dad has a strong sense of smell," I informed him, and Zak burst out laughing, wrapping me in his jacket and kissing the top of my head.

"We should go inside," I told him after a few blissful seconds. "The burgers will be ready soon."

"Yeah, I guess so." He breathed me in. "Just a couple more minutes."

It was warm inside his jacket, and I felt safe in his arms, and I could have stayed there for a lot longer than a couple of minutes. I didn't want my dad to find us, though, and besides I was hungry.

I patted Zak's bum. "Come on Studley McMuffin, let's go."

He chuckled. "Studley McMuffin. What sort of nickname is that?"

I shrugged. "It just came into my head. Don't you like it?"

"Love it." He then slapped my bum. "I'm starving, so yeah, let's go."

When we walked back into the bar, hand in hand. Dad winked at me. "Burgers are just coming out, sweetheart." He then raised an eyebrow at Zak. "And you should think about packing those cigarettes in. They're not good for you."

Zak nodded. "Noted, Mr N."

"Will," Dad deadpanned. "Now go and sit down, food will be there in five."

Smiling conspiratorially, and without discussion, we both went to the bathroom to clean up then, a few minutes later when the burgers arrived at the same time as Dad, my happiness doubled.

ZAK'S WHATSAPP MESSAGES

MADDY

Hey Studley. Spoke to Dad and he said London is fine, but he has to have the address. Oh, and I have to call him every couple of hours. And believe me he isn't joking xx

ZAK

That's great news. Still laughing at my new nickname but I kind of like it 😆. I'll send you the address and make sure you call him regularly. What are you doing now? xx

MADDY

Just got lost in the depths of TikTok. Started watching pimple poppers and now on stray dogs. What about you?

ZAK

Thinking about earlier!!!

MADDY

Yeah, those burgers were awesome 😏

ZAK

You know that's not what I'm talking about. I wish I'd been able to take you home and finish what we'd started. I really need to get my own car.

MADDY

Or your own house!!

ZAK

Imagine if we were both at uni together. We could have sex wherever we want, whenever we want.

MADDY

... (Maddy is typing)

MADDY

... (Maddy is typing)

ZAK

You still there, babe?

MADDY

Yes, still here. Just got a text from Emma. Yep that sounds amazing. I should get some sleep. Dad just came to bed.

ZAK

Okay. See you at school in the morning. I'll be the Studly McMuffin waiting by the gates xx

MADDY

Night night. See you in the morning Studly xx

ZAK

You still awake mate?

LIAM

Yeah, why? What have you done?

ZAK

How do you know I've done something? But I think I have!

LIAM

Tell me.

ZAK

I just mentioned to Mads about coming to Edinburgh. I think it freaked her out. Too forward? Too much? Too needy?

LIAM: 😂😂😂 😂😂😂

ZAK

Fuck! How do I take it back? Even though you know I'd love it if she came to Edinburgh with me

LIAM

Maybe don't mention it again, mate. Let her bring it up. If she doesn't go then you can always do the long distance thing.

ZAK

Yeah, I suppose so. Night mate. See you tomorrow.

LIAM

Yep later. Oh and I found us a party this weekend. Holly Smith is having a fancy dress party for her 18th.

ZAK

Excellent! Sounds good 👍

MAYA'S DIARY ENTRY

So excited I'm going to spend the weekend with Will!! Maddy is going to an 18th party so, as much as I love being around her, we'll have the house to ourselves. I bought new knickers and bra to celebrate.

CHAPTER 44
Will

As soon as Maya's car hit my driveway, I was at the front door yanking it open. The beautiful smile that she greeted me with was worth every part of the shitty day I'd had. There was never any trouble in my bar, yet earlier I'd had to stop a fight between two dickheads who couldn't take their booze. It had only been four in the afternoon, and they were supposed to be friends. Then to top it all off some prick had gone into the back of me at the traffic lights on the way home and tried to say it was because my brake lights weren't working. He had no case, as there was another car behind him with a dashcam that clearly showed my lights were working, and that the traffic lights were on red.

When I'd spoken to my insurance company they said he had no insurance, which meant that the police had to be involved. Thankfully, the number plate matched the car so at least they'd find him.

"Hey, handsome." Maya's arms went around my neck, and she leaned in to kiss me.

Instantly my rough edges were smoothed out, and I began to relax, forgetting everything except how good it felt to have her in my arms.

"Journey okay?" I asked when we finally pulled apart and I led her into the house.

"Yeah, the usual traffic on the M62, but once I'd got over the top it thinned out a bit." She gave me another quick peck on the lips. "Something smells good. What is it?"

"Curry. Maddy made it this afternoon when she got home from school?"

"She's a good girl." She dropped her bag. "Has she left for her party yet?"

I rolled my eyes. "No. She's up there with her friends, they should be down soon. I think Zak's picking them up."

"He's driving?" Maya asked, frowning.

"Driving there at least. I've already given her the talk about getting in a car with someone who's had a drink."

Maya laughed and patted my chest. "I'm sure he'll take care of her."

"Yeah, and don't I know it," I muttered.

"Will," Maya chastised.

"What?" I hissed, leading her into the lounge. "I was a teenage boy, Maya. I'm fully aware of what they'll be getting up to." I shuddered, wishing I had no awareness whatsoever

"And, as we've discussed before, Maddy will be careful." Red lips broke into a wry smile, and I immediately wanted to kiss her again.

"I actually want those girls to hurry up and go out." Looping my fingers in the belt loops of her jeans, I pulled her to me. "You're not in a hurry to eat are you?"

As I kissed her neck, Maya pressed her tits against my chest and moaned.

I'd totally discovered her hot spot a couple of weeks back. She had others, but they were more accessible with her clothes off.

"I can wait," she whispered. "When do the girls go out?"

"Soon." My hand went to her arse, and I cupped it, giving it a squeeze. "Although not soon enough."

Then, as if they'd read our minds, three pairs of feet could be heard thundering down the stairs. Maya and I pulled apart, but as the girls raced through the door, giggling, I moved her in front of me to avoid an embarrassment.

"What the hell are you wearing?" I asked as the three of them pulled to a halt. "And where's Liv?"

"Zombie schoolgirls," Maddy replied and beamed at Maya. "It's her mum's birthday. Hi Maya." Maya smiled back as Maddy continued talking. "And before you say anything about seeing my knickers, I have running shorts on underneath."

"Thank the lord for that." I looked between the three girls. They all wore the same school uniform, the skirt of which just about covered their backsides, and their socks were pulled up over their knees. As for their faces, they were made up in grey and white paint, to look like zombies, apparently. Maddy and Emma were grinning at me, but Ana was far from happy.

"You not loving the costume, Ana?" I asked. "Your face is kind of giving it away, love." Maya nudged me and I was reminded how bony her elbows were. "She looks miserable," I aimed at her.

"I wanted to go as ghost," Ana grumbled. "In fact, I didn't even want to go at all."

Maddy plastered on a smile and forced out a small laugh. "You can't just go in a sheet, Ana." Maddy's back stiffened, and it was clear that things between her and Ana hadn't improved. It was also clear that Ana was still suffering with her parents separation. It had only been a week since we'd talked, but I'd hoped something I'd said had sunk in.

Emma looked at her phone and broke out a grin. "The boys are here."

"Deep joy." Ana sighed heavily, her comment causing Maddy to flinch.

"Okay, girls," I said, clearing my throat. "Have a great time."

Emma skipped out with Ana following slowly behind, while Maddy came to kiss me on my cheek.

"Bye, Dad."

"Bye and be safe." I hugged her to me. "Is Ana okay, by the way?"

She shrugged alongside a frustrated sigh. "I don't know. I thought she was, but she's hardly said a word all day."

Maya ran a hand down Maddy's arm. "I'm sure she'll be fine."

Maddy nodded, already aware that I'd told Maya all about Ana and her parents. "Maybe. For some reason she's mad at *me* for calling Dad, yet *she* was the one who said it was okay. *And* she's been vile to everyone today, even the lovely lady in the Co-Op on the way home."

"Just keep an eye on her," I advised, kissing Maddy on the forehead, "but don't let her spoil your night. And make sure you don't drink too much, or that Zak doesn't drink and drive."

I got the eye roll. "I won't, I won't, and he won't. Okay?"

"*Okay.*" She then turned on her stupidly high heels and followed her friends. "Christ, teenagers."

"Teenagers, who," Maya said pausing as the front door banged shut, "have now left us alone."

She grinned and I grabbed her, continuing from where we'd been interrupted.

Craving her had become something that I'd gotten used to over the last weeks. Every single minute of every single day, all I wanted was her. It only intensified when I wasn't with her or hadn't seen her for a couple of days. With our work and the distance from our homes, a couple of days was the very least amount of time we were apart, generally it was five and I hated every single one of them.

With our hands tugging at each other's clothes, it was obvious Maya felt the same way. She couldn't get me naked fast enough, her fingers ripping at the buttons on my shirt.

"I've missed you so much," she rasped as she stepped out of her jeans and kicked them to one side. "Please can we just make this hard and quick, because," she said, reaching behind to unfasten her bar, "I'm desperate for you and some curry."

I paused momentarily to watch her, sure that my eyes were like that bloody heart-eyed emoji that Maddy sent me whenever I told her she could have something or do something. Basically, when she was creeping.

"I can go as fast and as hard as you like, gorgeous." Not able to wait any longer, I yanked off the rest of my clothes, racing with Maya to see who got naked first. It was a tie and we both moved at the same time, grabbing and smashing our mouths together.

My heart thundered as I grabbed her hair, pulling her head back to give me better access to her neck. Running my nose up the smooth length of her sweet smelling skin, my dick throbbed with need for her. My blood boiled with want, and when Maya cupped my balls with her long, delicate fingers, I thought I was going to explode.

Walking her backwards to the sofa, I put my hand between her legs and ran a finger through her wet pussy.

"Will." My name from her pouty lips sounded like a prayer. A plea. A pledge. It was everything or anything she wanted it to be because I would do anything for her. Give her whatever she wanted.

As she lay down, Maya's legs instantly parted, and she hooked one heel on the sofa and left the other on the floor. She was glistening with desire and her hips were moving to their own rhythm and I was desperate to join them. The ache in my dick urged me forward, and while I'd have loved to take my time and feast on her, I couldn't wait. Dropping to my knees between Maya's legs, I grabbed her hips, lifted her up, and then pushed inside of her. There was no sweet talk, or preamble, I thrust in quick and hard, only pausing to relish the feel of her wrapped around me. Grabbing her knee for purchase, I pushed in and out like my life depended on it. A sheen of sweat was already forming on my chest from the effort and exertion of making sure my woman was satisfied.

Maya mewled and reached behind her to grab the cushion that her head was resting on. Her tits lifted, her hard nipples enticing me to suck them. I leaned down and took one in my mouth and pulled on it, grazing it with my teeth.

"Yes," Maya gasped, turning her face into her bicep. "So good."

"*So,* fucking good," I echoed, keeping up my tempo, not missing a single beat. "And you're so damn sexy. Never met anyone…" I paused as feel the start of my orgasm pulled at my balls, before groaning, "Like you."

"Yes, that's it, just there. Yes, Will." She pushed against the arm of the sofa so that with each of my thrusts, her hips met mine, slamming into one another. Colliding in frenzy.

Watching her fall apart sent my heart into overdrive, she looked beautiful and free, her mouth dropping open into a gasp of elation. As her toes curled and her fingers gripped the cushion, I came with her, roaring out a curse of pleasure.

When I collapsed on top of Maya, her arms came around my back, and she hugged me tight, dropping a light kiss to my cheek.

"Amazing," she whispered. "Just what I needed."

Chuckling, I let my body sag, my bones feeling like jelly in the moment of peace in the aftermath of incredible sex.

"You hungry?" I eventually asked.

"*Yes*. Starving."

"Give me a minute and I'll get us some curry."

"Actually, any chance I could have a shower first?" Maya shifted her leg, and I remembered we'd stopped using condoms so she must be sticky.

"Mind if I join you?"

She gave a contented sigh and shook her head. "Not one bit. In fact, I'd love it."

CHAPTER 45
Maddy

Sweaty bodies swayed against each other on the makeshift dancefloor, while music blared, drowning out everything else. My legs felt like they could barely hold me up, so I was glad of Zak's strong hands at my hips, holding on tight.

We swayed to the rhythm, staring into each other's eyes, our lips inches apart, sexual tension whirling around us like a tornado, ready to rip up anything in its path. Anyone who dared to interrupt us was ignored, because all we could see was each other.

Admittedly, I was gradually starting to see two of Zak, but both were beautiful. "My legs are a bit wobbly," I told him and giggled. "Jelly legs."

Zak frowned. "How much have you had to drink?" He ran a hand down my cheek. "Do you want some water?"

I shook my head. "I'll be fine. I've had a couple of ciders, but they did taste a bit weird."

"Weird in what way?" He planted his hands on my shoulders, firmly, keeping me in place. "Do you think you've been spiked?"

I shook my head, the room immediately starting to spin. "Ana got them for me, and I never let them out of my sight. I didn't have much to eat for tea, maybe that's it."

He handed me his bottle of water. "Drink some of this, babe." He stooped down to look into my eyes. "Your pupils aren't dilated so I'm pretty sure you're right, you haven't been given anything. What did you eat at dinner?"

"I had a sandwich. I made Dad and Maya a curry but didn't fancy any of it. Plus, I didn't want to have garlic breath." I giggled, finding the idea funny for some reason. As I dropped my head back to laugh, I rocked unsteadily.

"Come on let's get you sitting down."

"No, honestly, I'm fine." I pulled my shoulders back and looked him in the eye. "Let's carry on dancing."

"Are you sure?" Zak frowned, but his body started moving with mine, and soon we were dancing again.

We carried on through various songs and gradually, with Zak regularly giving me swigs of his water, I started to feel a little better. To the point that I only felt slightly tipsy when Ana appeared with another can of cider.

"Got you this," she said, handing it to me.

"Are you sure you should?" Zak asked.

Ana blinked slowly at him and said, "Who are you trying to control?"

"No one, but she was feeling a bit dizzy before."

"I'm fine." I took the can from Ana and put it to my lips. "I've had loads of water."

When I took a drink, I resisted wincing and smiled instead, conscious that Zak was watching me carefully.

"Hey, Zak." Liam bounced up with Emma under his arm, wearing the same American Football kit as Zak. "The lads are having a darts tournament outside. Fancy it?"

Zak looked at me and when I smiled, he looked back at Liam. "Yeah, okay." He turned back to me and kissed me hard, his hand cupping the back of my head. "Won't be long, but if you want to go, come and find me."

Giving his bum a playful squeeze, I nodded. "Okay, will do."

As the boys walked off to play darts, Ana rolled her eyes, whereas Emma and I watched their arses in the tight, white, football trousers, until they disappeared out of the lounge.

"Have you been having sex upstairs with Liam?" she asked Emma. "Because you've been gone for ages."

I didn't miss the blush that coloured her cheeks, and I squealed. "Have you?"

"No," she snapped. "But we might have done other things."

"Fucking hell," Ana growled. "Why am I surrounded by you sad couples?"

I glanced at Emma, whose Zombie make up was, I now realised, smeared all over her face. She shrugged, and seemed as confused as I was. Ana's mood had been low when we left my house, but then she'd perked a little after an hour of being at the party, but after another half an hour, went back to being miserable and moaning that she didn't want to be there. That was when Zak and I went to dance, and Liam and Emma obviously disappeared for something else.

"Fancy a game of beer pong?" I asked, trying to think of anything to stop the negativity from becoming a full on rant.

"No." Ana response was short as she then whipped around. "More booze."

"I thought you were staying off it," Emma said, grabbing her hand.

Immediately Ana pulled her hand away and hissed over her shoulder. "You're not my parent, and if I want to drink I will."

As she pushed through the crowd, Emma and I heaved out a collective sigh and followed her, finding her in the kitchen cracking open a bottle of lager.

"I suppose we should stay with her," I said.

"Yeah. I suppose." Emma groaned and shook her head. "I just hope the boy's darts tournament doesn't take long, otherwise she's going to be shitfaced."

***

I couldn't stand up. My head was spinning, and I felt like I might puke. Zak was trying to force water down me, while Liam was trying to keep Emma on her feet.

"What have they been drinking?" I heard Zak ask.

"Cider," Ana replied.

"How come you're okay?" Liam grunted, and when I looked over, Emma had fallen forward from the fridge that he'd propped her against.

I didn't hear Ana's reply, mainly because Zak was talking to me and asking if I'd left my drink unattended at any point.

"Mads was fairly drunk earlier but she sobered up a bit," he said, presumably to Liam. "How can they get this shit faced in half an hour?"

"No idea, but if we take them home like this they're going to get a bollocking."

I managed to focus one eye on Zak and could see what looked like fear on his face.

"Dad will be fine." I waved them away. "Don't worry about William."

"Fucking hell," Zak muttered. "He's going to fucking kill me."

"Let's get them outside and take them for a walk, see if we can sober them up."

Ana started to laugh, too loudly, because it hurt my ears. "They can hardly stand, never mind walk."

"Ana, you're not helping," Zak snapped. "Although she's got a point."

Tiredness suddenly hit me, and I wanted nothing more than to sleep. I dropped my head against Zak's chest and closed my eyes. He held me to him as he continued talking to Liam, but I zoned out, concentrating on not being sick on his chest and trying to sleep at the same time. It was actually a comfy place to rest my head and I must have dropped off, because the next thing I knew, all I could hear was Ana and Zak yelling at each other.

"You stupid idiot, Ana. How could you do that?" He pulled me closer, wrapping his arm around my shoulders.

"You could have fucking killed them." That was Liam and he sounded just as angry as Zak. "Oh shit, she's going to be sick."

There was movement, and as I opened my eyes, I saw Liam guiding Emma's head over the kitchen sink. He held her hair back with one hand, while he rubbed her back with the other.

"What's wrong?" I asked, swaying as I tried to move towards Emma.

Zak kissed my forehead. "Ana spiked your damn drink with vodka. "Yours and Emma's."

"It was just a joke," Ana protested. "They were being boring, telling me how much I should and shouldn't be drinking."

"Not a very funny joke," Liam yelled and then turned back to Emma. "Come on, babe, get it all up."

Hearing him call Emma babe made me giggle.

"Aww he called her babe, Zak. Liam called Emma babe. He likes her."

Zak pushed my hair from my sweaty face, his thumbs lingering on my cheeks.. "Yeah he did. Do you think you need to be sick, too?"

I shook my head and instantly regretted it. "Oh, I think I might." He quickly pushed me towards the back door, but it was too late. Water flooded my mouth, quickly followed by the sandwich I'd had earlier and the gallons of booze I'd drunk. It projected all over my boyfriend's chest, hitting him smack bang in the middle, and then sliding down in big lumps and splatting on the floor.

"Oh, shit," I groaned. "I'm so sorry." I looked up at him, but his eyes were downcast, staring at the vomit covering him. His arms were still on my shoulders, though, making sure that I didn't topple over. "Zak, I'm so sorry."

Slowly, his gaze lifted to mine, and he gave me the softest of smiles. "It's okay."

Someone behind him yelled about the smell of puke, and then there was a roar of laughter, followed by someone screaming.

"What the hell." It was Holly whose party it was. "You dirty bitch. How could you?"

Zak whipped around. "Oi, you watch what you call her. It was an accident; she didn't do it on purpose."

"Of course she did. She—"

"I am so sorry, Holly. Get me some kitchen roll and I'll clean it up."

To my left, I heard Emma groaning as she continued to throw up into the sink. With each retch, Liam soothed her and told her to keep going.

"If anyone should clean it up, it should be you," Zak spat at Ana. "I can't believe you were so stupid."

"It's not my fault they can't take their drink."

I turned to look at her and felt another wave of nausea. Luckily, I was able to make it to the back door. It was a close call, but I got it open just in time before more vomit came up and splashed over the step leading down to the patio.

"You okay," Zak asked, rubbing my back.

"I'm so sorry," I sobbed. "I'm such a crap girlfriend."

He chuckled and pulled my hair over my shoulder. "No, you're not. You just have a shitty friend."

"I was here long before you, dick head," Ana yelled at him. "She's my friend and has been my friend since we were little. You've just come along with your nice teeth and your hot body and think you own her."

"Ana," I groaned, but said nothing else because another wave of vomit reared up.

"I don't think I own her, Ana," Zak retorted in a measured tone. "I care about her, and I certainly wouldn't spike her cider with vodka. That's stupid and dangerous."

"That's stupid and dangerous," she mimicked.

"Ana just shut the fuck up," Liam roared. "You're an absolute—"

"Liam, leave it mate," Zak butted in. "Let's get them home."

"I'll ring my dad," I said, in between spitting out bits of vomit.

"It's okay. I didn't drink."

"Your top." I pointed an unsteady finger at him.

Moving me towards the fridge, he propped me against it. "Ana, make sure she doesn't fall over," he ordered her. "I'm just going to take my shirt off."

I giggled. "Ooh naked chest."

Zak rolled his eyes and smirked. "I have a t-shirt underneath. It might not be too bad."

"There are carrier bags in that drawer," Holly said, "but who is going to clean it up off the floor? Because I'm not."

Ana sighed heavily. "I will. I'll get my mum to come and get me."

"I'll give you a lift," Zak said from over by the door. "I brought you, so I'll take you home."

"No, it's fine," she snapped, pressing a hand against my shoulder to keep me upright. "Mum will come."

"I'd rather not leave you." Zak appeared back in front of me, his eyes full of concern. "I'll help you clean up."

"I wouldn't," Liam offered. "I'd make her do it."

"Well, you're a prick," Ana replied, leaving me and pushing past Zak. "Where's your cleaning stuff, Holly?"

Leaning forward, I dropped my hands to my knees to steady myself and blew out a breath. "Can we go home, Zak?"

"Yeah, babe. Just let me sort my shirt out. You ready, Liam?"

"Yeah. I think she's more or less done." He leaned over the sink. "You finished, Em?"

"Hmm. My mum is going to kill me."

"You can stay at mine," I told her. "She thinks you are anyway."

"Your dad is going to kill me," Zak muttered as he came back, a plastic bag swinging at his side.

"No, he won't." I reached a hand out to him, and he took it, kissing the back of it. "I promise."

"We'll see, but we should go." He put his arm around my shoulders and guided me upright. "Okay?"

I nodded and made a couple of tentative steps, but then pulled to a stop. "I should take a carrier bag. Just in case."

Holly slapped one against my chest. "Here, and thanks again, *Maddy*."

"I told you, it wasn't her fault, so chill out, *Holly*." Zak threw a glare over to Ana who was on her knees wiping up vomit. Her head was turned away, and she was retching.

"We're ready," Liam said, Emma's hand in his. "Let's go."

"Okay, gorgeous," Zak said. "Let's get you home." He turned to Ana. "Are you sure about calling your mum?"

"I've already messaged her."

She held up her phone and Zak leaned closer to read the screen. Seemingly satisfied, he gave her a nod and then turned back to me.

"You ready?"

"Let's go," Liam replied and guided Emma out of the room.

As she heaved, I quickly passed her my carrier bag, hoping that I didn't need it on the way home.

CHAPTER 46
Will

Full of food and satisfied sexually, I couldn't remember when I'd felt so relaxed. Especially as Maya had agreed to watch *Wolf of Wall Street* with me. She was also enjoying it, which was a bonus. Although, I was pretty sure it had a lot to do with Leonardo DiCaprio.

"She's gorgeous, isn't she?" she said about Margot Robbie.

"Is there a wrong answer to that?" I asked with a smirk.

Maya flashed me a smile. "No wrong answer. I won't mind if you think she's the sexiest woman alive."

"Well, she isn't." As far as I was concerned, Maya was that. No question.

Maya's eyes twinkled, and she poked my arm with her toe. "You're such a smoothie."

I captured her foot with my hand and gave it a squeeze, trapping it on my lap. She was lounged out on the opposite end of the sofa, both of us having changed into pyjamas after a long shower together. A shower which had included more sex.

"What have we got planned for tomorrow?" Maya asked.

"I thought maybe a lie in to start with." I wiggled my eyebrows, making her giggle.

"Sounds good. Then what?"

"There's a really nice pub about two miles up the road. We could walk…" I saw her smile drop. "Or drive there for lunch."

She did a little dance with her feet, and I loved that she was so excited. I'd been worried that my life in a small town would be too boring for her, but she seemed genuinely enthusiastic about it.

"That sounds perfect. Then what? Can I meet Sam and Louise?"

"You want to?" She nodded. "We can do that. I'll message them and see if we can meet up tomorrow night. That okay?"

"Yes, I'd love that. Anyone else I can get to know?" She poked me with her toe again. "Any old girlfriends?"

"Definitely not." I grimaced at the idea of it. "There is no one else. Certainly not my father."

Maya frowned, folding her arms over her chest. "I can't believe he came here. It sounds like you were remarkably calm, though."

"Not really, but at least I didn't punch him."

It had been hard to keep my temper to just yelling at him.

"How *do* you feel?" Maya asked. "About him turning up. I know you told me you were angry, but there had to be some sadness there too."

Contemplating her words, I ran my hand slowly up and down her calf. She was right, there was, but it was much more than that.

"Every thought of injustice I didn't think I'd had, has come to the surface," I told her. "Every bloody job my mum had to slog at. Every foster home I lived in. Every birthday or Christmas I'd spent alone. All of it came back like one big ball of black bitterness." Rubbing at the bristles on my chin, I turned to see her green eyes surveying me. "I've always been a positive person. I had to play the cards I was dealt and made the best of them, never thinking about what could have been. Now, though," I sighed, "I can't help but keep wondering what did I miss? What if?"

Maya shuffled closer, moving to straddle me, instantly putting soothing hands against my cheeks. "That's all totally understandable, but don't let his appearance make you think that you've lived an inadequate life." She shook her head. "Because you haven't. Look at what you have—Maddy, the bar, this house. Do you really think having your dad in your life would have changed any of that?"

"No, maybe not." And I didn't think it would. It had been Miriam's generosity and my determination, to provide for Maddy that had given me everything. "Maybe him not being around is exactly why I have all this. Perhaps I'd have taken a different path, like a fucking car salesman."

Maya grinned. "I don't see it myself, but who knows. You in a suit and smelling of Lynx Africa might be sexy."

Laughter moved on to kissing, and the film was forgotten, until there was a banging on the front door. It wasn't just a knock it was a definite bang, and it was frantic.

"Who the hell is that?" Ushering Maya off my lap, I glanced at my watch. "It's half ten."

"Look through the window first, just in case," Maya urged, getting off the sofa and following me to the hallway.

I flicked on the main light, and through the frosted glass panels I saw a tall figure with a shorter one next to him. I knew instantly who it was and rushed for the door, yanking it open.

"What the fuck happened?" I asked, seeing Maddy lolling against Zak, who had his arm firmly around her shoulder, while his other hand lay against her stomach. Over his shoulder, I spotted Liam with Emma who was in a similar state to Maddy. "Get them inside."

"Bloody hell," Maya gasped behind me. "How much have they had to drink?"

As I led them down the hall towards the lounge, I could feel my blood getting hotter and my anger rising to boiling point.

"Get them both on the sofa for now," I snapped. "I'll get a couple of bowls."

"I'll get them," Maya offered. "Where are they."

"Under the sink, gorgeous. Ones got cleaning stuff in it, just tip it out."

Zak and Liam helped the girls to the sofa, who, luckily for the boys were still able to walk. If they hadn't been, it would have been a close call whether the boys would be, after I'd finished with them.

"I understand she's an adult and makes her own decisions," I said, turning on the boys and pointing an accusatory finger at them, "but I would expect you two to keep an eye on them."

"It's not their fault, Dad," Maddy groaned as she flopped back against the cushions, her hand gripping Emma's.

"So, what happened?" I asked again. "How did they get so wasted?"

"Ana," Zak said solemnly. "She spiked their cans of cider with vodka."

I blinked and then looked at Emma and Maddy, who both had their heads back and their eyes closed. "Ana, their friend?"

"She'd been doing it all night," Zak gritted out. "We had no idea. At one point, Maddy felt a bit drunk, so I got her to drink some water, and she sobered up. Then Liam and I went to play darts, for, how long, Liam?"

"Half an hour at most. Honestly, Will, they were fine and then we came back, and they were like this. Zak managed to get it out of Ana what she'd done."

"Is she fucking stupid?" I knelt down in front of Maddy and patted her knee. "Mads, sweetheart, are you okay."

"Feel sick, Dad. Want to sleep."

Sighing, I turned to her friend. "Emma?" I got nothing just a shake of her head.

It was then that Maya, appeared carrying two washing up bowls. "Are you putting them to bed or leaving them here?" she asked.

I stood up, grabbed the remote, and turned off the TV. "I think maybe we should leave them down here. At least they're sitting up." I took the bowls from Maya and thanked her. "Where's Ana now?" I asked, placing a bowl in each girl's lap.

"She stayed at the party," Zak informed me. "I tried to get her to come with us, to make sure she got home, but she got her mum to pick her up."

I rolled my eyes, hoping her bloody mother had stayed off the booze. "Was Ana drunk?"

Liam shrugged. "A bit, but obviously not as bad as these two."

"She was really drunk earlier, but Maddy told her to slow down." Zak moved towards Maddy as she made a groaning sound and took her hand in his. "You okay, babe?"

She gave him a strained smile and a little nod, and as much as I wanted to tell him to get his hands off her, I knew he was a good kid who cared about her.

"I take it they've already been sick?" I asked.

"Yeah, and on the way home in bags in Zak's car." Liam gave an empty laugh. "It was synchronised puking."

"I bet." I shook my head, knowing they were going to feel like shit the next day. "The zombie makeup didn't really survive, did it?"

"Poor kids," Maya said from my side. "Cider is crap at the best of times, but with vodka." She shivered.

"Liam, this is Maya, Maya this is Liam, Sam and Louise's eldest."

"Hi, Liam." She gave him one of her gorgeous smiles and then nodded at Emma. "You two are an item, are you?"

Liam hesitated, looking at me, and I grinned, holding up my hands.

"Hey, nothing will pass my lips to your mum and dad."

He looked back at Maya. "Yeah, we are."

Maddy giggled, held up a finger, and said, "I knew it." Then she slapped her hand back down and fell silent again. Zak chuckled and pushed some hair from her face which was sweaty and smeared with white and black makeup.

"I'll get them some water," Maya said.

Leaning over the girls, I pulled the woollen throw off the back of the sofa. "Liam, pass me the throw off that armchair." As I placed the one I had over Maddy, Zak picked up the bowl, putting it back down after tucking it around her. When I turned to Emma, Liam was sorting her out, with a damn stupid grin on his face. It seemed that he was a fucking smitten with Emma as Zak was with Maddy. Then, as Maya came back into the room with two pints of water, I knew I was in exactly the same boat.

She placed the glasses on the coffee table. "I wasn't sure where the painkillers were."

I cupped her face, once more thankful for meeting her. "I'll get them. Thanks."

"We are sorry, Mr Newman." I chose not to correct Zak on my name for once. I knew it wasn't really his fault, but it didn't hurt to let him feel a bit of my anger. "If I'd know what Ana was doing."

"If either of us had known," Liam added, "We'd have stopped her."

"I know," I said with a heavy sigh. "And I will be talking to her mum." I knew Ana was suffering, but what she'd done was stupid and dangerous. "You didn't drink and drive, did you Zak?"

"I would never do that," he told me with no uncertainty. "I was on water all night."

"Well, maybe you two should get off home," I suggested.

Zak looked at Maddy and then at Liam before opening his mouth to speak, but I beat him to it.

"You can come back tomorrow, but I think for now they need to sleep it off."

After a couple of beats, he nodded and turned to Liam. "I'll drop you off, mate." He then turned to me. "Could you make sure Ana's mum picked her up?"

"Yeah, sure. No problem." I scratched my nose, studying the boys and realising maybe I'd been a little hard on them. "Sorry, I yelled boys."

Zak shook his head. "Honestly, it's fine. I get it, and we should have probably kept a better eye on them."

"No, like I said, they're old enough to make their own decisions. Plus, Ana shouldn't have spiked them. I appreciate you bringing them back."

Zak pulled his car keys from the pocket of his jacket and gave Maddy one last look. He went to move away but then stepped back and kissed her cheek.

"See you tomorrow, babe." Maddy smiled softly and gave him a finger wave.

Liam leaned down to Emma and whispered, "Try and get some sleep." He brushed hair from her face and then kissed the tip of her nose.

Watching both boys gave me a little bit of peace. They were good lads, and Sam and Louise should definitely be proud of their boy, as should the Hoylands.

Once I'd seen them out and watched them pull away in Zak's mum's Mini, I wandered back into the lounge to find Maya turning the fire up.

"Okay?" I asked her.

She stood to her full height and moved over to me. "Yeah, I thought maybe if they're sleeping down here they might need a bit more warmth."

"Good idea." I peered at both girls who appeared to be sleeping. "They're both zonked. Let's hope they've got everything up already."

Maya's arm linked mine and feeling of her warm body leaning against my side filled my chest with something strange and warm. Something that I was feeling more and more each day.

"Fancy an early night?" I asked her. "Seeing as the pair of zombie drunks have taken our spot."

"Will they be okay? Should they be left on their own?"

"Believe me, they're fine. They're sitting up, they have a bowl each and they're warm." I kissed her forehead. "They're perfectly fine, but I'll check on them later. I promise."

"You sure?" Her brow screwed up in concern.

"I run a bar and have dealt with a lot of drunks in my time. Believe me they'll be okay."

"Are you going to ground her or anything?" she asked, looking at the girls.

"No. I'll give her the lecture, but she's seventeen. Who doesn't get legless and puke in a bowl when they're that age?"

"Very true." Maya laughed quietly and slapped my bum. "An early night sounds good."

Giving the girls one last check over, I left them a lamp on and then took Maya to bed, giving her one more orgasm before she fell asleep. After that I went back downstairs to find both girls still sleeping soundly.

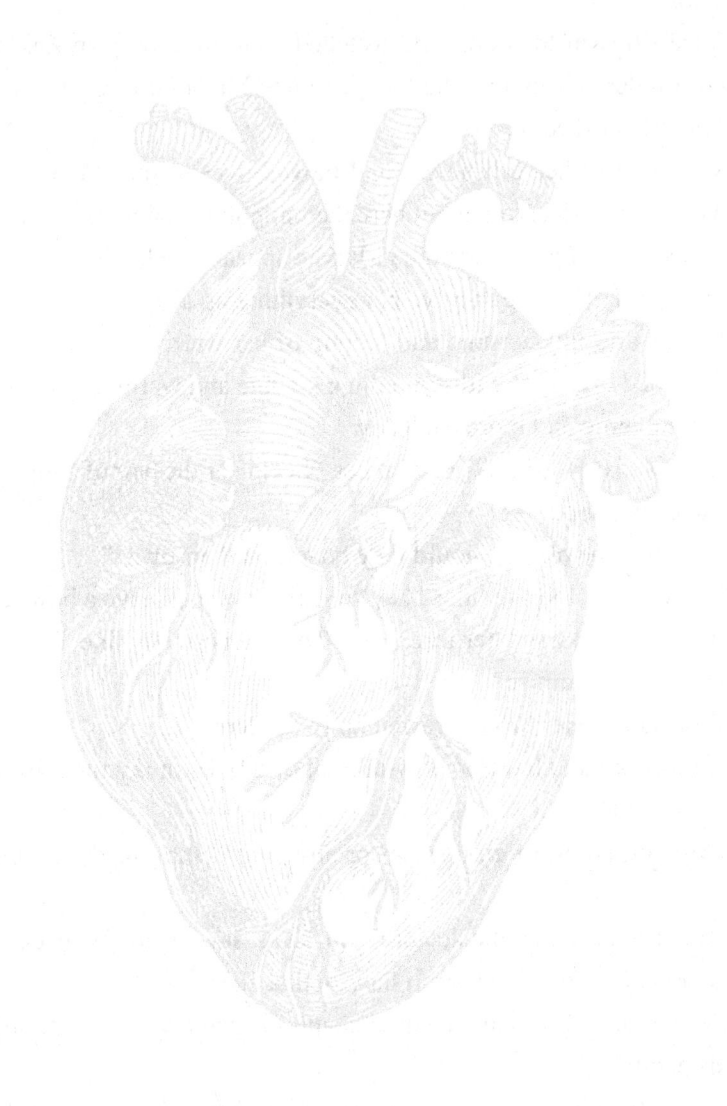

THINGS ARE GETTING SERIOUS

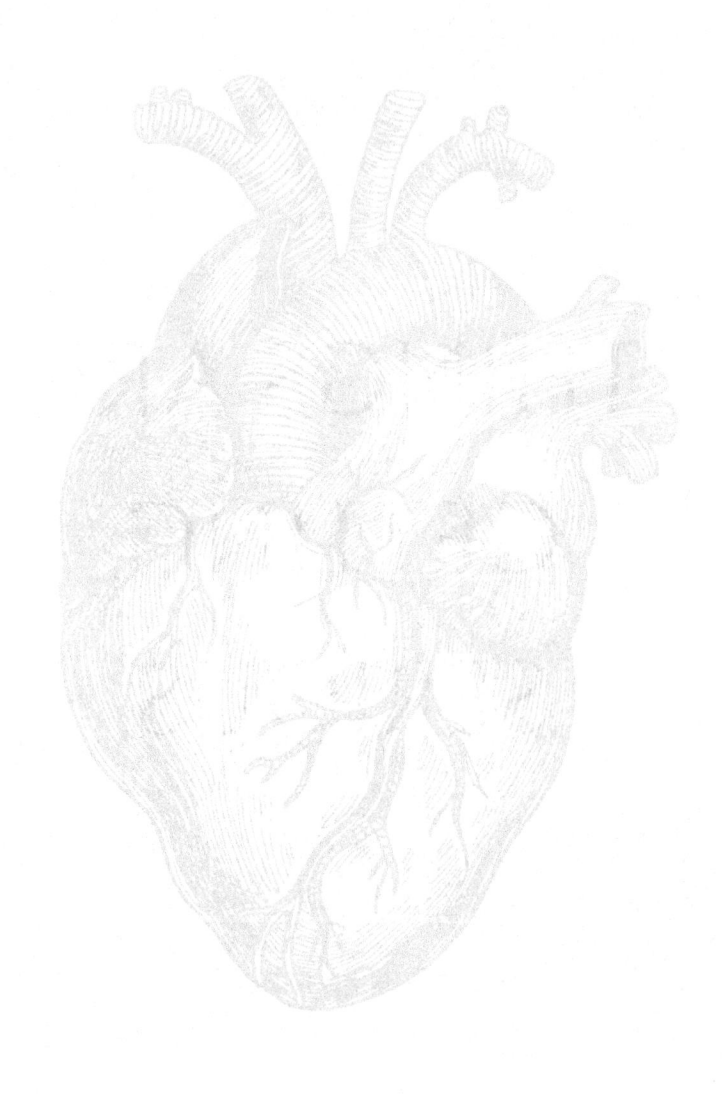

CHAPTER 47
Will

As I watched Maddy force dry toast into her mouth, I couldn't help but laugh. That earned me a nudge in the ribs from Maya.

"Don't laugh at her."

"Why not? It's funny."

Maddy's eyes lifted to mine as she placed a hand against her stomach. "Maya's right, it's not funny. I feel hideous."

"And it's not even her fault." Maya placed a glass of coke in front of Maddy. "Drink that sweetie, it'll help."

Maddy gave her a nod and a very small smile. "Thank you."

"Has Ana called you to apologise?" I asked, reaching for a piece of toast.

"Nope." Maddy picked up her glass with an unsteady hand. "I don't know whether I want to speak to her anyway."

"Yeah, well," I muttered, "I do. She was stupid and irresponsible and lucky that neither you nor Emma ended up in A&E. I hope she's going to tell her mum."

Maddy shrugged. "I don't know. I doubt it. We decided that we'll deal with it."

I shook my head. "Not happening. I will be talking to her and Emma's mum."

"Dad," Maddy groaned. "Please just let us sort it out."

I shook my head, turning my gaze to Maya as she'd placed her hand on my arm. She was chewing on her lip, clearly having something to say. "What?" I asked.

"Maybe let Maddy handle it how she feels—"

I didn't think anything would make me snap at Maya, but that comment instantly jarred on me. "Maya, if you don't mind, she's my daughter."

"Dad!"

Maya blinked and held her hands up in surrender. "Sorry, your dad is right. It's nothing to do with me."

I wasn't taking it back because I stood by it. Maddy was my daughter, and if I wanted to speak to Ana as well as Emma's mum then I would.

"Sorry, Maya. I didn't mean to snap, it's just—"

"Honestly, Will, It's fine. I shouldn't have said anything." She offered me a smile and then stood up. "I'll go and get a shower. What time are we going out?"

Asking about our lunch with Sam and Louise, seeing as they couldn't make it later, she sounded a little too bright. At least her smile looked genuine.

I took her fingers in mine. "An hour is that okay?".

She nodded but that time her smile was tight as she disappeared upstairs. As soon as we heard her footsteps up above us, Maddy turned on me.

"Why did you say that to her?" she hissed, glancing up at the ceiling. "Do you want to lose the best thing that's happened to you in years?"

"Don't be stupid." Was it stupid? What if I had hurt her? "Fuck!"

"Yes, Dad." She pointed upwards. "Go up there and apologise. Tell her you appreciate her input."

"But you *are* my daughter, Maddy. I *do* make the decisions and the rules."

"I know, but I can also make decisions because I'm seventeen. My decision is that I want to deal with Ana, and Emma doesn't want her mum to know. You know what Diane is like."

"Yeah, I bloody do, desperate to get me into bed." Emma's mum never failed to flirt with me and make comments about us having sex. She usually disguised it with innuendo, but I knew exactly what she was trying to say.

"Well, you won't want to have to speak to her then, will you?" She grimaced and rubbed her temples. "That's hurt my head."

"Good."

She narrowed her eyes on me. "Maya just understands what it's like for girls and their friends. We're not like boys, Dad. We don't like upsetting each other, even if we're mad at them. If you speak to her or her mum, or Emma's mum, it will change everything. There will be a huge argument, and things will never be the same again. At least if Emma and I argue with her, we'll do it in such a way that we can still be friends."

"I'm surprised you want to be after what she did." I was still furious with Ana, maybe not as angry as I had been, but I still thought she needed a good talking to. She was lucky I hadn't told her mum on the text I'd sent checking she'd got a lift home from the party. I'd listened to Maddy's request and was going to let her deal with it, so I'd given Susan some bull about Ana wanting to stay when the others were ready to leave. I didn't like lying to her, but I had to trust my daughter. Thinking about that text then made me realise that I should apologise to Maya.

Pushing my chair back, I stood up and leaning forward, kissed the top of Maddy's head. "I'm going upstairs to say sorry. Eat your toast and then get a shower, you stink. Plus, it will make you feel better."

"I don't think I'll ever feel better," she groaned.

"Do you want to come for lunch with us?" I asked as I deposited my dishes in the dishwasher.

"Ugh, no thanks. I think Zak is coming over later."

I stood to my full height and nodded. "Okay. If you feel better later, maybe we'll get takeaway tonight, or are you going out?"

She shook her head. "Nope. I may never go out again."

Chuckling, and deciding to see the lighter side of the situation, I scruffed her hair and then went upstairs to find out exactly how upset my girlfriend was.

When I opened the bedroom door, she was wearing a sexy set of coffee coloured underwear and rubbing cream into her legs, the ends of her hair wet against her shoulders.

"That was a quick shower," I said, moving further into the room, sensing the awkwardness in the air.

She glanced over her shoulder, but quickly put her attention back on her legs. Not sure I could blame her; they were well worth looking at. "You said an hour, so I thought I'd better make it quick."

There was tension in her voice, and I didn't like it. It unsettled me, made my stomach churn, something I'd never felt before over a woman. Alien though it was, I knew what I had to do to make things better.

"Maya, can we talk?"

She cleared her throat as her hand stalled on her thigh. "Yeah, sure." Putting her foot to the floor, she slowly turned to me. Her shoulders rose as she clutched the bottle of cream in front of her.

I had no idea why, but she looked ready to do battle. Like I was going to yell and scream at her, and she was going to yell and scream back. She chewed down on her bottom lip and watched me with a steely gaze.

"I'm sorry," I told her, taking a step forward and noticing the way she immediately straightened her spine and pulled her shoulders back. "I shouldn't have said what I did downstairs."

She shook her head. "I get it, but I only wanted to help."

As she inhaled slowly, her lips thinned, and I began to feel worried. Was she going to dump me? The idea made me feel sick and suddenly the distance between us felt so much more than a couple of feet. It was like a chasm, and I fucking hated it. With one stride, I was inches from her and taking the bottle of cream from her, throwing it onto my bed and then grabbing her hands.

"I know you were only trying to help, and I snapped your head off for it." When she exhaled, after what felt like a lifetime, I pulled her a little closer. "I'm just so used to dealing with everything on my own, it's hard to let go sometimes."

"I know, and I'm sorry if it felt like I overstepped, but if we are going to be in a relationship, I want to be able to help. Help without fear of being bollocked for it. I was a teenage daughter once, so maybe I can be a help to both of you." She shrugged and paused, I guessed to allow me to protest, but I remained silent, and so she carried on. "I know we haven't been together long, and who knows what will happen in the future, but while we are an '*us*', I want Maddy to know I'm here for her. I want *you* to know that I'm here for you, too. You don't have to do this on your own any longer, Will." She licked her lips and swallowed. "Unless that's what you prefer, because if it is—"

"Maya," I cut her off because I needed her to understand me. "It doesn't matter how long we've been together or how long we've known each other. At the risk of sounding like a corny romance hero and revealing my hand too quickly, I see a future with us. One where—"

"You do?" she said quietly, interrupting me. "See a future with us?"

Studying her, I saw the shock. She hadn't considered that I was serious about her. How could she not? I thought I'd made it clear. Hadn't I?

Moving a hand to the back of her neck, I pulled her closer, our noses inches apart. "Of course, I do, and I'm so fucking sorry I haven't made that clearer. Maybe deep down I was worried it would scare you off."

"Scare me off?"

"Yeah, seem like I was coming on too strong. Too soon." I shrugged. "Plus, I have no clue how to be a boyfriend. It's not exactly something that I've done a lot of."

She leaned into my touch. "You're doing a brilliant job so far, I promise you. But if you see a future for us then let me be part of the team. Let me take some of the load and if you don't like something I say, explain it to me, don't just bite my head off."

Her reinforcement of my boyfriend skills was a huge relief, because I really didn't have a clue what I was doing most of the time. I also took on board about not biting her head off. It had been wrong of me.

"And," she continued, "I wouldn't be scared off. I'm not scared off because I also want there to be a future with us, Will. I want this to go somewhere but I was scared to say in case that scared *you* off. And then downstairs, I was scared that was it, although I was really pissed off with you, too"

Chuckling, I kissed her forehead and then wrapped my arms around her, my heart picking up speed just being up close to her. Her scent, the feel of her soft, smooth, almost naked skin, it was all perfect.

"I think maybe we need to improve our communication skills," I told her.

"I think maybe you're right." She nuzzled into my neck and inhaled. "Truth and transparency from now on."

"If we are being honest and transparent from now on, then there's something I need to say."

Leaning back to look up at me, she frowned. "What?"

"I have a huge stonker because this underwear is fucking incredible." I pushed my hips forward making Maya giggle.

"I thought we only had an hour," she replied, running her fingers through my hair.

"That was a very rough estimate. Very rough indeed."

"Well," she said on a breathy sigh, "if that's the case."

We finally made it out over an hour and a half later.

***

I squeezed Maya's hand as we walked across the car park of the pub. "Apparently the food here is amazing."

"It looks a nice place." The Devonshire was an old farmhouse that had been converted to a pub with a load of money spent on it and the grounds, and it was where we were meeting Sam and Louise for lunch. "I bet it's lovely in the summer."

"We'll have to try it," I said, lifting her hand to kiss her knuckles. "I can see us sitting out here on long sunny afternoons."

"Sounds perfect."

It did, and I was sure that it would happen, now that we'd had *the* conversation. I wished I hadn't been so scared to do it before, but at least both our feelings were now out in the open. We could see a future with each other, and for once, I liked the idea of being with one woman for the rest of my life. With her.

"Sam and Louise said they'd meet us inside," I told her.

Maya blew out a breath and gave me a tentative smile. "I hope they like me."

"Of course they will." I wrapped an arm around her shoulders and hugged her closer. "What's not to like?"

Laughing together, we walked inside, and I immediately spotted my friends sitting by the open fire. Giving Maya another comforting squeeze, we walked over to them. Louise grinned from ear to ear, and Sam looked at me like a proud father.

"Hey." I gave them a chin lift and they both got out of their chairs.

"Maya, hi, I'm Louise." Before Maya had chance to respond, she was taken out of my arms. "It's so good to meet you."

Sam raised an eyebrow behind Lou's back and gave me a thumbs up. I clearly had his seal of approval for my girlfriend. After a little more hugging, Maya was finally let go and Sam took his turn. He didn't keep hold of her for as long as Louise had, but I did wonder if maybe she'd stopped breathing at one point.

"So lovely to meet you both," Maya was finally able to say as we all sat down.

"Same. We've heard a lot about you." Louise grinned at me, causing me to roll my eyes.

I took Maya's Puffa jacket and hung it with mine on a coat stand near to the table. She was wearing tight jeans with a long sleeve t-shirt, and she looked beautiful, her hair cascading down over her shoulders.

"The fire is gorgeous," she said, glancing over at the flames. I took her hand and pulled into my lap. She was obviously nervous but had no need to be.

"Being a woman of a certain age, I'm not sure whether it's a good spot or not," Louise said, fanning herself.

"What she means is she's forty-two and menopausal," Sam quipped, earning himself a glacial stare from his wife.

"You are asking for trouble, mate," I told him.

"He's asking for a considerable ban on sex, that's what he's asking for." Louise smiled at him with dead eyes. "Maybe you could go and get us some drinks. I'm ready for another. And take Will with you."

I grinned because she still had half a glass of wine, so she either wanted to get rid of Sam because he was pissing her off, or me because she wanted to find out the gossip from Maya. More likely, a mixture of both. I was happy to leave them to, it whatever the reason.

I stood and patted Sam's shoulder. "Looks like we've got our orders, come on. Wine, rum or beer, gorgeous?"

"Beer, please," Sam replied, and I rolled my eyes.

"I said gorgeous, not gormless."

Maya giggled and then said, "I'll have a beer too, please."

Dropping a kiss to her head, I went with Sam to the bar, hearing a gushing aww from Louise as we left.

"She seems lovely." Sam nudged me. "But you're definitely punching, mate."

I was totally aware of that. "That's two of us then."

"Don't let how average I am compared to my wife fool you. I, my friend am a great catch."

"What, like a huge scaly fish that needs throwing back into the water?"

"Fucking hilarious, dickhead." He leaned against the bar as we waited to be served. "Anyway, I heard about last night. How's Maddy?"

"Rough as a bear's arse. Emma actually puked on the pavement outside her house when I dropped her off this morning." I was just grateful she'd managed to avoid splashing my car. "Liam and Zak did well last night, bringing the girls home."

"Good, I'm glad that I taught him well. What's happening with Ana anyway? Have you told her mum?"

I shook my head, still angry about it, but I'd promised Maddy. "I'm not allowed. My daughter will never to speak to me again if I do."

"Someone needs to tell that little madam what she could have done." Sam sighed, shaking his head in disbelief. "Funny, isn't it, how when it's your kid, it's not right. I'm sure we must have done it to people when we were younger."

He was right, because it had happened to *my* daughter, I was furious. Yet working in bars and pubs over the years, I'd seen people slipping something stronger into their friend's drinks loads of times. I mean I'd stopped it happening a lot, but there'd been occasions when I'd found it amusing and gone along with it. I was happy to say that I'd grown up since then, and if I spotted it happening these days, I pulled the plug on it and threw the perpetrators out of my bar.

"Yeah, I suppose we all grow up eventually."

"Just not too quickly, though, hey." Sam shook his head. "You know, I'm glad that Liam isn't leaving home just yet. I'd hate it."

At least I wasn't alone. I thought it was just me who was a helicopter dad, freaking out about her leaving one minute and then angry the next that she wanted to stay.

"Who'd be a parent, hey mate." Sam slapped me on the back and laughed.

"I don't know," I replied, turning to watch my girlfriend as she laughed raucously. "It's not all that bad."

It wasn't, and I knew that I would do it all again if it was what *she* wanted.

CHAPTER 48
Maddy

"Do you think this is how it feels to die?" I asked Zak as he ran his fingers through my hair.

He chuckled, dipping down to kiss the top of my head. "It'll get better, babe."

Without moving my head because it hurt when I did, I looked up at him. "Thank you for the magic drink. It was disgusting, by the way."

"Blame my dad, it's his concoction. He was the one who suggested that I bring it over."

"He knows how drunk I was?" Lifting my fingers against my face, I groaned. "I won't be able to face them ever again."

"They know it wasn't you. They know it was Ana who spiked your drink." Smoothing a warm hand across my brow, Zak sighed heavily. "What are you going to do about her?"

"I don't want to have to think about it." The pain in my temples intensified for a few seconds. "Dad wanted to talk to her mum, but I think I've persuaded him to leave it. I really don't need that kind of trauma. She's in a bad enough mood as it is."

"I wouldn't care about what sort of mood *she's* in."

"Zak," I said on a sigh. "She's my best friend."

"Who did something that could have been dangerous." His exhale was harsh. "She was irresponsible, stupid and—"

"Zak!"

A spike of anger hit me, sending a shooting pain to my head and making my heart miss a beat. It was anger, disappointment, and betrayal all mixed together. Ana was my friend, and I'd known her a lot longer than I had Zak, and it felt wrong for him to be bad mouthing her. As much as she was in the wrong, no matter how angry I was with her, I still felt like I should defend her. I should have some loyalty to her.

"Maddy," he hit back.

Sitting up, I shuffled away from him, taking the thick woollen throw with me. "I'm sure she didn't know how bad we'd get," I said, all snippy and annoyed.

Zak frowned, spinning one of his rings around. "Are you pissed off with me because I'm pissed off with Ana?"

"No," I lied.

He raised an eyebrow. "What do you expect, Maddy? You were absolutely ruined because she slipped vodka into your drink. Enough to make you and Emma puke like I've never seen puke before." He turned to face me, lifting his knee to the sofa and keeping one foot on the floor. "Do you know how worried me, and Liam were about you both?"

"Yes, I know, so you've told me." I just about stopped at rolling my eyes, mainly because it hurt when I did.

"It was totally stupid. What if we hadn't been there? What if there'd been some dick lads who decided to take advantage of you both? Another couple of drinks and you wouldn't have been able to see, never mind stand." His jaw was tight as he gritted out the words, his fisted hand pushing into his seat as he emphasised the danger he'd considered us to be in. "The thought of that makes me feel sick."

"I'm sorry, I should have been more careful, but she's my friend, Zak."

He shook his head, disdainfully. "Friends don't do that sort of thing."

"It was a joke," I stressed.

"Well, I don't really see it that way." He shifted a little closer. "A joke makes you laugh, and there was nothing funny about last night."

"Seriously, Zak."

A tight knot developed in my chest as our eyes met. Zak's were full of fear, and I couldn't understand why. I'd been drunk, and yes, Ana had done got me in that condition, but I'd been safe. It wasn't like I hadn't been drunk before.

"Why are you getting so uptight about it." Grabbing a cushion, I hugged it to my stomach, pressing my fingers into it. "We were fine. You and Liam were there. Loads of people from our year were there."

"But what if we hadn't been? What if you'd been at a party with people you didn't know?" He gave a frustrated sigh. "Your best friend *was* there, and she was the one who got you into that state."

"And you've never spiked anyone's drink, *ever*?"

He shook his head, his lips tight and thin. "Never."

I scoffed and felt the sofa dip as Zak moved closer to me.

"I haven't and never would."

"Okay, I believe you, but you don't need to get so uptight about Ana. I'll speak to her."

"I know you think I'm overreacting Maddy, but I've seen what something like that can do to people."

I frowned. "What do you mean? When?"

His Adam's apple bobbed as he swallowed and then licked his lips. "My friend had her drink spiked at a party once and ended up being sexually assaulted. If it hadn't been for one of my mates walking in on them she would probably have been raped. She's been traumatised ever since. She never goes out and doesn't trust anyone." Inhaling through his nose, he shook his head. "That is not what I want to happen to you."

I felt a sudden flash of guilt as I saw Zak's fear replaced with sadness. It was clear that he'd been affected by his friend's trauma, and I understood a little more why he was so angry about what Ana had done.

Throwing the cushion to one side, I moved closer to him and grabbed his hand. Instantly, his fingers wrapped around mine and squeezed them tight, tension, fear and sadness coming off him in waves.

"I'm sorry about your friend."

Zak breathed out as he nodded. "She's still suffering because of it, and when I saw you like that, well it brought it all back and honestly, Mads," he said pulling me closer, "I was petrified about what could have happened. I wish that I'd taken more notice of what was happening at that party. If only I'd noticed how out of it Ruby was. But I didn't."

It made sense as to why he was so angry with Ana for what she'd done. Why he was insistent that I speak to her. "Did they get whoever did it?"

He shook his head. "When Oscar walked in and saw what was happening, he pulled the guy off Ruby. He punched Oscar and ran out, though. No one knew who he was and there was, and Ruby was the only one who'd spent much time with him, and of course, she couldn't remember anything about him. Oscar saw what he was doing and clearly how far he was going to take it." He sat back, taking me with him so that I was sitting in his lap. "Seeing you like that it just brought it all back."

When he brushed my messy hair from my face, I leaned into his touch, enjoying the coolness of his palm against my hungover heated skin.

"I'm sorry that you were scared for me. And I promise that I'll speak to Ana about it."

He sagged and breathed out, letting his forehead drop to mine. "Only if you want to do it for you. Please don't do it for me. I'm just being over protective." Placing a soft kiss on my lips, Zak's thumb stroked my jaw. "I'd hate it if anything happened to you."

"Nothing will." I grinned against his mouth. "Not with you taking care of me."

"Always."

As Zak kissed me again, his hold on me tightened, it was almost desperate, and I wondered how much blame he'd taken on for his friend.

I slowly pulled away from him. "You know what happened to your friend wasn't your fault, Zak."

He drew in a breath and then slowly let it out. "It was my party," he whispered. "I didn't know half the people I'd invited. I'd put it out on social media and thought I was Billy fucking big bollocks, inviting a bunch of dickheads to my parents' big house while they were on holiday." His eyes fluttered closed as he exhaled slowly. "If I hadn't had that party, Maddy, then Ruby wouldn't have gone through what she did. What she's still going through." He exhaled heavily. "Thinking about that night is why I don't sleep well. Why I take random midnight drives in my mum's car."

Stroking my hand down his face, I looked him directly in the eye. "Zak, you weren't to know. There's only one person to blame, and it's the boy who spiked her. It was not your fault. All you did was hold a party, so give yourself a break. Please, babe."

His handsome face crumpled, and my throat prickled with emotion. I hated that he felt the pressure of blame when he didn't need to.

"She's so different, Mads," he whispered.

I inhaled, breathing in his heady cinnamon scent and leaned closer to him. "And that really isn't on you."

Giving him a soft kiss, I wrapped my arms around him and hugged him tight, hoping that he would eventually give himself a break—that he knew how much I supported him. How I would always be there for him if he needed me.

"Fancy something to eat yet?" he asked me, stroking a hand down my hair.

I considered it for a moment and realised that my headache had subsided, and I actually felt hungry.

"Yes, that sounds good. Although, I don't know what I want."

Zak narrowed his eyes on me. "You don't know what you want? Are you actually my girlfriend?"

"Yes," I giggled. "Why?"

"Because you should know exactly what you want to eat." He nibbled at my jaw with his fingers digging into my hip. "What is *our* food?"

I could feel him growing hard beneath me, and while any other time I would be racing him up to my bedroom, I was still feeling a little too delicate for that. As Zak's mouth moved to my neck, I almost felt like I could give an equal contribution to sex, but my stomach growled and something sharp tapped my temple to remind me I would be less than useless.

"Chicken nuggets," I whispered as I dropped my head back to give him better access to my neck. "I'm hungry for chicken nuggets."

Zak smiled against my lips and gave my bum a squeeze. "There's my girlfriend. I knew that she was in there somewhere." Like some sort of sexy book hero, he stood with me still in his lap and carried me to the door, his mouth on mine the whole time.

"You know, you're very lovely," I told him.

Chuckling, he hoisted me further up his body and nipped my ear before whispering, "And so are you. Very, very lovely. Now let's get chicken nuggets."

And my hangover subsided just a little bit more.

CHAPTER 49
Will

Maddy was in bed after a trip out to get food with Zak hadn't gone too well. Apparently, she'd felt fine while she ate her chicken nuggets and drank her chocolate milkshake, but as soon as they'd got back in Zak's car, she'd thrown up in a carrier bag. Good on Zak, I say, for having the brains to put a couple in the dashboard of his mum's Mini.

It did mean, however, that Maya and I were alone, and not spending it with my daughter and her boyfriend as we'd planned.

"She's okay," Maya said giving me a smile as she came into the kitchen.

"Says she just wants to sleep, so we should eat without her."

I stopped chopping onions, pausing to drop a kiss to Maya's forehead as she wound an arm around my waist.

"Thanks for checking on her."

"Don't be silly, it's my pleasure." She reached for a piece of pepper that I'd already cut up. "She does look sorry for herself."

My shoulders stiffened. "God knows how much vodka Ana put in her drink if she's still feeling rough."

I turned back to the onions for the salad that I was making, thinking that if I concentrated on that, I wouldn't lose my temper.

As I chopped, Maya must have sensed that I was feeling uptight because she leaned forward and turned up the speaker which was playing some random music on Spotify.

"I love this song," she said, reaching for the knife in my hand and gently prising it from my fingers. "Dance with me."

Laughing, I shook my head. "I only dance when I've had few beers."

"Well, you've had a few swigs of that beer," she said with a flirty smile and a shrug. "So?"

"Okay," I told her, because I would do anything for *her*. "Let's go."

The music was slow and smoky, and the guy singing had a raspy voice that sounded like it came from too much booze and cigarettes. As he sang about Tennessee Whiskey, Maya led me by the hand into the middle of the kitchen. When she stood opposite me, so close I could smell her body lotion, I took control and pulled her against my chest. With one of my hands on her hip, I took hers and linked our fingers together, bringing it to my chest.

"Who's singing?" I asked, rocking us slowly from side to side.

"Chris Stapleton," Maya replied, laying her head on my chest. "It's one of my favourite songs."

"Country & Western girl, are you?"

"Hmm maybe. What about you?"

"Never listened to it that much, but this," I pulled her closer as the guy sang about his woman being sweeter than strawberry wine, "I like."

Our bodies swayed in time to the music, just looking into each other's eyes, not smiling yet, somehow, I knew it would be obvious to anyone watching that we were happy. That we were falling into something incredible.

I'd never felt that way about someone before. Like I was lost in her. How beautiful she was, how funny she was, how smart she was. How she was just her. Everything about Maya could quite easily become an obsession to me. Time apart was too long, time together too short and it had all happened so quickly.

The only other time I'd had similar feelings, they had hit me in my chest like a punch. That had been the moment I set eyes on my Maddy. While my love for my daughter was instant and unconditional, I knew that my feelings for Maya were growing into something just as huge. She'd brought so many different emotions and feelings out in me, and I relished every single one of them.

When her lips parted on a small sigh, her eyes shimmered and it was then that I knew exactly what had happened. Every feeling I had about her were ingredients. From the moment we'd met, I'd been adding a different one until I had the final, complete recipe.

"Maya," I whispered, hoping she could hear me over the thud, thud, thud of my heart.

She didn't say anything but nodded. A silent agreement that we were both in the same place. That maybe we were too scared to say the words just yet, but we both knew what they were.

"Good to know." And then I kissed her. A kiss that made it clear what the possibilities were. Where we were heading and that we would be doing it together. Despite my childhood, I'd had a good life with good things happening in it, but now I was moving on to *better* things, all because of her.

As the song on the speaker changed to Michael Gray's The Weekend, we tried to continue our dance but soon gave up trying to sway to the quicker beat. Determined not to be beaten Maya shrugged and started to bounce around. She grabbed both my hands, encouraging me to join in, but I shook my head and tried to pull away.

"Ah, come on, Will, I've seen your moves at Charlie's wedding. I know you've got this."

There was no point me denying it, and besides, her joy was infectious, so how could I not. Soon we were both jumping around like we were at the best party ever, not making a salad in my kitchen. As each song ended we carried on dancing, changing our style to the beat of the music and loving every single moment.

When we finally ran out of breath, we clung to each other laughing and I wondered whether, if I looked inside myself, I'd see my heart was actually glowing.

CHAPTER 50
Maddy

Walking along the corridor towards our study session, my stomach was doing nervous back flips. It was going to be the first time I'd seen Ana since the party, and I was hopeful that I'd persuaded Zak to let me deal with her.

"Stop complaining," I told him over my shoulder.

"I haven't said anything," Zak complained.

"I know but I can hear you thinking it."

"Well, if you ask me—"

"Zak," I whipped around, interrupting him. "We talked about this."

When he pouted, I wanted to kiss him, he looked so cute, but he needed to know that it was my decision where Ana was concerned.

"Okay," he finally said, throwing his hands into the air. "I'll keep quiet."

Giving him a tight smile, I continued walking. I knew he was following because I could hear him muttering behind me. His accent was more pronounced when he was angry, which was maddening. I loved his accent, it made me feel all squishy inside, so I hated that it was sounding all sexy while I was trying to be mad at him.

Pushing through the door, Ana was the first person I saw. She was sitting at the desk opposite the door and picking at her fingernails. There were a couple of text books on the desk in front of her, but they were closed. I knew that she was purposefully ignoring everyone while still taking in everything that was going on around her. It was the tilt of her head and the slight upturn of her lips that told me as much.

"Please don't let her totally off the hook," Zak said close to my ear. "I get that you want to deal with it, but make sure she realises how wrong she was. How dangerous it was."

I took a moment to exhale and then nodded. "I will."

Zak gave my hand a squeeze. "I'll go and sit over with Liam."

As I walked to Ana, she glanced up for just a couple of seconds, barely acknowledging me, before going back to examining her nails.

"Can I sit next to you?" I asked her, already pulling out a chair.

"Surprised you want to, but yeah, I suppose so."

My back stiffened because I knew if it was me, I'd be begging her for forgiveness. Evidently, Ana didn't feel the same level of remorse. Sitting down I cleared my throat, trying to give her a cue to say something, but she just sighed and reached for one of her text books. As she thumbed through it, she started to hum and bob her head, pausing on certain pages every now and again. We sat there for ten minutes, and still she said nothing. With each passing second of silence, I was getting more and more angry. Finally, I couldn't stand it any longer.

"You know I was still really ill last night."

Slowly, her head lifted, and she stared at me with a raised eyebrow.

"You're not the first person to get pissed and puke, Maddy." She looked over to where Zak was sitting with Liam. "Did he tell you that you should feel violated?"

"No," I snapped. "Not at all. He's angry because it was dangerous, and he was worried about me. Liam is too."

"Oh, for God's sake." She rolled her eyes. "They've been your boyfriend's for about two minutes. Sticking their bloody noses in. It was a joke, that's all."

"But we could have ended up with alcohol poisoning, you put so much in."

"I didn't," she scoffed. "It's not my fault you can't take your booze or know when your cider isn't just cider."

"You really don't think you've done anything wrong, do you?" She shrugged, making me shake my head in incredulity. "What the hell is the matter with you, Ana? We're you're friends. We helped you with your mum."

"I know." She leaned closer as the door opened and Miss Rubin, one of our teachers walked in. "And I'm grateful for that, but it was a bloody joke, and I'm sorry I made you sick, okay?"

I would have believed her apology if she hadn't been looking over my shoulder in the direction of Liam and Zak. If she hadn't then chewed on the inside of her mouth and looked bored. However, at the end of the day, she was my best friend, and I was determined we weren't going to fall into a habit of not talking or being bitchy to each other.

"Listen, we're all going to London at the weekend to a party. It's one of Zak's friend's and he says we can all go. Do you fancy it? We're staying at Zak's uncle's house." At first, Zak and I had disagreed about whether to include Ana in the invite. When we'd talked about what she was going through with her mum and dad, he eventually agreed that she deserved a second chance.

"I'll check with my mum." That was all she said. No thank you or I appreciate it, seeing as I was a bitch at the last party we went to. She just picked her book up and went back to reading it.

It crossed my mind whether to get up and move over to Zak and Liam, but when Miss Rubin called for us all to be quiet and start studying, I decided to stay where I was. I just hoped that the next party we all went to was a hell of a lot less drama.

***

"How are you feeling?" Liv asked, pulling me into a tight hug. "Em told me about what Ana did. I hope you gave her shit for it. Honestly, it's just not what you do. I mean, she's like your best friend." A few inches shorter than her, I was smothered by her chest.

"I'm okay, Liv. Honestly I'm fine, can you let me go." She held me tighter. "Okay Liv, I'm tapping out now." I smacked her back and groaned.

"Oh, sorry." She pushed me to arm's length and looked me up and down. "You do look a bit sickly."

"It was two days ago, Liv!"

Zak and Liam snorted a laugh behind me, so I twisted around and gave them a glare.

"She does, doesn't she?" Liv said to them. "Don't you think she's the same colour as that top I wore last week, you know, the one I wore with the navy leggings." She looked at the boys expectantly, but they both just stared blankly. Liv rolled her eyes and turned back to me. "Anyway, you don't look right, and I hope you gave her a bollocking."

"Yeah," I muttered. "I did." I'd already had a conversation with Zak, and he'd just raised an eyebrow when I'd told him what Ana had said.

"I'm so glad I didn't come to the party," Liv continued. "I am not good with sick. Anyway, what's happening with our trip to London."

We both turned to face Zak, looking at him expectantly.

"We're going to get the nine-fifteen train on Saturday morning and stay at my Uncle Mark's house, which is a ten minute walk away from the party, and also just fifteen minutes from where I used to live. Then we'll get the train back on Sunday after we've been into the city, and I'll take you to a few of the tourist places."

Liv clapped her hands together and jumped up and down on the spot. "Can we go to Harrods? They do this amazing perfume that you can't buy anywhere else. Not that I can afford it, but I could spray loads on for the party."

"Your uncle doesn't mind us all staying there?" I asked.

Zak shook his head. "He's pretty cool. He's my dad's youngest brother. He and his girlfriend are going on a skiing holiday, so he said we could stay there. With a few rules."

"No sharing beds?" Liam asked, looking pained.

"Who do you want to share a bed with?" Liv asked crossing her arms over her chest and smirking at him. "Emma by any chance?"

We all whipped our gaze to Liam and his red cheeks. He pushed his hands into his pockets and looked anywhere but at us.

"Why are you acting like it's not happening?" I asked him. "Like we don't all know about you both."

"Exactly," Liv cried and then leaned closer. "I heard you finger banged her in her hallway."

"I heard it was in her vagina," Zak muttered.

"Zak!" I elbowed him the ribs but could hardly stop the laugh from bursting out. "That's bad."

Zak shrugged and looked at Liam for confirmation. "What?" Liam asked with a shrug.

Zak stared at him again until Liam sighed. "Oh, for fuck's sake I am not talking about it with you three."

"If he won't discuss what he and his girlfriend are doing, he must like her," I suggested.

"She's not my girlfriend."

"So what is she?" Liv asked. "If you finger banged her, then why is she not your girlfriend."

"I didn't say I fin… I'm not talking about this. I told you." He stooped down to pick up his backpack and then walked off.

"Where's he going?" Zak asked, pouting. "We were supposed to be going to town for lunch and to pick up a new game."

"Ah, poor baby. Never mind I'll keep you company." I patted his arm. "As long as you get me chicken nuggets for my lunch."

A huge smile beamed over his face as he grabbed my hand, pulling me to him and kissing me hard. As I stood on tiptoe to get better contact, Zak slapped his hand against my bum giving it a squeeze.

"Please," Liv groaned behind us. "Can you not. We have London outfits to discuss."

Zak groaned against my mouth. "Go and have lunch with Liv and discuss London outfits, whatever they are."

"But my nuggets."

Another kiss and another bum squeeze. "I'll bring them back for you."

"Will you."

"Of course I will. For you, anything."

"God I love…" I almost said it. Even as a throw away comment, it felt too much. "Love chicken nuggets."

"I know." He wiggled his eyebrows and gave me a grin that made me want to push my thighs together. "Believe me I know."

As he raced away to try and find Liam, Liv started to laugh.

"What?" I asked turning away from gazing at Zak.

"You two are so damn cute. And he so wanted to say it back."

"Say what back?" I felt heat rise up my neck, hoping she hadn't realised what I nearly said.

She knew me too well. "You know, Madeline, and if it helps, I think if you'd owned it, he would too. Now," she said, linking arms with me. "London outfits let's discuss."

CHAPTER 51
Maddy

I hadn't led a sheltered life, even though I had lived in the same town for most of it. Going to London, though, I was grateful that my hand was firmly in Zak's. The masses of people pushing and pulling on the underground had been cloying, to the point that I wasn't sure I had enough breath in my lungs.

Sensing my tension, Zak had curled his fingers around mine and didn't let go as he pulled me through the crowds until we got onto the overground train, which we'd just gotten off. Heading for the exit, Liam had a hand on Emma's shoulder following us, while Liv dragged a huge suitcase behind her, evidently forgetting we were only staying for one night.

As we made it out into the cold grey day, I heaved a sigh of relief and Zak smiled down at me.

"Okay?"

"Yeah, I just can't believe how busy it is." I glanced back to where dozens of people were milling around, coming in and out of the station. "It's manic."

"Welcome to London, babe." He grinned proudly, clearly pleased to show us his 'home city'. "You alright guys?"

Liam wrapped his arm around Emma's neck and pulled her against his chest. "Yep, all good."

"I can't believe Ana didn't turn up for the train." I sighed, giving my phone yet another glance just in case she'd finally called me. "I hope everything is okay."

"You sure she's not in Liv's case," Zak replied sarcastically. "It's fucking big enough."

Liv rolled her eyes, running a hand down her pink wool coat with a deeper pink fur collar and cuffs. "Essentials, Zachary, and have I asked you to pull it?"

"No, but—"

"Then there's no need to discuss it, is there?" She did a ninety degree turn and pointed with a pink gloved finger. "I believe this is the direction we need to go in."

Blinking, I looked at Zak. "Do we?"

He scratched his ear. "Yeah, actually she's right."

As she took the lead, we all followed, and I couldn't help giggling. "How does she know where we're going?" I asked Zak.

"No idea. I mean I put it on the message for everyone to pass onto their parents, so maybe she googled it."

"She isn't even looking at her phone, though."

"I think she has a photographic memory," Emma said. "Because have you noticed how she never forgets anything."

"I don't think that means she has a photographic memory, Em," Liam replied. "That just means she holds a grudge."

"I heard that," Liv called over her shoulder making us laugh. "I wouldn't need to hold a grudge if you lot weren't such vile people. Right, it's just around here."

Zak shook his head and chuckled as we all trailed behind her and the bump, bump, bump of her suitcase on the pavement. Within ten minutes she pulled up at a wrought iron gate leading onto a black and white tiled path at the end of which was a black, front door with a shiny chrome letterbox and number seven. There were shutters at the bay windows and a holly tree standing proudly in a black pot next to the step.

"Very nice," Liv said pushing open the gate and standing to one side. "I presume you have the key, Zak."

He raised an eyebrow and moved past her, pushing a key into the lock. Once it turned and he pushed open the door, my stomach gave a little flutter of excitement. When Zak grinned at me and held out a hand to show me inside, I even did a little dance.

"This is going to be so much fun," I said over my shoulder.

"It is but there are some rules that my uncle has given."

As everyone pushed inside, congregating in the long thin hallway, we all dropped our bags and looked at him expectantly.

"Any booze that is drunk must be bought by us. Any of his that is used must be replaced and," he said, with a sigh, "his booze is expensive, so we really don't want to have to do that. Secondly, any beds slept in have to be stripped and the bedding put in the washing basket. Jules, his girlfriend, said we don't have to remake the beds, but she really doesn't want to find any, and I quote, 'jizz or puke stained sheets on her bed.'"

I snorted out a laugh, Emma giggled, and Liv gave a loud, "Yuk." Liam and Zak exchanged a smirk like they knew that was exactly what was going to happen.

"Is that it?" Liam asked, bouncing on the balls of his feet. "Can we pick rooms now?"

"Yes, but we're having the bedroom at the front." Zak grabbed my hand. "Get your bag, babe."

We were just about to dart up the stairs when there was a knock at the door. We all stopped and held our breath, staring wide eyed at each other, like we'd been caught out.

Zak looked at us all in turn and shook his head with a smirk. "It's fine, we're allowed to be here." Gently manoeuvring Liv to one side he moved to the front door, opening it wide. Liam and Emma picked up their bags ready to go up the stairs, while I peered around Liv to see who had knocked. Zak's hand gripped the handle and his shoulders lifted almost to his ears as his whole demeanour changed. His relaxed stance had gone, and he now looked as stiff as a board.

"What are you doing here?" he asked tightly. I couldn't see around him to see who it was, but whoever it was he didn't sound happy to see them.

"Nice welcome, hon." It was a girl's voice, and I don't know how I knew, but something inside told me that she'd been his girlfriend. Instantly, my insides curled in on themselves, bitterness biting at my throat. "I thought you'd have called me."

"I had no reason," he bit out, his shoulders heaving into a shrug.

"You were the one who wanted to try the long distance thing."

Emma nudged me and Liv gasped before hissing, "She was his girlfriend."

Biting on my lip, I glanced at her and shrugged. I knew nothing about her, other than he had an ex. We'd never discussed her, and Zak had never offered any information. He certainly hadn't told me that he'd suggested they have long distance relationship.

"I don't recall that," Zak snapped, probably for my benefit because I noticed how he glanced, albeit for a split second, over his shoulder

"I think we were you know, busy, at the time," she purred.

Zak took a step back, and I saw her palm was flat on his chest, and it may as well have been slapping me across the face. I mean I knew he'd had a girlfriend, that he'd kissed other girls, but being faced with the reality of it made me feel weird. I couldn't explain it other than it felt like nerves but in fact was pure green jealousy.

"Connie, I'll see you at the party later, okay."

We all jumped when Zak was pushed aside and a tall, gorgeous blonde girl stepped over the threshold.

"Oi oi," Liam muttered and grimaced.

She was beautiful. A halo of blonde hair, long legs in tight jeans and a leather biker jacket with a long white shirt underneath. It was bloody freezing outside, yet she didn't look like she felt it one bit. As she wafted in, we all got a whiff of her perfume and when I looked over at Liv studying the obvious designer clothes, it was clear my friend had fallen in love. Or lust, whatever it was when a girl fell for the looks and style of another girl without any sexual or romantic feelings.

"Oh hello," Connie gave a half smile, her eyes grazing across each of us. When they landed on me her smile dropped. "I'm Connie." She was telling all of us but staring specifically at me. I don't know how, but she knew that I was Zak's girlfriend. It was clear in her steely narrowed eyes and the way she thrust her tits out at me.

"How did you know that we were staying here, and more to the point we'd arrived?" Zak grabbed her forearm and pulled her back.

"Oscar mentioned it to Deacon who mentioned it to Nick who told Danny and he—"

"I get the picture." Zak interrupted her with a deep breath. "I heard you were seeing Danny."

Connie giggled and slapped her hand over the top of Zak's on her arm. "Not jealous are we, Zak?"

Zak pulled his hand away and pushed past her to stand next to me. "This is Maddy, my girlfriend."

Barely glancing at me she said, "Yeah, I heard." Giving a bored sigh, she turned to Zak and gave him what I imagined was supposed to be her sexiest smile. "Anyway, see you later at the party. In case you can't spot me I'll be wearing that red dress you love so much." She giggled and then swept away, back out of the still open front door.

When it slammed closed, Zak pinched the bridge of his nose. "That was Connie."

"Yeah, I got that," I snapped, desperately not wanting to sound bitchy, but unable to stop myself. Grabbing my bag, I headed for the stairs. "Front bedroom did you say?"

"Mads," he called after me.

I chose to ignore him and continued up to our room. It crossed my mind to tell him I was sharing with Liv, but I checked myself. He hadn't done anything wrong, except go out with a gorgeous girl and not tell me anything about her, other than she existed. When I threw open the door to a large, bright and airy room with shutters that matched those at the downstairs window, I instantly felt calmer. It was decorated in the palest of pink colours and had white furniture and bedding and at the ceiling was a small crystal chandelier that tinkled softly.

I moved around the room, thinking how understated yet beautiful it was. How it had clearly been created with love and attention, if the framed photographs, and the glass box of plane and concert tickets were any indication. When I looked at the photographs, I saw how like his uncle, Zak was. They had the same shaped face, the same dark hair and the same eyebrows, just like Zak's dad's.

"My two cousins, Henry and Thomas look the same, too. We Hoyland men clearly have a look."

Zak had come in and was standing behind me, and when he put his hands on my shoulders, I instantly relaxed. Thoughts and ideas of him and Connie vanished, or at least petered out to something of little importance. When he rested his chin on top of my head, I felt stupid for storming upstairs.

"Maybe I'd like to meet them," I told him, my tone light as I nudged him.

"Not a chance. Tom is a model. I don't want him stealing you away."

"But if you look alike why would I even consider him a better option?" My eyes stayed on the photograph as I marvelled at the amazing family genes if all the men looked that good.

"He's slightly prettier and has some strange irresistible charm apparently. Or so he tells me." He turned me around and cupped my face, tipping it up so our eyes met. "I'm sorry she came here. And I'm sorry she was so..." His eyes narrowed for a beat. "So, *Connie*."

I laughed. "And what is that like."

"A princess. A sarcastic, demanding princess."

I wanted to add, bitchy, but was determined to be the better person. Well, better than Connie at least.

"I was just taken by surprise. You've never told me much about her.

How gorgeous she is."

"You're more gorgeous," he replied instantly, his brow furrowed in a frown. "Believe me she puts a lot of effort in whereas you look beautiful even when you're puking your guts up."

"Thank for that, I think."

I rolled my eyes and Zak wrapped me in a hug, his chest rumbling as he laughed. "I mean it, Mads. You are."

Standing there with his arms holding me tightly, I felt more relaxed and more secure about Connie than I thought possible. Yes, she was beautiful and stylish, but she wasn't the one standing there with Zak. Then his head dipped and he took my mouth in a breathtaking kiss, and I knew that if I were in in her position, I'd be doing what I could to get him back, too. That didn't mean I wanted to be her friend, though, in fact it made me more determined to make sure we steered clear of her for the rest of the weekend. Zak was mine now and I wouldn't let her or anyone else spoil it.

ZAK'S WHATSAPP MESSAGES

ZAK

Fucking Connie turned up at Uncle Mark's just as we got here!! Was she waiting around the corner or something?

OSCAR

No way! Sorry mate. I messaged Deac to tell him you were here. Did he tell her?? What a fucking melt!

ZAK

She said he told Nick who told Dan. Why the hell would he tell her that her ex was back? He's the fucking melt.

OSCAR

You know what she's like she probably read his messages without him knowing. How was the 'reunion'.

ZAK

Shit. She was rude to Maddy and tried to flirt with me. God, I wonder sometimes what I saw in her.

OSCAR

She hid her fucking bitchy princess vibe well for a long time. Plus she's fit!

ZAK

Yeah well I think my new gf is fitter!! See you later mate.

OSCAR

Yeah look forward to meeting her and your new mates. And I'll make sure everyone knows to keep Connie away from you. What you planning today – going into London?

ZAK

Appreciate it. See you about 7. Gonna grab some food and chill this afternoon. Going into the city tomorrow before we leave.

OSCAR

Does chill include sex!!!

ZAK

I couldn't possibly comment! See you later 😉.

CHAPTER 52
Maddy

If I'd thought that Zak's Uncle Mark's house was nice, Nick, his friend's, house was incredible. They even had an indoor swimming pool with changing rooms and a spa pool. The party itself was in a room specifically for parties, with a bar at one end with proper bartenders. At the other end of the room, a hotdog stand was in one corner, and a taco stand at the other. Above us on a balcony was a DJ with a huge set of decks blasting out every type of music. It was absolutely wild; in fact, it was carnage. Food and clothes in the pool, people passed out everywhere and I'd seen more than one couple having sex in a dark corner.

"And I thought we went crazy at parties." Liv said shaking her head.

"I just walked in on a boy blowing another boy in a bathroom. They didn't even stop, just winked at me." Emma grinned. "It was quite hot, actually. I almost stayed to watch."

We burst out laughing and all jumped back when someone shook a bottle of champagne, spraying it in our general direction.

"Where are Liam and Zak with our drinks, anyway?" Liv asked and looked over to the bar. It was at least ten deep, and I couldn't see either of them. All the boys around here seemed to be six feet plus, which meant Liam and Zak mingled in too easily.

I shrugged and was just about to say they shouldn't be long, when Emma nudged me hard in the stomach.

"Ow, what was that for?"

"Bitch at three o'clock."

All three of our heads swivelled that way and I groaned. "Why can't she just leave me alone." Connie was walking towards us, a smarmy smile on her face.

"Hey, girls," she said in her sickly-sweet voice that I'd grown to hate over the last couple of hours. Any opportunity to speak to us and she had and each time it had been to relay some memory of her and Zak together. So much for me avoiding her. "Still having fun." She turned and waved at a girl who was taking it in turn to kiss two boys. "That's Hattie, she's hilarious." She leaned closer. "A bit of a slag, but hilarious with it."

Liv sighed heavily and crossed her arms. "Where's your boyfriend? Not seen you with him much."

Emma snorted and muttered, "Trust Liv to be to the point."

I couldn't help noticing how Connie rubbed at her neck before plastering on a smile. "Around. We're not joined at the hip. Unlike you and Zak." Her eyes pinned themselves to mine, and she thrust her hands to her hips, like she was waiting for a response.

I didn't immediately give her one because she was wrong. I'd spent some time talking to Zak's friend Deacon and the girl he was seeing, while Zak went to play a game of pool while I'd had a long, funny conversation with his other friend Oscar. The party was crazy, but I felt comfortable enough not to hang on Zak's arm the whole time, so she had it all wrong.

"Zak and I are fine spending time apart." I hated that I sounded defensive, to the point that it came across more like a protest than a fact.

Connie arched her perfectly waxed brows, the edge of her plump lips twitching up into a smirk. "Of course you are. It must be weird, though, him knowing everyone here and them knowing him better than you do. At least you've got your little group with you."

God, she was such a bitch. Every word she said an insinuation, and I had no idea what Zak had seen in her, because there wasn't much pleasant about her from what I could see.

"We're having a great time," Emma told her. "Especially as we're just country folk up in the big city."

Liv and I chuckled because you could always rely on Emma to be her sarcastic best when you needed it. Connie gave her a tight smile, flicking her hair over her shoulders. She looked around the room and then whipped her head back to me.

"Just need to talk to someone. See you later."

As she tottered off in her sky high heels, Emma leaned in close. "She hasn't got anyone to see. Look, everyone of Zak's mates turns their back on her."

We watched, and she was right—not one person spoke to her, but generally turned away and carried on talking to someone else. She walked the full length of the room, being ignored, until she reached her boyfriend, who barely gave her a glance as he continued playing pool.

"Sorry, the queue at the bar was fucking horrendous." Zak stood in front of me holding out a bottle of beer with a chunk of lemon stuck in the top. He pointed at it and shook his head. "Throw that if you don't want it."

"It's fine." Grinning and feeling relief that he was back in front of me, I pushed the lemon inside the bottle.

"Here you go, Liv." Zak passed her something that looked like it was radioactive. "Oh, and my friend Teddy was asking about you."

Liv instantly went on high alert, craning her neck and looking around the room like her head was a periscope popping out of the sea. "Who is he, and what does he look like?"

Zak chuckled and pointed over towards the hot dog stand. "That's him with a hot dog in each hand."

Liv's eyes narrowed on her prey. "Hmm, blonde, tall, broad, pretty. The two hot dogs are a problem, but I can sort that out."

We all watched as she stalked across the room, dangling her bottle between her fingers, in the direction of Zak's friend. When she stood in front of him she pushed her shoulders back, grabbed one of the hot dogs passed it off to a passing girl and then landed her lips on Teddy's.

"Fucking hell," Liam cried. "She's going for it."

"I think she was getting bored," Emma told him. "Did you get me a drink."

"Oh yeah. Here you go." He handed over a mini bottle of Prosecco with a straw sticking out of it. "Fancy a game of pool, it looks like the table is coming free."

When we looked over, Connie's boyfriend and his friend had put their cue's down on the table and were walking away. Connie was walking behind them, well more dragging really, with her arms firmly crossed over her chest.

"Doubles," Zak said, taking my hand. "Let's go and beat them, babe."

"I'm rubbish at pool," Em complained.

"She is," I told Liam, laughing and then turning to Zak. "We're going to smash this."

***

Sitting in a quiet corner, of which there were very few, I had been waiting for Zak to come back from the bathroom for about twenty minutes. I wasn't bored, given there was a lot of people to watch, but I was starting to get a little concerned about where he was. Emma and Liam had disappeared straight after we'd annihilated them at pool. I had no idea where they were but had an idea it was a dark corner. He'd leaned over her quite a lot during our game, trying to teach her how to hit the balls. There was more rubbing up and down on her arse than teaching going on. As for Liv, she was kissing the face off Teddy against the wall opposite. I had a good view of her and knew that she was okay. As well as the necking on, there was a lot of laughing too, so I wasn't worried about her.

Taking another look at my phone screen, I saw another ten minutes had passed since I'd last seen Zak. He'd promised he wouldn't be long, mainly because it was almost two and we wanted to get some sleep before we needed to get up to investigate London.

I still felt okay, until I saw Connie's boyfriend walk past with a couple of his friends. The realisation struck me at the same moment my stomach bottomed out and my heart missed a few beats. The last time I'd seen Connie was just before Zak had gone to the bathroom. She'd been watching us from across the room, her eyes never leaving us, even when she dragged her boyfriend to her—Dan, I think his name was—and started kissing him. My hands began to shake as I stood up from the chair and stood to look around the room. The crowd had thinned out a little, but it was still busy, maybe just a little less wild. but there was no sign of Zak. Chewing on my lip, I started to push through everyone to make my way to the bathroom which was next to the pool.

"Excuse me." A guy wearing a hat shaped like a birthday cake looked at me and then tried to pull me to him. "I need to get past."

"Dance with me," he slurred. "Just one."

When he grabbed my arm, I snatched it free and threw him a glare as I carried on walking. The whole time I pushed past and dodged people, I was on high alert for both Zak and Connie, my heart thudding in time with the music pounding in my ears. The longer time went without spotting them, the sicker I felt. The harder my heart slammed against my breast bone. I had no idea why or how I knew that they were together, but I just did. When I rounded a corner there they were. I was right.

Zak was leaning with his back against the wall, and Connie with her side to it. She was twiddling her hair around her finger and giggling. My gaze snapped to Zak, and he was smiling and gesticulating with his hands, evidently telling her some funny story. He didn't look at all like he didn't want to be near her, that he thought she was a demanding, sarcastic princess. I didn't know what to do. When she placed her hand against his chest, bile rose in my throat. When that hand then trailed down towards the waistband of his jeans, I wanted to rip my eyes out. Zak moved a step to the side, but he continued chatting. He didn't pull her hand away or tell her to stop, he just carried on talking about whatever it was she found so fucking hilarious.

When she stood on her tiptoes, and Zak lowered his head, I stopped breathing. Would my heart give up if they kissed? Would I scream or just burst into tears? When she whispered something into his ear the relief was huge, until he smiled. It was *my* smile, yet he didn't look in my direction, didn't sense my presence and that caused a pain in my chest like I'd never felt before. The moment he entered a room, I was aware of him. I knew that he was there and yet he didn't have that same second sense about me.

Knowing I had to do something I tried to take a step, but my legs felt like they were made of lead. I wasn't even sure what sort of step it would be if I could take it. A step towards them or away from them? Did I stay and confront them, or just run and pretend I hadn't seen anything, giving him the opportunity to lie about where he'd been. Then again maybe he'd tell me the truth.

I knew I shouldn't be warring with myself about it. I was strong. My dad had brought me up that way. He'd told me never to let anyone walk all over me or to make me feel inadequate. Yet, the idea of going over there and telling him that he was a dick for leaving me alone to speak to her, well, it scared me because of what he might say. What if he told me to go away? What if he said he'd realised that Connie was the one for him? What if…

It was too late Zak had spotted me, and as he lifted his eyes to mine he smiled at me. It wasn't forced, but it felt like he was surprised, so I did what instinct told me to do and what my legs finally allowed me to do…I turned around and ran away.

CHAPTER 53
Maddy

I knew I couldn't go back to Zak's uncle's house. I had no idea how to get there, or what the address was. The best thing I could do was find Emma and Liv and come up with a plan, but scanning the room there was no sign of them. I did spot Oscar, though, so headed for him.

"Hey, Mads." He greeted me with a huge, drunken smile. "Having a good time?" He peered at me and then frowned. "What's up, darlin'?"

I took a huge breath, unsure what to say. Zak was his friend, and he knew Connie better than he knew me, so I couldn't really expect his support, but there was no one else around, and I was on the verge of bursting into tears. Shaking my hands out at my sides, I looked over his shoulder towards the spot where I'd seen Zak and Connie talking. Then it kind of hit me—they were *only* talking…

"Maddy?" Oscar prompted.

"I just found Zak and Connie together," I blurted out.

Oscar's eyes went as wide as saucers as he leaned his upper body forward, like he wasn't sure he'd heard me properly.

"Together?" Scrubbing a hand over his face he placed his other on my shoulder. "Like together, together?"

"Talking together?"

He placed both hands on my shoulders as he looked me in the eye, swaying slightly as he did. "Talking?"

I nodded and watched as he blinked slowly. He was a good-looking boy, not quite as dark as Zak, with slate grey-eyes that glinted with mischief. His style was very much like's Zak's, wearing rings and a necklace, but instead of short, cropped hair, his was longer on top and messy. He'd had plenty of girls following him around all night, but his eyes seemed to always be on a tiny, pretty redhead who stayed closed to her friends, warily watching the room.

"If they were just talking."

"It was the way they were talking." As he scratched his head, I knew that I shouldn't have told him. Zak was his friend, and I was putting him in a difficult situation. "It's fine, I'm just being an idiot."

"No, if it's upset you, then it's not fine."

"Mads." A hand reached for mine, and Zak appeared in front of me. He turned to Oscar. "Thanks, mate."

Oscar shook his head. "Sort it out because I mean it, Connie is not worth the shit." He ruffled my hair and left, heading in the direction of the redhead.

"Who's that?" I asked Zak. "Oscar seems to like her."

Zak looked over to where I pointing and sighed. "That's our friend, Ruby, who I told you about. The one who was drugged. This is the first time she's been out in ages; she was really nervous about it."

My gaze shot over to her. She was looking up at Oscar who was a respectful distance from her. When he reached out to touch her cheek, and she visibly relaxed, giving him a beautiful smile, my heart did a little leap.

"He likes her," I stated.

Zak nodded. "Yeah, he does. Has done for a long time, since we were about ten." He laughed and then turned to me, signalling a full stop to the conversation. "Why did you run away?"

I pulled my hand from his and crossed my arms over my chest. "Why do you think?"

"We were only talking."

"For about half an hour while I was waiting like an idiot." Swallowing, I waited for Zak to turn it on me, to make it seem like my fault, like I should have gone to the toilet with him if I didn't want to be left alone, like I should have gone looking for him sooner.

He dropped his head and sighed. "I'm sorry. I should have come back to you sooner. I shouldn't have left you for so long."

It wasn't what I expected. But he was still talking to her, though. He still looked like he was enjoying their conversation.

"It wasn't just that, it was how you were talking to her."

Saying the words again didn't make them sound any less stupid than they had the first time. They didn't make me seem any less neurotic.

Zak studied me, opened his mouth, and then closed it again. After licking his lips, he nodded. "Okay, I know how it must have looked, but I know Connie. Me being harsh with her back at the house and ignoring her didn't seem to have worked, she's been following me around all night." I thrust my hands to my hips, annoyed that she hadn't taken the hint. "Yeah, I know. Whenever I went to the bar, the toilet, when I went to get you some food, when I went outside for a smoke, she followed me and each time I practically told her to fuck off. When I came out of the toilet this last time she was there, waiting. So," he said with a huge sigh, "I thought I'd try being nice. Try talking to her and explaining that it wasn't going to happen because of how I feel about you."

Before he said that, it felt like my heart had been deflated, like a dinghy, and then it unfurled with each pump of air it received. It expanded to the point of pain, because I was in no doubt that I was in love with him. Deep, bone crushing love that no matter what happened would stay with me forever. He was my first love and the idea of him even talking to his ex-girlfriend had hurt more than I could imagine.

"And did it work?" I asked quietly.

"I think so. I told her about school, about our circle of friends, about the parties we've been to, the laughs we have, and the shit that we talk about." His arms came out and wrapped around my shoulders, and instantly I was plastered against his chest, his mouth against my forehead. "And then I told her I was happy and loving my new life, and it was mainly because of you. I told her what I had with you was different than what I'd had with her."

Leaning back, so that I could look at him, I asked, "How?"

"It's real, Maddy. What we have feels like the start of something. I know we're young and we're about to start on the next big step in our lives, but I just feel like maybe..." He blew out a breath. "I don't know, I'm shit at words."

It didn't matter because I knew exactly what he was saying because I could see it in his eyes. The honesty.

"When you came over," he said, "I was telling her about and me and Liam trying to get Liv's case out of the rack on the train and how it got wedged in. That's what we were laughing at, but I know it must have looked bad and I should have come to find you."

"And what did she whisper in your ear?" I asked, unable to stop myself from poking at the sore that was still festering in my chest. "What was it that made you smile?

He rubbed his bottom lip with his thumb, his silver ring brushing against his chin, and he looked so worried it was quite cute. "She asked me how I felt about you. Whether it was the real thing or not."

The relief was instant. That smile *had* been for me.

"It's fine," I said. "Let's forget about her. I believe you." I was about to move in for a kiss when I saw Connie approaching us. She was smiling, but I wasn't totally convinced. I wasn't sure that one conversation would sway her from chasing my boyfriend. I cleared my throat. "Connie is coming this way."

"Fucking hell." Zak groaned. "I didn't tell her we could be best friends."

"It's fine. We can be nice for a few minutes, but then can we go home? *Please*."

"Yes, sure," He took his phone from his pocket. "I'll message everyone and get them to meet us at the front door." He plastered on a grin. "Hey, Connie."

"Hey you two. I'm just heading home, so thought I'd say goodb—"

"Shit!"

"What the fuck," Zak groaned as we found ourselves covered in beer from a guy who had lurched into us.

"Oh, sorry, geezer," he slurred, laughing as he stumbled away.

"You okay?" Zak asked me.

"Yeah." I shook the beer from my hands and then brushed it away from the short, red jersey dress I was wearing—yes, I'd chosen a red dress, too. "Did he get you?"

"My phone is soaked, I'm soaked."

"Pass me your phone," Connie said. "I have tissues in my bag." She unzipped the blue Pom Pom London bag that she had across her body. When she took out the packet of tissues, she held her hand out to Zak. "Phone."

Zak handed it over and then turned his attention to his t-shirt and jeans. When he looked up at me he started to laugh. "You're a bit wet, gorgeous."

"Just a bit." I giggled, throwing myself into his arms and kissing him hard.

I wasn't sure how long we were kissing for, a fair while, but we were interrupted by Connie clearing her throat.

"Sorry," I said, pulling away from Zak and biting my bottom lip.

Her smile was tight, but it was a smile. "Here you go." She handed Zak his phone back. "It's all cleaned up and dry."

"Cheers, Connie." Zak wrapped an arm around me and pulled me into his side. "Been good seeing you."

"Yeah, you, too." She turned to me. "Nice to meet you, Maggie."

"You, too, Carrie."

With a tight smile she ran a hand down Zak's arm and then left throwing her hair over her shoulder. As we watched her go Emma and Liam appeared, both looking more than tipsy.

"Finally," I said, looking Em up and down and noticing her dress was on back to front. "Had fun have you?"

"So much fun," she giggled. "So much fun and wine."

Liam swayed with a stupid grin on his face, and I noticed that he was holding on tight to Emma's hand. I wasn't sure if that was to stop him from falling over or because they'd obviously moved on a step in their relationship. Whatever it was, it was cute.

"Have you seen Liv?" I asked. "We're thinking of leaving now."

"Oh, thank God," Emma sighed. "I'm knackered and so ready to sleep."

"I've messaged her." Zak pulled my hair over my shoulder and kissed my neck. "She was outside, she's coming in now."

Within a few minutes she appeared at our side, holding hands with Teddy. He was looking at her like she was made of diamonds or something equally glittery, while Liv was smiling, and her lipstick was gone from all the necking on she'd been doing.

"Hi peeps, are we all okay?" She pulled her shoulders back, shaking her sheet of long blonde hair. "Ready to go?"

"Yeah. Hi Teddy." Zak nodded at his friend. "You coming back with us?"

"No, he is not," Liv cried, extremely put out. "He's lovely and everything, but we're nowhere near that close."

Zak chuckled and fist bumped Teddy. "Good seeing you, man."

"You, too, catch you again soon? Manchester is my first choice uni, so I'll be around a lot of weekends and stuff."

"Nice one," Zak said, placing his hand in the small of my back, "Anyway, we'd better go, our Uber will be outside in five."

After more goodbyes to Teddy, we all trailed outside, a little drunk and feeling tired. I realised that I hadn't once thought about Ana and that made me feel bad—but something else, I hadn't worried about my dad and whether he was okay—so maybe I was ready to go away to university after all. When Zak hung his arm around my neck and pulled me close to kiss the side of my head, I knew I was.

HEARTBREAK

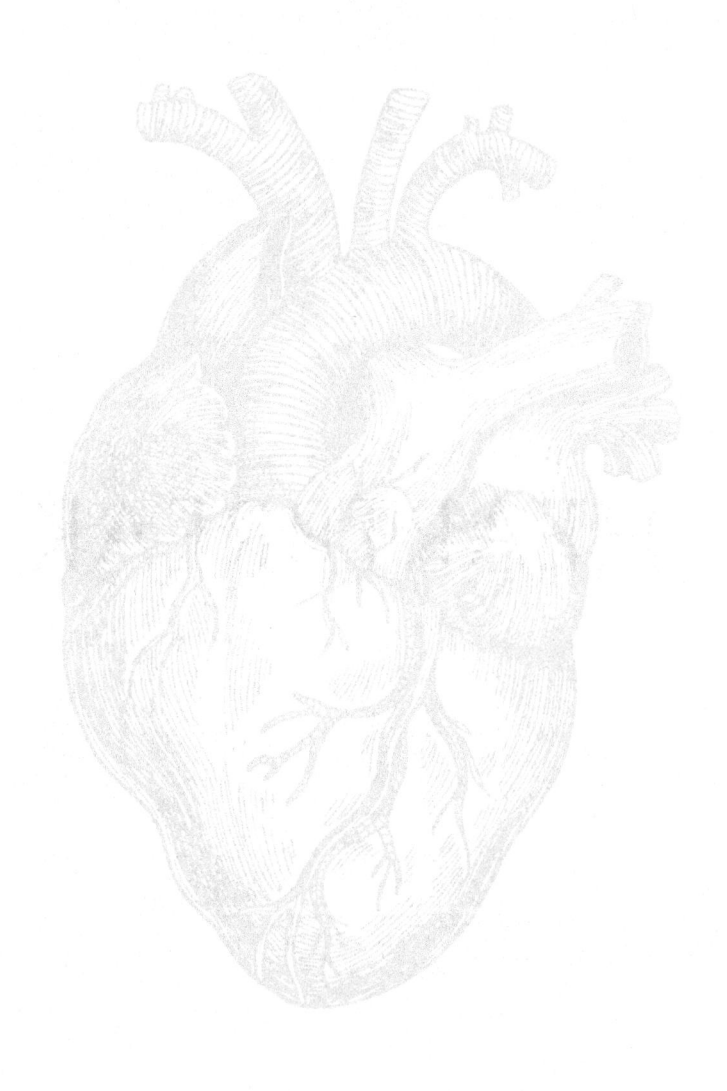

CHAPTER 54
Will

"Twelve-eighty," I told the guy holding his bank card up. He tapped the card reader, pocketed his card, then picked up his drinks and walked back to his table. "My pleasure, don't mention it, dickhead."

"I don't know why you get so upset," Marcus said as he wiped the bar down in front of me. "You know most pissed-up people have no manners."

I did know, and that was one of the few reasons why I hated owning a bar. There weren't many others, but rude customers were definitely one. Not seeing Maya was another. I couldn't not take my turn on the rota for a

Saturday night, it wouldn't be fair, but it didn't mean I liked it.

"That hen night are getting a bit lairy as well," I ground out, everything getting on my nerves. "Maybe we should cut them off."

Marcus burst out laughing. "It's not like they're ordering quadruples or anything like that. They're just enjoying themselves."

"Yeah, well when the mother of the fucking bride thinks it's okay to squeeze my arse like she's testing the juiciness of an orange, I think that I'm entitled to be a killjoy."

He laughed again and called over to a serve one of our regulars. "Two pints, Joe?" When he got the thumbs up, he pulled two pint glasses from under the bar and set them under two pumps, and pulled them at the same time. "Are you grumpy because you've got blue balls, seeing as you haven't seen Maya since last weekend."

We'd both had busy weeks and had only managed our nightly phone calls; no lunchtime meetups or evening dinners. So, yes, I was grumpy because I hadn't seen Maya, and yes, I had fucking blue balls.

"She's coming over tomorrow morning."

"She won't be waiting at home for you when you've finished?" He finished pulling the pints and set them down in front of Joe, taking the cash from him and programming it into the till. "Keeping the bed warm."

"Nope," I replied like a sulky teenager, moving down the bar to the next customer.

While I served them, Marcus carried on down his end of the bar and Dilly worked the tables, carrying on with a usual Saturday night. Thankfully we were busy, so it didn't drag, but when it reached last orders, I was still relieved.

"I'll Z the tills and then stick the trays in the safe," I told Marcus. "We can bag it all tomorrow."

He saluted me and then turned to watch Dilly lean over the bar and grab a cloth to clean down the tables. I shook my head, despairing of his bloody desire to hook up with her, no matter how many times I'd told him it wasn't happening.

"Dills, leave that, love," I told her. "You get off. Your car is by the door, right?"

"Yep." She placed the cloth on the bar. "Sure, it's okay to go?"

I waved her away. "Me and Marcus can wipe down."

As she left, shouting a final goodbye, Marcus narrowed his eyes on me. "You knew I was going to make a move tonight, didn't you?"

"No," I laughed. "And I've told you, don't."

"Why not?" he smirked, like he thought I was the most stupid person on earth.

"Because she'll say no, and your ego won't take it. Then you'll sulk for days and be a pain in my fucking arse."

He gave an empty laugh as if the idea of her saying no was absurd. I threw the cloth at him.

"Get wiping, stud."

As we both set about cleaning up my phone rang in my pocket. It was almost midnight, and there were only two people who would call me—Maya or Maddy. I pulled my phone out, expecting either of their numbers, but it was unknown. I almost didn't answer it, but something inside of me told me I had to.

"Hello."

"Will, it's Jack, Maya's brother."

"What's wrong?" I knew something was. I just felt it. My heart was racing. With my legs feeling like jelly, I grabbed for a stool. "Is Maya okay?"

"She's had a car accident," Jack said, his voice shaky and breathless. "She was on her way to see you and some fucker rear-ended her on the M62."

I literally felt the colour drain from my face as my stomach dropped. "Is s-s-she…"

"She's in hospital. Manchester General. I'm on my way there now, but you'll probably be able to get there sooner than me. I've told them you're her fiancé so you can get information. Mum and Dad are leaving Scotland now, so should be at the hospital in about four hours."

"Right, okay, I'm going now." I pushed up from my stool and had to force my legs to move. If her parents were on their way, it had to be bad. "Message me any details that you think I might need. I know her date of birth but I…" I blew out a breath as I turned full circle, no idea what I was looking for. Marcus had clearly picked up on the fact something was wrong because he threw me my keys that I hung up behind the bar.

"Will, just drive carefully. She's going to be fine."

"You know that?" I grasped at the idea like I was drowning, and it was a lifebelt because that was exactly how I felt—like I was drowning. My lungs were tight, and I could barely breathe.

As soon as the call ended, Marcus ran to the door and pulled back the bolts, and swung it open.

"Maya's been in an accident," I told him as I ran a hand through my hair.

"I guessed." He slapped my back, gently pushing me outside. "Go and be fucking careful."

Then everything melted into the background because the only thing in my head was getting to Maya.

***

I made it to the hospital in record time, knowing full well that a speed camera had flashed me. Thankfully I'd found a parking space, and with Jack telling the hospital that I was Maya's fiancé, I'd been allowed onto the ward. I was waiting for the doctor to come and talk to me. All I'd been told was that she was comfortable.

My knees bounced as I sat and waited, seeing as pacing hadn't helped at all. I leaned forward, hoping to alleviate the pain in my stomach, but it wasn't helping in any way. Looking down at my phone, I saw I had been there almost forty minutes, which meant that Jack couldn't be far away. Standing up, I went to the door and looked through the glass. There was no one around, and I was getting more and more anxious. I started pacing, which still didn't help, and carried on waiting.

After a few more minutes, the door was flung open, and Jack came barrelling in breathing hard.

"What's happening?" he asked, trying to catch his breath.

"They've just told me that she's comfortable. That's all I know."

Suddenly I was dragged into his arms and into a strong hug and back slap. "She's going to be alright, bud. She's strong."

As we pulled apart the door opened, and a small guy with his shirt sleeves rolled up smiled at us both.

"Maya's fiancé and brother, is that right?"

We nodded, and I took his outstretched hand. "Will."

"Jack, Maya's brother," Jack offered as he then greeted him.

"Dr Young. Please take a seat."

Jack and I exchanged worried glances as we took a seat opposite the doctor. Thank fuck he was smiling.

"Okay, so the situation is this," he said. "Maya has a broken left wrist and three cracked ribs. She's got some stiffness in the neck, which would indicate she has whiplash, so don't be alarmed when you see her wearing a collar, it's just a temporary measure."

"Is she awake?" Jack asked.

"Yes, she is. She's a bit battered and bruised, so she's in a fair amount of pain, but we are giving her something for that. That means she may fall asleep soon. Which is why I'm going to let you see her for a few minutes before she does."

Both of us stood up immediately while Dr Young stayed seated. He grinned and held his hand up.

"One second, guys." We both sat back down, and my knees started bouncing again. "She's been very lucky it was only her quick thinking to veer into the hard shoulder when the other car hit her that stopped her from ploughing into the truck in front."

Nausea hit me, and when Jack groaned and grabbed my arm, I knew that piece of information had hit him hard, too.

"So," Dr Young continued, "we don't think there'll be any reason to keep her in. However, when she goes home, I need you to keep a look out for some form of post-accident trauma. What *could* have happened may hit her hard once she's got time to think about it."

"I'll keep a close eye on her," I said.

"We'll watch her like a hawk," Jack said at the same time.

Dr Young slapped the wooden arms of his chair. "Okay, let's take you to her."

Leading us to the side room that Maya was in, I was desperate for him to quicken his steps. I needed to see her—the woman I loved. There was no point in denying it any longer.

Finally, we reached the room. There on the bed Maya was lying, looking tiny and pale against her pillow

"Fuck," I muttered.

Her eyes fluttered open, and a smile ghosted over her face. "Hey."

Jack rushed over to her and bent to kiss her forehead. "What the hell, Mays."

"I know. I'm sorry."

I stood back to let them have a few moments, watching as her brother brushed her hair from her face. Looking down at her, he took in a deep breath and then slowly blew it out, and I noticed how his hand was shaking at his side.

"I'll leave you for a few minutes," Dr Young whispered to me. "She's in a temporary cast at the moment, so tomorrow we'll put her in a permanent one, but she needs some sleep for now."

I grabbed his hand and shook it. "Thank you, Dr Young."

"My pleasure and she's going to be fine."

As he slipped out of the door, Jack turned to me and then back to Maya. "Will's here, Mays." He took a step back, and I immediately rushed forward to take his place.

"Hey, gorgeous." Leaning closer, I placed my arm above her head and took her good hand in mine. "What were you doing driving on the motorway so late?"

Her eyes drooped but then she took a breath. "Coming to see you. I wanted to be there when you got home."

"Oh, sweetheart." I swallowed back the huge lump in my throat, hoping that the tears which were threatening didn't come. Now was a time to be strong. "I heard you acted brilliantly when the car hit you."

"I just knew I couldn't go into the back of the lorry." Her words were slow and deliberate. Her pain meds were kicking in. "I didn't know what else to do. I hit the bank."

"I know, but better that than the truck." Glancing over at Jack, I gave him a tight smile, and he gave me a sharp nod. "We're going to leave you to sleep, but I'll be here when you wake up if they let me."

"Go home, baby," she murmured, barely awake.

Kissing her forehead, I moved back and let Jack take my place to say his goodbye. When we walked through the door, I glanced back, not sure that I could leave her but knowing that I had to.

"Do you think they'll let me stay?" I asked Jack.

He shrugged, his hands deep in his pockets, his gaze on the door of Maya's room. "Maybe. I don't know. I think I'm going to find a Travelodge or something close by and see if I can get a room, and then Mum and Dad can use it when they get here."

"You don't need to get back home tonight?" I glanced at the clock on the wall, and it was almost two-thirty. "Or should I say this morning."

"Heather told me to stay as long as I'm needed. She's taking the kids to her mum's today anyway. Why don't you do the same? Find a room."

"Yeah, it wouldn't be a bad idea." I scrubbed a hand over my face, suddenly overpowered by tiredness. "Maddy is away so I don't need to get back for her. I just need to let my head barman know he'll have to sort the bar out tomorrow."

"Come on then." He beckoned to the corridor with his head. "Let's go and find somewhere. I just want to have a quick chat with the doctor if he's still around."

My shoulders sagged with relief. "Good, I wanted to, but didn't want to overstep. I just want him to clarify that she's going to be fine."

Jack nodded and gave me a pat on the back. "Let's go and find him."

It took everything for me to walk away from Maya's room, but I just kept telling myself that she would be there the next day, because the alternative was unthinkable.

CHAPTER 55
Will

The very moment the sun rose, I was up and out of bed getting dressed to go to the hospital. When I popped into the hotel restaurant to grab a takeaway coffee Jack and his and Maya's parents were already there. They were sitting at a table laid for breakfast, all staring into mugs.

"Hey, Debra, Ian, great to see you again, although obviously not under these circumstances."

Ian stood up and put a strong hand on my shoulder, squeezing it reassuringly. "Good to see you, too, Will."

"You don't look like you've had a minute's sleep, love." Debra gave me a sympathetic smile. "Sit down and have some breakfast with us."

I looked over towards the buffet, where all the food was laid out under heat lamps, not sure it was what I wanted, or if I could eat anything at all.

Ian looked me in the eye. "It's going to be a long day. We can't go in until nine and then she's got to have her cast on before we can take her home, so you may as well eat something, son."

"Okay," I said with a sigh, taking the empty seat at the table. "You're probably right."

"We should all just go and help ourselves," Jack replied, yet no one made a move.

Apart from a couple of guys in work gear and high-vis jackets and a woman wearing a bright pink trouser suit, we were the only people in there, and no one spoke for a great amount of time. Finally, Debra picked up her phone and looked at the screen.

"Still too early to go. Maybe we should eat something."

We looked at each other and then made a half-hearted effort to get up from our seats. Each of us sighed as we trooped to the buffet and added food to our plates, just enough to satisfy that we'd tried to eat as though everything was normal.

"Have you thought about what the plan is for when Maya comes out of hospital?" I cut my sausage, even though I had no intention of eating it.

"She can come to us," Jack offered. "We can put George in with the girls."

"I could come and stay with her for a wee while," Debra suggested. "I've only got my volunteer work at the hospital. I can easily rearrange that. I mean you've got work, love," she said to Ian, "but there's nothing stopping me from staying with her."

"We're supposed to be going away next week, but maybe the holiday company will let us swap to a later date." Ian patted Debra's hand, telling her silently that he would do whatever it took to take care of their daughter.

I cleared my throat. "She can come and stay with me. I can easily take time off from the bar, and if I'm not there Maddy will be."

"We couldn't expect you to do that, Will," Ian replied, shaking his head.

"No, son, honestly, we'll sort it."

Jack chuckled. "Maybe we should ask Mays what she wants to do."

"There is that," Debra replied with a sigh. "But I honestly think that I should be the one to take care of her. There'll be things she might need doing." A blush rose up her neck. "Lady things."

A snort came from Jack, and I almost choked on my coffee when he said, "I'm sure that Will has that covered, Mum."

The blush spread to Debra's cheeks, and she quickly hid her face behind her cup of tea. Ian's back stiffened as he started to cut his bacon like he was sawing a piece of wood.

"Maddy can help her with whatever I can't, but I honestly would prefer to have her close by." I held my hands up. "But you're her family and like Jack said, we should probably ask Maya." I chuckled, unable to keep the smile from cracking my face. "Because knowing her she has an opinion on it."

"Too bloody right." Jack drained his mug of tea and then slapped the table. "Right, I don't know about you, but I can't eat this luke-warm shite. Let's get to the hospital and see if we're bringing our Mays home."

All in agreement, we stood up, leaving our barely touched plates of food. As I followed them out, I was determined that Maya would be in my house later. Not a chance she would be anywhere else.

***

Maya winced as she dropped her feet to the floor. "Was it a tank that ran over me?" She rubbed her neck, and I would have worried if the doctor hadn't said it was okay for her to take the collar off. It was minor whiplash, thankfully.

"You nearly were, well, by a truck," I replied. When she gave a groan of pain, I almost lost it. "Shit, Maya, I don't know what I'd have done if anything had happened to you."

Dropping my gaze to the pale grey tiles on the floor, I studied a long crack in the one next to my foot. It went from one edge to the other, breaking off into a series of small cracks in the corner. A tiny piece was chipped away, too small to be replaced, reminding me of my heart. It also had tiny veins of damage, not big enough to stop it beating, but enough to make it stall on occasions. That tiny chip which was missing would have been like losing Maya—irreplaceable.

Maya's fingers tangled with mine and she tugged on my hand. "I'm going to be okay. One broken wrist and a few broken ribs aren't the worst thing in the world."

"Yeah, but it could have been so much worse." I swallowed back the anxiety again, silently begging it to stay away. She was fine. She was going home. There was nothing to fear.

"Come and sit down," she begged me. "My lot won't be back with coffee for ages yet."

We were waiting for her to be discharged and as there'd been a major emergency— another car crash—we'd been delayed. I took a seat next to her on the bed.

"Please don't worry, Will." She dropped her head to my shoulder, wrapping her arm around mine. "They wouldn't let me go home if they weren't sure I was okay."

"I know that. It was just the idea of…" Maya moved closer, and I didn't miss another quiet groan; instantly, I was on high alert. "Are you sure you're okay?"

"It's just my ribs. Oh, and my wrist and my neck." She tried a quiet laugh, but it was quickly followed by a wince. "Seriously my ribs are more uncomfortable than anything."

"Come and stay with me," I whispered, staring at the pale yellow wall in front of us. "While you're getting better, stay with me and Maddy. Let me take care of you."

"Mum said she'd stay with me."

I turned to look at her, wanting to see in her eyes what she really wanted. "I know, but I want you to come home with me. I can't stand the idea of you being away from me while you're feeling like this. I just want to be able to help you, Maya. Besides your mum and dad are supposed to be going on holiday."

"I know, but you don't need me under your feet." She gave me a tight smile, while chewing on her bottom lip. "I'd just be in the way, getting you to open things for me, or helping me to get my clothes on."

I grinned. "That's a good enough reason for me to want you to stay."

She giggled and shook her head. "What will Maddy say? What if she doesn't want me there?"

My stomach was clenching in time with my heart because the idea of Maya saying no was almost as scary as the possibility of losing her.

"Maddy loves you. Maya, I…" The words stopped, wavering on the precipice of being out in the open or locked away. But if the night before had taught me anything, it was that time could be too short. "I love you." The words burst out of me like I had seconds to say them before they died on my tongue forever. Hardly able to catch my breath, I carried on telling her everything that was in my head and my heart. "I think I fell in love with you the minute I saw you. If it wasn't then, it was within a few days of knowing you. You're so beautiful and funny and kind, and you're everything that I had no fucking clue I wanted. It was like fate us both being in that bar. If we'd left a few minutes earlier, I would never have seen you standing there looking so damn beautiful." I carried on even though I was practically breathless. "These last couple of months have reminded me that happiness is possible, that love for someone other than my daughter is possible. I realise this might be quick and that maybe you don't feel the same way, but I had to tell you Maya. I had to let you know that I'm sick of being just me—I want to be us."

When I stopped speaking and looked at her, my stomach dropped. Her eyes were staring at me and her mouth in silent "o". In the time I'd known her, she'd never been silent. She always had an answer.

"Maya," I whispered. "Say something, even if it's, Will, shut the fuck up."

Finally, a small smile whispered across her lips and tears brimmed at her lashes. It was partly the response that I'd wanted, the smile at least, but not the tears.

"Forget I ever said anything."

Shaking her head, a little grimace of pain on her beautiful face, she leaned in and kissed me softly. It was short and closed lipped, but it was everything, it was my favourite kiss, because of the words that followed it.

"I love you, too."

"You do?" Gently brushing her hair from her face, I ran a tender finger over the bruise on her left cheekbone, hating that it was there, even though it didn't take anything away from her beauty.

She nodded, a tear crawling down the side of her face. "Just so you now, I'm only crying because I hurt a lot, not because you're the most gorgeous man I've ever met, and you've just made me happier than I realised I could be. I've had some shitty boyfriends in my life, including one I told you about. The one who cheated all through our relationship, and well, it made me wary. But you," she said, shaking her head and smiling. "You've made me realise that there are some good boyfriends in this world and you, Will Newman, are the best."

"You do know we sound like a couple from one of those shitty films that you and Maddy talk about. We sound almost poetic."

"Those films are great," she replied with a giggle, swiping at the tear on her face with her plastered hand. "Ow, that hurts."

"Why have you taken your sling off? That's supposed to be in it."

Maya rolled her eyes. "Are you going to be this bossy while I'm staying with you?"

The hairs on my arms stood to attention, excited and happy, but a little scared. I'd never lived with a woman before, not counting Maddy. I could be really shit at it.

"You're sure?" I asked.

"Yeah, although not so sure what my mum will say about it, plus, you have to double check with Maddy." She narrowed her eyes on me. "Call her before she gets back from London. She's back at nine isn't she? That's what she messaged me the other day."

"Yeah, she is." I grinned, finding it adorable that Maya knew Maddy's train time because my daughter had messaged her to let her know. "I'll speak to her when she gets home—she'll only worry about you all day otherwise."

"Okay, but if she says no, or even shows a hint that she doesn't want me staying, then you have to tell me." She studied me for a few seconds. "I mean it, Will."

"Okay, I promise."

At that moment, the door swung open, and Jack, Debra, and Ian walked in with Dr Young.

"Time to go home, love," Debra said.

Maybe she would argue about her daughter staying with me, maybe she wouldn't, but one thing was for sure I would be the one caring for Maya for the foreseeable future.

CHAPTER 56
Maddy

A warm hand landed on my stomach, slowly edging its way into my knickers as lips kissed my neck and along my shoulder.

"You smell all warm and cuddly," Zak whispered in my ear. "Sexy, warm and cuddly."

Moving onto my back, I opened my legs, bending one at the knee and then dropping it to the mattress. When he pushed his fingers inside of me, I lifted my hips urging him for more, and so he could take my knickers off.

"What do you want to do today?" he asked in between kisses and nips, as his fingers stroked my inner muscles. "Anything at all and I'll make sure it happens."

When his thumb rubbed against my clit, my back shot up, like my spinal cord had been replaced with a live electric cable. His fingers moved in and out slowly and leisurely, as his mouth went to my nipple, flicking his tongue in time. I felt the wave starting in the pit of my stomach, swelling slowly like waves lapping on the shore.

Reaching for Zak's dick, I wrapped my hand around him and started to pump. It was hard to keep the rhythm while I was concentrating on my own orgasm that was getting bigger with each second.

Picking up on my attention being disturbed, he chuckled against my skin. "I can wait, babe."

When I looked down at his flat stomach with the thin line of hair disappearing inside his boxer briefs, I licked my lips. He was gorgeous and sexy, and he was my boyfriend, and now excitement mixed with the intense ring of pleasure deep in the pit of my stomach.

"Do we have any condoms left?" I asked.

"One," he whispered, kissing a path down my cleavage towards my stomach. "We used two yesterday before the party and I gave Liam three."

"Three to Liam?" I tried to sit up, but when Zak moved his fingers up and down inside of me, I gasped with pleasure and lay back down, opening my legs wider, and gripping the headboard behind me.

"Want me to use it?" he asked with a grin.

The deep cadence of his voice was soothing most of the time, but when he spoke while he did amazing things with his fingers, there was nothing soothing about it. It sent me into a frenzy, rapidly moving my hips backwards and forwards chasing the orgasm I was so desperate for.

As I reached my peak, Zak's strong arm wrapped around my shoulders with his hand cupping my head as he kissed me. Our tongues entwined, teeth nipping, as we swallowed each other's moans until mine broke free as a scream.

Immediately I pushed Zak onto his back and yanked down his boxers as he reached across to the bedside table for our one remaining condom. Straddling him, I lifted onto my knees so he could kick his underwear off while he ripped the packet open.

"You want to do it?" he asked, palming his rock hard dick.

I nodded and took it from him, licking my lips as I rolled it on. "I want to go on top," I told him. I hadn't done it before, but I was desperate to try. Zak nodded, and I guided him inside of me. The change of angle felt different, it was good, it was deeper.

"Move your hips, babe," Zak groaned. "I'm dying here."

Giggling, I did as he asked and started to move. At first I wasn't sure of what my rhythm should be, but with Zak's hands on my hips guiding me I soon found it. It was like I was dancing to my favourite tune, moving in time to music playing in my head. It was Helium by Sia, and its slow beat was perfect for the lazy pace of a Sunday morning.

"Fuck," Zak ground out as his fingertips pressed into my bum. "So good."

His eyes fluttered open, and his gaze met mine, as we moved in time, and when I felt the beginning of another orgasm, I grasped his shoulders and clung on. Zak did an ab curl to sit up and the angle changed again. It was just as good, better in fact because his arms wrapped tightly around me while he sucked on my collar bone.

As his hips started to move faster, I matched him thrust for thrust. As his fingertips dug deeper, so did mine. As his breaths became more ragged, so did mine. When he moaned my name, I moaned his, until finally he stiffened and gently bit down on my shoulder and as he did, he gave my clit two strokes, and I went with him. As the tremors ebbed away we held on tight, desperate not to let each other go.

His chest heaved, brushing against my sensitive nipples making me shudder. He wrapped me up tighter against his warm body, dropping soft kisses on my collar bone which I knew would be marked.

"That was perfect," Zak said, leaning his head back to look at me while running his fingers through my messy hair. "You're perfect."

I rolled my eyes. "No, I'm not. Far from it."

"Yeah, to me, you are." He flopped back against his pillows, while I stayed sitting up, our fingers linked together, hands pushing against each other's. Our gazes locked. "I think I—"

"Come on you two, stop shagging and get up." It was Liam, banging on our bedroom door. "We have places to go and beds to strip of jizz stained sheets."

"God he's a dick," I groaned, dropping my head to Zak's chest, my hair spilling over it.

"I don't want to have to come in there, kids," he called, banging the door one more time.

"Okay, okay," Zak yelled back. "Give us ten minutes."

"Up and dressed you two, no more canoodling." Emma clearly thought she was as funny as her boyfriend.

"I suppose we need to get showered," I groaned, looking over to the ensuite bathroom.

"Yeah, I suppose." Zak chuckled. "Pity there are no condoms left. Talking of which." He pointed down to where we were still joined together. "We need to get rid of this, too."

With a groan of disappointment that we couldn't stay in bed any longer, we got up and, even though we didn't have any condoms left, we showered together. I was tempted to say sod it, let's do it without, after all, I had the implant, but I still wasn't quite ready. After all, my dad had been lucky to have an Aunt Miriam and as much as I really, really liked, okay loved, Zak I wasn't ready to be his baby mummy.

***

"Bloody hell," Liv squealed as we flopped into seats on the train. "I thought we were going to miss it."

"Yeah because we had to drag that bloody case down the platform." Liam turned his arm over and looked at the back of his sleeve. "I thought I'd ripped my coat. I could have sworn I heard it rip."

"You didn't, so stop complaining." Liv dug a brush from her bag and started running it through her hair. "I didn't know the wheel was going to come off."

"Do you think it's all the clothes you bought today?" I asked her, the memory of spending an hour and a half in Urban Outfitters still vivid.

"I had my birthday money, so of course I'm going to spend it."

"Anyone want a drink?" Zak asked. "I'll go down to the buffet car." He stood up and took his jacket off, throwing it onto the seat next to me. "Hot or cold, babe?"

"Coffee, please." I reached into my bag and pulled out my purse. "I'll get them."

Before I had chance to take any money out, he took it from me and threw it back into my bag. "I'm getting them. Anyone else?"

"I'll come with you," Liam told him. "Do you want anything to eat, Em?"

"Crisps and chocolate please." She grinned at him, giving him an eyebrow wiggle. "Get yourself something, too, because you're not eating mine."

Liam laughed and ruffled her hair. "God, you're tight. Liv?"

"No thanks. I'm going to have a sleep."

"No snoring," we all chorused. Going back to the house in the Uber the night before, she'd made a noise like a chainsaw.

"Whatever." She gave us all a dirty look and then settled down, resting her head against the window. "Wake me up at Stockport."

"Well, that's where we're getting off, so I hope you'll wake up," I told her.

"That's good then. Night, night."

As the boys disappeared down the aisle, I turned to Emma and raised an eyebrow. "Well?" I ask.

"What?" She shrugged, but I didn't miss the smirk.

"You and Liam. What's happening? Finger banging, or just banging?"

She gave a loud burst of laughter, and when someone tutted further down the carriage, we both giggled and ducked down, leaning closer together.

"So, what method does Zak use," she asked, grabbing hold of my jumper. "Ready To Rock or Scout's Honour." She showed me each hand shape in turn, and I started to giggle. "Well?" she prompted.

My mind flittered back to that morning when Zak had given me an orgasm, and I had to admit I had a little flush. "Ready to Rock."

"Oh my God," she gasped. "Same! Do you think they compared notes, or googled it or something, because Liam definitely used Scout's Honour the first time."

"Maybe. I can't remember the first time, but then I was kind of nervous because, well, it was the first time." I honestly couldn't recall what technique he'd used; I just knew it had been good. "I don't know whether I'd even know anyway."

"I think you'd know if he'd suddenly changed his method." She gave me the rocker sign with her hand and then flicked her tongue like a snake between her fingers. "It's a bloody game changer," she whispered.

We put our heads together and cackled conspiratorially. "Have you had sex, then?" I eventually asked her.

"Yeah," she squeaked. "Last night was the first time."

"And?" I bounced in my seat, desperate for information. It might make me a little uncomfortable hearing it, after all Liam was like a cousin to me, but I was excited for my friend.

"It was so good." She fanned herself. "How have I not seen this boy for the last three years since he grew a couple of feet and got muscles.

"You saw he'd grown and got muscles, so he clearly didn't go that far under the radar."

She shrugged. "Clearly."

"And he took care of you?" It was her first time, as far as I was aware anyway.

She took a deep breath, a silly grin on her face. "Oh yeah. He put his hoody under me, in case I bled, which I did a tiny bit, and then afterwards, he cuddled me all night. Then this morning we did it again. He thought I'd be sore, but I was more than ready." Emma bounced in her seat and grabbed my hand. "Why did I never do this before?"

I shrugged. "Because you didn't like anyone enough, and we probably weren't old enough."

"Very true." She leaned into the aisle and looked towards the doors into the next carriage. "I think they're coming."

"Okay, but quickly tell me, do you like him, and are you actually girlfriend and boyfriend now?"

She nodded. "Yeah. He asked me at the party last night and then he double checked before we had sex again this morning."

"So you've got one condom left," I stated, with a wiggle of my eyebrows.

"Hmm, well, not really Liam put it over his head and mouth and blew it up."

As we both cracked up, the boys arrived back and put various drinks and snacks on the table.

"What are you two laughing at?" Zak asked, leaning down to give me a quick kiss.

"Nothing," Emma and I chorused.

Then a voice behind us chirped up. "They're discussing your fingering techniques boys, and now if you don't mind, I'm trying to sleep until we get to Stockport."

CHAPTER 57
Will

As Maya winced, my hands gripped into fists. It was almost time for her pain medication, but each time I saw hurt ghost over her face, it killed me. She was on the sofa propped up with pillows, lying under a duvet. She kept dropping off to sleep, but when she woke she assured me that she was fine.

Her eyes fluttered as she lifted her arm with the cast on it. "What time is it?" she asked.

"You ready for your pain killers?"

"Not yet, I was just wondering whether it was time for Maddy to get back."

Getting up from my chair, I went over and kneeled at the side of the sofa, smoothing a hand over her hair. "She will be totally fine about you being here, honestly."

"I just feel like I've been forced upon her." A small grimace swept over her face. "I don't want to ruin the relationship I'm building with her. I love you and she's your daughter and so I want to be friends with her."

"Exactly, she's my daughter and I know her. I know how big her heart is, and there is no way she would want you anywhere else but here. I love you and having you here makes me happy and that's all she'll want."

At that exact moment, I heard a key in the door and, as it always did when I knew my daughter was home safe, relief flashed through my body.

"And here she is." I pushed up from the floor and went into the hallway. As I stepped into it the front door swung open and my beautiful daughter stepped inside. She looked tired but happy as she stepped into my arms. "Hey, Mads, did you have a good time?"

"It was the best, Dad. We had such a good time and the house where the party was, God Dad, it was unbelievable. They had a swimming pool, and a bar, and a proper DJ and—"

"Okay, okay," I said with a laugh. "Take a breath."

She let out a breathy laugh. "Sorry." She grinned. "How was your weekend? Miss me?"

I cleared my throat and glanced behind me, towards the lounge door. "Maya is here."

"Still? Ah brill. What did you do?"

She took a step to move past me and I caught her hand.

"I didn't call you, because I didn't want to worry you, but she had a car accident so is going to stay here for a while. Is that okay with you?"

"Of course, I don't mind. She's okay, though?" Her voice was almost a whisper as she clutched her jacket in the region of her heart.

"Broken wrist and cracked ribs—oh, and a few bruises. Really, she was lucky because she veered onto the hard shoulder."

Once again, the horror of what might have been, appeared like a ghost on my shoulder, making me shudder. Thank Christ for Maya's quick thinking.

"Is she in there or in bed."

I thumbed over my shoulder. "She's awake, but I'm just about to get her painkillers. Go in and see her."

Without any hesitation, Maddy skipped past me and into the lounge. I paused for a few seconds, listening and felt my heart warm when I heard Maddy ask if she could give Maya a hug. The way they'd taken to each other so quickly was just perfect; I could have so easily have got it wrong by introducing them so soon. I guessed that now the L word had been used it was official that we were serious about each other, and it was more important than ever that Maddy and Maya liked each other.

When I went back into the lounge a few minutes later, with a glass of water and Maya's pills, Maya was telling Maddy what happened. I'd only heard bits and pieces, not wanting to put her through reliving it, but she sounded okay as she spoke.

"I saw him in my rearview mirror, getting closer, and was I yelling at him to just overtake me, but I think he was coming off at the next junction because I vaguely remember his indicator going." She sighed. "I didn't want to move lanes because it was quite misty and raining."

"I don't blame you," Maddy replied. "And what happened? He just went into the back of you?"

"I braked, because the lorry in front of me did, but dickhead behind didn't. He went into the back of me and shunted me forward, so I just about managed to steer away from the lorry. I braced on the steering wheel, but when I hit the bank, I lurched forward, and my wrist was caught at a funny angle when the airbag went off."

Having heard enough, I stepped out of the shadow of the door and went to stand next to the sofa, trying to quell my anger.

"I hope the police do him for dangerous driving," I grumbled, handing Maya her water and pills.

"Jack says that the police said he doesn't have insurance." She smiled up at me and popped the pills in her mouth. "He'll get into real trouble for that."

"Good," Maddy snapped. "What a dick. It's intimidation as well as shit driving."

Maya smiled, but I could see that it was laced with pain. "I think maybe you should go up to bed, gorgeous."

"God, Dad, you're so mushy, it's icky," Maddy groaned.

"Whatever, Madeline, but I don't care." Grinning at Maddy, I crouched down beside Maya and rubbed her thigh over the duvet. "You look shattered."

She nodded as she swallowed the pills with a sip of water. "Yeah, I think I will."

"Get in my bed, and I'll get in the spare one to give you some space for your wrist." When she frowned, I smiled. I didn't want to sleep in a different bed either, but I still thought she'd have a better night without me. "Just for tonight, at least."

"Yeah, okay." She threw back the duvet and swung her legs off the sofa. She was wearing cute pink and white striped shortie pyjamas, and even with a cast on her arm and bruises on her face and shins, she looked incredible. "Night, Maddy, and I'm glad you had a good time in London. And don't worry about that mean ex-girlfriend."

"I won't, don't worry."

I made a mental note to ask about that once I'd settled Maya in bed. Even so, her feeling happy to tell Maya was another reason to feel like life was good.

Ten minutes later, with Maya already asleep, I went back into the lounge to find Maddy frantically texting.

"How the hell do your thumbs go so fast?" I asked her, flopping down next to her.

"Practice, Daddy. That's all it takes."

"Who you texting anyway. Surely not Zak, you've been with him all weekend."

"Nope. Ana."

I rolled my eyes, still not sure why she would want to be friends with her after what she did. Over reaction on my part? Maybe.

Expressive eyes looked up at me. "She bailed on us at the weekend."

"You never said when we spoke over the weekend. You just said you were having a great time."

"We were." She shrugged. "I didn't think to tell you." Biting on her lip, Maddy pulled her feet up and sat crossed-legged, facing me. "She just didn't turn up, Dad. We waited as long as we could at the station, and me, Em and Liv all called her loads of time, but she didn't answer any of them."

"It's her own fault that she missed out, sweetheart. There wasn't much else you could do about it." Her eyes were full of worry, and I wished that she had a few more years' experience. Then she'd realise that none of it was her fault. "Take my hand."

She gave me a withering look but took it, anyway, smiling when I wrapped my other around it.

"Ana is a troubled girl at the moment. You've tried to help her with her mum, suggesting she go away for the weekend with you. You didn't even really kick off when she got you pissed."

"Dad, I was pissed already."

"I know that but," I said, patting her hand still in mine, "I know you, and I know that you're sensible enough to know when you've had enough to drink. Her spiking your cider with vodka wasn't funny because it took away your control, and we all know how you like to have control." I smile wryly and earned myself a grin.

"I don't *always* have to have control, but I do know you're right. Zak and I even argued about it." She shook her head. "And he's on your side."

"Good lad."

"As if he'd do or say anything opposite to you. He loves you."

She shook her head, but her grin told me she liked the idea.

"Like I said, he's a good lad." Grinning, I pulled her close, so that her cheek was resting on my chest. "I'm glad you had a good time, Mads, but I'm also glad that you're home, safe and sound. As for Ana, I personally would be avoiding her." I heard her take a breath to speak, but I jumped in before she had chance. "I'm not saying cut her out of your life totally, but I do think you should maybe keep your distance. At least while she's in the head space that she's in."

"Dad, I can't *not* be there for her. She's my best friend. What if she needs my help?"

"Then be there for her. Check in with her, but make sure you don't let her take her advantage of you again. Be on your guard and make sure she knows no more stunts, or I'll be speaking to her mum and dad."

She contemplated it for a few seconds and then nodded. "I will. I'll speak to her tomorrow and try and find out why she didn't turn up." Her head shifted against my chest. "Am I an awful friend, Dad?"

I looked down to see worry in her eyes. "Why, sweetheart?"

"I didn't think of her once, the whole weekend."

"Don't feel bad about that. It's understandable, the ways she's been recently, and no one begrudges you having a good time. You're seventeen, that's what you're supposed to be doing."

"I know, but she's my best friend, and she never entered my head."

Maddy had a big heart, and she loved Ana, but she needed to realise it was okay to have fun.

"That's okay, Mads, because you should be able to have fun without worrying about it or anyone else." I hugged her tight. "Life is too short, and it's not like Ana will know."

"I suppose." She sighed. "Anyway, did you save me anything to eat? I'm starving."

"You haven't eaten already?"

"A crappy sandwich before we got on the train."

I kissed the top of her head. "Good job I saved you some lasagne then. Garlic bread?"

"Oh yes please, and mayo on the side."

"You're a weird child," I told her, even though I would give her anything she wanted, even mayonnaise with lasagne. It was good to be taking care of her, because if she went away to uni, I wouldn't have many more opportunities for a while.

Later, I went to check in on my other girl and was surprised to find her awake.

"Hey, gorgeous." I knelt by the side of the bed and ran a hand down her hair. "You in pain?"

"Hmm, a bit. Nothing major. I only just woke." She gave me a sad little smile and reached up to place her hand on mine. "Can't I sleep with you?"

Chuckling I ran my finger over her pouty lips. "No, you need to get some proper sleep, and I don't want to roll onto your arm."

"You can sleep on the other side."

"But you know I like to fling my arm over you, then what about your ribs?"

Maya sighed heavily, followed by a little grimace.

"See," I told her. "You can't even sigh without pain."

Her eyes fluttered closed, and then she nodded. "I know. I just miss you."

The feeling that swept through me felt like warmth had been injected into my veins. The heat reached every single pore, every single nerve ending, and mixed with the excitement that hadn't stop swirling since I'd met Maya. Being a kid on Christmas morning had nothing on how waking up every day with Maya as mine felt.

"I miss you, too." I kissed her forehead. "Now, go to sleep and shout if you need anything. Do not get out of bed."

"Okay." Her response was resigned as she pulled the duvet up.

"Pills are next to the bed." I didn't want to leave her, but she really did need to sleep.

"How's Maddy. She told me about Zak's horrible ex-girlfriend."

"She's fine. I think she's more worried about Ana not turning up to go with them. Her words to me about the ex were, 'She's insignificant to me, and if he chooses her over me then he's not the boy I thought he was.'"

Maya chuckled, and when her eyelids slowly closed, I knew it was time to let her sleep.

"Night, gorgeous," I whispered. "I love you."

And I did. More than I thought possible so quickly. More than I'd expected.

"Love you, too," she whispered back, and that warmth just spread wider, filling ever corner of my being.

MAYA'S DIARY ENTRY

I can't write much because I'm so tired and in a fair amount of pain. I had to write this down, though. We told each other that we love one another. I know he first said it after the accident, but he's said it again since. I love him, too and I can't believe how happy I am – apart from the pain. Maddy doesn't seem to be bothered about me staying here while I get better, which is a huge relief.

I really need to sleep. I just wish it was with Will in his bed :)

CHAPTER 58
Maddy

"Maya still asleep, Dad?" I asked, as I gathered my school books together.

"Yeah."

He rubbed a hand over his face, and I noticed how tired he looked. "Did you sleep at all last night?"

"Yeah," he said with a yawn, "but I kept waking up thinking I'd heard her moving around. I just checked on her, though, and she's fast asleep."

"Just leave her as long as you can. Sleep is good for healing the body."

He reached out and pulled me closer, kissing my forehead. "I know."

When he let me go he scratched at his chest and yawned again. "I might just try and catch a bit more sleep once you've gone."

I glanced at the clock on the cooker, to see it was only half seven. "You didn't need to get up with me, you know."

"I know, but I haven't seen you all weekend, plus I wanted to be sure that you're okay with her staying."

My eyes almost bulged out of my head. "What? Of course I'm okay with it. I would have been disappointed if you hadn't brought her back here."

Dad's shoulder's sagged in relief. "You're a good girl, Mads."

"I know I am. Be very grateful for me, and now go back to bed." I gave him a hug. "I need to go because Zak will be here soon."

"Is he in his mum's car today?"

"Nope, he's riding his bike over and then walking me to school."

Dad's eyes rolled. "Suck up."

Laughing, I gathered my stuff and walked towards the front door, knowing that secretly Dad loved that Zak was taking the time to walk me to school.

And, when I got outside, there he was, about to push his bike up our path with a huge grin on his face. He looked as gorgeous as ever, wrapped up in his coat with a black beany hat pulled down over his dark hair.

"Morning." As I approached, gripping the handle bars, he leaned the top half of his body forward to kiss me. "You smell nice."

"It's my usual perfume." I gave him another quick peck. "Want to give me a croggie?" I pointed at his bike.

"What the hell is a croggie?"

I laughed at how it sounded in his accent. "A croggie, a seaty. Basically, you sit on the seat, and I sit on the crossbar."

Frowning, he looked at me and then the bike. "We can if you want to give it a go, but…"

"I'm joking, Zak. I think it's illegal anyway."

"We'd better walk, then." Smiling he held out his hand, which I took, loving how his big one curled around my much smaller one. "So, tell me about Maya. All you said in your text was that she had an accident and was staying at yours."

"It was a car accident," I told him. "Someone went into the back of her, and she broke her wrist and a couple of ribs. She's been lucky, and is going to be fine, but I think Dad wanted her close."

"That's understandable." He squeezed my hand and led me across the road. "Thank God it wasn't worse."

He was right. I'm not sure how Dad would have taken it. Maya was going to be fine, but it was obvious he was worried sick. I was glad she was staying with us, for Dad's sake as much as hers.

"Have you heard anything from Ana since we got back?"

All I seemed to do lately when talking about Ana was sigh. My response to Zak's current question was no different, a long drawn out exhale that held a mix of frustration and sadness. I felt a twinge in my chest at the thought of seeing the girl who'd been my best friend for what seemed like forever. I hated that things weren't right between us, but I wasn't sure what else I could do. We'd tried to help her, but she didn't seem to want to make things better.

"No and I'm nervous to see her," I reply. "I have no idea how she's going to be on a day to day basis."

"Hmm, there's got to be more going on than just her mum and dad. I mean your dad went out of his way to help her with that, yet she's still being awkward."

Aware of the steel in his tone, I decided it was better to change the subject. I knew how he felt about Ana, but she was my friend, and I didn't want to argue about her.

"So," I said, looking up at him with a smile. "Heard any gossip about the party?"

***

"How are you feeling?" I asked Emma as we filed into the canteen at lunchtime. I hadn't had chance to talk to her all morning. "Bit sore down there."

She giggled. "I'm fine." Looking around, she leaned in closer. "He called last night, and we had phone sex. Well, I say phone sex, I was knackered, so just made a few moaning noises while he had a wank."

I burst out laughing, grateful that Emma knew just how to brighten my day, seeing as Ana was barely talking to any of us again. She'd sat next to me in study period in total silence, but she definitely wasn't studying. When I asked her why she hadn't turned up for the trip to London, she'd muttered something about having better things to do.

"You're an idiot," I told Emma as we joined the queue for food. Then something struck me. "Not that I don't trust Liam, but you didn't do it over video chat did you?"

"God no," she snapped back, elbowing me in the side. "How stupid do you think I am?"

"I mean, I don't think he'd do anything bad, but people can get hold of stuff like that and—"

"It's fine, Miss Cautious. I didn't and I won't, and I won't send him any nudies either, and I certainly don't want any dick pics from him." She picked up two trays and passed me one. "I mean it's a beautiful thing he has in his pants, but I don't want to clog my phone up with images of it. Besides, what happens if we split up, I'll be tempted to look at the photos all the time, and I'll never move on. I'll always remember the good days."

When she raised an eyebrow, we both burst out laughing, and were still clutching our sides when we got to the front of the queue.

A few minutes later, Liv joined us at the table and slammed her salad box down.

"What's wrong?" I asked her, forking a tomato from my plate.

"Ana." Was her short, curt reply.

"What's she done now?" Emma shook her head. "What the hell is wrong with her? I thought we'd sorted everything out."

"Clearly not." Liv flicked her hair over her shoulder. "I told her about the party and all about Teddy and she told me I was stupid because he'd clearly be, and I quote, 'Fingering someone else by tomorrow.' Not that I let him do that to me."

"Take no notice of her." I patted her arm. "He didn't seem like that at all. Didn't you say he's already texted you?"

"Yes, but she's probably right. It's not like I'm going to see him again, is it?"

"You might." Emma didn't sound convincing.

Liv shook her head. "No, he'll probably go to Oxford or somewhere else just as posh. He's not going to slum it in Manchester. Did you know his dad is a barrister?"

"And?" Emma shrugged. "Zak's dad is a surgeon, and Zak still gets in Maddy's pants regularly."

I nudged her in the stomach. "Oi."

"But he does."

"I object to your insinuation that he shouldn't just because his dad is a surgeon. I'm just as good as him."

"I know, that was the point I was making to Liv. She shouldn't think she's not good enough for Teddy just because of his dad's profession."

"Oh bloody hell," Liv groaned. "Here's Little Miss Sunshine now."

We all looked over to see Ana walking towards us. Her mouth was turned down into a grimace, and she was practically dragging her bag on the floor.

"Brace yourselves," I muttered. "She doesn't look happy at all."

A few seconds later, it was confirmed that Ana was definitely in a bad mood. "Are you all still talking about that shitty party you went to?" Her face twisted into a scowl and the atmosphere at our table shifted instantly.

"It wasn't shitty. If you'd come with us you, might have enjoyed yourself," I replied, trying to keep my voice calm despite the building tension.

She gave me a disdainful look, like I'd suggested she should have climbed Everest or something. "We can't all swan off and have a fun little weekend, can we?"

I glanced questioningly at Emma and then Liv. "I thought your mum and dad had sorted things out." I put a hand on her forearm. She'd pissed me off, but she was still my best friend. "Is it still all going on? Your mum isn't drinking again, is she?"

Ana's expression was hard, not the happy, cheeky smile I'd always been used to over the years. I hadn't seen that look for a long time. It's disappearance had been sudden, and she didn't seem to be in any rush to bring it back.

Frowning, she pulled her arm away from me. "No, she isn't."

"So, what's wrong?" I asked, biting back a sigh of frustration. "Tell us and maybe we can help you."

"Everything is fine. And for your information I don't need yours or anyone else's help."

Emma raised an eyebrow, and Liv cleared her throat. We all knew that she was far from fine. The respite from her bad moods had been very brief. It seemed like her mum drinking wasn't the main issue. Her parents splitting up was awful, and it must have been hurting her more than I could imagine, but we were her friends, and I couldn't understand why she didn't want our help. Why she didn't feel like she could be open about how she was feeling.

"Ana, why don't y—"

"No, Maddy, I don't want to talk about it. You did your good deed sorting the house out, I don't need any of you sticking your noses in."

She looked at each of us and with a shake of her head, stormed away.

"What the hell is her problem?" Liv took the lid off her salad box and peered inside. "She should count herself lucky that she had her mum and dad together for so long, poor Emma here doesn't even know who her dad is, and your mum died before you were even on solids."

"Liv!"

"She does have a point," Emma added, flicking her food around on her plate like she was looking for something.

"I know, but…" I had no idea what the but was. Liv was right, at least Ana still had both her parents.

"Maybe we should organise a night out or something?" Em suggested.

"Em, she was just invited to a weekend away and didn't bother turning up." Liv stabbed a prawn with her fork—her mum always made her lovely lunches.

Sitting back in my seat, I surveyed the canteen, trying to catch sight of Ana, but she'd disappeared. I had a horrible feeling we weren't going to get back to normal with her any time soon and the truth of acknowledging that fact, made my chest ache.

CHAPTER 59
Will

Maya gave a disgruntled huff as she tried to get comfy on the sofa. I'd heard the sound a lot already, since the minute she woke up, in fact. When she needed help in the shower, help drying herself, getting dressed, and as she was currently trying to do, get comfy.

"Would a pillow or cushion help?" I asked, aware that I was hovering and had been all day. I wanted to tell myself to stop being like fucking clinging ivy, so I could put money on Maya feeling the same way.

"No." She put her good hand to her side. "I'm due a painkiller soon."

Forcing myself to sit down, I gripped the arms of the chair to stop myself from getting back up to help her.

"Do you want it now?"

I heard an almost imperceptible sigh of frustration so, not waiting for a response, pointed the remote at the TV.

"Anything you want to watch?"

"No."

Short, sharp and snappy.

We were only on day one and things were already feeling tense. Well, Maya was. I was more Mother Hen with a case of serious unease.

"Just say when you want anything, you know pain killers, a drink or—"

"Yes, Will, I know."

She let out another deep sigh, so turning off the TV, I turned in my seat to look at her. "What's wrong?"

"Nothing."

She chewed on her pouty bottom lip, shaking her head with a look that said, 'disagree with me if you dare'. I felt for her, but if she started to take it out on me, things were going to get even more tense between us. We were still basking in the glow of new love, and I didn't want anything to spoil that. I also didn't want us to bottle up how we were feeling to the point where one or both of us boiled over.

I wasn't experienced in relationships, but I knew enough that I couldn't leave it to fester.

"I know you're in pain, Maya. I know you're frustrated, so instead of trying to act like everything is okay, tell me what you need to help make things feel a little better." I raised an eyebrow. "If you want me to shut the fuck up, tell me. If you want me to stop asking what you want, tell me. If you want something, ask me, but don't sit there bottling it up and getting more and more pissed off with me."

"I'm not," she protested.

"Maya, you are. You're being snappy, and I fully understand why, but give me some indication about what it is. If it's your pain, then I can get you pain killers. If you're uncomfortable, I can get you a pillow. Just give me a clue."

Then she burst into tears, and I felt like the biggest shit on the planet. I hadn't even raised my voice. I'd kept my tone soft and light, yet big fat tears were rolling down her pale cheeks.

Moving to her side, I used my thumbs to wipe the wetness from her cheeks. "Hey, hey, what's wrong? I didn't mean to upset you."

"You haven't," she snivelled. "I'm just so fed up and miserable."

"Staying here?" I asked wryly.

Maya's tears splashed my skin as she shook her head before dropping it against my shoulder. Gripping onto my jumper, she gave great big gulping sobs, making her body—and mine—shake as she held on tight.

"It's j-j-j-just painful and I f-f-feel so useless."

Gently wrapping her in my arms, I kissed the top of her head and made soothing noises to try and calm her down. I knew she was uncomfortable, but I was also aware of what the doctor had said about suffering from post-accident trauma.

"I hate that I can't even get dressed." She hiccupped.

"I like that you can't," I joked. "It means I get to help you put your bra on."

She snorted, a cross between a laugh and a sob, then wiped her nose with the back of her hand. "Trust you."

"I must admit I had a sneaky look at them while I helped you. And, when I help you take it off, I might even cop a feel."

I got a smile from her, even though she continued crying quietly, wrapping both arms around me.

"I'm being stupid," she said with a sniff.

"No, you're not. You've had a shit experience that scared you, and it's all just got a bit too much." I kissed her hair and inhaled a relieved breath. "It could have been so much worse."

After a few minutes, Maya's cries subsided, and her grip on me loosened.

"Bit better now?" I asked.

She nodded. "Yep. Thank you."

"Anything for you." And I meant it. I would do anything for her. I'd do whatever it took to make her happy. From the minute I'd met her, it was if I'd been ordained to. "So, tell me what you need."

"Painkillers and a pillow or cushion, please." Her bottom lip was pouty, like a small child's who was being forced to do something they really didn't want to, in her case, admit that she needed help.

"Okay, sit back and I'll get everything you need." I helped her ease back against the sofa, then slowly stood up, my eyes pinned to her the whole time, until I was sure that she was okay. "Want some chocolate or ice cream?"

She considered it for a second, and then shook her head. "No thanks."

"Okay." I dropped another kiss to her head. "I'll be back in two minutes."

After getting her some pain killers, I ran up the stairs to get another pillow. My phone started to ring. Just as I reached the bedroom door. I gave it a cursory glance, ready to ignore it, but saw that it was Marcus. He'd been good enough to take on my shifts so I could take care of Maya, so didn't want to ignore him if it was urgent.

"Marcus, what's up mate?"

"Will, that guy who reckons he's your dad, was here again. I told him you weren't working today, and he said it was fine, he'd come to the house. Sorry, bud, I'd have lied and said you'd slipped out for a bit if I'd known he had your address."

"For fuck's sake," I groaned, running a hand over my head. "Can he not take a bloody hint? How long since he left the bar?"

"Two minutes ago."

That gave me ten or so to figure out how I was going to tell him to fuck off and actually be heard this time. I was just glad I'd told Marcus everything, otherwise he might have turned up and I wouldn't have been prepared.

"Okay," I sighed. "Cheers for that. Everything else okay? No problems?"

"No. Except the bread order was short."

"Great, that's all we need seeing as Robbie's sandwiches are so popular." I hung my head wondering what else could go wrong.

"It's fine; Robbie came up with an open sandwich that takes less bread. It's been a big hit so far." Marcus chuckled. "You really need to send that kid on some courses so we can increase our menu."

"Yeah, I send him on the courses and then a big pub in Manchester knicks him from us. No, we're fine with sandwiches and burgers for now."

I glanced at the bedroom door, conscious that Maya was still waiting for her pillow. "Anyway, thanks for letting me know, mate. Call me if you need anything."

"Will do. Speak later."

As he ended the call, all I could think about was how to get rid of the man who donated sperm to my mum, because I knew there was nothing he could say that would make me welcome him into my life. Scrubbing a hand through my hair, I went back downstairs to take Maya her pillow.

"What's wrong?" she immediately asked. She rubbed a finger between her eyes. "You've got that little crease that you get when something is bothering you."

I had decided to try and keep it from her, but clearly wasn't very good at it. "It's nothing I can't sort out." Going over to her, I gently pushed her forward, putting the pillow behind her. "Is that better?"

She shuffled a little, then nodded. "Yeah, but don't think you're getting away with not telling me what's going on."

Dropping to my haunches, I took both her hands in mine. "It's Steven Brownlow."

"The man who says he's your dad?"

"Yeah, he's on his way round here. Marcus just called to let me know he'd been in the bar looking for me, and when I wasn't there, he said he was coming here."

"For what?" She reached up and smoothed her finger along the crease that she said I had. "Stop it, or it'll stick, and you'll look permanently puzzled."

Chuckling, I turned my head and kissed the inside of her wrist. "Don't worry, I'll make sure I don't let it spoil my good looks."

"Good because I really can't have a boyfriend I can barely look at." She started to giggle, then winced. "Ooh that hurts."

"Well, I'd better make sure that I don't make you laugh then."

"No." She sighed heavily. "I need you to keep doing that because if I don't I might cry." Her bottom lip trembled. "And I don't want to, not again."

"If you want to cry, then cry. It's fine." Kissing her forehead, I wished that she wasn't having to go through everything.

She took a deep breath. "No, I don't want to cry."

"But do you need to?" I cocked my head on one side and raised an eyebrow, waiting for her response.

She thought about it for a few seconds, wiped her nose with her hand, then shook her head. "Nope. As long as you're here, I don't need to cry."

"Just remember that if you do feel like crying, then do it and I'll still be here."

Brushing Maya's hair from her face, I thought about kissing her, but when the doorbell rang, I knew my window of opportunity was gone.

"Shit," I groaned, resting my forehead against hers. "He's here."

Her hand smoothed down my cheek, and instantly the anger that had been building started to subside, just a little.

"Go and see what he wants and don't lose your temper."

"Okay." I stretched to my feet. "I'll try not to lose it with him."

With a last kiss to Maya's head, I slowly made my way to the door shouting that I was on my way when the doorbell rang again.

When I swung the door open, Steven's hand was reaching out, as though he was going to knock or ring the bell again.

"I said I was coming, now what do you want?"

"Seems like you knew I was on my way here." He looked me up and down and I didn't fail to notice the slight smirk on lips. He certainly didn't come across as a man who was desperate to reconcile with his long-lost son.

"Marcus called me, so what do you want?"

"Can I come in?" He placed a foot on the doorstep, but I pulled the door to me, closing the gap.

"No." I jutted out my chin in defiance. "So?"

There was a resigned sag to his shoulders, and for a moment, he looked like an old man. Defeated and old. If I'd been a better person, I might have felt a glimmer of sympathy, but I didn't. Not one little bit.

"This would be much better if I could come inside."

I cleared my throat, using the pause to consider how I kicked a sixty-odd-year-old bloke from my property without causing him any harm.

"I really need to speak to you, William." I shot him a glance. "Sorry, Will."

He was persistent, I'd give him that. "Just say what you've got to say and then leave."

It was obvious he was about to argue again, but something in my expression must have warned him not to.

"I didn't want to ask you…" He rubbed a hand over his face. "Tell you like this."

"What?" I asked impatiently, almost ready to just shove him off my doorstep.

"Your brother needs a kidney, and I was wondering if you'd be willing to donate one of yours."

CHAPTER 60

Will

If Steven had smacked me around the head, I don't think I'd have been as dazed as I was by his announcement—or question, whatever it was. I had no idea, but what I did know was that he had a fucking cheek.

"You've got some neck on you," I finally managed to growl. "How fucking dare, you."

"William, if I hadn't been desperate… If *he* hadn't been desperate…"

Shaking my head in disbelief, I moved to shut the door, but he placed a big meaty hand on it.

"Will, please it's for my son," he yelled.

I'd been stoic as a kid, never really dwelling on my dad not being around. Never upset or questioning why he didn't want me in his life. It was what it was, and as far as I was concerned, his loss not mine. Yet, in that moment, listening to him pleading for his son, I knew exactly what rejection felt like. I knew the weight in my heart felt to the point of pain, like I was being crushed. The emotion I tried to hold back scratched at my throat and made my eyes sting.

Those feelings of loneliness that I'd pushed away as a kid, for fear of appearing weak, now washed over me like a cold, wet fog, making me shiver throughout my whole body. I hated that he'd evoked emotions I'd managed to stave off for years. He had no right to do that. He didn't deserve it, and I wanted to punch myself for letting him take away my control.

"I don't give a shit," I ground out. "Now, get off my fucking property before I call the police," I leaned into his space, "or worse."

He tried to hide his anger and disdain, but I saw it. I saw the disappointment that I wasn't willing to help his precious offspring. That his bastard wouldn't help the one with his name.

If I'd ever had any regret at saying no, then it disappeared in the split second that a sneer appeared on his lips.

"I told you once," I said, my tone low and menacing. "And I won't tell you again."

He finally got the message and took a step back, leaving me with one last look of pure anger and distaste before I slammed the door. With my chest heaving with the weight of it all, I laid both palms against the wood and rested my forehead, relishing in how the glass cooled my heated skin. My anger was at the point of explosion, with the pressure building in my head and buzzing in my ears. I wanted to rip the door off its hinges and then chase after him and demand to know why he thought he had the right to fuck about with my life.

"Will?" The voice behind me was tentative and quiet, but it still managed to instantly calm me down.

When I felt a hand on my back, I slowly turned around and asked, "Did you hear any of that?"

"Bits."

Maya's arm was wrapped around her waist, and there was pain etched across her face, so I put my hand to her back and gently turned her around. "Come on, let's get you back on the sofa."

"Will, I'm fine. What did he mean it's for his son? What is?" She looked over her shoulder and immediately winced. "Tell me."

"Sit down first."

I helped her back to the sofa, making sure she was comfortable. Sensing her impatience, I started to talk. "His son needs a kidney and wants me to give it to him."

"Woah."

With wide eyes, Maya looked as shocked as I felt. My heart was pounding against my chest as my head tried to unscramble everything that Steven had told me, that he'd asked me for.

"Yeah, I know." Saying it again didn't make it sound any better. Didn't make him sound any less of a wanker for asking, or me a twat for saying no. "Should I have said yes?"

Maya chewed on her lip and shrugged. "My instinct says no, but…"

I knew exactly what she meant. As the seconds passed by, the more I was questioning my response. Not telling him to fuck off, but I could have least told him to get my 'brother' to contact me. Because surely he couldn't have expected me to decide there and then. *Surely,* he'd have known that I'd have to think about it… wouldn't he?

Maya must have read my mind. "Maybe if his son had asked you'd have felt different."

"At least then I'd know he really wanted it. Maybe he doesn't know he asked me."

"Maybe he doesn't even know about you," Maya said, grabbing for my hand. "It might explain why he's never tried to contact you or asked you for a kidney himself."

"I wouldn't put it past Steven to hide my existence. He's hardly got a good track record where honesty is concerned." Suddenly, I felt embarrassed for saying no, which made me angrier. I dropped my head into my hands and groaned. "Why the fuck am I feeling guilty about this?"

"You've nothing to feel guilty about. You're entitled to say no, Will."

"But what if..." My words trailed off as I considered what might happen to the brother I'd never met. "Should I have said yes?"

"No," Maya protested. "Not if you're unsure. Besides which, you may not be a match, and," she said with a sigh, "it's a dangerous operation, babe."

I reached up and rubbed a finger gently over her frown, giving her a small smile. "I'd be fine."

"I'd still worry. And think about Maddy. Would she want you to do it?"

***

"No, absolutely not," Maddy said later that evening when I mentioned the transplant. "You don't even know him, so why should you?"

I didn't argue because she was right, I didn't owe Cameron anything, so why should I? I also knew that, like me, Maddy would start to feel guilty and by the end of the night would have probably researched everything to ensure that it was safe for me to say yes.

"And why hasn't he asked you himself?" She echoed the same question that Maya and I had been tossing back and forth earlier. "If he wanted your kidney, he should have come here, told you who he was, and asked politely, 'can I have your kidney?'"

"You dad doesn't think that his brother knows about him."

Maddy's head whipped back and forth between us. "That's just messed up if it's true." She slumped back in her chair. "You really think your dad would do that?"

I shrugged. "I don't know him, so no idea. What little I do know; I wouldn't put it past him."

"What a vile thing to do." Maddy chewed on her thumbnail, and I knew she was thinking.

"What?" I asked.

"What if he doesn't really need a kidney and he's just going to sell yours?"

I burst out laughing, as did Maya, but she quickly stopped as it clearly hurt. Trust Maddy!

"What the hell sort of things do you watch on TV?" I shook my head, still chuckling.

"Hey," she protested, sitting up straight. "It happens, Dad. People go out for a drink and then wake up in an abandoned multi-story car park on an old operating table with a foot long scar across their back."

"A foot long?" Maya asked, grinning, but holding her side. "Is that even possible?"

"Are you two doubting me?" Maddy picked her phone up from the arm of the chair and started to tap away at the screen. "I'll show you."

"Mads, sweetheart, it's fine. I believe you, but I'm sure that's not what Steven is doing."

"You just said you don't know him," she protested, looking up at me through her long lashes as she continued tapping on her phone. "He might be a real weirdo."

"He might, but I believe that it's his son who needs the kidney." From my spot on the end of the sofa, I reached for Maya's feet and pulled them into my lap, resting my hand on her calf. I just needed to be touching her whenever I could, even if it was only her feet. "I think I'm going to sleep on it and see how if anything miraculous comes to me in the night to help me to decide. I'm sure he'll be back anyway."

"Maybe ask to speak to Cameron yourself," Maya suggested. "Then see how you feel?"

"Yes, do that," Maddy added and when her eyes narrowed, I knew she was already feeling sorry for my 'brother'. "But I don't want you in any danger."

"If, and it's a big if, I say yes, then I'll make sure it's all completely safe. It won't be happening in an abandoned multi-story car park."

"I promise you it happens." She rolled her eyes and stood up. "I'll go and start the pasta for tea."

"No Zak tonight?" I asked, secretly hoping she was staying home so we could all watch a film or a comedy together. I wasn't sure how many more of those kind of nights we would have if she changed her mind and went away to uni, so any opportunity was gratefully received by me.

"No, his mum and dad are out so he's babysitting his sister."

"He didn't want you to join him?"

"No, Dad, because contrary to what you think, we're not joined at the hip." She leaned down and gave Maya a gentle hug. "I'm glad you're okay and look much better today, and I'm glad you're staying."

As she left the room, I wasn't sure I could speak. The lump in my throat was huge. The gratitude I felt for Maddy caring about my girlfriend was more than I could express. Then, when I glanced at Maya and saw her swipe away a tear, I knew she felt it, too. To be honest I think we both needed more sleep.

"You okay?" I asked, rubbing a hand up and down her leg.

Maya nodded and sniffed. "She's so lovely."

"I know she is." Maddy made me proud and glad that I hadn't been the drop out that I'd thought I was seventeen years ago. "She makes great chicken pesto pasta, too."

"I'm not sure I'm hungry." Maya's lips pouted; she knew full well I'd make her eat.

"Not happening. She can make you a small bowl."

She gave me an eye roll and then a little smile. "Okay, just a small one."

"Good girl." I patted her leg, which earned me a disgruntled sigh.

"I'm not a five-year-old who's just finished her greens, William."

That made me chuckle. I knew she would have stamped her foot if it hadn't been resting in my lap.

"Okay, Maya, duly noted." I leaned closer and gave her a quick kiss. "Right, I'm going to help Maddy. Will you be okay?"

"Fine. You're only a few feet away if I need anything. Want to get some walkie talkies so we can keep in touch?"

"Okay, I get it. I'm smothering you."

At least she laughed. "Go and I'll take a snooze while you do."

I narrowed my eyes on her. "I knew you were tired. Have a sleep, and I'll wake you when the food is ready."

As I left the room, she had already snuggled down. What was great was that she didn't wake until the next day, not even when I carried her to bed and tucked her in with a kiss to her forehead, or when I stood in the doorway, watching her sleep and being grateful for her coming into my life.

CHAPTER 61
Maddy

"What's he going to do?" Zak asked, his arm around me, and his thumb softly rubbing my shoulder.

We were at the party of some boy Liam knew from his football team. Even Ana had come with us. The atmosphere was still a little bit frosty, but she'd thawed enough to agree to come out.

"He said he's not going to do it, but I know he's starting to feel guilty."

"You can't just give a kidney to someone you don't know." Zak frowned and shook his head. "It's flipping bonkers, isn't it. I bet your dad's head must be mashed."

"His dad turning up is one thing, but him asking for his bloody kidney is…" I shrugged, unsure how to find the words for what was going on.

"You wouldn't offer yours would you?"

I couldn't help but laugh at his worried tone and the deep crease between his brows. "No way. I don't want Dad to do it, it's too dangerous." I leaned in and gave him a quick kiss. "So, stop worrying."

"Want me to speak my dad and ask him what he thinks?"

I hadn't thought about that, but it was a brilliant idea. "It might make me feel a bit better, just in case he says yes."

Zak hugged me closer. "I'll do it tomorrow. And for the record, I don't think you or your dad should feel guilty."

I narrowed my eyes on him. "How did you know I felt guilty?"

"I just know," he chuckled. "It's who you are."

And I loved that he knew that about me. It was one more reason to make my little heart sigh.

It was like I knew that when he rubbed his temple with one finger, he was about to say something that he thought might upset me. Like now.

"What?" I asked.

"About you feeling guilty, you shouldn't with Ana." He flashed a glance across the room to where Ana was scowling at a boy who was chatting to her. "I know you think you should be the one making the effort and feel bad that you're annoyed with her, but you shouldn't. All you've tried to be is a good friend. She's the one who—"

"I know," I said, cutting him off, not wanting to argue, but knowing we would if we continued talking about Ana. "I know, Zak, but *you* know she's my oldest friend and I can't just cut her off." Irritated, I sat forward so that his hand fell from my shoulder.

"Mads." His fingers wrapped lightly around my bicep. "I'm sorry okay, but you have no idea how scared I was for you. You know, after what happened to Ruby."

Turning to face him, I was surprised at how worried he looked. His eyes were hooded, and he was chewing on his bottom lip as he watched me carefully.

"Zak, I was never in any danger. It was just vodka, babe."

He started to spin one of his rings around and there was no denying the tension and worry on his face and in his eyes.

"It might not have been. Plus, Ana had no idea whether you would have a bad reaction or not."

"She's seen me drinking vodka before, Zak. She knows exactly what I can and can't drink." I cupped his face and he leaned into it. "She was never going to put me in real danger, but I understand your worries, especially after what happened with Ruby."

His hand moved down my arm until our fingers linked and he pulled me back against his chest. "I promise not to mention it again."

"I do appreciate you worrying about me." Kissing him quickly, it felt good to feel his lips lift into a smile. "Fancy a dance, I love this song."

Zak tipped his head back and listened as Snakehips' All My Friends started to boom out. "Yeah, okay, let's go."

Taking his hand in mine, with his arm draped over my shoulder, we made our way onto the makeshift dancefloor in the conservatory. It was heaving with people and smelled distinctly of sweaty bodies and weed. Emma and Liam were in the midst of the crowd, slow dancing and necking on like they'd run out of oxygen. Liv was standing and talking to a couple of girls who left our school the year before, but she gave us a wave as we looked over.

Zak took hold of both my hands, lifting them and moving them and his hips in time to the music. Dancing was something else he was good at, the way he moved made me feel all hot and gave me butterflies deep in the pit of my stomach. He had great rhythm that wound its way through his whole body as he mesmerised me with every single move. I followed his lead and when he put a hand against the small of my back and pulled me closer, we were practically joined. I loved that with each sway and thrust he grew harder against his jeans his gaze growing more intense.

As the song built up towards its end, Zak's hand moved to my bum, and he pulled me even closer so I could feel the outline of his erection.

"Do you know how much I like you," he said close to my ear, sending a shiver down my spine. "You're like no one I've ever met before."

"Is that a good thing?" I asked, pushing my hips forward and rubbing myself against him. It earned me a groan, and his grip on my backside tightened.

"Very." His teeth nipped my earlobe, and I could feel myself getting wetter with every single second.

"Do you think there's somewhere we could go?" I asked, raking my fingers through his hair, gently scratching his scalp. "I really need to be alone with you now."

Instantly his lips were on mine, and his tongue pushed inside, slowly seducing mine with every sweep. Without saying anything he lifted me up, and my legs wrapped instinctively around his waist as he pushed through everyone, all the time his lips on mine.

"Seriously."

I would have ignored the comment and carried on to wherever we were going, but a hand in the middle of my back stopped our progress.

Zak groaned and sighed heavily. "What, Ana?"

Dropping my head to his shoulder, dread swirled in my stomach. I knew from her tone that she was not in a good mood. It was hard, angry and drunk. Tapping Zak's back, I dropped my feet to the floor and turned to face my friend.

"What's wrong?" I asked her.

She rolled her eyes and growled as somebody jostled her from behind. "Fuck off," she snapped before turning back to us. "Do you two always have to be so fucking gross, sucking face all the time."

"It's not really hurting you is it," I retorted, feeling around for Zak's little finger and linking it with mine. "So, I don't know what the problem is."

"Do you know how disgusting you look, mounting him like some cheap tart on heat?"

"Oi, watch your mouth," Zak warned. "Don't speak to her like that."

Looking up at him, I saw his jaw tense, the muscles popping as he ground his teeth. He took a big breath and then turned to me.

"Let's go and get a drink, babe."

"Oh, let's go and get a drink, *babe*," Ana mocked in a bad copy of his accent.

"Ana." I stamped my foot, trying to get her to listen. She whipped her head in my direction, a sneer on her face. "What the hell is your problem? You're being a complete bitch, *again*."

"Better a bitch than a slut, hey, Maddy?"

"Right, that's enough," Zak said, pointing at her. "You do not speak to anyone like that, least of all Maddy. She's been nothing but good to you, helping you as much as she can, and all you've done in return is to be exactly what she said, *a bitch*."

"Oh fuck off, Zak."

"Ana, what the hell." I grabbed her wrist, not hard, but she instantly snatched her arm away.

"Leave me alone, don't touch me."

"Why are you being like this? What's going on? Is it your mum again?"

"I've told you, no. Stop sticking your nose in to my business." She turned in a flash and started pushing people out of the way.

"Ana!"

"Leave her." Zak tugged on my hand. "She's just going to give you more shit."

"You don't think I should check on her?" I got on my tiptoes, looking over the heads of people trying to spot her. "Because there's clearly something really wrong with her."

"Yeah, she's fucking awful." His nostrils flared. "She's leaving." He nodded towards the general direction of the door, out into the garden.

"She's not walking home on her own is she?" Anxiety washed through me as I looked up at him. "She can't do that, Zak. Maybe I should go with her, make sure she gets home okay.

"She's not your responsibility, Mads." He heaved out a resigned sigh. "I'll go and check on her. If she's going home I'll make sure she calls for a lift. Unless you want to go, and we can both walk her home."

She was my best friend and she'd been going through a lot at home. "Should I come with you to check on her, make sure she calls for a lift?" She had been awful, though, vile to me and Zak, in fact. "Then again, why should she spoil our night?"

Zak nodded. "Okay, you stay here." He reached through a couple of people and grabbed Liam by the shoulder. "Lee, just stay with Mads for a minute will you."

Liam nodded and dragging Emma with him joined us. "What's up?" he asked with a chin lift.

"Ana has kicked off with Mads, and now she's stormed off. Maddy is worried she's walking home on her own."

Liam frowned and Emma rolled her eyes. "I'll come with you. Stay with Maddy, Em, we won't be long."

"Well, I'd leave her to it," Emma complained. "She told me I looked fat earlier."

"She what?" I asked, my eyes almost popping out of my head.

Emma linked my arm. "Yeah, said I looked fat in this skirt. Normally I'd let it go, with all the shit she's got going on, but I've had enough of her, so I told her to piss off."

Emma was right, Ana had gone too far. "Maybe we should leave her to it, like Em said."

"No, it's fine. We'll be back in a minute," Zak said, clearly frustrated.

As he and Liam made their way out to find her, I spotted a couple getting up from a sofa, pulling up the lad who was sitting next to them. He was only semi-conscious but awake enough to be able to stumble along with them.

"Quick, free sofa," I hissed, grabbing Emma's hand and dragging her with me. When we got to it, we both flopped down with a sigh.

"She's a fucking nightmare," Emma groaned. "I thought Liam was going to blow a gasket when she called me fat."

"Same with Zak. He was fuming."

"What did she say to you?"

"Called me a slut and told me to stop sticking my nose in her business."

"A slut? Wow, she really is an arse."

I sighed heavily. "I know but am I bad for not wanting to go after her?"

"God, no," Emma scoffed. "Your night shouldn't be spoiled just because of her. You tried to help her. You sorted out her house, got your dad to help her mum. Then she got us absolutely wasted." She shrugged. "So..."

"Yeah, you're right," I replied with a determined nod. "I've tried and if she's not willing to meet me half way then that's her problem, not mine."

"Exactly." Emma lifted her bum and pulled out a pair of boxer shorts. "What the hell?"

Holding them up we both stared at them. They were huge and slightly stiff. With a screech, she threw to over her shoulder, and we both burst out laughing.

"Where's Liv anyway?" Emma asked, wiping her hands on her skirt.

"Talking to Millie Johnson and her friend. You remember Millie, she left last year. The girl who went out with Chris Dickinson."

"Oh yeah, I remember her. Didn't know Liv knew her."

"I think they used to go to dance classes together when they were little." I looked to where Zak and Liam had disappeared, hoping to see them coming back, but there was no sign. "I think Millie is at Manchester Uni, so they're probably talking about that."

"Ah yeah, probs. Fancy going running tomorrow?"

I frowned. "Running? When did you start running?"

"Tomorrow." She burst out laughing. "Liam has amazing stamina. I think I need to get fit."

"No," I cried. "That's gross, he's practically my cousin."

"You know we're having sex," she exclaimed. "So, what's the big deal?"

"You saying about his stamina has made me queasy."

She rolled her eyes, and we continued chatting for a few minutes until she pointed behind me. "They're back, but no Ana."

I looked over, and Zak shook his head with a shrug. My stomach rolled because he didn't look happy, and I wondered what else she'd done.

"Nowhere to be seen," Liam said, sitting down next to Emma.

"I think she's gone, babe." He took my hand and pulled me up, took my place and then patted his knee. "We couldn't find her anywhere. My guess is her mum picked her up."

Hesitating to sit down, I looked out towards the garden, but Zak tugged on my hand.

"Jack Grayson said she went through the gate after yelling at Marcus to fuck off."

"Christ," I groaned. "What the hell is wrong with her?" I finally sat down. "Do you think we should go after her?" I asked half-heartedly.

"No," Zak said sternly. "She'll be fine, besides she's been horrible to all of us tonight."

"He's right," Liam said. "Let her cool down and then speak to her tomorrow."

They were both right. She had been awful, and she did need to cool down, so I wasn't going to let her spoil my night any further.

CHAPTER 62
Will

There were times in my life when I'd wished that Maddy and I could pack up everything we own and move to somewhere hot and foreign. This was one of those times, except that wish now included taking Maya along, too. I suppose Maddy would insist on taking Zak, as well.

Although, she was walking around like a bear with a sore head, which I was sure wasn't all down to a hangover from the party she'd been to last night. I had noticed that she'd kept looking at her phone then huffing and throwing it to one side. When I asked her what was bothering her she told me nothing and stormed off to her room.

Once she was in a better mood maybe I'd broach the subject, but in the meantime she could stay up there and sulk. I had other stuff that I needed to think about, like my kidney and whether to donate it to someone I didn't know.

"Why don't you call him?" Maya cupped her hands around her coffee mug and snuggled down into her dressing gown. "I'm sure you'll be able to find his number. Didn't you say he works for the franchise that bought Steven out?"

"Yeah, he does."

"So, it'll be easy to get his number." She gave me a gentle smile, which made me think everything would work out okay, whatever my decision. Because, I had to be honest, that was how she affected me. It was if as soon as we met, she'd put a spell on me, one that demanded that I forgot about my life before her, and that I saw only her as my anchor.

"It will, you're right." I blew out a cleansing breath, determined that I would contact my brother and speak to him directly before I made any other decision. "I'll call him after the weekend." Maya's brow rose. "Not because I'm putting it off, but because I want to dedicate time to you and Maddy this weekend, and as soon as I speak to Cameron I have a feeling the shit will hit the fan."

Maya nodded. "Okay. Good plan."

"Right," I said, clapping my hands together. "Do you feel up to going out for lunch. Food might just drag Maddy from her bedroom."

"Yes, sounds good. Maybe not too far, though."

"There's a great café in town that do loads of different things. Then we can come back, you can have a little nap, and then this evening I thought maybe I'd ask Maddy to get Zak round and we could play cards."

Maya's eyes lit up. "I am so good at Poker."

Chuckling I kissed her cheek. "I was thinking more like Hearts or Rummy."

She shrugged. "I'll still beat you."

"I'll go up and speak to Miss Grumpy." As I started for the door my phone began to ring in my pocket. "Shit, that better not be Steven again."

"Just send it to voicemail."

About to do as Maya suggested, I was surprised to see it was Mike, Ana's dad, calling me.

"Hey, Mike," I answered, frowning.

I hadn't spoken to him in ages, not even before he'd left Susan. We weren't exactly mates but exchanged the odd text or call about the girls. Instantly, I wondered if he'd heard about what Ana had done to Maddy and Emma.

"Will." His voice sounded hollow and distant, like he was distracted, or I was the last person he wanted to speak to.

"Is this about Ana?"

He drew in a shaky breath. "Y-yeah, how did you know?"

"Well, Maddy told me. I mean it wasn't like she could hide it from me, Zak had to hold her up and—"

"I'm not sure... shit, I think we're talking about something different, Will."

Then it hit me. He didn't sound hollow or distant, he sounded broken, grief stricken, and my heart started thumping.

"Mike, what's happened? What's going on?"

There was silence on the other end of the line. At least I thought there was and then I heard a barely audible high-pitched squeal of agony. Gripping the phone tight, I sank onto the armchair and glanced over at Maya who was looking at me quizzically.

"Mike, tell me what's wrong? What's happened? Is Ana okay? Is she in some kind of trouble?"

There was a noise like he'd dropped the phone, and then I heard faint crying.

"Mike?"

Silence stretched out for what felt like ages until I heard a long drawn in breath. "It's Theo, Mr Newman, Ana's brother."

My stomach bottomed out as goose bumps broke out over my skin like I'd been doused in cold water. "Theo, what's happened?"

"She's dead, Mr Newman. My sister is dead."

***

"No." Maddy shook her head and stared at me with wild eyes. "You've got it wrong. She's not dead."

Maya and I were sat either side of her, Maya holding her hand while I had mine gently cupping her cheek. We'd just told her one of the worst things you could tell any kid: her best friend had died after taking a short cut across the railway track to get home. The times I'd drummed into Maddy not to do that, no matter how late she was. Everyone had taken the shortcut at some point, and we were lucky that there had been only one other fatality in fifty years. It was a recognised crossing point, but you still had to have your wits about you—your ears and eyes had to be sharp. It was not a safe place if either of those senses were impaired.

"I'm so sorry." My hand smoothed down her hair and then moved to rub small circles on her back. I offered my other hand to her. "Take my hand, sweetheart, please."

Taking it, Maddy's gaze lifted and met mine. "Why was she going that way? She knows not to Dad. We always say *never* go that way, no matter how late you are, *never* cut across the railway line. We—"

Her words were coming out quick and fast, and I was afraid she was going to hyperventilate. Her shoulders and chest were rising and falling. Painful. Ragged.

"Maddy, sweetheart, please just calm down. Take a deep breath and—"

"We always say, never go across the railway line. You've always told me." Maddy's grip tightened, and I saw Maya wince. I reached over and gently loosened her hand so Maya could free hers, but she didn't. She kept hold and hugged it to her chest. "I wanted to go with her. She was so mad, Dad. She was so nasty, and she left, and I told Zak we should go after her, but he said she'd be fine." She let out a sob. "But she wasn't. She went across the line and…" She turned to me. "What happened, Dad, did it…"

Her words trailed off into more sobs as she threw herself at me. Wrapping her arms around my chest, she clung on tight, her whole body shaking with grief. Sadness engulfed me, because apart from holding her, there was nothing that I could do to soothe her. I couldn't take the pain in her heart away. I wouldn't be able to stop the guilt she was bound to feel, or the sorrow that would always be there whenever she thought of her last year at school. And I would never, ever, salve that deep grief the mere mention of Ana's name would bring for the rest of her life.

As I held Maddy, Maya placed a warm comforting hand on my knee and gave it a gentle squeeze to gain my attention.

"I'll leave you both to it," she said

"Babe, it's fine."

Maddy then gave another heaving sob and gripped my jumper tighter. "She can't be dead, Dad, she can't be."

Maya chewed on her bottom lip, and her eyes filled with tears as she sat on the edge of the sofa. She looked like she didn't know what to do, or what her role was, but as far as I was concerned, she was exactly where I wanted her to be. Where I needed her to be. I understood her need to be able to do more, though. That had been exactly how I felt when I first moved in with Miriam and she was Maddy's primary carer until I got the hang of things. I'd hover around feeling useless and looking a lot like Maya did at that moment.

"Could you call Zak?" I asked her. I fished my phone from my jeans pocket. "I took his number when they went to London. Ask him if he can come round."

Maya nodded and as her bottom lip trembled, she gently cupped my face. "Of course I will."

It hurt to think that maybe Maddy needed him, but this wasn't about me and my heart. It was about my daughter and what she needed, and I believed that Zak was it.

Stroking a hand down her hair, I gently rocked her and made soothing noises that I knew wouldn't help one little bit, because this was the worst thing she'd ever been through. When Mrs P died, she'd been upset because she was like a grandmother to her, but this was another level. Ana had been her best friend since they were little girls, and no one expected to lose their best friend at just seventeen.

"I'm so sorry, sweetheart. So, so sorry."

"We argued Dad," Maddy gasped out. "We argued and she went home on her own. I knew I should have gone home with her. Zak and Liam went…"

"Mads, no one was to know what would happen. It was a horrible, horrible accident."

According to Theo, she'd been just a foot from safety, almost across the line, when the train hit her. The poor driver had tried to put the brakes on but hadn't been able to stop in time. He must have been in a real state, no one expects something so tragic to happen when they go off to work in the morning.

"You want a glass of water or something?" I asked when she finally calmed down.

"No," she said shaking her head. "I don't want anything."

"Do you want me to call Emma for you?" Theo said he was going to call Emma and Liv's parents. I didn't envy him one little bit. No brother, or parent should have to do that.

"Yes," she murmured, swiping her hand across face. "And Liv. I want to see them." She took a deep breath. "Zak, I need to call Zak."

"Maya's calling him for you."

She looked up at me with tears brimming at her lashes, and she looked just like she used to when she was upset as a little girl. All big eyes and snotty nose. I wanted so much to be everything she needed but I was aware that times were changing, and I was no longer her whole world.

"He'll be here soon, Mads."

She nodded against my chest and curled in closer and that's how we stayed until Zak turned up. The one thing that made me feel better was that she didn't let go of me immediately when he walked in. She hugged me tighter for another minute or so and then slipped onto his knee, so I left them alone as for the first time, Zak took my place.

CHAPTER 63
Maddy

Emma was curled against Liam's side while holding Liv's hand, and I clung to Zak as he held me tight in his lap.

"Do you need anything?" he whispered, stroking my hair.

"No, thank you." I swallowed back the sob that was constantly on the edge of breaking out of my chest.

We were all devastated. It felt like that we'd cried so much that there were no more tears to shed. It was like we were all in limbo, without any clue what to do or say. We hadn't even spoken about her. Not mentioned her name or what happened, we'd simply sat in a state of disbelief and grief.

Then Liv suddenly spoke, breaking the silence. "You know, we actually need Ana here."

I gasped and lifted my head from Zak's chest. "What?"

"We need Ana. She would break this awful, shitty silence. She would be talking about what happened and saying how fucking stupid she was for going over the track when we know you just don't do that. She'd be talking non-stop and telling us that we should just get pissed and deal with it."

I narrowed my eyes on her. "But she isn't, Liv, is she?"

As my body tensed, one of Zak's hands smoothed up and down my thigh, while his other moved in between my shoulder blades. His touch would normally calm me, but all it did was add to my irritation as I stared at Liv.

"Liv, how can you be so insensitive?"

"I think she's—"

"No, Zak." I didn't even look at him. "What she said is wrong. She can't talk about Ana like that."

"Maddy." Emma sat up and pushed away from Liam. With one hand still tethered to Liv, she reached for me with her other one. "What Liv says is right; you know it is. Ana would be the one doing all the talking and encouraging us to as well. You know she would."

"Doesn't mean we should say that, though." My chest felt tight as I thought about my best friend. "It's disrespectful. It's not right. She's not here and…" I started to breathe heavily as pressure built up inside me, culminating in a huge ball of sorrow in my throat.

"Hey, babe, take a deep breath," Zak coaxed.

I shrugged him off and stood up. "And you don't care either." I swung around to face him. "You were the one who told me to leave her. "You said she'd be okay, and, and—" my hands clenched into fists as I produced more tears from somewhere— "and she wasn't, Zak. She fucking died." Zak's expression looked like I'd accused him of killing Ana. His face had lost all its colour as he sagged back, dropping his hands either side of his thighs.

"Maddy," Liam snapped. "There's no need."

I couldn't even look at him. I didn't want to look at him or anyone else, all I wanted to do was talk to Ana. To find out that it had all be a huge mistake. That they'd got the wrong person.

"Mads," Emma said tentatively.

I didn't wait to hear what else she had to say because there was too much anger inside of me. If I stayed, I'd say something that I could never take back. Something that I might regret for the rest of my life.

Kicking Liam's outstretched leg as I stormed past him, I wrenched the door open and strode into the hall. I looked towards the kitchen, where my dad and Maya were sitting at the kitchen table. They were both nursing mugs, their eyes pinned to me.

"You okay, sweetheart?" Dad asked, already half the way out of chair.

Staring at him I shook my head. "No. I'm not," I sobbed. "I'll never be okay again. My best friend has been killed by a fucking train, so how can I be okay?"

In my periphery I saw Zak appear in the doorway, holding onto the wooden frame. When I looked at him, his gaze was on my dad, but he quickly looked back at me, his eyes pleading. I couldn't give him what he wanted, though. I couldn't say it was okay and that I didn't blame him. That even if I'd gone after her, she would have stormed off and still taken the short cut. I mean I knew that was a possibility because of how she'd been behaving the last few weeks, but I wanted to believe that I could have done more, that I could have saved her life.

"I just want to be on my own," I told whoever was listening.

"Babe—"

I didn't answer him but turned and ran up the stair, slamming my bedroom door behind me, wanting to close myself off from everyone.

Will

As I heard Maddy's bedroom door slam, I saw Zak flinch in the doorway to the living room. His gaze dropped to the floor, and his whole body slumped against the doorframe.

I pushed my chair back and moved towards him, giving Maya's shoulder a gentle squeeze as I passed her.

"What happened?" I asked Zak as I stood in front of him.

There were muffled whispers from the living room as he thrust his hands deep into his jeans' pockets. His whole demeanour was of someone in pain, someone who'd just been hurt by the person he cared about the most. His chest heaved, and he made a quiet groaning noise from the back of his throat.

"She blames me," he said so quietly I almost missed it. "She said that I should have let her go after Ana."

Placing a hand on his shoulder, I gave him a shake. "Zak, look at me."

Slowly, he lifted his head to show me blue eyes filled with sadness. He took a deep breath. "She was being so awful, Will. I didn't want her to upset Maddy more than she already had."

"This is not your fault. Maddy is lashing out because she has no idea how to deal." I cupped the back of his head, forcing him to look at me. "It's a fucking awful tragedy and if Mads had gone after her, we may have been suffering her loss as well today."

Maddy would no doubt have tried to persuade Ana against going over the track, but who was to say she would have succeeded? Besides, the poor kid standing in front of me didn't need to know that.

"We looked for her, but she'd already disappeared," he said, his throat bobbing. "You can ask Liam."

"Hey, hey, I know you did. None of you could have known what was going to happen."

Liam appeared behind Zak and placed a hand on his back. "Will's right, mate. It's no one's fault. She knew not to take that short cut, especially not at night."

Zak glanced at my best friend's son, but his expression remained black and full of hurt at my daughter's words. "Maybe we should have—"

"Zak, no," Maya said, coming up to stand next to me. "Do not think about the what-if's. It won't change anything. Maddy is just lashing out because she's grieving. She has a whole host of emotions rushing around her body and her head; she doesn't know how to deal with them, so anger has come out on top. She can't be angry at Ana, so you're the one in the firing line."

His face crumpled momentarily, but he quickly inhaled and schooled his features and turned to Liam.

"We did search for her, didn't we?"

"You know we did." Liam looked to me, and I could see the uncertainty in his eyes. These kids shouldn't have to be dealing with something so tragic at their age. No wonder they had no fucking clue how to express themselves.

"Why don't you all go back in there," I suggested. "We can order some food and then I'll see if I can persuade Maddy to come back down." I doubted that I would, she could be stubborn when she wanted to be.

Maya rubbed Zak's bicep. "It might be a good idea for you all to be together and talk about her. It might help a little."

"Is it okay if Mum, Dad and Darcy come round?" Liam asked. "They'll just worry about me otherwise."

I smiled because he couldn't admit he needed his parents, and if I knew Liam, especially a hug from his mum.

"Yeah, sure. Give them a call." I turned to Maya. "If I give you my card can you order some pizzas or something?"

She nodded. "Yes, but I don't need your card. I'll sort it." Then she leaned in and gave me a quick kiss to the lips. "Go and speak to Maddy."

Shit, I had no idea what I'd done to deserve her, but whatever it was I was glad I'd done it. She was clearly in pain and probably desperate to sleep for a little while, but my daughter and a bunch of kids she barely knew were her priority, and I didn't think I could love her more.

"I'll go and see how she is," I told them and then slowly made my way up the stairs, wondering how I was going to help my little girl because I couldn't stand to see her with a broken heart, and I would do whatever it took to heal it for her, even if it meant sitting for hours holding her hand.

ZAK'S WHATSAPP MESSAGES

OSCAR

Hey mate, didn't get to speak to you much at the weekend. Was great to see you though. Oh and your gf is a sort!!

OSCAR

You okay, Zak? Bit worried as you haven't replied to my messages. Hope it's not the comment about Maddy lol.

ZAK

Sorry mate. Got a lot going on here. Maddy's best friend died. It's been fucking shit. She's in bits and I don't know how to help her.

OSCAR

Fuck! One of the girls who came to the party?

ZAK

No her friend Ana. She was supposed to come with us, but didn't make it. She got hit by a train, mate! It's so fucked up. I don't know how to help her, she won't talk to me or about it.

OSCAR

Fuck, I'm so sorry. She must be devastated. Just give her time she'll talk to you eventually once the shock has worn off. Not sure what I can do to help but buzz me if there's anything.

ZAK

Thanks, Ozzy. I'll call you soon.

CHAPTER 64
Maddy

February was a shit month. I hated it. I hated how dark and miserable it was. I hated that it was raining outside. I hated that that it was cold outside. I hated that it was almost lunchtime, and I was still in bed. I hated that Zak has sent me a thousand messages and I couldn't bring myself to answer any of them.

My phone beeped with another one, and Emma sighed next to me.

"You're going to have to speak to him at some point," she said, tugging at the duvet.

"She's right," Liv chimed in from the blow up mattress on the floor.

Her hand reached up to my bedside table, snatched up my phone and then threw it at me. It landed on my stomach.

"Just put him out of his misery, Maddy."

I slammed my hand over it just as it vibrated with another oncoming message. They were right, I should speak to him, but I couldn't. I picked up my phone as many times as he messaged me every day, but when I pressed on his picture, ready to dial his number, my mouth became dry, and a huge ball formed in my throat. No matter how much I tried, I just couldn't form the words.

As for the thoughts, well they were there in abundance.

It was Zak's fault.

He should have let me go home with her.

I had a choice and chose not to go with her. I should have.

He and Liam should have looked harder for her.

I should have ignored her bad mood and not argued with her.

I missed my best friend.

I'm angry with my best friend.

He should have let me go after her.

"Maddy." Emma lifted onto her elbows and stared at me. "The boys tried to find her, and as much as I love her, she was being a bitch to us all. We were right to let her leave. She wanted to leave, and if you'd gone after her you know she'd have said something vile to you. If you'd followed her, you might not have persuaded her to go the long way home, and then we'd be grieving for both of you."

Her last comment caused me to gasp. "Stop quoting my dad." He'd said it to me a couple of times since we'd heard the news, and he was wrong, I'd have persuaded her easily. She'd have gone back to the party with me. I know she would have.

"Your dad is hot and right," Liv added with a yawn. "And we should really get up. We've been in our pyjamas for almost forty-eight hours, and we can't keep eating the food your dad leaves on the dressing table."

We could, as long as Dad kept providing it for us. On the night that we found about Ana, we all decided that we wanted to spend the night together. Dad had persuaded me to go back downstairs and be with my friends after my initial tantrum. But then, when after fifteen minutes of awkward silence, interspersed with sobs from me, Emma and Liv, pizza arrived, I totally lost it. I stormed back to my room to be joined about ten minutes later by my friends telling me that Liam, his family and Zak had gone home with a pizza courtesy of my dad. The girls stayed the night and still hadn't gone home. Their parents had visited and checked in on us, but we just wanted to be together to cry and talk about Ana.

"I don't want to ever leave this room," I told her.

"We need to soon, Mads," Emma said softly. "I think we'd feel better if we went back to school. My mum said Miss Rogers in Pastoral Care told her we can have more time, but if we go back they'll give us any help we need. Plus, you do need to speak to Zak. Liam said he's really worried about you."

"Liam or Zak?" I deadpanned.

"You know who."

She sat up, taking the duvet with her, and I snatched at it, pulling it up to my chin. "I just can't," I muttered.

Liv groaned and got up to her knees, leaning her forearms on my bed so her head was close to mine. "Madeline, Zak is worried about you because he cares about *you*. He more than cares about you."

Any other time that statement would have had my stomach in the best kind of knots, but my heart was currently too full of grief to care.

"She's right," Emma added. "Liam said that Zak is crazy about you. He told Liam that he's never felt like this about anyone before, and that he's dreading leaving you when he goes to Edinburgh."

I didn't respond, just turned on my side, so I was facing the wall, away from Liv. Unfortunately, though, I was in direct eyeline of Emma's boobs which were almost spilling out of the side of her vest top. In frustration, I pulled the duvet over my head.

"You can't hide forever, Mads. We all have to face the outside world at some point, and maybe today should be the day." Emma tried to drag the duvet back down, but I held on tight.

"Please." Liv pleaded. "Listen to Emma and call Zak."

As I lay in quiet contemplation, there was a knock on my door. It opened slightly and I heard my dad's voice.

"Can I come in?"

With a grunt, I threw the duvet over Emma, and yelled, "Come in."

He popped his head around the door, his eyes immediately going to me. "Do you think you girls should think about getting out of bed. It's almost one and you've been in here for two days now."

The ache in my heart increased for a split second as I remembered why we'd been in my bedroom for two days. Dad took a step inside and even in the dim light of my room with the curtains closed, I could see how tired he looked. His hair needed a cut, there was grey under his eyes, and his hand was pushed deep into his jeans' pocket while the other clutched the door.

"I've made some chilli so how about you all come down and get some?"

"How's Maya?" I asked, rubbing my eyes. "Is her pain any easier?"

"She's getting there, sweetheart." His face softened as he looked at me. He then walked over to the curtains and pulled them open. "Let's at least get some light in so you know what time of day it is."

The rain-spattered window gave us a view of the grey skies, and the heaviness in my heart and body increased. The girls and Dad were right, though; we had to leave the room at some point and maybe it was the right time.

"We should go and see Ana's mum and dad," I suddenly announced.

"What?" Emma sat up, and then remembered she was barely wearing a top, and lay back down. "Are you sure?"

I nodded. "Yep."

Dad cleared his throat. "W-what about Zak? Are you ready to speak to him? Because I've got to be honest, Mads, he's called me about a million times and sent just as many messages." He stepped over Liv and sat on the stool at my dressing table. He held out his hand, silently asking me to take it. When I did, a huge sense of love and safety swept over me. "He really isn't to blame sweetheart. And I'll be honest with you, if I'd been in his position, I'd have done and said the same. Remember the things she did and said over the last month or so, things that worried him, and made him angry. His reaction was exactly how I would want a boy who cares about you to react."

I knew he was right. If Zak hadn't given a shit about the vodka or the bitchy comments, I'd have probably been disappointed. When he told us to let her go home, he had no idea what would happen, none of us did. Hindsight was definitely a wonderful thing, and if that had been one of his friends, I'd have probably given him the same advice.

Picking up my phone I nodded. "I'll call him."

"Halle-flipping-lujah," Liv cried from the floor. "Can we now get dressed and get some chilli; I'm starving."

"That's a relief," Emma groaned. "I think I have bed sores."

I whipped my head around. "You both could have gone home at any time. You didn't have to stay here with me."

Emma's mouth dropped open. "As if we'd be anywhere else. We stick together." Her eyes instantly filled with tears, and I knew what she was thinking.

"We weren't to know, Em." Everyone had been right. We weren't to know. And none of us were to blame. None of us, including Zak.

"Okay, girls," Dad said, clapping his hands together. "I'll go and sort out some garlic bread for the chilli."

Once the door clicked shut, we all seemed to breathe a sigh of relief. Like we'd finally been released from a prison of our own making.

"You're really going to call Zak?" Emma asked, picking up her own phone from under her pillow, no doubt to message Liam.

"Yes, I'm really going to call Zak. Once I've had a shower, but I'll message him first."

I had no idea why, but instead of opening WhatsApp, I flicked to his Instagram account. He never used it, and so I didn't know what made me look at it, but I was surprised to see he had a story. Dad said he'd been messaging him, Emma had told me, via Liam, that he'd been holed up in his room worrying about me. When I clicked on it and saw the image, I felt like I might puke. I felt like another ton of grief had been landed on me.

"What is it?" Emma asked as I made a painful groan. "Maddy?"

With tears rolling down my cheeks, I clutched at my t-shirt; Zak's t-shirt which I slept in. "Check his Insta story."

After a few seconds, when she saw what I'd seen, I heard her say, "Fuck."

"What is it Liv?" asked. "What's on Zak's story?"

What was on Zak's story was a picture of him, hugging Connie and kissing the side of her head. The caption was me and my bae together again and the song playing over the top was Sia's Helium. The song that had been one of my favourites… until now.

CHAPTER 65
Will

What had happened in the few minutes between talking to the girls and me going back into the kitchen, I had no idea. Now I was listening to Emma and Liv rant on about Zak and what a dick he was. All that while Maddy stormed around upstairs, also yelling about Zak being a dick.

If what I was hearing was true, then the little prick would be best keeping his distance from me in the future. Although, I had real trouble believing it. He adored Maddy, you only had to see the soppy grin on his face when he looked at her. How worried he'd been about her the last couple of days.

"And this girl is the girlfriend he had in London?" I asked the girls, standing in front of them with my arms firmly folded across my chest.

"Yes and he said they were finished, and when we went to London he told her to leave him alone. She kept flirting with him, but he knocked her back and—"

"Emma, love." Sighing, I ran a hand across my face. "Take a breath before your lungs give up the ghost."

She took a huge breath, and then tagged team Liv with a look. "And in his story they're hugging, and it mentions that they're back together and he's put Maddy's favourite song over the top."

"Yeah, I got all that." I took my phone from my back pocket and flicked through to Zak's number.

Maya, who clearly already knew me well, said in a warning voice, "Will."

My eyes flicked up to hers. "What?"

"Do not call him." She was wearing a sling because the weight of the plaster cast was getting her down. Tucked inside it was a bag of Maltesers.

"Why do you have chocolate tucked in your sling?" I asked, trying to hide my grin.

"They're for Maddy. In times like this, a girl needs chocolate, not her dad calling up the boy in question." The raised eyebrow persuaded me to put my phone back in my pocket. "Now, will I take them up, or will you?"

Emma and Liv were looking at Maya like she'd just farted a rainbow or something, and I realised we'd never had boy trouble before. Otherwise, I'd have known about the chocolate. I mean, I knew about it during the week of her period, but never when a boy was involved.

"You go," I told Maya. "I may say totally the wrong thing about the little fucker, and if it's all a mistake, and she doesn't break up with him, I'll be the bad guy."

Maya grinned and nodded towards the hallway. "Are you coming girls."

Emma shook her head. "I should go home."

"She means that Liam is coming round." Liv rolled her eyes. "I should go home, too, though. I've run out of clean underwear. I thought we were only coming round for a few hours."

To be honest I thought it was a good idea, it wasn't doing any of them any good being holed up in Maddy's room. They absolutely needed to grieve, but the longer they stayed in Maddy's room, the harder it would be for them to leave it.

"Okay, but let me feed you first." I looked at them each in turn. "Good plan?"

"Do we still get garlic bread?" Emma asked.

"Absolutely."

"Yes, please," they both chimed.

"Right, go and sit in the lounge, and as soon as Maya and Maddy come down, we'll eat."

As they walked away, I exhaled and looked up at the stairs, hoping that Maya was able to get through to Maddy. Despite still being able to hear quiet sobbing, I had high hopes that she would.

A little while later, after the girls had gone back home, Maddy was still upstairs. She hadn't wanted to talk about it with me. She hadn't wanted to talk to anyone, she hadn't wanted to eat; she hadn't wanted to do anything except have a bath and get ready for school the next day. All she'd done was snatch the Maltesers from Maya, and then asked to be left alone. As for Maya, she was sitting on the sofa with me. She looked tired, and I knew it wouldn't be long before we went up to bed, too. It had been a hard day, a hard couple of days one way or another. Maya's pain seemed to be under control, but she had a stiffness about her shoulders and that crease between her brows was back.

"You okay, gorgeous?"

She nodded but there was a sulky pout to her lips. "Yeah, I suppose so."

"I know I haven't been able to give you much attention today, but tomorrow will be better."

Maya's mouth dropped open, and she gasped. "God, no, that's not it, love. Honestly."

"Are you in pain?" From my chair, I dropped to my knees and shuffled over to her, placing my hands on her thighs. "Do you need more painkillers?"

She shook her head and breathed in. The swell of her breast rose and fell with each inhale and her eyes turned dark as she stared at me.

"What then?"

She chewed on her lip. "I don't want to say. It makes me sound like a horrible person."

"What does?" I leaned up to give her a soft kiss. "I can't imagine anything making you sound like a horrible person."

"This would," she said quietly. "After everything those poor kids have gone through, saying this would make me feel like a vile, selfish cow."

She lifted her cast wrist with her other hand and cradled it against her chest. She winced a little, so I reached for her sling that she'd thrown to one side.

"Put this on."

"It's so unattractive, though." She rolled her eyes but still took it from me.

"Is that what's upsetting you, that you think your sling is ugly?"

She squirmed a little and shook her head. "Don't judge me for this but…" When she paused, I waited patiently until she finally blurted out, "I'm so horny, Will. I'm so angry."

When her bottom lip trembled, I burst out laughing. "Seriously?"

"Yes, and don't mock me. It's been awful. I have this constant throb between my legs, and touching myself just isn't doing it for me, well actually, I can't because my ribs hurt when I do."

"Well maybe we should do something about that." At the idea of easing her ache, my dick moved behind the zip of my jeans. "I can make you feel much better."

"You don't need to. I shouldn't have said anything. I should jus—"

I cut her off when I ran my finger up the inside of her thigh and then whispered it between her legs over the thin fabric of her leggings.

"Will," she gasped as I pushed her legs further apart and ran my nose along the same path.

Without saying anything, I reached up under her oversized t-shirt, and hooked my fingers in her waistband. I tugged gently, silently asking her to lift her hips. When she did, I dragged them down her legs all the way to her ankles, pulling them over her socked feet. Her legs trembled with anticipation as I did the same thing to the pretty pink knickers she was wearing until she was bare in front of me. Bare and beautiful.

"What about Maddy?" she asked, as her eyes fluttered closed. "What if she comes down."

As if timing couldn't be any better, I heard Maddy's bedroom door close. I pointed to the ceiling and we both listened as footsteps padded above us and then the bed creaked.

"See, nothing to worry about," I told her and then kissed the inside of her thigh.

"Are you... shit... are you sure?"

"Hmm," I hummed against her skin as I travelled closer to her pussy. My thumbs pushed into the softness of her thighs as my fingers parted her lips. She was so wet, the thin strip of hair she had was glistening with her arousal. I'd barely done anything.

"Christ, Maya," I said looking up at her. "You weren't lying, you're soaked."

"I've been so desperate for you since I dreamed about you last night."

"Really? And what was this dream about." Unable to wait any longer, I gave her one long lick from bottom to top and then sucked on her clit. Her good hand went to my hair and gripped it. As her nails scored my scalp, my dick got harder to the point of painful, so I reached down and undid my jeans. I was desperate to be inside her, but she wasn't well enough for that so my pleasure could wait.

"You fucked me," she replied breathlessly. "Fucked me against the wall, hard."

I tasted her again, this time flicking my tongue against her tiny bud of nerves and her hips lurched up. I could feel the wince she held back, and I tried to pull my head away, but Maya pushed me back.

"No. I need this more that it hurts."

Smirking, I went back to feasting on her, eating her out and making her pant. Hearing her whimpers, seeing her nipples tight and hard, pushing against her t-shirt, and feeling how she thrust her hips closer and closer to my face, made me feel like I'd just been pronounced King. It made my heart full and my dick rock hard.

"You taste so fucking good," I told her, and nipped at her clit causing her to cry out a curse, and tug on my hair again. Licking, nipping and sucking I drove her right to the edge and over it, until she came, and I tasted every single inch of her release.

"Will," she panted. "I…"

"I know." I kissed the inside of her thigh which was sticky and damp and wondered how I'd managed without her for so long. "I'll get you some tissue."

"What about you?" she asked, her chest heaving. "You need me to—"

"No, I'll be fine."

I wouldn't. I would have to go upstairs and sort myself out in the bathroom, there was no way I could sit for the rest of the evening with a boner as hard as steel.

"Will," she pleaded, her eyes flaring.

"It's fine, gorgeous." Pushing up on my knees, I cupped her face and smiled at her sheer beauty and my heart stuttered. "I love you so much. You're it for me, you know that don't you?"

Her gaze softened even more than I thought possible, and she gave me a single nod. "Same," she whispered. "I can't believe I found you. What if I hadn't gone into that bar?"

"You did, so don't worry about it." I reached for her knickers. "Lift your legs up." She did as I asked, and I pulled them and then her leggings halfway up her legs. "Want tissue or the bathroom?"

"Bathroom," she replied, so I finished redressing her and then helped her to her feet.

"You go first," I told her. My dick would have to wait for some attention.

As she left the room, I decided there and then I was going to marry her, I just had to speak to Maddy first to make sure she was okay with it. Then she and I were going ring shopping. First, though, I needed to wash my face and then check on my daughter.

"Can I come in?" I asked, poking my head around Maddy's bedroom door a few minutes later.

She was on her side with the glow of her phone lighting up her tear stained face. Her lips were curled inward, and her little face was so sad I desperately wanted to kick Zak in his nuts.

"Hey, Dad." Maddy put her phone on her chest of drawers and gave me a sad smile.

"Good bath?" Sitting on the edge of her bed, I ran a hand down the long plait that she'd put her hair into.

"Yeah, okay." She sniffed, a single tear creeping down her cheek.

"Oh, sweetheart, I'm so sorry. I know it's all too much for you. Ana and now this with Zak. Have you spoken to him?"

She shook her head and dropped to her back, resting her forearm over her eyes. "He's called me a few hundred times. I'm guessing Liam told him that I've seen the picture." Her breath was shaky as she placed her hand on her stomach. "I don't know what to do, Dad. It's bad enough that I'm sad about Ana, and I'd just decided to speak to him instead of blaming him, and then…" Her voice broke, but she held it together. "And then I saw the picture of them together and it just broke my heart even more."

At that moment *my* heart broke, too. My poor little girl she was absolutely devastated. She'd been dealt two hard blows in a matter of days; her grief being doubled by Zak's actions. How could he not realise what it would do to her putting that picture up? How could he do that to her, my baby? Because I had to admit, it didn't seem like the sort of thing he'd do. Yet the evidence was there to see.

"Take my hand, sweetheart." Maddy laid her tiny one in mine, and I wrapped it up tight. "Are you sure you're ready to go back to school?"

"I've got to go back sometime and apparently we're having a special assembly for Ana tomorrow. Millie Burton messaged me, Em and Liv."

"How are you going to deal with Zak?"

She tried to disguise the whimper, but I heard it and felt a pain in my chest.

"I'll have to speak to him," she finally said. "Find out why and," she shrugged, "and when?"

"Yeah, I can't get my head around when he met up with her again, are you sure it was him." Zak was a good kid, and I found it hard to believe he'd do that to Maddy. That didn't mean I wouldn't kill the little fucker and bury his body where no one would find it if he had.

"I'm sure," Maddy replied, her voice almost a whisper.

"Well, I still think you should listen to what he has to say but stand your ground and remember you're a Newman. We don't let people treat us without respect."

Nodding silently, she pulled up into a sitting position and threw her arms around me. "Thanks, Dad. I love you."

"I love you, too." Inhaling I recognised the smell, it was the baby shampoo I always used on her when she was little. When things were going on in her life, like exams, or her first dance recital, which was also her last, and when her boyfriend broke her heart, she always used it. It was like it gave her comfort.

"You know this is all your fault," she muttered against my chest.

"What is?" I pulled back and frowned at her.

"The Zak thing."

I sifted through my brain trying to think of what I'd done to cause Zak to be a little wanker to her. "I don't know what I did, but—"

"You're just too good, Dad," she sighed with a roll of her eyes. "You're a high bar to reach and he didn't make it."

My chest went tight as my heart grew with the amount of love and pride that had just been pumped into it. If ever I'd doubted that I'd not managed to do my job as a father properly, then Maddy measuring every boy against my qualities, proved me wrong.

"Maddy, you are my greatest success in this life. My most treasured gift. From the moment I set eyes on you; I loved you. I knew I would love and protect you until my dying day, and I will. Wherever you are, whoever you're with, however old you are, that, is my promise to you." I kissed her forehead, already dreading the days she wouldn't be around for me to do this, yet also wanting her to soar. "I love you, Madeline."

"I love you, too, *Dad* and thank you for being my dad."

"Anytime sweetheart, anytime. Now," I said, brushing her hair from her face, "get some sleep."

She snuggled down under the duvet. "Thank Maya for the chocolate for me, it really helped."

I gave her a wide smile, glad that it had and glad that Maya had known exactly how to help my little girl. It just proved that she was made for me.

CHAPTER 66
Maddy

Emma's hand tightened in mine as Liv linked my arm, the school gates a couple of feet in front of us. There, leaning against the wall, in his usual spot, drawing hard on a cigarette, was Zak.

"He looks like shit," Emma announced.

"He looks like he's been crying." Liv added, tugging on my arm. "I think you should listen to what he's got to say."

"Liam said he's adamant that he isn't back with her and that he hasn't seen her since we all went to London, or that he didn't post that photo."

"Yes, well, I know what I saw." I bit down on my lip desperately trying not to cry. Just the sight of him made me want to sob. He looked terrible—like Liv said, he looked like he'd been crying, or at least not sleeping.

"Just speak to him," Emma urged.

As we moved closer, Zak pushed off the wall, stamping down on the cigarette. "Mads, please," he begged, holding out his hand. "You have to believe me. I did not post that picture. I am not still seeing Connie. I swear to you."

"I know what I saw, Zak, so if you didn't post it, who did?"

"I don't know, I have no idea. Connie, maybe?"

"How the hell could she do it? Unless, of course, you were with her and let her have your phone."

Emma cleared her throat. "Come on Liv, let's go." She hugged me and whispered, "We'll see you in assembly. Just listen to him."

"See you in while," Liv added as she uncurled her arm from around mine.

And there I was, alone with Zak, staring at me with red-rimmed eyes, swallowing hard so that his Adam's apple bobbed.

"You look awful," I told him, giving him a sweeping gaze from head to foot.

"I feel awful. I've hardly slept and I…" he ran a hand over his face and released a long, exhausted breath. "Why wouldn't you answer my calls?"

"Why do you think?" I shook my head in disbelief. "I'm grieving my best friend, and then I see a picture of you and your ex on your Insta. Posted only yesterday. Why would you do that, Zak? If you're back with her, that's the fucking shittiest way of telling me."

Looking over his shoulder at everyone milling around us, he groaned and then took my hand in his. "We need to get out of here."

I stood my ground, planting my Doc Martens firmly on the pavement. "No, Zak. We have Ana's assembly in half an hour, or don't you care about that either? You know, like you didn't care that she walked off from the party."

"That's not fair."

"No, it's not fair that she's dead. That's the most unfair thing in the world."

"Right," he said in a no-nonsense tone. "We're going to talk."

He gripped my hand harder and marched me away from the gates towards the bus shelter across the road. There was one girl in there, searching through her bag.

"Do you mind leaving?" Zak asked, his usual well-mannered self. "We need some privacy."

She stared wide eyed at him and then me. I didn't know her, but she looked like she might be a couple of years below us, so I smiled hoping she realised we weren't there to hurt her. Picking up her bag, she threw it over her shoulder and left us alone without even a backward glance.

"Sit down," Zak urged, pointing to the bench seat. "And listen to me."

"What if I don't want to?" Yet I sat down anyway.

"Please, Maddy. I need you to listen to me. I swear to God, I never posted that picture. I don't even know when it was taken. I haven't spoken to Connie since we left the party in London."

Looking down at my feet, I noticed that my right boot was dirty, so I reached down and rubbed at it with two fingers.

"Maddy," Zak cried, putting his hands on my shoulders. "Listen to me."

"I'm listening, okay." I blew out my cheeks. "I'm listening."

He exhaled and linked his hands at the back of his neck. "Thank God." Taking two paces back he crouched down so that we were eye to eye. "On my life, I swear to you that I'm not back with Connie, I didn't post that picture, and I haven't seen her or even spoken to her since London."

As I looked into his eyes, it was like looking into a shimmering pool of clear blue water, but instead of my own image reflecting back at me, it was something else, a whole host of things. It was his protectiveness, his morals, his affection for me, his beautiful nature, and his kindness; it was truth and honesty.

"How can I trust you and what you're saying, Zak?" I knew deep down he wasn't lying, and instinct told me that he had done nothing wrong, but sometimes you have to ask the questions—just to be sure you're not stupid and you do have the right answers after all.

He closed his eyes with a sigh, and as his shoulders sagged, he looked back up at me and licked his lips.

"Because." He hesitated and then shook his head. "Because you're the best thing that's *ever* happened to me Maddy, that's why. You're everything to me."

My mouth dropped open, shocked by his admission. I'd had no idea that he felt like that. Or maybe I did. Maybe that was why I was so shocked by his supposed betrayal. I knew I was there with us, but…

"I-I am?"

He nodded, putting one knee to the floor, resting his forearm on the other. "Yeah, you are. To the point that I know I'll never get over you if you dump me now, not ever."

"You're not just saying it, so I won't set my dad on you, are you?" I asked with a grin, my veins pumping with excitement and happiness.

"No, of course not. Although he does scare the shit out of me." His perfect lips pouted. "I wanted to tell you in London, but I wasn't sure that you would want to hear it. I know we're young and it's quick, but if me telling you now makes you trust me, then I'll take the risk."

"What risk?"

"Of you telling me to stop being a weird twat and to fuck off."

I couldn't help giggle at that. "I wouldn't say that."

Never ever. Not in a thousand lifetimes.

"You wouldn't?" He looked up at me with hopeful puppy eyes, which just made the stupid idiot even more attractive.

"No, but I would say, get up off that dirty pavement because you're kneeling in chewing gum."

"Ah, shit." He jumped up quickly, brushing down the knees of his jeans, muttering about dirty skanks spitting out chewing gum.

As I watched him, my body sighed with relief and I couldn't stop my smile as I said, "You're just lucky that stream of pee didn't travel far."

Zak looked where I pointed and groaned. "It's not the most romantic place to tell you I'm obsessed with you, is it?"

"Not really." It didn't mean I didn't like it, though. In fact, my heart was thudding in time with the wings of the butterflies in my stomach. "But thank you for the thought."

Sitting next to me, Zak tentatively took my hand and pulled on it until I looked at him.

"What?" I asked.

"You really do believe me?"

I nodded. "Yes, I do." Maybe it was the overpowering grief of losing my best friend that had blinded me. My heart had already been suffering and had no immunity to stupid tricks and lies. Now I was with him, though, looking into his eyes, seeing his truth, it was clear how stupid I'd been.

"Thank God," he whispered, rubbing a hand over his face. "I've been shitting myself that you wouldn't."

"Well, I do, but, if you didn't post the picture, who did?" I asked, not pulling my hand away from his. "Who could have got into your Insta?"

Zak shrugged. "No idea. I think it was taken at some family party of hers, but I know that the shirt I'm wearing went to charity when we moved here." He narrowed his eyes on me. "And you can ask my mum if you want to."

"No, I don't want to." I gave his hand a squeeze and earned myself a gorgeous smile. "Who else knows them?"

"Amelia?"

"Amelia wouldn't do that would she?"

"Not a chance, she's more obsessed with you than I am."

Grinning, I asked him, "You're obsessed with me?"

"You know I am," he replied, rolling his eyes. "And if you don't then I haven't done my job as your boyfriend properly."

Laughing, I shook my head. "You sound just like my dad."

"I am Luke to his Darth Vader. He taught me well."

"Shit, you are turning into him."

As I slapped a hand to my face, he chuckled deeply and put his arm around my shoulder, hugging me closer. "Thank you for believing me." He drew in a breath and looked at me tentatively.

"What?" I asked. "What aren't you telling me?"

"Fuck it, I'm just going to say it."

"Say what?" I asked, my voice quivering with trepidation.

"That I love you, Maddy," he said quietly, his gaze fixed on me. "And

I'm an idiot because I should have said it before now. Because that's what I really wanted to tell you in London. You're not just everything to me. I love you."

My stomach tumbled as I stared at his lips, not sure if I'd heard him properly. "Say it again," I whispered, watching him carefully. "Tell me again."

He reached for my hand and pulled it against his chest. "I. Love. You."

His words were slow and definite so that there was no doubt what he was saying. And every single syllable made perfect sense. He. Loved. *Me*. This clever, kind, gorgeous boy loved me, and I knew that even if it didn't last he would always be ingrained in my soul. That was how special he was, how special what we had was. It was the perfect first love.

Our eyes met in an intense stare and all the excitement rolling around in my stomach intensified. It wasn't heated or lustful, but much deeper than that. It was a silent recognition of how we felt about each other. Of the excitement and joy of first love.

My heart hammered as adrenaline coursed through my body, and his intense blue gaze stole my breath. This boy was everything to me. He was the best part of my life. The best part of my heart. "I love you, too," I told him, hoping my words didn't sound as shaky as they felt in my throat, because I needed him to hear them and understand them. "That is my truth, and I'm sorry that I doubted you for one second, because I know how amazing you are."

"Amazing?" He had a wry grin on his face, and it was so cute it made my heart flutter.

"Yes, amazing. And perfect and ho—"

I didn't have a chance to finish because Zak jumped up, cupped my face, and held it in his strong hands while he kissed the breath from my lungs. It was passion and sweetness mixed together as he bit my bottom lip before sucking on it gently. His fingers tangled in my hair as he urged me to stand with him. Once I did, we lost ourselves even more in a kiss that was a recognition of the feelings we'd fallen hopelessly into.

"I love you," he said breathlessly in the seconds between kisses.

"I love you."

It was like we couldn't get close enough, pushing against each other, our hands clutching and grabbing.

Being there in that moment with Zak made me wish that I hadn't been so angry about Ana's death, or so furious with myself for not going home with her, and so full of resentment at Zak. All those feelings had been stupid and damaging. What I really should have done was let myself need him. Because all that fury and bitterness had squashed down the grief, and I'd let it because that was so much easier to deal with. In return, I'd suffered more. My relationship with Zak had suffered, too.

"Please don't ever doubt me again," he said, leaning in to kiss me softly. "Because of all the people in this world, Maddy, I only want and need you. And I would never hurt you." He breathed out slowly, like he finally felt at peace.

"I know." And I did know, and I had to say the words one more time. "I love you."

Smiling, we stared at each other, our gazes drinking each other in as we memorised the moment that would be the defining one of our relationship. The moment where I'd stopped over thinking and just let myself feel.

"We should go," I said, conscious of the time of Ana's assembly.

He nodded, his thumb brushing my cheek, his ring cold against my skin. "Yeah maybe you're ri…"

"What?" I asked, when he trailed off.

"My passcode. Connie knows it."

"Connie?"

"Yeah, she does."

"But it was your Insta password, not your phone." I didn't understand what he was getting at. "How would that help her? Or does she know that, too?"

"No, but maybe she got into my phone and checked my password. I don't have it hidden because I always forget it."

"Zak," I cried. "You told me all your passwords are Hoyland123, how the hell do you forget that?"

He shrugged like he had no idea what the problem with that was. "The point is," he replied, "she might have got into my phone and checked my password and then she posted it."

"Would she go to those sort of lengths?" I asked and then remembered the party. "Yeah, she would."

"I'll kill her," he growled about to push up off the bench seat when I pushed him back down.

"We need to be sure first. And, I can't believe I'm saying this," I shook my head and rolled my eyes, "but does it matter? If she did, the reason was to break us up and it hasn't worked, so…"

Zak shook his head. "It does matter. She made you cry, and I had the shittiest weekend of my life."

"Who said I cried," I argued.

He circled my face with his index finger. "You look beautiful, but I can see hints of tears."

"My friend died, Zak. Do you not think that maybe that's why my face is blotchy and my eyes like slits."

Shame and regret fell over his features. "Shit, I'm sorry. I can't imagine how bad you must feel. How sad and heartbroken. Fuck," he cursed under his breath. "I'm so sorry, Mads."

"It's fine." It wasn't fine, there were still vestiges of anger inside me, but it was time to let it go.

"I know that you're angry at me for not chasing after her the other night, but honestly I didn't know she would take that short cut. I didn't even know it existed."

"I wasn't angry at you, well, not just you. I was angry at everything; at Ana, at me, at you. Just because it was easier than the alternative which was grief. Grief and acceptance that she really is dead."

"I'm so sorry." Zak stroked my cheek and gave me a half smile. "But I understand that totally. I promise you, though, Liam and I looked hard for her. We even went out onto the street, both in different directions, but neither of us saw her."

"She probably cut through the allotment, another stupid thing she used to do." Scuffing the toe of my boot on the pavement, I thought about Ana and some of the stunts she used to pull. "She'd often go off on her own, take short cuts and the darkest roads home. She was the first one to sneak drink out of her parents' drinks cabinet, she was the one who jumped a taxi when we went to a gig in Manchester one time. She did a lot of stupid things, so her storming off from a party wasn't your fault, not at all."

He gave me a single nod and sighed. "We should get to the assembly. Go and pay tribute to her."

It was only when Zak reached up and wiped my cheek with his finger that I realised I was crying, but it felt good to have him there to comfort me.

"I'm doing a speech," I told him. "I just hope it's okay."

"It'll be perfect," he replied. "You'll make her proud, I know you will. And then, after that I'm going to call Connie and find out what she's been doing."

"Zak, it's fine."

"No," he said determinedly. "She could have split us up, and I won't ever forgive her for that."

We then walked back to school and as Zak squeezed my hand, it felt good to have a small level of normality. Even though the next couple of hours were probably going to be the saddest of my life so far.

CHAPTER 67
Will

Holding Maya's good hand, we filed into the school hall, slow-footed and sad, like everyone else. After Maddy had gone to school, Sam had called to say he and Lou were going to Ana's assembly and asked if I wanted to tag along. I didn't think Maya would want to come, but she'd said she'd be honoured. She'd only met Ana the once, but she mattered to Maddy and that was enough of a reason for Maya.

"There's Mike and Susan at the front, with Theo," Lou whispered to me as we took our seats. "I can't imagine how they're feeling."

The idea of what they were going through, filled *me* with a fear that I'd never felt before. Thinking that could have been me sat at the front of the hall made panic rise in my chest, and I hoped to God that it was never would be. It made me think about Steven and his son, and what he must have been going through. I needed to decide about the transplant, but more importantly I needed to contact his son, my *brother*.

"Is that Ana's brother?" Maya asked, rousing me from my thoughts.

Theo looked just as shattered as his parents, yet he was the one with his hand in his dad's and his arm around his mum. He was holding them up even though he looked like he was ready to collapse in a heap himself.

"He's a couple of years older," I told her. "Poor kid."

"Emma's mum is waving to you," Sam hissed from the side of his mouth. "She never gives up does she, even on a day like today."

She was waving her fingers and smiling, and it was totally inappropriate considering why we were sitting in the hall. At least when I gave her a chin dip, she turned back to the front to watch the staff and kids taking part in the assembly troop onto the stage.

"Oh bless." Maya sighed and clutched her sling. "Maddy."

My gaze followed Maya's, and my heart dropped to my boots with a thud. My little girl looked so damn sad. She, Emma and Liv were all holding hands, and they looked so small standing next to Mr Anderson, their head of year, and Miss Coombs, the head of school. There were another couple of teachers who I didn't know, and Becky Marshall, the head girl, who was clutching a book. All of them looked desolate, but the girls were by far the most overwrought with sadness.

"I can't stand this," I muttered, feeling my gut clench. I was halfway out of my seat when I spotted him.

Zak Hoyland.

When he placed his foot on the first step up to the stage, I stood to my full height and took a half stride. That was all it took for Maya to grab my hand.

"Don't Will. Just wait."

I looked down to see a raised warning brow. She then looked back at the stage, her eyes urging me to look for myself. When I saw him pull Maddy into his arms and kiss the top of her head, exactly what I would have done, a sense of relief washed over me.

"They made up," I whispered.

"I had no doubt." She gave me a knowing smile. "He's a good boy and he likes to think he models himself on you, so of course he was going to grovel for something he probably didn't do."

"You don't know he didn't do it," I grumbled, my eyes still on the scene playing out on the stage. "The evidence was pretty damning."

"Believe me when I tell you this," she replied with a smirk, "there are some awful girls out there, and if he didn't do it—and I believe he didn't—then I'm pretty sure one of those awful girls in this world did. Either that or she got some weaselly suck-arse little boy to do it."

"Christ, you know some horrible people," I laughed and settled back in my chair watching as Zak held Maddy's face and said something to her. After she nodded, he kissed her forehead and then went back to his seat. My eyes then moved to Emma who was crouched at the edge of the stage where Liam was reaching up his fingers linked with hers as they talked. "You have a good kid there," I said to Lou as she shifted in her seat.

"Takes after his dad," Sam said leaning forward to give me a self-congratulatory smile.

"You know him?" Lou asked.

Maya and I snorted a quiet laugh. "Bloody hell, I love her," Maya said, placing her hand on my thigh and giving it a small squeeze.

"Yeah, she knows how to keep him in his place."

Sam leaned forward and tapped Maya's knee. "I am Liam's dad really. It's a running joke that she thinks is funny."

"Shut up, Sam." I pushed him back with my arm. "It's about to start and we all know that you're not Liam's real dad."

Louise and Maya laughed quietly and then we all sat back to pay tribute to a girl who had always held my daughter's hand when I couldn't. Now she was gone but at least Maddy had Zak now, as well as me and Maya. There were a lot of kids who couldn't say that, so I was happy that my daughter was one of the lucky ones.

***

"Ana was my friend, my best friend since we were little, and I will always treasure that."

As Maddy took a deep breath, Liv rubbed her back, giving her what she needed to continue. Liv and Emma had done their tributes, Liv's had been a funny story about the four of them getting locked in the school, something I hadn't known about. Emma had read out a poem that she'd written herself, all about friendship. It was beautiful and poignant, leaving more than one person crying at the end of it. Now, Maddy was battling her tears to read out her tribute.

When she didn't continue, my hands clenched, wondering whether I should go up there and hold her hand. Her bravery won through, and after glancing into the audience, I suspected at Zak, she carried on.

"We did so many things together," she looked up and grimaced, giving a little shrug, "sorry parents about this next bit. We had our first taste of alcohol together when we skipped Mr Kings geography lesson once." Then she looked over at the staff who were sitting against the wall. "Sorry, Mr King, but rock formation wasn't doing it for us."

"Did you know that?" Maya whispered to me.

"No, I didn't. Now I know why she dropped geography the minute she could."

"Ana and I also went to our first gig together and we both fell in love with Shaun Peters together when we were eight and he was fifteen." A murmur of laughter spread around the hall, and Maddy's shoulders relaxed. "Shaun never knew, so if he ever arrests you, please don't tell him." When there was more laughter, the pride I felt for her was huge. Even Ana's family had smiles on their faces. Susan was wiping her nose with a tissue, but she was definitely smiling behind it. "Ana was also the first person to tell me if my outfit didn't look right, or if my hair needed cutting and she was the first person to notice that I had the hots for the new boy in school." She looked in Zak's direction, her features softening, and I was glad that he hadn't been a dick. He was a good kid and was good for Maddy. "The point is we might have argued from time to time," she stumbled on those words, "but she was always there for the important parts. I can't believe I'm going to have to go through those in the future without her. It doesn't seem right or fair. Not for her parents, her brother, her family, her friends, me," her voice broke but she carried on, "but mostly for her. She would have taken life by the reins and lived it to its fullest but, because of one stupid decision, she won't get the opportunity." Folding her notes she pushed them into her pocket and smiled at the audience. "I will never forget Ana. She will always be in my heart and when I graduate, get my first job, get engaged, married, and become a mother, I will tell her all about it. Then she'll still be with me for the important parts." She then looked directly at Ana's family, placed a hand on her heart and finished by saying, "Thank you for giving me the best friend in the world."

"Oh Will," Maya whispered. "That was beautiful, you must be so proud of her."

I couldn't speak for the lump in my throat but just nodded. I was proud, proud and grateful because she was my daughter, and I'd had a part in making her the person she was.

Without thinking about it, I leaned into Maya. "Want to move in with us?"

She blinked and pulled back to look at me eye to eye. "What?"

"Want to move in with us? Me and Maddy, well, until she goes to uni because I have a feeling she might change her mind about going to Edinburgh."

"H-have you asked her?" she whispered as Miss Combs took over on the microphone. "And how do you know about her changing her mind about uni?"

"Not yet but I know she'll be fine about it. She loves you. She'll be happy for us, I promise you." I leaned in closer. "As for Edinburgh, she tried to hide a letter from me and there's a certain boy who is going there."

Maya's eyes widened, wary as she glanced towards the stage.

"Well?" I prompted.

"I-I mean it's a shock and I'd love to, but can you ask me again once you've spoken to Maddy." She dropped her head, leaning closer to my ear. "And this is a strange place to ask me."

I shrugged. "Maybe, but today is all about the end of a life and the end of a chapter." I looked over to Ana's mum, dad and brother who were hugging the girls, glad once again it wasn't me. "The end of one chapter usually means the beginning of another," I continued, "so it seems as good a place as any."

Rolling her lips inwards, Maya nodded and then placed her hand in mine. Exactly where it was meant to be.

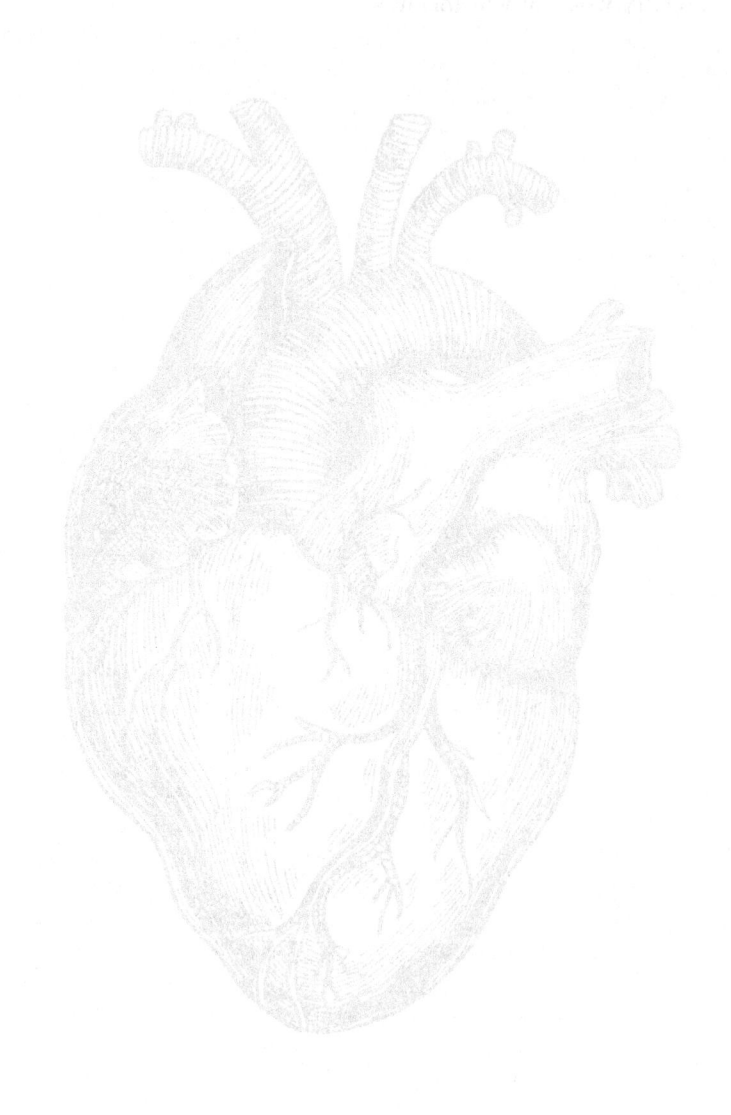

THE FUTURE

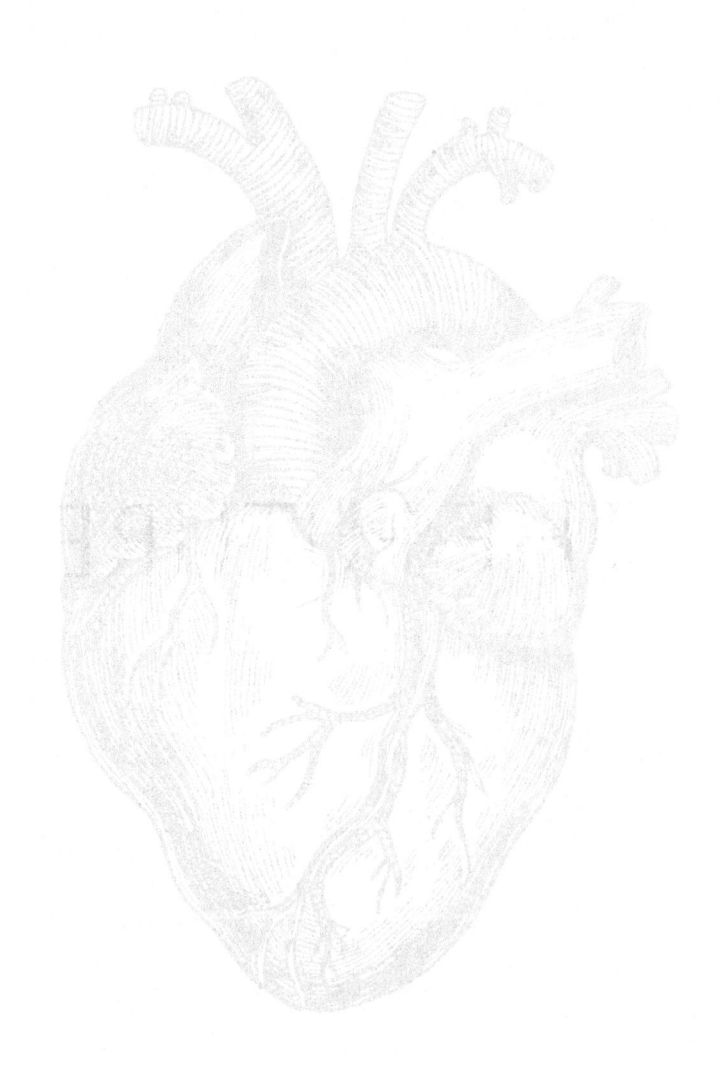

CHAPTER 68
Will

Maddy and Zak were curled up on the sofa, watching some mindless reality TV show based on a luxury yacht. I had no clue what was going on, only that some people had millions in the bank but no taste whatsoever. What I also knew was that Zak hadn't let go of her hand in the two hours that they'd been sitting there. They'd even eaten their pizza one handed.

"Any chance we can have a chat?" I asked, leaning down to pick up the TV remote and pausing the program.

"Do you want me to go?" Zak asked, looking like he might burst into flames if he had to leave my daughter's side.

I shook my head. "It's fine because I reckon this affects you as well."

Maddy scooted to the edge of the sofa, concern in her eyes. "What's wrong? Is Maya okay, did she go to bed because she doesn't feel well?"

"No, no. It's all fine. She just needed a nap. Those painkillers knock her out." I sat down and patted Maddy's knee reassuringly. "It is about Maya, though."

"Is she pregnant?" Maddy gave me the first smile she'd offered in days. "Please yes. I've always wanted a little sister."

"No, sweetheart, she's not pregnant." Although, I wouldn't be averse to it if she was. And that thought took me by surprise. I'd never thought I'd have any more kids, mainly because I'd never imagined meeting anyone I'd want them with. Now there was Maya.

"What then?" Maddy's smile disappeared into an expression of disappointment.

"I was wondering how you felt about her moving in with us." I had no idea why, but I grimaced, scared of her reaction.

Maddy's eyes widened. "Really?" I nodded and braced ready for rejection, but had no need to worry. "That's the best news ever, Dad." She launched herself at me, finally letting go of Zak's hand, and wrapped her arms around me. "I'm so happy for you."

Hugging her back, my body sagged with relief and then pumped back up with the joy and love. This girl, the one squeezing the air from my lungs, was my world. My greatest achievement, my greatest love and whatever she did with her life, wherever she went I would support her and be proud of her. Whichever man was lucky enough to spend the rest of his life with her had better take care of her because I would always be waiting in the wings, ready to take over and kick the shit out of him if necessary. As I looked over her shoulder at Zak and saw the way he looked at her, I had a feeling he might well be that man. If meeting Maya had taught me anything, it was that when you fell in love with someone you never wanted to be without, you don't stand a chance. You can't stop it, just because you're deemed to be too young, or too old, too poor, or not suitable. When you find a deep, soul embedding love it hits you with force and sends you reeling. Maybe that was what Zak and Maddy had, and who was I to tell her he wouldn't be her last, most important love, because maybe he would be.

"I can tell her yes then?" I asked when Maddy finally let me go.

"Of course you can. The sooner the better." She edged back on the sofa bringing her legs up and grabbing Zak's hand again. "Go and tell her now." She bounced up and down, and I was happy to see her excitement at having Maya move in.

"She's sleeping, besides which I think we have other things that we need to talk about."

"We do." She frowned at me, then at Zak, and finally back to me. "What?"

"What went on with the ex-girlfriend, Zak?"

"Dad, it's all sorted," Maddy protested.

"You sure?" I raised an eyebrow at Zak. "She didn't just decide to forgive you? You didn't spin her some tale?" I was pretty sure he was being honest. I'd thought it odd that he'd do anything to hurt Maddy anyway. I'd just done the Dad thing; assumed that he was guilty and threatened the existence of his balls. Now I just needed to check that he really was a good kid after all.

"I swear, Will, I didn't do anything. I wouldn't do anything to hurt Maddy."

"He's telling the truth. We're pretty sure it *was* the ex-girlfriend who did it."

Zak explained everything about his passwords and passcodes and how he though she got into his phone somehow and made the post.

"Any idea when she got hold of your phone seeing as you're here as she's in London?"

Zak. "No idea."

"When was the last time she had her hands on it?"

"His phone or something else?" Maddy asked dryly.

"His phone." I shook my head in disbelief. "You need to take this seriously, Maddy. If it is this girl, then she'll do it again, and next time *he* might not have any proof it wasn't him. Or she'll do something that hurts you even more than this did."

"Your dad has a point, Mads."

"Yes, but what do we do?"

I wasn't sure how, but Zak did need to get her to admit it. It was true what I'd told Maddy, if he didn't, and it happened again, she'd always be wondering.

"Maybe just ask her," I suggested.

"She's too sneaky for that." Zak sighed and lifted his gaze to the ceiling, clearly frustrated. "I'll think of something."

I clapped my hands together. "Good. Now, who wants a drink?"

"Yes please." Maddy reached for the remote. "Beer?"

"Okay, Zak, the same?" When he nodded, I heaved myself up from the chair. "Right, and then this shit gets turned off."

"Dad."

"No Mads, I'm not watching this crap for the rest of the night. Maya will be up soon, and she gets seasick."

They both looked at me and frowned. "What the hell are you talking about, Dad?"

"She gets seasick she won't want to watch something about boats."

Zak grinned and scratched his head. "You do know it doesn't work like that, don't you?"

"Not sure, do I?" I said and winked at him leaving the room.

In the hallway I listened out for any noise from Maya and when I heard nothing, I started to walk to the kitchen but had barely walked two strides when the doorbell rang out. Not wanting it to wake Sleeping Beauty, I ran back to the door. I barely had it open when Steven came barrelling in, his face fixed in a sneer.

"You couldn't just say yes, could you. You had to say no, and now it's too fucking late," he screamed at me.

"What the fuck." I pushed him with both hands against his chest. "How dare you storm into my house and shout at me."

"I dare because you're nothing but a fucking bastard, and now I've lost my son because of you."

I took a step back blinking rapidly. "What?" I didn't know my brother, his son, yet shock and sadness hit me in the chest. "What happened?"

Steven gripped his hair with both hands and then bent at the waist and let out what I could only describe as a howl.

"Dad?" Maddy appeared in the doorway and looked at Steven. "What the hell is going on?"

I rubbed a hand over my mouth, not sure what to tell her. Then movement caught my eye and I saw Maya walking down the stairs.

"Babe, what's happening?" Her arm wasn't in her sling, but she was cradling it against her chest.

Steven stood up straight and turned to her. "He killed my son," he spat out, his finger pointing at me. "He didn't say yes to the transplant, and now my son is dead."

I rubbed a hand across my mouth, not sure where the guilt was coming from. I didn't owe him, or his son, anything, yet I felt an element of truth in his words. Maybe I could have saved his life.

Maya took the last couple of steps and as she got closer, I could see fire in her eyes. Her good hand was clenched into a fist; she was mad.

"How dare you come into Will's home and speak to him like that." Her growl was so low and angry even I was scared of her. "You only asked him a few days ago, how could you expect him to say yes immediately?"

When she winced and put her hand to her ribs, I took a step forward. "Maya."

"No, Will," she snapped. "He doesn't get to speak to you like that. He doesn't get to storm in here and accuse you of something that isn't your fault." She wheeled back around to Steven and pointed a finger at him. "If he'd said yes, only a few days ago, do you really think it would have happened that quickly? That your son would have had his kidney by now?" She stared at Steven, but when he didn't answer, she poked him in the chest. "Well, do you?"

"Shit," Zak muttered behind me. "She's scary."

"Yes I am," she hissed, her eyes still on Steven. "When someone accuses my boyfriend of something that is beyond his control and," she said, thrusting her good hand to her hips, "they wake me up from one of the best sleeps I've had in days."

I was sure that was a lie because she'd told me only that morning that she was sleeping better. I didn't care, though, Maya was angry, and she was sexy as hell when she was angry.

"If his kidney has finally given up then he was obviously seriously ill. Will couldn't have helped."

The way Steven looked at her made me want to punch him. He was looking her up and down with disdain, like she was dirt under his shoe.

"You need to go," I told him. "Out of my house, and I never want to see your face ever again."

He turned to me and gave me the same look of contempt, if not a harder one. "He was twice the man you'll ever be."

"Oi," Maddy butted in. "Don't you dare speak to my dad like that."

When he said, "I should have known you'd be dragged up, just like him." I'd had enough.

"Right, get out now. I'm not to blame for your son, I couldn't have saved him. Even if I'd said yes, there was no way we could have had tests and a transplant in a matter of two weeks. I'll let what you said about me go because you're grieving, but I will not have you speak to the people I love like that. Maddy is my daughter and Maya," I said pointing to the angry woman seething at the bottom of the stairs, "is my girlfriend, and this is their home. They deserve respect, and if you can't give them that, then shut your damn mouth."

"His heart gave up," Steven practically whispered. "He had a massive heart attack because of the drugs and booze, all when he was going to give up, and that's not fair. I'd got him out of the squat he was in, and he wanted to do better. He wanted to get back working, be good at his job again, like he was before the drugs. None of it is fair."

"What's not fair is you blaming Will for that," Maya said softly. "It's a terrible situation, and I feel sorry for you, but you can't come here yelling blame where it's not justified."

I was shocked to hear that my half-brother had been an addict. I'd automatically assumed he'd be some sort of executive in his dad's business, and that he'd done well with his life. Maybe he had a family and a home. I'd assumed that because he'd had a father in his life. How wrong could I have been? It seemed I was assuming a lot of shit the last few days.

Steven looked at each of us in turn, and then went to the front door, and pulled down the handle. I breathed a sigh of relief. He was about to walk out, when he stopped and turned around, pointing his finger at me. "It should have been you," he snarled. "You should have been the fuck up, not him."

Then he was gone, slamming the door behind him.

"I think that'll be the last you'll see of him," Maddy commented.

Reaching out an arm, I wrapped it around her and pulled her to me, kissing her temple. "You could be right, sweetheart, but can't say I care."

"Are you okay?" Maya asked, cautiously.

"Fine, babe. Absolutely fine." When she gave me a soft smile, I didn't feel one ounce of regret. "We're just having a beer. You want one?"

"That would be lovely. A toast to Ana," she said looking lovingly at Maddy.

"Yes," Maddy said on a sigh. "And you."

"Me?" Maya asked. "Why me?"

"Moving in with us, of course."

"You asked her?" Maya rolled her eyes at me. "I thought you weren't going to do it today. You said you'd leave it a couple of days."

"Maya, it's fine. I needed some good news after today." Maddy slipped from under my arm and went to Maya and hugged her. "It's going to be great having two of us to gang up on him."

I knew that they would do exactly that, but I really didn't give a shit. In fact, nothing would make me happier.

CHAPTER 69
Maddy

"Now you know exactly what you're going to say, don't you?"

Zak rolled his eyes and then with the drawstring of my hoody pulled me in for a soft, gentle kiss which made me sigh with satisfaction.

"We've been over it a hundred times," he said. "I know exactly what I'm going to say."

My nerves were jangling as Zak pulled his phone from his pocket. He was going to call Connie and try and get her to confess. With Dad, we'd come up with a plan, because he was right, I did need to hear her say it. I knew that Zak was telling the truth, I trusted him, but if I didn't hear it, maybe there would always be a tiny niggle in the back of my mind.

"I've got this," he added, looking at me with a raised eyebrow.

"I know." It was my turn to kiss him and then I patted his chest. "Okay, let's do it."

He gave me a short, sharp nod, and then pressed the screen. A couple of seconds later the ringtone sounded out.

"Don't forget we're on speaker," Zak said quickly. I nodded and we waited for her to answer.

Finally, she answered. "Zak," she said breathlessly, and I could just imagine her flicking her hair over one shoulder and checking her lip gloss, like he could see her. "What's wrong?"

"Nothing, I just wanted to check in with you." His face was hard but his voice soft and cajoling. I almost felt jealous, but he reached for my hand and pulled me closer. "I also have something to tell you."

"You do? What?" I detected a waver in her voice, and it was clear she was nervous. Surely she must have wondered if he'd seen the picture. Then again, she probably didn't even care if he had.

"Maddy and I split up." Zak swallowed hard and I knew it was because he hated saying the words. We'd argued about it. He just wanted to confront her, but I knew a sneaky bitch when I met one, confrontation didn't always work with them, sometimes you had to be just as conniving.

"Oh no. God, why?"

I had to give it to her, she was a good actress.

"The picture on my Insta story." Zak's nostrils flared as his anger continued to build.

"Your Insta?' she questioned, and I detected a quiver of nerves in her tone. "You never use your Insta. I've never known you once use your Insta." Which was exactly what she'd been hoping for.

"I don't, I haven't, so I'm not sure how the picture ended up on there. It was one of us, I think it was one at your auntie's party."

"I don't think I know which one you mean."

I had to slap a hand over my mouth to disguise the gasp of air I took. Zak looked at me and shook his head, knowing that if she discovered I was there, she'd probably end the call.

"Lying bitch," I mouthed, and he grinned back at me.

"The one your dad took. The one you said we could use as an engagement picture, if we ever got engaged.

I swivelled around in my seat, and my eyes nearly popped out of my head. If she'd been there, I might have changed my stance on violence, at least pulling out some of her hair extensions—because no one's hair was that soft, thick, and beautiful naturally. Apart from Maya's, but she was gorgeous inside as well as out. Zak patted my knee to calm me down, but my blood was red hot and surging in my veins, and not likely to cool down until Connie was totally out of our lives. I couldn't believe that she'd talked about getting engaged to him. To think Zak could have ended up saddled with the conniving little…

"Oh, that one." She giggled. "I remember it. What about it?" Now her acting skills were waning quickly.

"It was on my Insta story," Zak gritted out with a forced smile. "Maddy saw it and dumped me."

"What? Oh no, that's terrible. Why would she do that?"

I could practically hear the laughter in her voice, and I hated her even more.

"Because of what it said." He took a deep breath. "Because of what you wrote on it."

"Me? What I wrote? I have no idea what you mean."

Zak laughed, and even though I could hear how hollow it was, I hoped she didn't. "Connie, I know you. I know it was you, *babe*." The last word was practically spat out, so I waved my hand at him and silently told him to calm down. He nodded and continued, "It has to be you, because I didn't do it. Not that I'm mad at you, I mean, Maddy and I weren't going anywhere. I was ready to call it a day, so it did me a favour really."

"Honestly?" the conniving witch asked.

"Yeah, honestly. I think after seeing you at the party, she realised that we probably weren't as serious as you and I had been." Zak's fingers curled tighter around mine, his wordless promise that it wasn't true. "That and the picture, well, you know the rest."

"Did you show it to her?" Connie's tone was high and excited, like a child getting the treat that they'd been begging for. "Or did she see it herself?"

"She saw it herself. You know I never go on my Insta." Zak gave a false chuckle. "Did you do it, Connie?"

"Zak, as if."

Her giggle made my spine stiffen and every vein in my body pulse with hate and anger. I'd never experienced such nastiness and vindictiveness in my life. Maybe it was because I lived in a small town or maybe I chose my friends more wisely than Zak chose girlfriends. That thought made my chest clench, and as Ana's face flashed before my eyes, I wished things that weren't nice to think.

"Well," Zak continued. "Like I said, whoever it was, did me a favour."

There was a moment of silence, and his gaze met mine. The air crackled around us as we held our breath, because instinctively we both knew what was about to happen.

"If it was me would you be mad?" she asked, huskily, like she was trying to seduce him. "Or would I be your best friend, forever?"

"Maybe more than my best friend," Zak replied.

"Well, it was me." She said the words with confidence and pride. "I posted it. Remember at the party when I held your phone after it got covered with beer?"

"Yeah." Zak swallowed, and I could see he was holding tightly on to his temper.

"I checked your Instagram login and password, and I posted it a couple of days later." Another giggle set my teeth on edge. "I could see you weren't totally happy, so I thought, why not help you lose the baggage."

That almost sent me through the roof, and as I moved to stand up, Zak placed a calming hand on my knee. He tipped his head on one side and widened his eyes, pleading with me to let him finish what he'd started. With my blood boiling, I practically threw myself against the back of the sofa, holding on precariously to the arm because what I really wanted to do was launch his phone and symbolically throw Connie against the wall.

"And you thought that maybe we'd get back together, did you?" Zak's voice was light, with a hint of laughter as he tried to coax Connie's motivation out of her. "Thought we'd go back to how we were?"

"Well, I hoped."

That fucking laugh of hers was driving me mad. I had no idea how Zak had put up with it.

"I mean I know you're going to Edinburgh, but Newcastle isn't a million miles away."

My heart stuttered and suddenly, I wanted Zak to end the call. I was desperate to talk to him about what came next for us. I dropped my gaze from his, over thinking about things that hadn't even happened, but when he placed a finger under my chin, forcing me to look at him, my heart thudded. He gave me the most beautiful smile and nodded, like he knew what was going on in my head.

With his eyes still on me, he spoke again. "So, tell me your full plan."

"Post a picky of us, get the Northerner to dump you, and leave you free to come back to me, then we see each other at weekends while we're at uni and then maybe…" Connie trailed off and more tinkling laughter echoed down the line, filling in the gaps for Zak presumably.

Zak licked his lips and took a deep breath before pulling me closer and wrapping an arm around my shoulder.

"Connie," he said in a deep authoritative tone, "there's many things that are going to happen in our futures, but I can assure you, you and I getting back together is not one of them."

"What?" She sounded genuinely shocked, like her actions were a perfectly acceptable way of getting your ex-boyfriend back.

"I think you heard. I'm not getting back with you. If this fucking dick trick of yours had worked, I still wouldn't be getting back with you. We ended things because our relationship was toxic."

I blinked and straightened my spine, he'd never told me that, only that they'd grown apart.

"We were *not* toxic," she cried.

"You sleeping with some random boy on our school ski trip, and then telling me about every detail, wasn't toxic? You telling me that my friends hated me, wasn't toxic? You telling my parents I was stalking you, wasn't toxic?"

"*She's* the toxic one," I cried, no longer caring if Connie heard me. "What a bitch."

"Is she there?" she demanded with a screech.

"Of course she is." Zak grinned. "As if you could split us up."

If I'd know exactly what she was like, known the things that Zak had just mentioned, I would never for one minute have believed he'd cheated on me with her. She was truly vile, and I couldn't understand why he'd never told me everything.

"But she's just... just... nothing," Connie screamed.

"That's where you're wrong," Zak said with a sigh and a smile for me. "She's everything."

"Zak ple—"

"No, Connie," he snapped, his smile gone. "I don't want to hear it. Just stay out of my life and don't ever contact me again."

Then he looked at me and I took great pleasure in leaning forward and ending the call.

"Why didn't you tell me about her?" I asked, finally feeling the knot in my chest unravel. "I would never have believed it if I'd known what a cow she was."

Zak shrugged as he sat back against the cushions of the sofa. "She wasn't always that bad. She was lovely at the start, but when that initial excitement of getting together wore off, she started her antics. She did whatever she could to humiliate me. Luckily I have a good relationship with my mates, so I asked them if it was true that they hated me. Of course, they laughed their arses off. As for my parents instead of believing her, they told me that I should distance myself from her. My dad called her troubled."

"And what about the boy she slept with? You didn't just take that did you?"

"Fuck no. I ended it there and then. I was already thinking of doing it, but it doesn't mean it didn't hurt. I felt embarrassed and I was glad that we moved here not long after."

"God, what an absolute bitch, and you were so nice to her at the party. I would have taken great pleasure in ignoring her."

"I was never going to act like best friends with her, but she doesn't mean enough to me for me to go to the effort of being nasty to her." He leaned in and kissed me softly. "Let's forget about her, she's not going to bother us again. Tell me about you deciding to go to Edinburgh instead."

I gasped and slapped playfully at his chest. "How did you know? I didn't even tell my dad just in case I wasn't accepted. I didn't think I had, but I got the letter yesterday offering me a place, they said it was an administrative error. And it all depends on my grades."

"Which you'll get."

I rolled my eyes. "We'll see, but how did you know?"

Zak shrugged. "I just saw it in your face when Connie mentioned she'd be in Newcastle."

"And would you be okay with that if I went there?" I looked down, rubbing at some non-existent stain on my jeans, not daring to see the expression on his face.

"Mads," Zak said, regaining my attention.

"What?" I looked back up at him and chewed on my bottom lip.

"Of course, I'd be happy if you went there, if it's right for you. I want you there for me, but I don't want you just to go because of all this with Connie, because nothing at all is ever going to happen there ever again." He cupped the back of my neck, threading his fingers through my hair, the intensity in his gaze making me want things that I shouldn't at my age. "If you don't go then we'll just have to make it work."

I took a fortifying breath, not sure I should give him my honesty, but I was so in love with him it was impossible not to.

"I want to go there. It's a great course and I want to be with you. I don't think I could stand not seeing you every day, but if we don't work out, then I won't stalk you around campus or anything, I promise."

Zak frowned. "Well, that's not happening anyway. You know we're going to work out, and if we didn't, I'd definitely stalk you."

We both laughed softly, and as our gazes locked on each other, the atmosphere changed. There'd been a shift in our relationship one way or another the last few days, and I think we both knew that we were a serious 'us'.

"You know my dad and Maya have gone out to dinner and won't be back for ages, don't you."

Sadness about Ana still overwhelmed me, but whenever I was with Zak the pain was slightly less. Intimacy was something I was desperate for. Not just for the thrill of the orgasm, but because it felt right being in his arms. It felt safe.

Pushing me on my back, Zak hovered over me, his hands caging my head, and dropped his mouth to mine.

"I love you," he said as he slowly unzipped my hoody. "And I can't wait until we get to Edinburgh."

"Me neither," I whispered, pushing up his t-shirt, relishing the feel of his warm skin.

"Good."

It was then, as he started to undress me, I realised that apart from my dad, Zak Hoyland, was the only man whose hand I wanted to take.

CHAPTER 70
Will

My nerves were jangling as Maddy and I leaned against the counter of the jewellers we were in.

"Dad, your hands are shaking," she said, laughing as she placed hers on top of mine.

"I'm not sure whether it's the thought of Maya saying no or the amount of money I'm about to handover," I replied with a groan.

"The money, definitely." She gave me a huge grin and held her hand, palm up. "Take my hand, Dad."

Exhaling, trying to rid myself of tension, I placed my hand in hers, and her small fingers wrapped around mine. "I love you, sweetheart," I told her. "And I'm so proud of you."

A shy blush appeared on her cheeks, never one to like too much attention. "Dad, it's university, that's all."

"It's a big thing," I protested. "You're going out of your comfort zone and leaving home."

Maddy was going to Edinburgh, not staying at home and doing some online course. My relief was huge, only tempered by the knowledge that I was going to miss her.

"I'm only going because I know you have Maya to take care of you," she told me.

Maya had been living with us for three months and it had been perfect. Well, almost. There'd been a couple of teething problems over how I left the bathroom after a shower, and how she got makeup powder everywhere. Money had also created a heated discussion because I didn't think she should pay half the bills. Seeing as Maddy's habit of leaving lights on, and Zak eating every meal with us most weekends, contributed the most to our bills. After an hour of ignoring each other, though, we discussed it calmly and we finally agreed on Maya paying a third. I'd have been happy with zero, but my woman was bloody stubborn.

"How are you going to do it anyway?" Maddy asked, peering in the glass case at some diamond earrings. "And yes, I am changing the subject."

"You little turd." I ruffled her hair. "And I have no idea."

"Dad," she exclaimed. "You have to have something fancy planned out." She shook her head disdainfully and gave an exhausted sigh. "You're hopeless."

"No, I'm not," I protested. "Maya isn't into fancy. She likes normal, but romantic, and so it will be."

"Just don't do it when you're cutting your toe nails or anything like that."

I did have an idea, but it involved us being naked, so I wasn't going to tell Maddy about it. All I knew was the question would be asked soon. Now I'd made my mind up, I didn't want to wait.

I'd only told Maddy a couple of days before what I was planning on doing, in case her stupid grin gave it away, and she'd insisted coming with me for the ring. She said it was to give her guidance, but I knew it was more to make sure I shelled out a fucking heap load of money. Between us, we'd narrowed it down to three rings, all diamonds with a diamond encrusted white gold band. One was a pear shape, one round and one what the jeweller had informed me was princess cut. I knew which I liked but I hadn't said anything, because I wanted Maddy's honest opinion.

"We can go and get Maccies after this," I told her.

"With an eight grand ring in your pocket." She looked at me wide eyed. "Maybe we should do the drive thru."

I chuckled at the idea of dumping it in the bin with left over burger by mistake, then my skin went cold. "Yeah, maybe you're right."

As we continued to wait for the jeweller to come back, I looked at Maddy's profile. She was the image of Andy from that angle. The same tilt of her nose and little elfin like chin. In fact, she was a good mixture of both of us and I knew her mum and Aunt Miriam would be proud of her and her decision to go to Edinburgh. I didn't even think Zak being there was the biggest part of her reason for going. We'd been to visit the campus with Zak and his parents, and they both fell in love with the place. Maddy more than Zak. I was quite glad they would be studying a bus or bike ride away from each other, because at least then they wouldn't be in each other's pockets. Zak's parents, however, had decided to invest in a property near to the uni and Maddy was moving in with him; him, two lads and a girl who were going to rent rooms from them. I hadn't been totally in raptures about it, but I couldn't have everything, the main thing she was going to be spreading her wings.

"Right, sir," the jeweller said, coming back and placing a pad on the counter top. "Here's the three you requested a closer look at."

He talked to me about diamond clarity, and which would retain the most value, but I couldn't take my eyes off the pear shaped one. It was clearer and sparkled more, and the glint reminded me of Maya's eyes when she found something funny. It wasn't huge but it wasn't small, it was perfect, like her.

"Mads?" I asked her. "Which do you like?"

Beaming at me she pointed to the pear shaped one. "It reminds me of

Maya's eyes."

God, my daughter. I couldn't express how much I loved her.

"My choice, too."

She giggled. "And the most expensive, so it's perfect."

It really was and so was everything else in life. All I needed now was for Maya to say yes.

***

"Did you have a nice day with Maddy?" Maya asked as I rubbed her back with the bath sponge.

I watched the bubbles trail slowly down the groove in the middle of her back and disappear into the water. Her hair was up in a messy bun and some of the strands that had escaped stuck to her neck and cheeks as she rested her head on her knees. She was the picture of beauty.

When she'd been in plaster, taking a bath together had become our favourite thing to do with Maya sitting between my legs so I could wash her. It wasn't as easy as a shower, but it was more fun because it usually ended in me giving her an orgasm with my fingers.

I'd lit candles and placed them around the bath and the room, and I'd even brought the speaker in to play music softly in the background. We had a bottle of wine, and it was the most relaxed I'd felt in months.

"Maddy and I had a great day. She cost me a fortune, though." Maddy and Maya, but I didn't mind one bit.

"Aww she deserves to be spoiled. She'll be gone too soon."

"Ugh, don't remind me." I dropped a kiss to Maya's shoulder. "The house will seem a lot quieter without her and Zak blasting music and eating us out of house and home."

Maya didn't say anything but hummed her agreement. Maybe Maddy leaving was upsetting her more than I thought. They'd become close since Maya had moved in, their own little girl gang who picked on me relentlessly; I loved every single minute of it.

"Lisa is already talking about a trip to see them," I said, talking about my conversation with Zak's mum.

She glanced at me over her shoulder. "He's a lovely lad and such great parents. I can't believe they bought a house to make life easier for them."

"I know, I wish I could help more."

Maya shifted around and putting a wet palm against my cheek, smiled softly. "Baby, you don't have to buy a house to show how much you love and support them. And what you have done for that sweet girl all her life is incredible. You've been her mother and her father, and she has the confidence to move on to the next chapter because of you. Because of every single time you told her she was strong, she was brave, and she was beautiful."

A lump formed in my throat as I thought about the years when it had just been me and my Mads. At times it had been hard, but in the most she'd made it easy for me. She'd been a great kid to bring up. My little teammate and now she was leaving me.

"Shit, if I feel like this now, how will I cope the day she leaves?"

Maya kissed me gently. "I'll hold your hand, don't worry. Always."

Now was the time to let Maddy go and start a new team. I reached down the side of the bath underneath the towel I'd placed there and pulled out the small black velvet box. As Maya washed her arms, I flipped open the box, and cleared my throat of the nerves, and moved my shaking hand in front of her.

She didn't notice immediately, but when I kissed the back of her neck she looked up and instantly squealed.

"Oh my God, Will."

Turning around to face me, water sloshed over the sides of the bath onto the tiled floor as a small tidal wave formed around us.

"You mean it?" she asked, her palms flat against her cheeks. "Really?"

"Yes, gorgeous," I whispered. "I mean it. I love you and I can't wait to spend the rest of my life with you. I can't imagine *not* spending it with you." Mesmerised by her beauty, I drew in a breath, unsure how I'd been so lucky. "Love wasn't something I was looking for. I didn't think I wanted it, but you, shit, Maya, you changed all of that. I love everything about you, your heart, your laugh, your jokes, your body, your lips, everything, but most of all I love how you love my daughter. So," I said, blowing out a breath, "will you marry me?"

"Yes," she screamed. "Yes, of course I will. Please put that beautiful ring on my finger."

As soon as it was on, she threw her arms around my neck and kissed me like she needed it to survive. More water splashed over the sides and when Maya straddled me, we were left with only a small amount left in the bottom of the bath.

"I love you," I told her. "So, fucking much."

Maya's bottom lip trembled as she traced my eyebrow with her finger, her gaze fixed on me. "I love you, too and I can't wait to be your wife."

Then, in a few inches of water, I made love to my fiancée and made her scream my name as the diamond on her finger twinkled just like her eyes.

MAYA'S DIARY ENTRY

I can't believe it, I'm engaged! Will proposed and it was perfect. The ring is beautiful and he's incredible and I am the luckiest person in the world. My mum and dad went crazy on the phone. As for Morgan and Loretta they're already talking about what colour bridesmaid's dresses they want. Maddy was so happy for us, but she already knew because she went with Will to choose the ring. Well, she's got good taste.

I didn't think I could ever be this happy. Well, there is something else, but I don't know for certain which is why I haven't told Will, but I think I'm pregnant. It had to be when I was on my pain meds, I think I might have missed a pill. I probably should have got a test today while he was out with Maddy, but I can go tomorrow. And flash my engagement ring at the pharmacist lol!

I'm so unbelievably lucky and happy and it's all down to him. Will. The love of my life.

ZAK'S WHATSAPP MESSAGES

ZAK

Hey Oz, you okay mate? Just wondering if you fancy coming up for mine and Mad's leaving party. Maddy's dad is putting it on in his bar for us. It's all on him, beer and everything. Mention it to everyone, except Connie of course. It's on the 19th of next month. You can all stay at ours, sleeping bags and stuff in our basement – don't worry it's nice down there!

Oscar

Sounds great mate and you don't even need to mention her. No one is talking to her after that stunt she pulled. Even Dan dumped her, and he's desperate to work for her dad.

ZAK

She's a piece of work and Maddy is worth a thousand of her.

OSCAR

Pretty serious between you and Maddy then seeing as you're going to uni together!!!

ZAK

I guess so. We're going to be living together but I've seen my schedule and it's fucking crazy. We've agreed to still enjoy the uni life and go out with friends, plus we're studying in different places, but I'd hate it if she wasn't there... so yeah, pretty serious (Smiley face emoji). IYKYK

OSCAR

Pleased for you mate even if you are a soppy melt 😆.. I'll let you know who's up for coming to the party.

ZAK

Great. Speak soon mate.

EPILOGUE
Maddy

I wasn't sure standing at a graveside at a wedding was the done thing, but I had to come and talk to Ana. It had been a few months since I'd last been, so I had a lot to tell her. There were fresh flowers already in the pot, but I had some of my own to leave.

"Hey, Ana," I whispered, crouching down to touch the small stone angel which marked where her ashes had been buried. "Sorry it's been a while, but things have been a bit manic as you can imagine. There's loads to tell you, though. Firstly, the wedding. It was beautiful. I cried of course, because you know me, and Dad did, but you know him, too." I laughed with a little sniff because unbelievably there were still some tears left. "Emma and Liam are back together, at least I'm pretty sure they are. Seeing as I walked in on them having sex at her mum's house the other day! I went to talk about some last minute things for today and she'd already messaged me to say just come in as she was painting her nails. So, I did, but if Liam's bare arse pumping between her legs was her painting her nails I don't ever want a manicure from her."

As the leaves of the tree that I was standing next to rustled, I placed a hand against my heart. I wanted to think it was Ana laughing with happiness seeing as we'd already been through the trauma of their breakup, six months into uni. The distance had been too much, they'd both been pretty heartbroken about it, but it appeared things had changed

"Liv has a new boyfriend. We haven't met him yet, but she seems happy and apparently in her words, 'he's very adept at oral sex.'" When the leaves rustled again I knew for sure it was Ana.

"As for me," I continued, "I'm so bloody happy, especially today. Everything seems to have fallen into place for us, and I can't believe how lucky I am." I sighed heavily and laid down the flowers. "I wanted you to have these because you should have been here in person, Ana. You should have been the one standing by my side so hopefully these make you feel a part of it."

When I heard a noise behind me, I looked over my shoulder to see Zak leaning against the church wall, watching me. The smile which he gave me was brighter than the sun, and held so much love and tenderness, I felt more tears well. As I stood to my full height, he pushed off the wall and started to walk towards me.

"You okay?" he asked, taking my hand in his when he reached me.

"Just filling her in," I told him, glancing at Ana's angel. "I always said she'd be part of the important parts, no matter what."

"I think leaving your bouquet for her is a beautiful idea." He leaned in and gave me a soft kiss. "I love you, Mrs Hoyland."

I exhaled a breath which was a mixture of content and joy, my heart feeling full to bursting. Today was our wedding day, and I had desperately wanted Ana to be with me in some way, so inside the bouquet was a photograph of us laughing together when we were about fifteen. It was hard to believe it had been almost seven years since she'd left us, because the pain still felt as raw as it had that day.

So much had changed since that day. Emma, Liv and I had become closer than sisters, no matter how many miles were between us, my family had grown from just me and Dad and now, as of half an hour ago, I was married to Zak. We already lived together in Manchester where we both worked, me as a social worker, and Zak as a vet in a city centre practice, but today was the day I'd been waiting for since he'd proposed a year ago. Apparently, he had planned a romantic meal and some soft lighting, but we were out walking in the park and got caught in a summer storm. He said the joy on my face as I made him dance with me in the rain, persuaded him to ask me there and then. We then ran home, and he got the beautiful square cut diamond ring from his sock drawer and put it on my finger.

"We should get back," Zak said, taking a tendril of my hair and holding it between his fingers. "The photographer wants to do the shots with us and our siblings."

I grinned thinking about the fact I even had siblings. For so long it had been me and my dad and while I'd loved it, I loved it even more now.

"Okay, let's go."

As I gave one last look at the angel, Zak held out his hand and I happily took it, grateful for the abundance of love in my life and my heart.

Will

As people milled around outside the church, I was taken back to a similar scene five years before. Maya and I had married here, and while it had been a much smaller affair, it had been just as happy. We also had an eight month old baby at the altar with us as we took our vows, but who gave a shit. I certainly didn't. Now that baby, Ivy, was a bossy five year old, who along with her three year old sister, Dolly, were running around and squealing while Oscar, Zak's best man, chased them around, threatening to eat them if he caught them.

"He's going to be a great dad," I said to his pregnant fiancée, Ruby, who was standing next to me.

"I know," she sighed, flicking her long red hair over her shoulder. "I'm not sure he's realised he's not actually a child."

As I laughed and continued to watch my youngest children, I felt her presence behind me. My beautiful Maya. When she put her hand between my shoulder blades, my skin warmed, even though her touch was over my shirt and jacket.

"They're having fun," she said, her expression one of awe as she watched over her daughters. "Let's hope it tires them out for tonight."

They were both good sleepers, but when Maddy and Zak were home, they wanted to be constantly by their side, even sneaking into their bed on occasions. That meant they wouldn't want to leave the party tonight when it was their bedtime.

"It's good of Liv's cousin to babysit them in the hotel room," I replied, turning to her. "Although I think the fifty quid I offered her helped."

Maya rolled her eyes. "I told you it was too much, and we could have put jackets on the floor under the table if they fell asleep."

"Have you forgotten my eldest daughter is a family social worker?"

Maya burst out laughing. "As if she'd report her own parents, besides it was her idea."

My heart swelled at Maya referring to us both as Maddy's parents, because they really were like mother and daughter. Maya had always let Maddy know she could rely on her for anything, because she loved her like a daughter. She'd also made it clear she didn't expect to replace her mum. Maddy said that she didn't know or remember her mum, so Maya wasn't replacing anyone and even if she was, Maddy was glad it was Maya because she loved her. She didn't call Maya mum, but that was how she referred to her when asked, as well as writing Mum in any cards or messages she sent. As for her little sisters, she adored them almost as much as they adored her. We were just one big, happy family who occasionally argued, often laughed and rarely cried.

"I wonder if we might be attending another wedding soon." Maya nodded towards the side of the church. Liam and Emma were gazing into each other's eyes as he held her hand against his chest.

"Mads said they were back together." I laughed and pointed to Sam and Lou who were talking to Marcus and his latest girlfriend. "He'll have a dicky fit if he's got to shell out for a wedding, he's a tight bastard."

"You really think Louise will let him skimp on anything." Maya grinned, knowing exactly what the answer was.

"Well, I doubt Emma's mum will be able to pay towards it, seeing as she's living it up in Tenerife." I for one was glad she was in a different country. Me being married to Maya hadn't stopped her from flirting, or groping me, whenever she saw me.

"The problem is, love," Maya said with a smile, "you've got two more to pay for."

I rolled my eyes. "Christ, don't remind me. I think I'd better start saving now." Zak and Maddy had been going to pay for their wedding themselves, but—call me old -fashioned—I told them no. I was Maddy's dad, so it was my responsibility. Lisa and Jim, Zak's parents, had insisted on paying for the party at night, but everything else had been Bank of Dad, and I wouldn't have had it any other way.

"Ah here's the happy couple now," Maya said softly, gripping my forearm. "God, she's so beautiful."

And she truly was. Maddy's sleeveless dress was fitted to mid-thigh and then flared out with a short train and made of blush coloured lace, or so I was informed, it was an exquisite compliment to my daughter's beauty.

"Hey, Dad," she said, getting on her tiptoes to kiss my cheek.

My heart stuttered as I looked down at her hand in Zak's because I knew he had taken my place as her protector.

"You okay, love?" Maya asked.

I nodded; not sure I could get any words out past the lump in my throat. "Yeah," I eventually managed and turned my gaze on Zak.

"It's your turn now, Zak," I said, my voice breaking.

He nodded and brought their joined hands to his chest. "I know."

"And you make sure you do it right because it's an honour and a privilege."

Another nod. "I know that, too, and I swear nothing or no one, especially not me, will ever hurt her."

It was my turn to nod before I turned my attention to Maddy. "You saw Ana?" She nodded. "And you're fine?"

"I'm okay, Dad," she replied, grinning at me. "I'm not sad, I'm really happy. Are you okay? You look a bit serious."

"I'm fine, sweetheart, but I want you to know that even though you have Zak, I will always be here for you." I drew in a shaky breath and lifted her hand, the one not in Zak's, and kissed the top of it. "You, Madeline, are my first born, my first love, and with your sisters, my greatest achievement. I don't know if you have any idea how precious you are."

Maya squeezed my arm and sniffed, and I smiled, knowing that she was crying— again. My gorgeous wife the big softy. When I then looked at Zak, I knew my daughter had chosen well, because his eyes were lit up with wonder and love as he watched Maddy. There was no doubt he would do as I asked.

Then smiling at Maddy, I said, "Take my hand." And, without hesitation, for one more time, my daughter gave it to me, and I felt a sense of peace that only a man whose life was full of love could feel.

The End

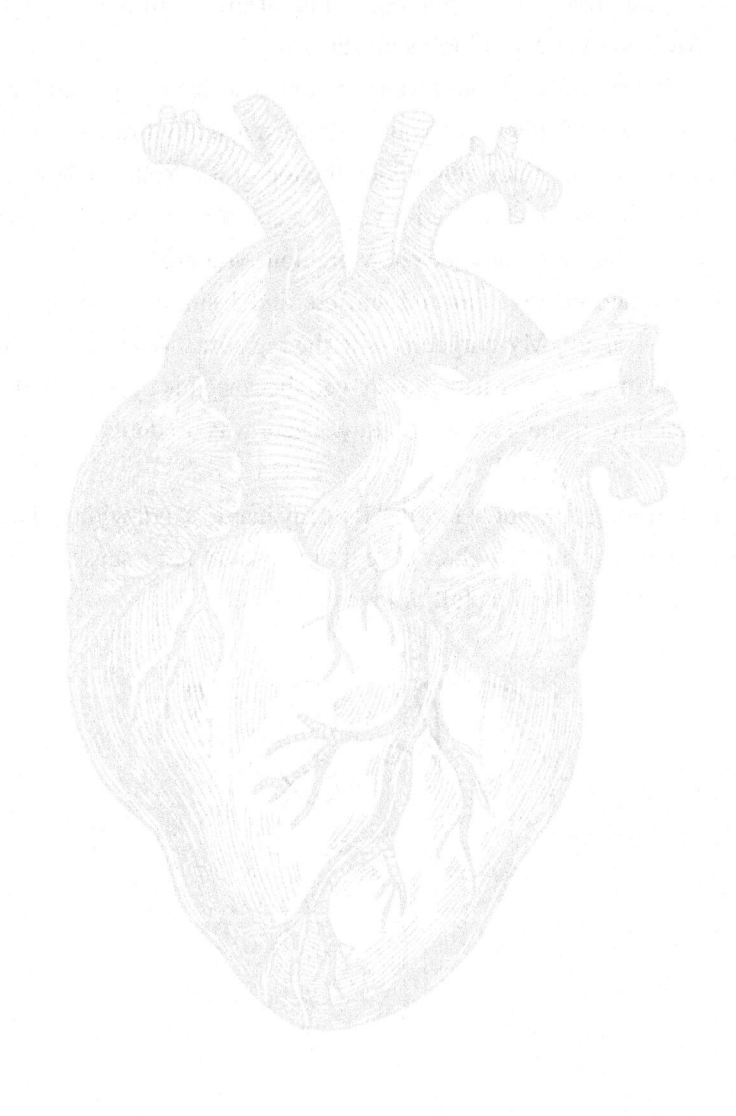

ACKNOWLEDGMENTS

Thank you all for reading this book, it really has been a true labour of love, in the best way.

Your continued supported is appreciated and has allowed me to continue to follow the dream I've had since I was eight years of age.

The biggest gratitude to Lily and Nancy for giving me the help I desperately needed with the 'teenage speak'. As well as explaining how relationships work these days.

David, I just love you, nothing else to say.

Finally, the most important thank you goes to my dad. Gone but never ever forgotten.

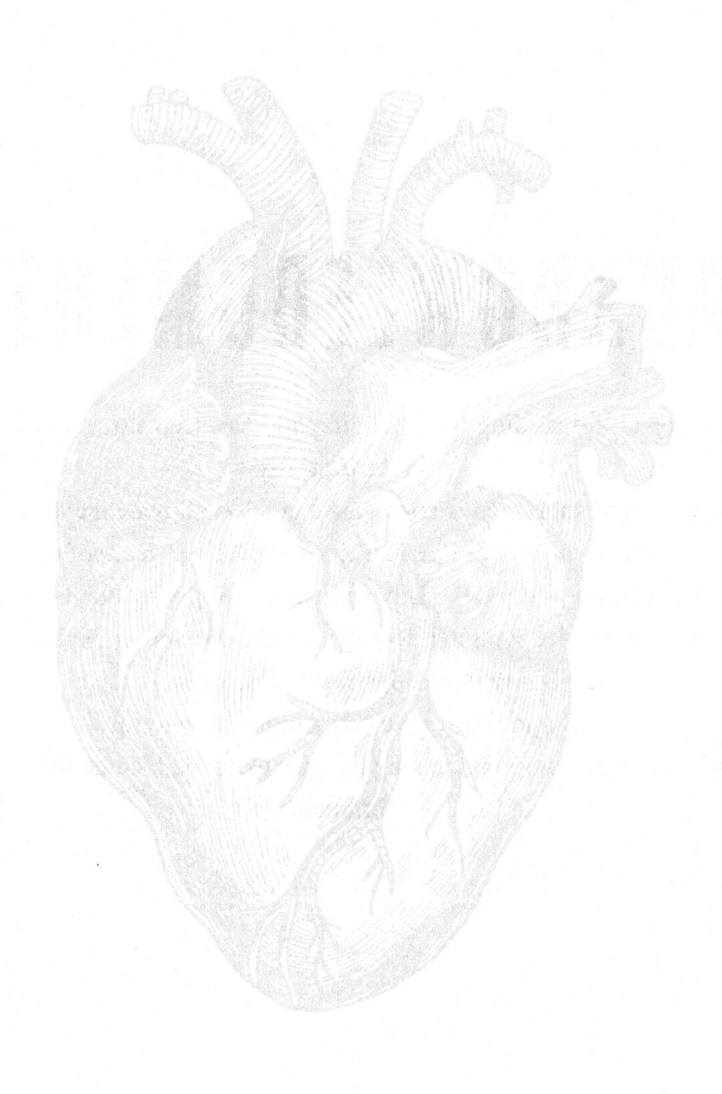

TAKE MY HAND PLAYLIST

Found on Spotify
https://shorturl.at/hpE8a

Not Nineteen Forever – Courteeners
Lovers In A Past Life – Calvin Harris, Rag 'n' Bone Man
Jealous – Nick Jonas
All My Friends – Snakehips, Tinashe, Chance the Rapper
Dakota – Stereophonics
Naïve – The Kooks
Dive – Olivia Dean
One Kiss – Calvin Harris, Dua Lipa
She Moves In Her Own Way – The Kooks
Made For Me – Muni Long (With Mariah Carey)
The Weekend – Michael Gray
Last Request – Paolo Nutini
Hell N Back – Bakar ft Summer Walker
Helium – Sia
Never Let Me Go – Florence + The Machine
Tennessee Whiskey – Chris Stapleton
Too Lost In You – Sugababes
Levitating – Dua Lipa
Sailor Song – Gigi Perez
Fix You – Coldplay
Take My Hand – Picture This
Beneath Your Beautiful – Labrinth, Emeli Sande
These Words – Natasha Bedingfield

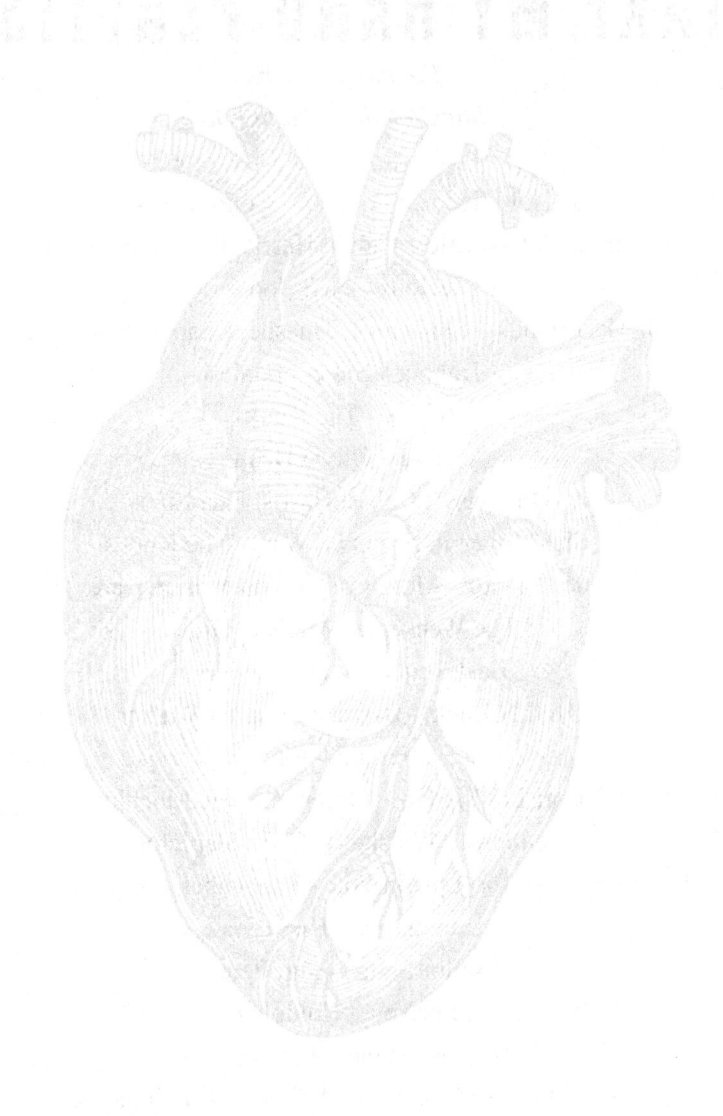

NIKKI'S LINKS

If you'd like to know more about me or my books,
then all my links are listed below.

Website
www.nikkiashtonbooks.co.uk

Instagram
www.instagram.com/nikkiashtonauthor

Facebook
www.facebook.com/nikki.ashton.982

Nikki Ashton's Angels Facebook Group
www.facebook.com/groups/1039480929500429

Amazon
viewAuthor.at/NAPage

Audio Books
preview.tinyurl.com/NikkiAshtonAudio

nikki ♥
ashton

Made in United States
North Haven, CT
04 October 2024

58299798R00290